A GUNFIGHTER GROWS OLDER

It had happened before—so many times before. Now Nathan decided to speed up what was going to happen anyway. He walked to the man's table and said, "You've been taking my measure ever since I came in. Do I know you?"

The stranger laughed. "I doubt it. But I know you. You're Nathan Stone, the killer."

"I'm Nathan Stone," Nathan replied coldly. "What do you want of me?"

"I'm Mitch Sowell, and I'm callin' you out. I'll meet you on the street."

"I have no fight with you," Nathan said.

"Oh, but you do," Sowell said. "You have a reputation, and I aim to fight you for it."

How many more times would he have to do this? Nathan wondered as he followed Sowell out of the saloon. How many more times would he have to kill before he died . . . ?

AUTUMN
OF THE GUN

Ralph Compton

A SIGNET BOOK

SIGNET
Published by New American Library, a division of
Penguin Group (USA) Inc., 375 Hudson Street,
New York, New York 10014, USA
Penguin Group (Canada), 90 Eglinton Avenue East, Suite 700, Toronto,
Ontario M4P 2Y3, Canada (a division of Pearson Penguin Canada Inc.)
Penguin Books Ltd., 80 Strand, London WC2R 0RL, England
Penguin Ireland, 25 St. Stephen's Green, Dublin 2,
Ireland (a division of Penguin Books Ltd.)
Penguin Group (Australia), 250 Camberwell Road, Camberwell, Victoria 3124,
Australia (a division of Pearson Australia Group Pty. Ltd.)
Penguin Books India Pvt. Ltd., 11 Community Centre, Panchsheel Park,
New Delhi - 110 017, India
Penguin Group (NZ), 67 Apollo Drive, Rosedale, Auckland 0632,
New Zealand (a division of Pearson New Zealand Ltd.)
Penguin Books (South Africa) (Pty.) Ltd., 24 Sturdee Avenue,
Rosebank, Johannesburg 2196, South Africa

Penguin Books Ltd., Registered Offices:
80 Strand, London WC2R 0RL, England

First published by Signet, an imprint of New American Library,
a division of Penguin Group (USA) Inc.

First Printing, December 1996
40 39 38 37 36 35 34 33 32 31 30

PUBLISHER'S NOTE
This is a work of fiction. Names, characters, places, and incidents either are the
product of the author's imagination or are used fictitiously, and any resemblance
to actual persons, living or dead, business establishments, events, or locales is
entirely coincidental.
    The publisher does not have any control over and does not assume any re-
sponsibility for author or third-party Web sites or their content.

"Nathan Stone, someday, in some town on the frontier, you'll die with your boots on, going against impossible odds, for what you believe is right."

—from *The Killing Season*

PROLOGUE

Southern Arizona Territory
April 18, 1877

"Yonder he is," Tasby shouted. "Git him!"

Nathan Stone plunged headlong back into the thicket from which he had just emerged, the shackles on his wrists impeding his progress. Lead whipped through the foliage above his head. Nathan wondered where his dog, Empty, was. While the hound had aided in his escape from Tasby and Doss—the men delivering Nathan to Yuma territorial prison—Nathan was now on his own. He was afoot, wounded, his wrists manacled, half starved, and without a weapon. When the firing ceased, he crept deeper into the thicket. Nearing the end of his second day as a fugitive, having had no food since the morning of his escape, there was weakness in his body and dizziness in his head. He could hear the voices of his pursuers, and they sounded far away.

"He's in there, by God, an' he ain't armed. We got him now."

Nathan Stone lay still, overcome by weakness. Sundown was two hours away, but if he evaded them until then, what would it avail him? By morning, weak from hunger and loss of blood, he would be at their mercy. As he lay there, his mind drifted back over the years. Again it was 1866, and following his release from a Yankee prison, Nathan Stone had returned to find his father, mother, and sister dead, murdered by renegades. On their graves, Nathan had taken a blood oath, vowing to track down and kill the seven renegades to the last man. The killers had fled west, and for seven long years, Nathan had ridden a vengeance trail. When the last of the seven were dead, Nathan Stone had the reputation of a fast gun, the name of a killer. He had tried to settle down, distinguishing himself as a telegrapher and troubleshooter for the railroads. He took for his wife a young woman he had rescued from a band of renegades in Indian Territory, only to have the outlaws abduct the girl and brutally murder her. After taking his vengeance— gunning down the outlaws—Nathan had given up his position with the railroad and become a drifter.

But Nathan Stone had been unable to escape his reputation as a fast draw. Wherever he went, he had been forced to live by the gun. When Texas Ranger Captain Sage Jennings had been shot in the back from ambush, Nathan had again ridden the vengeance trail, killing the outlaw who had murdered his friend. He had been stalked and ambushed by a bloodthirsty female whose gun-slinging brother he had been forced to shoot, while a price had been put on his head by the wealthy family of a renegade he had killed in Missouri.

Finally, Nathan's mind drifted back to that dark day in Pueblo, Colorado, where his friend, Harley Stafford, lay near death. Nathan had become involved with Vivian, Harley's sister, and his ensuing friendship with Harley had gotten him a position with the railroad. But Harley had been gunned down by outlaws during a train robbery, and again Nathan Stone had taken to the vengeance trail. Leaving Vivian with the critically wounded Harley, Nathan had taken the trail of the outlaws, tracking them to southern Arizona Territory.

Reaching a town, Nathan had discovered too late that it was inhabited entirely by outlaws, including the judge and sheriff. This time even Nathan's fast draw couldn't save him. He had been forced into a gunfight, charged with murder, and sentenced to hard labor. In chains, he had fought with and killed a brutal guard, and his punishment was more terrible than anything he could have imagined. To his horror, he was being sent to the territorial prison at Yuma as part of a profitable scheme devised by crooked officials at the prison and the outlaw Judge Ponder. For ten thousand dollars, an inmate at Yuma would be allowed to "escape." The prison would report the escapee had been captured, but the man actually being returned to Yuma would be Nathan Stone.

Judge Ponder had selected Doss and Tasby to deliver Nathan to Yuma territorial prison, and on April 15, 1877, the trio had ridden west. One morning beside the Gila River, when they had been about to resume their journey,

Nathan had made his move. Empty, the hound, had attacked one of his captors, while Nathan had gone after the other. His hands still manacled, Nathan had escaped by leaping into the river. Fearing the wrath of Judge Ponder, Tasby and Doss had not given up the chase, and now they were closing in.

Hearing a rustling of leaves, Nathan was about to struggle to his feet, but to his relief, he saw only his faithful hound. Tasby and Doss had taken to shooting at the dog, and since they were mounted, there was little Empty could do except avoid them. But the hated duo had dismounted. Counting on Nathan being wounded, weak, and manacled, they were pursuing him into the thicket. Empty stood beside Nathan, his teeth bared, and the instant one of the searchers appeared, the hound was on him in a fury. When Doss dropped the Colt, Nathan seized it. Weak as he was, he needed both hands, but he shot Doss through the head. Nathan went belly down, and when Tasby fired, his first shot missed. He had no chance for another, for Nathan shot him dead.

"Old son," said Nathan, struggling to his knees, "if it wasn't for you . . ."

Empty sat there watching him as Nathan searched both the dead men. With a sigh of relief, he found the key to the cruel manacles and freed his hands.

"Come on," Nathan said. "First thing we do is find the horses the varmints was ridin' and fix us some grub."

Nathan took the Colts and gun rigs from both the dead men, and when he found their saddled horses, there was a Winchester in each saddle boot. He went through the saddlebags, finding bacon, coffee beans, hard tack, and most of a bottle of whiskey. With trembling hands, he started a fire, filled the blackened coffeepot at the river, and hacked off chunks of bacon. Sharing the bacon with Empty, he ate it half raw, drinking the coffee right from the pot. His hunger satisfied, he removed his muddy shirt and examined his wound. It was clean; the lead had missed the bone, and there appeared to be no infection. He heated some water in the coffeepot, cleansed the wound, and, after dousing it with some of the whiskey, bound it with a piece of a shirt from one of the dead men's saddlebags. Nathan then mounted one of the horses and, leading the other, rode upriver until he found his own horse where his pursuers had picketed it. The grulla nickered as Nathan picketed the other two horses alongside it.

"We'll rest a day or two. Empty," said Nathan, "and allow this wound some time to heal. Then we have some unfinished business with Judge Ponder, Sheriff Hondo, and the rest of those coyotes in that outlaw town."

A day after regaining his freedom, Nathan released the horses belonging to Tasby and Doss, their cartridge belts with empty holsters thonged to the saddle horns. The horses would find their way back to Ponder's town, and Nathan expected their return to trigger a massive manhunt, for Nathan Stone knew too much. When every available man had been mounted and sent in search of him, Nathan would ride in and settle accounts with Judge Ponder. Nathan had kept the Colts and Winchesters taken from the dead men, along with all their ammunition, and had transferred their food and supplies from their saddlebags to his own. Two days after releasing the horses, Nathan crossed the Gila and rode east. The searchers would be forced to ride west until they discovered what had become of Tasby and Doss. That would allow Nathan to settle with Judge Ponder and prepare a reception for the searchers when they returned. Concealing his trail, Nathan kept well to the south of the Gila River. Once he had ridden far enough eastward, he headed north. Empty was somewhere ahead of him, and when Nathan was within a mile or two of Ponder's town, he circled it. To the south, he found what he was seeking. There were the fresh tracks of many horses, and the trail led west. Nathan reined up, and Empty came trotting out of the brush.

"Looks like the judge mounted everybody that could ride," said Nathan. "Empty, it's time we called on Judge Ponder and showed that old coyote the error of his ways."

Somewhere a mule brayed, and Nathan could hear the distant thunk of an axe. Ponder evidently had kept his chain gangs at work, and that meant guards were on duty. Nathan picketed his horse in a thicket and made his way on foot toward Ponder's quarters, which also served as a jail. Coming in behind the building, he paused. He saw no horses at the hitch rails in front of any of the buildings. He pointed toward the dirt street, and Empty bounded ahead. If there was unseen danger, the dog would warn him.

Empty trotted the length of the street, then returned, and Nathan stepped around the corner of the jail. Two horses were tied at the hitch rail before the building and, ignoring the entrance, Nathan stepped up on the porch from one end. He eased up beside the door, listening, and from within he heard voices. The loudest belonged to Judge Ponder.

"Damn it, Roscoe, if they don't ride him down, we're finished."

"They won't ride him down," said Roscoe, "because he won't be there. Them hosses comin' in with empty saddles is proof enough he's cashed in Tasby and Doss. Now he's got a hoss and a gun, and he's on his way here."

"I fear you may be right," Ponder said. "I want you to remain here in this office until Sheriff Hondo and the posse returns."

Roscoe laughed. "Keeno, I can take him. That's why I didn't ride with the posse. I'll gamble they ain't a man in the territory faster with a Colt than me."

"You lose," said Nathan, kicking the door open.

Nathan stood in the doorway, a Colt belted to each hip. Roscoe managed to recover from the shock, but Nathan fired twice, and the man died with his pistol barely clear of the holster. Judge Ponder dropped to the floor, seized a shotgun, and fired over the desk, but Nathan was belly down on the floor, and the deadly load went over his head. He fired once, and the slug struck Ponder between the eyes. Outside, Empty was barking furiously; without a backward look Nathan was out the door. Across the street, a man stepped out of the saloon. He fired twice and, the slugs slammed into the wall to Nathan's right. He returned the fire, and his second shot drove his attacker against the saloon wall. The man slid to the ground and didn't move. Nathan could hear distant shouts, a fair indication that some of the guards were coming to investigate. Nathan circled around and headed for the site where the dam was being built. Normally there were two guards, and if one of them had gone to investigate the shooting at the jail, Nathan would be facing only one of them at a time. When Nathan neared the dam, he could see the men had ceased work, and Sanchez, the remaining guard, was awaiting word as to what the shooting had been about. Within pistol range, Nathan stepped out of the brush and shouted a challenge.

"Sanchez!"

Sanchez had a Winchester in the crook of his left arm, but went for his Colt. Nathan allowed him more of an opportunity than he deserved, and then gunned him down.

"Stone," one of the prisoners shouted, "God bless you. Get us out of these chains so we can help you."

"Some of you search Sanchez; see if he has the key to your irons and free yourselves," said Nathan. "That other guard will be comin' back on the run. I aim to welcome him."

"Damn it," said one of the prisoners, "he ain't got the key to these irons. Gustavez must have it."

"He'll be comin' back," Nathan said, "and I'm sure he won't object to us havin' it."

"He sure as hell won't," said one of the men who had taken the Winchester from the fallen Sanchez.

"Where's the other work gang?" Nathan asked.

"Workin' the fields," said one of the men. "What's happened in town?"

"I talked some sense to Judge Ponder and one of his gun-throwers in a language they could understand," Nathan replied. "Once we've rid ourselves of these guards, we're going to prepare a reception for Sheriff Hondo and his posse that's out lookin' for me."

Suddenly a slug zipped past Nathan's head. Two men, their horses at a gallop, had drawn their guns and were firing at Nathan. He returned the fire, but the prisoner who had the Winchester shot one of the men out of the saddle. The second man wheeled his horse and tried to run, but was gunned down by one of the captives who had taken the Colt from the fallen Sanchez. Quickly the men searched Gustavez and came up with keys to their leg irons.

"While you're freeing yourselves," said Nathan, "I'm going after that other guard. If there are more of these coyotes around, you now have weapons. Use them. I'll be back."

Nathan took a horse belonging to one of the dead guards and rode toward the distant fields. He must get within gun range before the remaining guard recognized him. But his luck didn't hold, and lead ripped the air over his head as soon as he was within range. It became a dangerous situa-

tion, for the other man was kneeling, firing a Winchester.
But some of the prisoners came to Nathan's aid. They piled
on the guard from behind and seized his Colt, and he was
dead before Nathan reached him. Quickly the men went
through the dead guard's pockets, found the key to their leg
irons, and freed themselves. Most of the men remembered
Nathan, and they shouted a joyous welcome.

"Come on," Nathan said. "Sheriff Hondo's out with a
posse, and we have to be ready when they return."

"What happened to Judge Ponder?" somebody wanted
to know.

"He came after me with a shotgun," said Nathan, "but
he missed. I didn't."

When the groups came together, there were almost a
hundred men, and they looked at Nathan expectantly.

"Somewhere in this town there'll be guns and ammunition," Nathan said. "It's up to us to arm all of you. We'll
start with Ponder's quarters and the jail."

Ponder and Roscoe lay where they had fallen. One of
the freed prisoners took the shotgun from Ponder's dead
hands, while another seized Roscoe's Colt and pistol belt.
They found two more Colts, two Winchesters, and a supply
of ammunition, but it was far short of what they needed.

"God," said one of the men, "there's fifty riders with
Sheriff Hondo. We'll be outgunned near ten to one."

"Maybe," Nathan said, "but Ponder has dynamite somewhere. He used it building the dam. Let's find that dyna
mite, and we'll even the odds."

They searched the jail and Ponder's quarters without result. In the outer office, a faded, dirty rug covered most of
the floor. Shoving Ponder's desk against the wall, Nathan
kicked the rug aside, revealing an iron ring flush with the
floor. Two men seized the ring and raised the door. There
was a lamp on Ponder's desk. Nathan lighted it and held
it above the yawning hole. Wooden steps vanished into
the darkness.

"Anybody down there?" Nathan shouted.

There was no response.

"Gimme the lamp," said one of the men. "Some of you
cover me, and I'll go down and light the way."

There was no other way, and Nathan surrendered the
lamp.

"My God!" the man shouted from below. "There's gold down here!"

"I wouldn't get too excited," Nathan said. "It's stolen. What about the dynamite?"

"One full case an' part of another," came the response. "There's caps an' fuses, too."

"Some of you get down there," Nathan said, "and bring up the dynamite, caps, and fuses. We have work to do, and we may not have much time."

After they had brought up the dynamite, Nathan took the lamp and went below. He wanted his own Colts and Winchester, given him by Texas Ranger Captain Sage Jennings. He quickly found the weapons concealed under canvas. When he reached the head of the stairs, he found the men had broken out the dynamite.

"We'll fuse and cap single sticks," said Nathan. "Short fuses, not more than six or seven seconds. We'll spread out all over town, each of us with a few sticks of dynamite. I found my weapons below, so you can have the pair of Winchesters and the Colts I took from Tasby and Doss."

"When that bunch rides in, we'd best throw the dynamite while they're bunched," one of the men said. "Elsewise, they'll scatter, and we don't have the guns for a standoff."

"That's the idea," Nathan said. "If nothin' else, the blast should stun them long enough for us to take their guns."

Nathan returned to his picketed horse, taking the Winchesters and extra ammunition from the saddlebags. He had all but forgotten Empty when the dog loped out of the brush and growled deep in his throat. Something was definitely wrong, and when Nathan looked to the south, he knew what it was. There was a faint plume of dust against the blue of the sky. The outlaw posse was returning! Nathan hit the steps to the jail on the run.

"They're coming," Nathan said grimly. "A couple of you stay here with me and the rest of you spread out and take cover. Drop some of that dynamite in their midst, and their horses should pile them. Some will be stunned by the blast, giving you time to grab their guns. The others will come up shootin', and it'll be up to those of you with guns to cut them down."

Each man grabbed two or three sticks of dynamite and they scattered like quail. Two of the men remained with Nathan. Standing near the door, they could see the first horsemen topping the hill to the south. With open fields on each side of the trail, there was no cover for the defenders except the few buildings on the edge of town. By the time the outlaws were close enough for the dynamite to be thrown, they would be within range of Nathan's Winchester. Once the approaching riders were close enough, the defenders wasted no time. Dynamite rained on them, much of it exploding in the air above them. On the heels of one explosion there was another. Horses screamed and pitched, men cursed, and those who had been thrown rose from the dust only to be gunned down. Sheriff Hondo lit out in a run for the jail, only to have a thrown stick of dynamite explode right over his head. He sprawled in the dirt to rise no more. Half a dozen of the outlaws who had stayed in their saddles wheeled their horses and rode for their lives. Taking advantage of the thrown dynamite, the defenders rushed into the street, seizing the guns of the confused outlaws. Those who had survived the dynamite blasts staggered to their feet, only to be shot down without mercy, most of them with their own weapons. When the dust settled, forty-five outlaws lay dead. Not one of the defenders had been hurt, and there was a victorious shout. The men gathered in front of the jail. They owed their very lives to Nathan Stone, and they listened respectfully as he spoke to them.

"Men," Nathan said, "what becomes of this town is of no interest to me. I want just one thing. Part of that gold under Ponder's office was stolen from the AT & SF Railroad, and I want it returned. A friend of mine almost gave his life for it."

"What happens to the rest of it?" somebody asked.

"I don't know," said Nathan. "If nobody comes along to claim it, I reckon it belongs to those of you who have had part of your lives stolen by Ponder and his outlaws."

Raiding Ponder's stores of food, the men prepared a meal such as none of them had enjoyed for months. Near sundown, two riders approached from the north, and some of the men readied their guns.

"It's all right," said Nathan. "They're friends of mine."

Harley and Vivian Stafford reined up their horses, surprised at the presence of so many armed men.

"Get down," Nathan said. "It's a long story."

*   *   *

The next morning, Nathan and Harley loaded the gold into the same wagon the thieves had used after stealing the shipment from the railroad. Nathan bid farewell to the men with whom he had shared captivity, and took the trail north with Harley and Vivian. Nathan drove the wagon, his grulla trailing behind on a lead rope, while Harley and Vivian rode alongside. Empty loped well ahead of the wagon.

"The railroad owes you for this," Harley said, "and I owe you a lot more."

"The railroad owes me nothing," said Nathan. "I did this for you because you're my friend, not because I see it as a debt to be paid. I'll see you back to Pueblo, where all this gold will be the responsibility of the railroad."

"Where will you go from there?" Vivian asked.

"I don't know," said Nathan.

She had stopped short of asking him about his intentions toward her. He had—as her brother well knew—shared her bed for months. Now, after the gold had been safely returned to the railroad, could he just ride away? His mind drifted back to those early days on the frontier when he had been riding a vengeance trail, when Eulie Prater had been part of his life. Nathan had gone to New Orleans to kill a man, and it was there that Eulie had died in an ambush that might have been avoided. Every woman Nathan Stone had ever cared a damn about had somehow died a violent death as a result of her relationship with him, Nathan thought dismally. Somehow, by the time they reached Pueblo, Nathan must reach a decision regarding Vivian Stafford. She and Harley had no family, and he believed they should remain together. But he was at a loss as to how he might convince them. They were more than five hundred miles from Pueblo, and even with mules pulling the wagon, they might be on the trail as long as a month. Harley made himself scarce at night, and it became more and more difficult for Nathan not to resume his former intimate relationship with Vivian. Finally the girl became impatient and hit him with a direct question he couldn't possibly evade.

"You're avoiding me, Nathan. Why? Are you tired of me?"

"Yes," Nathan admitted. "I'm avoiding you, but not because I'm tired of you. It's for your sake that I'm backing off, and now I reckon I'll have to tell you why."

He talked for an hour, the two of them sitting on the wagon tongue, and when he had finished, he had the feeling he hadn't gotten through to her. She quickly confirmed his suspicion.

"All right," she said, "you've warned me that you're bad news. I know about your fast gun, your sometimes uncontrollable passion for saloon gambling, and your pride that often kicks common sense out the window. But I still believe in for better or worse. This is the frontier, Nathan. I could get shot by somebody that's gunning for Harley. I'll never complain about where you go or what you do. I'm willing to take my chances with you, and I can't see anything wrong with that. Unless you don't want me."

"Damn it, Vivian, it's got nothin' to do with me not wantin' you," said Nathan. "What I've tried to tell you is that I can't stand the thought of somethin' happening to you as it happened to the others. My conscience can't handle any more."

"I think you're blaming yourself unfairly," she argued. "Perhaps it's a gamble, but *you* gamble. Why can't I?"

"Because you're . . . you . . . I . . ."

"Because I'm a woman," said Vivian.

"No," Nathan said angrily, "because we're talkin' about two different things. Gambling for money is one thing, while gambling your life is another. Trailing with me, you're risking your life, and nothing you can say or do will ever change that. I don't know where, when, or how it'll happen, but it will. It's a feeling that comes over me, and it's never been wrong yet."

They parted in anger, and barely spoke for an entire week. Nathan found himself telling Harley what he had already told Vivian, and he found Harley sympathetic.

"I reckon I can understand your feelings," said Harley, "and I don't know what to tell you. Why don't we just wait until we get to Pueblo and see if anything changes?"

It proved to be good advice.

Pueblo, Colorado
May 21, 1877

The railroad showed its gratitude by hosting a dinner at one of the hotels. It became a joint honor for Nathan and Harley, and they were forced to attend.

"Damn," Nathan complained, "why can't they show their gratitude in some way that don't force a man into a boiled shirt, tight britches, and a necktie?"

When the affair was over, some of the railroad personnel insisted that Nathan and Harley accompany them to a fancy saloon for drinks.

"Go on," Vivian urged. "I'll stay here at the hotel."

So Nathan and Harley went, and Nathan became interested in a high-stakes poker game that was in progress. The big winner appeared to be Drew Collins, a little man with thinning dark hair, black eyes, and diamond cufflinks. In a solid black suit, he looked like a preacher or an undertaker, and Nathan developed an instant dislike for him. It was Collins who suggested a twenty-dollar limit, and at that point Harley dropped out.

"Too rich for my blood," Harley told Nathan. "Maybe we ought to mosey back to the hotel."

"Not yet," said Nathan

Only four men remained, and the pot quickly reached five hundred dollars. Finally it reached a thousand dollars, and two more men folded, leaving only Nathan and Collins.

"Your turn to fold," Collins said with a smirk.

"I'll raise you five hundred dollars," said Nathan.

There was twenty-five hundred dollars in the pot when it was time to show their hands. With a flourish, Collins laid down four face-up aces.

"Beat that," the smug little gambler said.

"I can," Nathan replied. He dropped five cards on the table. Four of them were kings and the fifth was an ace of spades.

Collins had reached for the pot, and when Nathan seized both his arms, two more aces fell from the sleeves of Collins's coat.

"Collins," said Nathan, "where I come from, that's called cheatin'."

"By God, that's what we call it here, too," said a man who had been forced out.

Half a dozen angry men seized Collins, dragged him through the saloon, and flung him out on the boardwalk.

"Mister," a bartender said, "you'd best take your money and get out of here. Collins is ever' bit as touchy as Ben Thompson. He'll kill you."

"Come on, Nathan," said Harley.

Nathan and Harley returned to the hotel. To Nathan's dismay, he found Vivian in his room, and she refused to leave.

"Harley," said Nathan, "tell her—"

"Tell her yourself," Harley said. "She quit listenin' to me a long time ago."

Harley had refused breakfast and Nathan thought he knew why. He didn't intend to involve himself in the hassle between Nathan and Vivian. Suddenly, as they neared a vacant building, there was a rattle of gunfire. One slug burned its way along Nathan's neck, under his left ear. With his Colt in his hand, he was off and running, but by the time he reached the old store building the bushwhacker was gone. Nathan could hear shouting behind him and he turned back. Vivian Stafford lay on the boardwalk, blood rapidly soaking the left side of her shirt.

CHAPTER 1

Nathan had little doubt that Drew Collins had been responsible for the ambush, and in due time he would find the vindictive little gambler. But not until he knew that Vivian was out of danger. While they waited for a verdict from the doctor, he talked to Harley.

"What's just happened can happen again," Nathan said. "Now do you understand what I've been trying to tell Vivian?"

"I reckon I can," said Harley.

"As soon as I know she's going to live, I aim to ride out," Nathan said. "It's up to you to convince her it's for her sake."

"You'll be taking care of Collins, then."

"Yes," said Nathan, "and when we meet again, I don't aim for him to have anybody to throw lead at except me."

By the next morning, Vivian was sleeping peacefully, out of danger. Nathan joined Harley Stafford and Foster Hagerman for breakfast.

"First thing I need to know," Nathan said, "is whether Collins took the train after the shooting. It would be the logical thing, unless there was too much time before the next train."

"I can answer that for you," said Hagerman. "While you and Harley were concerned with Vivian, Sheriff Brodie began looking for Collins. The next train east was more than four hours away. The sheriff found a livery that had sold Collins a horse and saddle. It's a safe bet that your man is almost to Denver by now."

"Thanks," Nathan said. "Now, can you take it a step farther? Before I saddle up and light out for Denver, can you wire the Kansas-Pacific terminal and find out whether or not Collins has taken a train east?"

"It's a two-day ride from here to Denver," said Hagerman. "If Collins is headed that way, he won't be there until late this evening. Before you go galloping off anywhere, why don't you talk to Sheriff Brodie? He's having the Kansas-Pacific terminal watched by the law in Denver. If Collins shows up there, he'll be arrested. Why don't you wait another day, until Brodie hears from Denver?"

"I reckon that makes sense," said Nathan. "I just don't like waiting, and if he fails to take the train from Denver, the little varmint's got a two-day start on me."

"He could ride to Cheyenne and take the Union Pacific to California," Harley said.

"My God," said Nathan, "that's even worse. Cheyenne's a just a hundred miles north of Denver. He could reach Denver sometime tonight and be in Cheyenne late tomorrow."

"Then you'll never catch up to him on horseback," Hagerman said. "If Brodie gets no response to his inquiry to Denver, have him wire the Union Pacific terminal in Cheyenne. If Collins doesn't take the train at Denver or Cheyenne, he could have gone anywhere."

It made sense, and Nathan waited. Denver was a hundred and fifty miles north, while Cheyenne was a hundred miles farther. A wild-goose chase of such magnitude wasn't very appealing. After supper, Harley and Nathan went to the sheriff's office, but Brodie could tell them nothing positive.

"No sign of Collins at the Kansas-Pacific terminal in Denver," said Brodie.

"Will you wire the Union Pacific at Cheyenne?" Nathan asked.

"Yeah," said Brodie. "If we don't catch him there, you might as well give up on him taking a train, unless he headed for Hays when he left here. But I wouldn't consider that likely. It's more than two hundred and fifty miles."

"If he don't show at the Union Pacific terminal in Cheyenne by tomorrow," Harley said, "we've lost him."

"Like hell," said Nathan. "He left here on a horse, and there's been no rain. That trail I followed into southern Arizona Territory was twelve days old. This one will be three days old at the most."

"I'm riding with you," Harley said. "It was my sister he shot."

"But he was shooting at me," said Nathan. "I want you here with Vivian."

Harley laughed. "I reckon I know why. But if you're

goin' to be around until sometime tomorrow, you'll be able to talk to her. You owe her that."

"No sign of Collins at the Union Pacific terminal in Cheyenne," Foster Hagerman said.

"About what I expected," said Nathan.

"Vivian's awake and asking for you," Harley said.

"Damn," said Nathan with a sigh.

Nathan and Harley reached the small hospital where Harley had been laid up.

"I've already talked to her this morning," Harley said. "Your turn."

Removing his hat, Nathan went in. Vivian Stafford sat on the edge of the bed.

"You surprised me," she said. "I expected you to ride out while I was sleeping off the laudanum."

"I aim to track down that skunk of a bushwhacker," said Nathan uncomfortably.

"I suppose you aim to do it without me."

"I do," Nathan said. "Do you need more reasons, or is the one you've had enough?"

"It's enough," she said, surprising him. "When will I see you again?"

"When I get back to Dodge," said Nathan. "Hagerman's checked out every possible railroad connection, including the Union Pacific. I'll have to find the little varmint's trail and ride him down."

Not wasting any more time, Nathan took his horse from the livery, and, with Empty following, he rode out. Estimating that he was five miles from Pueblo, he began circling the town. With the mostly barren, unsettled Utah Territory to the west and a railroad to the east, Nathan expected Collins to ride north or south. When he finally found what he hoped was the trail it led southeast. Nathan reined up, and Empty doubled back.

"The way he's headed," said Nathan, "the first town will be Amarillo. That's at least two hundred and fifty miles, and Fort Worth's twice that. Amarillo's not much more than a wide place in the trail, so he can't hide there. We'll ride the varmint down before he gets to Fort Worth."

Nathan rode on. Near the end of his third day on the trail, he crossed the Cimarron, and there he came upon the camp of some soldiers from Fort Elliott, Texas. There was a lieutenant, a sergeant, and five privates. As Nathan rode in, his hands shoulder high, one of the men—Sergeant Willard—recognized him.

"Come on," said Willard, "and step down."

Nathan dismounted, and Sergeant Willard introduced him to Lieutenant Bruxton, the officer in charge of the patrol.

"It's late," Bruxton said. "You're welcome to join us for the night. We'll be returning to Fort Elliott in the morning, and you can ride with us, if that's where you're bound. I've heard Captain Selman speak of you. He credits you with helping to establish a twice-weekly stage from Dodge to Fort Griffin."

"I reckon it's livened things up a bit," said Nathan.

"It has," Bruxton agreed. "There's already another saloon, a whorehouse, and a livery at Mobeetie."

"The last time I saw Captain Selman," said Nathan, "he was having problems with just one saloon. I reckon he's not looking forward to a second one."

"He ain't," Sergeant Willard said. "We hear he aims to celebrate by enlarging the post guardhouse."

Nathan shared his bacon with the soldiers, and it wasn't until after supper that he got around to telling them where he was bound and why.

"We met your man yesterday, just before we crossed the North Canadian," Lieutenant Bruxton said. "His horse was lame, and he seemed relieved when he learned there's a livery at Mobeetie. There's nothing but a general store to the south, beyond the Canadian."*

"That should slow him down enough for me to catch up to him," said Nathan.

"A word of caution," Lieutenant Bruxton said. "Unless you plan to have him placed under military arrest, I'd advise you not to confront him on post. The last bunch of civilian hell-raisers kicked up such a fuss the noise was heard in Washington."

"The Dismukes," said Nathan.

"My God, yes," Bruxton said. "You've heard of them?"

"I can answer that," said Sergeant Willard. "After Captain Selman banned that bunch from the post, they snuck

---

*Site of present-day Amarillo, Texas, which didn't become a town until 1887.

back with dynamite, with plans to level Fort Elliott. Stone rode back and warned us. Them Dismukes was just plain crazy. We had to shoot 'em down like dogs. If it hadn't been for Stone, Fort Elliott would have been rubble, and some of us would have been coyote bait."

"I don't look for any trouble at the fort," Nathan said. "This varmint's the kind to get himself another horse and ride on. The last thing I want is to involve the military in a purely personal matter."

"You have no conclusive proof, then," said Lieutenant Bruxton.

"Nothing that would stand up in court," Nathan replied, "but enough to satisfy me. He had a motive, and he's running like a scared coyote."

"I can understand your position," said Lieutenant Bruxton. "This is the frontier, and I suspect that for every case taken before a court of law, there are a thousand settled with fast guns."

For the thousandth time, Drew Collins cursed himself for not having taken the train to Kansas City. Before reaching the North Canadian, his horse had thrown a left front shoe. That would have been bad enough, but the thrown shoe had struck the animal's left rear leg, causing a deep, painful cut. He had managed to stop the bleeding, but the horse was unable to bear his weight. He would be lucky, he thought grimly, if the animal held up under the saddle until he could buy another horse. The soldiers had seemed suspicious of him, and meeting them, his pursuer would learn he was afoot. He paused, sleeved the sweat from his face, and squinted along his backtrail. Seeing nobody, he sighed in relief and trudged on toward Mobeetie.

His fourth day out of Pueblo, Nathan rode out with the soldiers toward Fort Elliott. Nearing the North Canadian, Lieutenant Bruxton reined up.

"This is where his horse lost a shoe," said Bruxton.

"His problem went beyond a thrown shoe," Nathan said. "There's dried blood on that clump of grass."

"Sir," said one of the privates, "that horse had dried blood on his left hind leg."

"You're an observing man, Private," Lieutenant Bruxton

said. "That's a hazard of having a horse throw a front shoe."

"We should catch up to this gent before he gets to Mobeetie," said Sergeant Willard.

"Maybe not," Nathan said. "He'll know I'm gaining on him, and he might have gone on, not stopping for the night."

"If that's the case," said Lieutenant Bruxton, "he'll reach Mobeetie ahead of us."

"As liveries go," Sergeant Willard said, "that one in Mobeetie ain't nothin' to get all excited about. They rent horses to the girls from the whorehouse and the saloons, but I'd be surprised if they got any for sale."

"That won't matter to Collins," said Nathan. "A coyote that's low-down enough to back-shoot a man ain't above stealin' a horse."

"From the sign," Sergeant Willard said, "he's resting more often. The horse may be weakening, and this gent ain't wantin' to tote that saddle."

When at last they could see the distant buildings that made up Mobeetie, nothing seemed amiss. But as they drew nearer, Lietenant Bruxton pointed toward the livery. A roan horse stood with head dropping. A man stepped out of the livery with a bucket in his hand, halting when he saw the riders approaching.

"That's Ike Hollister, the livery owner," said Lieutenant Bruxton.

Hollister set the bucket down before the spent roan and turned to face the riders.

"Well, Ike," Lieutenant Bruxton said, "I see you've been horse trading."

"Hoss tradin', hell," said Ike. "I gits up this mornin' and finds this poor critter just a-standin' here near dead. Next thing I knows, some skunk's behind me with a pistol in my back. He near knocks my brains out, and when I wakes up, he's done took my bay. Best damn hoss I had."

"What can you tell us about the thief?" Lieutenant Bruxton asked.

"Nothin'," said Ike sourly. "Damn it, I told you he come up behind me. I never laid eyes on the skunk. Since we ain't got law here, what do you aim to do about it?"

"Speaking on behalf of the army, there's not much we

can do," Lieutenant Bruxton replied, "but here's a man who might be able to help you. This is Nathan Stone."

Ike eyed Nathan skeptically, and Nathan quickly repeated his reason for following Drew Collins.

"I hope you gut-shoot the varmint," said Ike, "but that won't help me none, after he's rode my hoss to death."

"I'll catch up to him before he's had time for that," Nathan said, "and I'll return your horse. How far ahead of me is he?"

"Maybe two hours," said Ike.

"Lieutenant," Nathan said, "I'll need a fresh horse. I'll leave my horse here, and clear it with Captain Selman."

"You don't have any time to spare," said Lieutenant Bruxton. "Come on to the post and I'll see that you get a horse. I don't believe Captain Selman will object to that, do you, Sergeant Woodard?"

"No, sir," Sergeant Woodard said.

At Fort Elliott, Lieutenant Bruxton had one of the privates cut out a big dun from the quartermaster's corral. Quickly Nathan removed the saddle from the grulla and one of the privates took it away to be rubbed down, fed, and watered.

"Thanks, Lieutenant," said Nathan. "Tell Captain Selman I'll see him when I return."

Nathan mounted and rode out, Empty loping along behind. Since he had no idea what might be the fugitive's destination, Nathan prepared to ride in a circle until he eventually found the trail. To his surprise, he found the trail immediately; it headed due north.

"Well, by God," Nathan said to himself, "unless he changes course, he's headed for Dodge, and since it's less than sixty miles, he'll get there ahead of me. If Mr. Wyatt Earp is still town marshal, this ought to be interesting."

Nathan rode at a slow gallop, sparing the horse, knowing he couldn't overtake Collins. There was little doubt the bushwhacker intended to take the train, but unless the schedules had all changed, his luck had run out. The eastbound would have already passed through Dodge, and the westbound wouldn't arrive there until two o'clock in the afternoon. Nathan doubted that Collins would travel west, for that would return him to Pueblo, the scene of his failed ambush.

*   *   *

Two days after Nathan rode out of Pueblo, the doctor pronounced Vivian Stafford able to travel. The next morning, she and Harley, accompanied by Foster Hagerman, boarded the eastbound, returning to Dodge. It so happened that Harley Stafford had gone to the railroad depot to talk to Foster Hagerman. He looked out Hagerman's office window just in time to see Drew Collins riding toward the depot.

"By God," said Harley, getting to his feet, "yonder comes that damned back-shootin' gambler, Drew Collins."

"That can't be," Hagerman said. "It makes no sense."

"Sense or not," said Harley, "he's here. I don't know how he escaped Nathan, but he won't escape me. Damn him, he's goin' to die."

Harley stepped out the door. "Collins," he shouted, "you're covered. Get down off that horse."

Ignoring the challenge, Collins kicked the horse into a gallop. Mounting his own horse on the run, Harley galloped in pursuit. Drawing his Colt, he blasted two shots at the fleeing Collins. But fate took a hand on behalf of Drew Collins. Marshal Wyatt Earp stepped out into the street, a Colt in his hand, forcing Harley to rein up.

"Damn it," Harley shouted, "he's a killer. He shot my sister from ambush in Pueblo."

"Can you prove that?" Earp asked, in his most infuriatingly calm manner.

"No," said Harley, "but he did it."

"Not good enough," Earp said. "Put the gun away or I'll jail you for disturbing the peace."

Furious, Harley holstered his Colt and rode on in the direction Collins had gone. But Earp followed and hailed Collins as he was about to enter Delmonico's. Collins waited, and Harley couldn't believe the nerve of the man.

"Mister," said Earp, "the gent on the horse claims you shot his sister in Pueblo. What do you have to say for yourself?"

Collins laughed. "I just rode in from Texas, Marshal. I've never been in Pueblo in my life, and I've never seen this man before, until he took to throwin' lead at me."

Earp glared at Harley and, without a word, he rode back to the railroad depot, where he found Hagerman waiting for him.

"That bastard, Earp," said Harley in disgust, "takin' that

coyote's word over mine. He threatened to jail me for disturbing the peace."

"I'll admit he seems kind of slow witted at times," Hagerman said, "but for the sake of the railroad, we have to get along with him."

"Maybe you do," said Harley, "but I don't. I'm no longer with the railroad. I quit, as of right now."

"Oh, damn it," Hagerman said, "you don't have to quit. Collins can't hide behind Earp forever. When he moves on, you follow. Earp's jurisdiction doesn't go beyond Dodge."

"When I follow, I'll have Nathan Stone with me," said Harley. "Unless Collins set up another ambush and pulled it off, Nathan will be here."

A little more than two hours later, Nathan reined up before the depot. Dismounting, he stepped into Hagerman's office without knocking.

"He's here," Hagerman said. "Harley went after him, and Earp got in the way."

"Where's Harley now?"

"Stalking Collins," said Hagerman. "For the sake of the railroad, I warned him against antagonizing Earp, and he threatened to quit the railroad."

"I don't blame him," Nathan said. "Is Dodge that hard up for a lawman?"

"I didn't accept his resignation," said Hagerman. "He has my permission to follow Collins when he rides out, beyond Earp's jurisdiction."

"He won't be riding out," Nathan said. "He'll hunker right here and wait for the next eastbound."

"Where are you going?" Hagerman asked as Nathan turned toward the door.

"Fortunately, I don't work for the railroad," said Nathan.

"I can't stand behind you if you go against the law," Hagerman said.

"I don't recall asking you to," said Nathan as he mounted his horse.

Hagerman watched him ride away. He genuinely liked Nathan Stone, and rued the day Nathan stepped over the line and went against the law.

Nathan found Harley leaning against a hitch rail, across the dirt street from the Long Branch Saloon.

"He's in there, I reckon," said Nathan, dismounting.

"Yeah," Harley said, "and so is Earp. He's had a mad

on for me ever since I came here. With Hagerman's help, he's using this Collins coyote to put me down."

"I don't work for Hagerman," said Nathan, "and since Collins was shooting at me, this is my fight. I came here for Collins, and I'll get him, if I have to take Earp's pistol away from him and bend it over his skull. Come on."

With Harley following, Nathan crossed the street to the Long Branch. Wyatt Earp leaned against the bar. Involved in a poker game, Drew Collins sat at a table with three other men. Ignoring Earp, Nathan stalked to the table, where Collins sat facing the door. Collins rose to his feet, his hands shoulder high.

"You got nothin' against me, Stone, and I ain't armed."

"You back-shootin' son," said Nathan, through clenched teeth, "I'll kill you with my bare hands."

"Back off, Stone," Earp shouted, his hand on the butt of his Colt.

But Nathan might not have heard. He seized Drew Collins by his shirtfront, dragging him across the table. He drove his right fist into the gambler's face, and Collins went back across the table, slamming into the wall. He stood there, head sagging, but before Nathan could go after him, Earp had drawn and cocked his Colt.

"One more move out of you," said Earp, "and I'll shoot you. Now you turn around and do it slow. Then you loosen your pistol belts and let 'em fall."

Nathan turned around slowly, between Earp and Collins.

"Nathan!" Harley shouted.

Nathan dropped to the floor and rolled, coming up on one knee, his Colt spitting lead. Collins had drawn a gun from beneath his coat, and his slug ripped into the bar, inches to the left of the startled Earp. Both of Nathan's slugs had struck Collins in the chest, and he slumped back against the wall and slid to the floor.

"The back-shootin' little varmint got what he deserved," said a railroad man.

Nathan got to his feet, holstered his Colt, and fixed his cold eyes on Earp. When he spoke, it was loud enough for every man to hear.

"Mr. Earp, that little sidewinder was about to finish what he started in Pueblo, when he ambushed me and gunned down Vivian Stafford. If it hadn't been for Harley, he'd have shot me in the back, with you allowin' it to happen. I'm claiming self-defense."

Earp was in a bad position and knew it. Most of the saloon's patrons were railroad men who, along with the two bartenders, remembered Nathan Stone. Their faces reflected their disgust, and Earp yielded with poor grace.

"I'm callin' it self-defense," said Earp. "This time. You're not welcome here, and I want you out of town."

"I have friends here," Nathan replied, "and I'll go when I'm ready. I'm not ready."

Some of the men who knew Nathan laughed and others grinned, not so much at what Nathan had said as at the change it had wrought in Earp. His face had gone red; without a word he stalked out of the saloon.

"Everybody to the bar," said Harley. "The drinks are on me."

Nathan and Harley left the Long Branch, mounted their horses, and rode back toward the railroad depot.

"That was smooth," Harley said. "You showed Collins up for the back-shootin' coyote he was. Even Earp could see that."

"But he didn't like seein' it at his expense," said Nathan, "and he'll be watching me. I could end up in his *juzgado* from spittin' on the boardwalk."

"Vivian's goin' to be glad to see you," Harley said. "She won't hardly leave the Dodge House unless I'm with her. She can't stand Earp, and he follows her like a shadow. Since I'm with the railroad, I can't antagonize Earp without Hagerman comin' down on me. I'd as well warn you—she's decided she'd rather risk bein' shot with you than have Earp follow her around when I ain't here. I've talked to Hagerman but he claims he's in no position to discipline Earp. Hagerman's just one of ten men on the town council, and the rest of them are sold on Earp. I'm thinking of quitting the railroad, taking Vivian, and moving on."

"For the times," said Nathan, "it's a good job. Nothing else pays as well. If you quit, where will you go and what will you do?"

"I have no idea," Harley said. "I'll be doing it for Vivian. I ran out on her once, and I won't do it again."

"I understand," said Nathan, "and I agree with you. Something must be done. We're stuck with Earp until he moves on or the town council gets enough of him, and I don't see you quitting the railroad as a solution. If you're willing to risk it, and she wants to go, I'll take Vivian with me."

"She wants to go and I'm willing for her to," Harley said. "We just don't want you feelin' like you've been boxed in, that she's become a burden."

"She's never been a burden," said Nathan. "If I didn't care for her, I wouldn't be concerned about something happening to her."

"Like what happened in Pueblo," Harley said. "We understand and appreciate your concern, but she's willing to take the risk. I'm willing, because she needs a man like you. I know you would fight to the death for her, and no man who ever lived could do more than that. Take her, with my blessing. She's at the Dodge House. Why don't you ride over there and tell her what you've decided?"

"I will," said Nathan. "Tomorrow I'll be riding back to Fort Elliott. I left my grulla there and I promised to return the horse Collins stole from the livery at Mobeetie."

Nathan rode on to the Dodge House and wasn't surprised to find Earp slouched in a chair in the lobby. He glared at Nathan through slitted eyes, but Nathan ignored him.

"Oh, I'm so glad to see you!" Vivian cried when she opened her door. "Come in and tell me what's happened."

She closed and locked the door, and Nathan told her everything, up to and including the showdown with Drew Collins.

"Wyatt Earp may be a wonderful town marshal," she said, "but I can't stand him. Now he'll make it as hard on you as he can, because you've made him look small."

Nathan laughed. "He doesn't cast as long a shadow as he thinks. Harley and me just had a talk, and we've decided you're better off with me, bein' shot at, than bein' stalked by *Señor* Earp while Harley's away."

"Do you mean it?" she cried. "Do you *really* want me?"

"I mean it," said Nathan, "and I do want you. I just don't want you shot, but neither do I want Earp hounding you. I'll buy you a horse, a saddle, and saddlebags. We'll leave for Fort Elliott and Mobeetie in the morning."

"I'll be ready," she said. "Will you be joining Harley and me for supper?"

"Yes," said Nathan, "and for now, you'd best stay where you are. Earp's out there in the lobby."

CHAPTER 2

"Grandma, why can't you tell me somethin' about my pa? Who was he?"

Young John Wesley Tremayne would soon be eleven years old. John Tremayne—his grandfather—had been dead a year, leaving Anna to raise the boy as best she could. Now it was up to her to lie to the boy, and she sighed.

"John, I can't tell you what I don't know."

"Don't call me John," he begged. "Call me Wes, like Wes Hardin, the outlaw."

"I will not," said Anna. "You were named after your grandfather, John, and my own father, Wesley."

The boy stomped out in disgust. Anna Tremayne removed her spectacles and rubbed her eyes. Now that John was gone and her own health was failing, what was going to become of the boy? He had been given his grandfather's watch; inside the cover was the only photograph they had of Molly Tremayne, John Wesley's mother. She had died at the boy's birth, and all they knew of the affair that had led to the child's arrival was the little she had written in her diary. There were the dates—the days Anna and her husband had been away, leaving Molly alone at home—and a man's name. Nathan.* They hadn't known the diary existed until Molly was dead. She had told them nothing. The final entry, written the day before Molly had died, had been a message to John and Anna Tremayne:

I am truly sorry. Sorry for what I have done, and sorry to so burden you. The child is to be told nothing.

*The Dawn of Fury (Book 1)

Approaching her time, Molly Tremayne had been deathly ill, screaming as she awakened from her sleep, and troubled with premonitions of her own death. John and Anna had fulfilled her wishes, telling the boy not even the little they knew or suspected. Now, more than ever, Anna Tremayne regretted having lived a lie, for she feared the bitterness she could see in the cold blue eyes of young John Wesley Tremayne.

Fort Elliott, Texas
May 28, 1877

"While we're here at Fort Elliott," said Vivian, "I want you to buy me a pistol and a supply of shells. If I'm going to be shot at, I intend to shoot back."

"You should have told me before we left Dodge," Nathan said. "The .31-caliber Colt pocket pistol is a mite easier to handle, but the sutler's store may not have them."

Nathan had returned the stolen horse to the livery in Mobeetie, and the horse that Lieutenant Bruxton had loaned him to the quartermaster's corral. Vivian led her horse as they walked back to the orderly room and the post commander's office. Sergeant Willard grinned at them as they entered the orderly room.

"Captain Selman's expecting you," said the sergeant.

Nathan opened the door to Selman's office, and he and Vivian stepped inside. Except for more gray in his hair, Selman had changed little. He stood up to greet them.

"Lieutenant Bruxton told me you had stopped long enough to borrow a fresh horse and had gone on your way," Selman said. "I trust your mission was successful."

"It was," said Nathan. "I've returned your horse, along with the one stolen from the livery in Mobeetie. Do I owe anything for the loan of the horse?"

"We'll call it even," Selman replied, "since you recovered the horse taken from Ike's livery. With the army bein' the only law in these parts, he'd have never let us forget we had fallen down on the job. Will you folks be staying the night?"

"If you can put us up," said Nathan. "My dog didn't make it any farther than the mess hall."

Captain Selman laughed. "The cooks haven't forgotten him. They never have anything to throw out while he's here."

"I've been away from the newspapers and the telegraph for a while," Nathan said. "Is there anything of importance happening?"

"Congress finally got together long enough to agree on one sensible bill," said Selman. "Reconstruction is over, and the people are again in control of their local governments."

"Thank God," said Nathan. "It's been hard times."

"It's been hard on the military, too," Selman said. "We've had to enforce an unpopular law that most of us thought harsh and vindictive. I doubt we'll ever live it down."

"I think you will, Captain," said Nathan. "Most folks are coming to realize that many of their problems originate in Congress. I came west right after the war and I've always been treated fairly by the military."

"It's kind of you to adopt that attitude," Selman replied, "but it seems we no sooner put out one fire than Congress starts another. According to the telegraph, there are small ranchers in Wyoming calling for soldiers to prevent a range war."

"Why, hell," said Nathan. "Wyoming's still a territory."

"Of course it is," Selman said, "but there are petitions for statehood cropping up all over the frontier, and it's only a matter of time until those territories become part of the Union. Supposedly, that's why the Congress passed the Desert Land Act back in March."

"And it's already causing trouble?"

"In spades," said Captain Selman. "The act provides for the sale of a hundred and sixty acres of land at twenty-five cents an acre to anyone willing to irrigate a portion of the land within three years, and at the end of that time, to pay an additional dollar an acre to secure ownership."

"That sounds reasonable enough," Nathan said, "but I reckon it ain't workin' out that way."

"No," said Selman. "While the bill was passed supposedly to help pioneers, it is doing exactly the opposite. Apparently, it was lobbied through Congress by a few wealthy cattlemen as a means of acquiring enormous tracts of land for next to nothing. As the small ranchers have pointed out, a man with money can gobble up thousands of acres. He needs hire just four men and get their signatures on the proper papers, and he has control of a full section. Six hundred and forty acres."

"And that's what's happening in Wyoming," said Nathan.

"In the Powder River Basin," Selman replied. "Some of them have picked up blanket Indians, had them sign the necessary papers, and claimed land in their names. Have you ever known an Indian to even get close to anything resembling work?"

Nathan laughed. "Such as irrigation?"

"You get the idea, then," said Selman. "With Congress on the outs with President Hayes, there'll be no soldiers deployed, but there'll be trouble in Wyoming for somebody. The Powder River may run red."

On that somber note, Nathan and Vivian left Selman's office. Sergeant Willard then led them to a cabin that had been assigned to them for the night.

"Supper's at five," Sergeant Willard said. "I'll see you then."

"You get along well with the military," said Vivian when Willard had gone.

"They've been more than decent to me," Nathan said, "and on the frontier a man needs all the friends he can get. Besides, they've had the telegraph and I've often needed it. I never know when I'll have need of it again. Remember how it got word to us when Harley had been shot?"

"I'll never forget that," said Vivian. "Where are we going when we leave here?"

"First to Fort Worth and then to New Orleans," Nathan said. "I like to leave word with Captain Ferguson where I can be reached. Then we'll go on to New Orleans. When I'm tired of drifting, of shooting and being shot at, I spend a few weeks—or months—with my friends Barnabas and Bess McQueen. They have a horse ranch, and Eulie's buried next to the horse barn."

"They'll always remember you being there ... with her," said Vivian. "Do you think I'll be welcome?"

"Of course you will," Nathan said. "That's where I told Harley he could reach us if he needs to."

"It sounds nice," said Vivian. "What will we do there?"

Nathan laughed. "As little as possible. We'll eat, sleep,

and maybe attend a horse race or two. Barnabas trains horses and races them."

Nathan and Vivian spent a pleasant hour over supper in the enlisted men's mess hall and then went to the sutler's store, seeking a weapon for Vivian.

"We don't get much call for the .31-caliber Colt," they were told, "so we don't sell 'em new. But we got a second-hand piece. Belonged to a gambler that couldn't back up his bluff with his gun."

"We'll take it," said Nathan, "along with two hundred rounds of ammunition, a pistol belt, and a holster."

"It's still early," Vivian said. "What are we going to do now?"

"We're going back to the cabin," said Nathan, "and for the next several hours, you're going to practice drawing and cocking that pistol. It won't be worth a damn to you until you can draw and fire without shooting yourself in the leg or foot."

Fort Worth, Texas
June 1, 1877

"I reckon we'll stay the night," said Nathan, "and give you a chance to meet the post commander, Captain Ferguson."

Ferguson welcomed them, and after visiting with the captain in his office, Nathan and Vivian were assigned quarters for the night.

"You have impressive friends, Nathan," Vivian said.

"Captain Ferguson was lacking a post telegrapher once," said Nathan, "and I filled in until he could get a man assigned. The captain hasn't forgotten."*

"How far are we from New Orleans?"

"About five hundred miles," said Nathan. "Taking our time, we're a week away."

Leaving Fort Worth, they rode eastward, bearing a little to the south. There were no large towns, and many of the villages through which they passed had no hotel or board-inghouse. Often they cooked over an open fire and slept near a spring or a creek. Empty ran on ahead, and their

The Dawn of Fury (Book 1)

journey was without incident. They crossed the Mississippi at Natchez, and spent the night there before riding on to New Orleans. As they followed the river south, one of the big boats passed, its paddle wheel churning as it headed north.

"They're so grand looking," said Vivian. "This is the closest I've ever been to one."

"When we're ready to leave New Orleans," Nathan said, "maybe we'll take one to St. Louis."

"I'd like that," said Vivian. "There's so much I've never seen or done."

New Orleans
June 9, 1877

"We won't spend any time in town," Nathan said. "I'm fair-to-middlin' sure there's at least a few hombres here that would like to see me dead."

They rode on until they could see the roof of McQueen's horse barn. Empty ran on ahead, and without hesitation took the tree-lined road toward the distant McQueen house. A breeze whispered through the leaves of the majestic oaks, and their shade offered pleasant respite from the sun.

"It all looks so peaceful," said Vivian.

But looks were deceiving. Empty began barking, and a buzzard flapped sluggishly into the sky, coming to rest atop the horse barn.

"Something's wrong," Nathan said, kicking the grulla into a gallop.

Vivian followed, reining up behind Nathan as they neared the house. It had a vacant look, and the front door stood open. Empty awaited their arrival, growling deep in his throat. Nathan's heart sank when he discovered what had attracted the buzzards. Near the house lay the mutilated remains of Barnabas McQueen's four hounds. As unnerving as the sight was, the odor was worse. Nathan's horse shied at the smell of death and, reining up, he dismounted. Vivian reined up, waiting, as Nathan went closer. Quickly he turned away and returned to the grulla.

"What killed them?" Vivian asked.

"They were shot," said Nathan. "We'll leave the horses next to the barn and go on to the house on foot. Keep your pistol handy; I don't know what's waiting for us."

Remembering the McQueens had always entered the house through the kitchen, Nathan ignored the open front door. Vivian followed him around the house, waiting as he tried the back door. It opened readily, and she followed him into the kitchen. A chair lay on its side and fragments of a broken dish were scattered on the floor. A length of stove wood lay under the table, while on the otherwise clean white tablecloth there were flecks of dried blood.

"They put up a fight," said Nathan, "but they were taken away. The dogs have been dead maybe two days."

"What could have happened to them, and why?" Vivian asked.

"I don't know," said Nathan, "but I have an idea. Barnabas bought and trained horses. Expensive horses. Let's have a look in the barn."

There were no horses in the barn. Vivian stepped out ahead of Nathan, and he closed the door. Immediately he began looking for tracks, and there were plenty.

"The trail's two days old," Nathan said. "What I don't understand is why they didn't kill Barnabas and Bess instead of taking them along."

"Empty's found something," said Vivian.

The dog ran toward them, and with a yip turned and ran back the way he had come.

"Let's ride," Nathan said. "He's found a trail."

They rode at a slow gallop, Empty keeping well ahead of them, and when they reached a patch of bare ground, Nathan reined up, studying the tracks.

"Ten horses," said Nathan, "four of them on lead ropes. Allowin' mounts for Barnabas and Bess, there's four of the varmints."

The trail led to the south; occasionally the distant blue of the Gulf of Mexico could be seen through the trees.

"This makes no sense," Nathan said. "The way they're headed, there'll soon be water everywhere except behind them. That leaves just one possibility."

"A boat," said Vivian.

"Yes," Nathan replied, "and that's where we'll lose them."

But the trail began veering back to the west, following

the shore line, and the blue of the gulf was clearly visible to their left. Entering a profusion of undergrowth, willows, and cane, they were forced to dismount and lead their horses. Suddenly, before them was the desolate remains of a cabin. The shake roof was gone, and the standing walls were so mossed over they were all but invisible.

"We'll have to take it slow," Nathan said softly. "They could be holed up here."

But somewhere within the ruins, Empty yipped three times.

"Empty says it's safe," said Nathan. "Come on."

They found Barnabas McQueen first. He lay face down, his hands bound behind him, and he had been shot twice. In the back.

"Vivian," Nathan said, "see if you can find Bess."

Cutting the bonds, Nathan tried both wrists, but failed to find a pulse. Frantically, he sought the big artery in the neck, sighing with relief when he found a spark of life.

"I found Bess," said Vivian.

"How bad?" Nathan asked.

"Bad enough," said Vivian. "She's been stripped, brutalized, and shot, but she's still alive. She's burning up with fever."

"So is Barnabas," Nathan said, "but at least they're alive. We must get them to a doctor, pronto, and we'll need a buckboard. We're only three or four miles south of town. I'll leave Empty with you, and I'll be back as soon as I can."

Nathan galloped away. The only livery he knew of was across the street from the St. Charles Hotel; he had no time to search for one any closer, so he went there.

"I need a buckboard and team," he told the liveryman. "I'd like to leave my horse with you and claim him when I return the buckboard. I have some sick folks in bad need of a hospital. Where's the nearest one?"

"Five blocks down St. Charles, on the left," said the liveryman. "It's the Le Croix."

"Thanks," Nathan said. Climbing to the box, he flicked the reins, guiding the team into the cobbled street.

Waiting for Nathan, Vivian looked around for Bess McQueen's clothing. Finding none, she wrapped the unfortunate woman in a blanket. She then went to see about

Barnabas, and was startled to find his eyes open, watching her.

"Who ... are ... you?" he croaked.

"Vivian Stafford. I'm with Nathan Stone. He's gone for a buckboard."

"Bess ...?"

"She's alive," said Vivian.

"Thank ... God ..." Barnabas mumbled. His eyes closed and he was again lost to a burning fever.

It seemed hours before Vivian heard the welcome rattle of the approaching buckboard. Vivian had a blanket ready, and they lifted Barnabas onto it and took him to the buckboard first. Bess was within the ruins of the cabin and would have to be carried farther. When they had her in the buckboard beside Barnabas, Nathan climbed to the seat, flicked the reins, and started the team toward town. Vivian rode alongside while Empty followed. Nathan turned on to St. Charles and soon reined up before the Le Croix Hospital. By the time Nathan was off the box, attendants were there with stretchers. Empty remained with the buckboard while Nathan and Vivian followed the stretcher-bearing attendants into the hospital. A nurse approached Nathan with pad and pencil.

"Barnabas and Bess McQueen," said Nathan. "They've been shot."

"Who are you?" the nurse asked. "Are you responsible for them?"

"A friend of theirs, Nathan Stone, and yes, I'll be responsible for them. Do what you must. They're burning up with fever."

Barnabas and Bess were taken away, and it was almost an hour before Nathan and Vivian had any word. Finally a doctor approached them.

"I'm Dr. McKendree. I have removed the lead, and fortunately their vitals have been spared. But they've lost a lot of blood, and infection has already taken hold. We're doing our best to save them. Have you notified the police?"

"No," said Nathan. "We have no idea who shot them. There'll be time enough for that when they're able to talk. When will you have another report on their condition?"

"We should know something by noon tomorrow," McKendree said.

Nathan and Vivian returned to the buckboard, and only then did Nathan speak.

"Wait here until I return the buckboard and get my horse. Then we'll find us a hotel or boardinghouse. We'll be here until Barnabas and Bess are able to talk. I'm hoping they can tell us who's responsible for this."

"And then?"

"Then we go after the varmints," said Nathan.

They found a boardinghouse with a stable across the alley, not far from the Le Croix Hospital. While Nathan and Vivian approached the front desk, Empty sat near the door. The old lady looked at Nathan, at the dog, and back to Nathan.

"He makes a mess," she said, "you clean it up or pay to have it done. Two dollars a day. Meals is extra."

Nathan paid for two days in advance and accepted the key; then the pair left to stable their horses. That done, they returned to the boardinghouse. Their room was in the rear with an outside entrance.

"We might as well get some rest," Nathan said. "I don't know of anything to do in this town except visit the saloons, drink, and gamble."

"I think we can do better than that," said Vivian. "Besides, if you've had trouble here, you shouldn't be seen any more than necessary."

"My thoughts, exactly," Nathan said. "I don't know that I still have enemies here, but I don't want to confirm it by being shot in the back."

Rather than attract too much attention, Nathan and Vivian left their horses stabled and walked back to the Le Croix Hospital. They waited half an hour before the doctor could see them.

"Another day," said McKendree, "and the infection would have been too far advanced. But you got them here in time, and unless they take an unexpected turn for the worse, I believe they'll recover."

"How long before we can talk to them?" Nathan asked.

"Not for another forty-eight hours," said McKendree, "and maybe not then. It will depend on their progress."

McKendree ended the conversation and went about his business, leaving Nathan and Vivian with time on their hands. For the lack of anything better to do, they returned to their room at the boardinghouse.

"Now," said Vivian, removing her boots, "aren't you glad I came with you?"

"I am, for a fact," Nathan replied. "I've never been very good at waiting around with nothing to do. Can you keep me busy until suppertime?"

"I reckon," said Vivian, "but not with you standing there in your boots, britches, hat, and gunbelt."

They slept, awakening an hour before sundown.

"I know a cafe near the Pioneer Hotel that serves fried catfish," Nathan said. "I'm willing to risk gettin' shot for a mess of catfish."

"Is that all they have?"

"Oh, no," said Nathan. "They have 'gator tail, crab, oysters, and just about any kind of critter that can be hauled out of the river or the gulf."

Vivian shuddered. "I've always been partial to catfish, myself."

Time dragged, but somehow they survived, and the fourth day after the McQueens had been taken to the Le Croix Hospital, Dr. McKendree allowed Nathan and Vivian to spend a few minutes with them. Barnabas and Bess, in separate beds, were in the same room. Nathan wasted no time introducing Vivian, and after a glad welcome from Barnabas and Bess, Nathan questioned them and Barnabas replied.

"Remember the big black, Diablo, that Eulie trained?"

"Yes," said Nathan.

"He's never lost a race. On Sunday, June fourth, we raced him at Natchez, and every other horse ate his dust. A gambler from Shreveport, Rutledge Jackman, offered us twenty thousand dollars for Diablo, and we refused to sell. It ended in a cuss fight, with Jackman swearing he would have Diablo. Four of them came after us, and they struck just before first light. Two of them gunned down the dogs while the other two came after us. First they shot me. Likely would have killed me, but Bess brained one of them with a stick of stove wood, and they went after her. That's when I blacked out."

"It's well that he did," Bess cut in. "They tore my clothes off. If he'd seen them do ... what they did ... hurt as he was, he'd have fought them. And they would have killed him."

"You're both alive," said Nathan, "and that's worth any sacrifice. They're going to pay for what they've done, along with Rutledge Jackman. Your horses will be returned, too."

"Nathan," Barnabas said, "you've saved our lives, and that's all we have any right to expect. This is my fight."

"You're in no condition to fight," said Nathan, "and by the time you are, this damned Rutledge Jackman may have sold your horses, or hidden them where you can't find them."

"I must admit that bothers me," Barnabas said. "The other three horses aren't quite in Diablo's class, but they have the potential. They represent seven years of hard work."

"That's why I'm going after them," said Nathan. "Is there anything more you can tell me about Rutledge Jackman?"

"Only that he's ruthless," Barnabas said. "God only knows how many men he hires, and they may all be killers. I can't let you go up against such odds alone."

"You have no choice," said Nathan. "Besides, I work better alone."

"You're not going alone," Vivian said.

Bess laughed. "Nathan Stone, she's a strong woman. You ride with him, my dear, and watch his back."

"Barnabas," said Nathan, "the doctor has already mentioned the law. Since you have no proof to support what you've told us, the law won't be much help. Anything you tell them now could point to you as a suspect when I'm done with Rutledge Jackman."

"We won't be telling the law anything, except that four men shot and robbed us," Barnabas said. "We can truthfully say we've never seen them before."

"Good," said Nathan. "That leaves me free to use whatever manner of persuasion may be necessary. I know Diablo, but how can I identify the other three horses?"

"There's another black that could be Diablo's double," Barnabas said. "The other two are chestnuts, and all four are branded with a crown on the left hip."

"I want you and Bess to remain here in the hospital for a few days," said Nathan, "and when you're allowed to go home, lock your doors at night and arm yourselves. We'll return as soon as we can and bring your horses."

"I don't know how to thank you," Barnabas said.

"You don't owe me any thanks," said Nathan. "Any wrong done to my friends is a wrong done to me. *Vaya con Dios.*"

Nathan stepped out of the room, followed by Vivian. Neither spoke until they had left the hospital.

"All we know is a man's name and where he is," Vivian said.

"I've hunted men with a lot less," said Nathan. "We'll ride to Shreveport and have us a look at this Rutledge Jackman."

"What do you intend to do, beyond recovering the horses?" Vivian asked.

"I aim to teach Jackman and his bunch the error of their ways," said Nathan. "Those four who robbed and shot Barnabas and Bess won't ever do that again."

CHAPTER 3

"First," said Nathan, "we'll find us an out-of-the-way boardinghouse. Then we'll set about investigating this Rutledge Jackman."

The boardinghouse wasn't as isolated as Nathan would have liked, but within walking distance there was a livery. The hostler had a female hound that struck Empty's fancy, and it would be a convenient place to leave Empty when it became inconvenient to bring the dog along

"Pardner," said Nathan when the liveryman had stabled their mounts, "I'm interested in fast horses, and I hear there's an hombre in these parts who buys, sells, and races 'em. Can you tell me anything about him? His name is Rutledge Jackman."

"Nothin' to tell," the hostler said, a little too hurriedly. "Owns the Five Aces Saloon here in town, and Jackman Stables, just north of here on the Red."

He hurried away, unable or unwilling to say more.

"Which are we going to visit first?" Vivian asked.

"I'm going to visit the Five Aces Saloon," said Nathan. "You're going to wait for me in our room at the boardinghouse."

"It won't be easy for me, watching your back from there," Vivian said.

"We're not in deep enough for that," said Nathan. "It may be best if Jackman doesn't know we're together."

"I've had saloon experience," Vivian said. "I can always hire on at the Five Aces."

"I don't think so," said Nathan. "Somehow, I believe Harley expects better of you, and of me."

Despite her protests, Nathan left her at the boardinghouse and went looking for the Five Aces Saloon. Somehow he must learn what Jackman intended to do with the horses taken from Barnabas McQueen. Was Jackman going to sell the animals or race them? With the McQueens being left for dead, Nathan was inclined to think Jackman intended to keep and race the horses. Nathan needed time, for his was a threefold task. Not only were the four who had robbed and shot the McQueens going to pay, but so would Rutledge Jackman for having sent them. Finally, Nathan intended to recover McQueen's four horses. The Five Aces could only be described as elegant. The mahogany bar was fifty feet long, and even in the early afternoon three bartenders were on duty. There was a poker game already in progress, but that didn't interest Nathan. Three men sat at a table near the far end of the bar, and on the shirtfront of one of them was a lawman's star. The other two were well dressed in town clothes. One of them beckoned to a bartender.

"Yes, sir, Mr. Jackman," said the bartender, breaking out a new bottle.

Nathan made his way to the bar and ordered a beer. It allowed him a few minutes to study Jackman. The lawman laughed at something Jackman said, and it was obvious the two were on good terms. Such information might prove useful. Nathan finished his beer and left the saloon. Suppertime wasn't far off, so he returned to the boardinghouse.

"Well?" Vivian said.

"I had a look at the mighty Rutledge Jackman," said Nathan, "and he's drinking with the sheriff. That pretty well eliminates the possibility of us depending on the law, but his being on good terms with Jackman may work in our favor. Through him, we're going to force Jackman to lead us to the four no-account coyotes who robbed and left Barnabas and Bess for dead. Then we're going to make it so risky that Jackman will try to dispose of the four horses stolen from Barnabas. When he does, we'll get the horses and him."

"You make it sound so simple," Vivian said.

"It's anything but simple," said Nathan. "We're going to need a telegram sent from New Orleans to the sheriff here in Shreveport. I'm counting on him being aware of these four horses Jackman has, and I want him to know those horses were stolen from Barnabas McQueen. To really spook Jackman, this telegram from Barnabas will offer a five-thousand-dollar reward."

"My God," Vivian said, "how are we going to accomplish that? You'd need to talk to Barnabas, and it's a four-day ride back to New Orleans. Even if Barnabas agreed to sending the telegram, Jackman could dispose of the horses before we could return here."

"We're not going to New Orleans," said Nathan, "and Barnabas won't be sending that telegram. I have a friend in Washington—Byron Silver—who can arrange to have this telegram sent from New Orleans. But to reach Silver, I need the unrestricted use of the telegraph. The nearest access will be through Captain Ferguson at Fort Worth."

"How far?"

"Not quite two hundred miles," Nathan said. "Two days there and two days back. I'll have Silver delay the telegram until we've had time to return here. I'm counting on our friend the sheriff to make the connection between Jackman and the stolen horses and to warn Jackman. McQueen's signature on the telegram will tell Jackman that the varmints who took the horses bungled the killing of the McQueens."

"Then Jackman will lead us to the four who shot the McQueens and took the horses."

"I'm counting on it," said Nathan. "He may have the stolen horses at his stable, but he won't feel safe leaving them there. I look for him to distance himself from the horses as well as the men who took them. Where they go, we'll follow."

"We'll still be up against four men."

"That's cutting the odds about as fine as they're likely to get," Nathan said. "Jackman is the kind who might have a dozen or more hired guns. Our only chance is to force him to cut out the four varmints we want, along with McQueen's horses."

"Then you'll settle for that, leaving Jackman alone?"

"I didn't say that," said Nathan. "First things first."

They found a quiet cafe and had supper, after arranging to have Empty fed in the kitchen. There was little talk, and they were almost at the boardinghouse before Nathan finally spoke.

"You're mighty quiet. I reckon you don't care for my plan."

"Oh, I do like it. All but the last part. Must you go after Rutledge Jackman?"

"Yes," Nathan said. "That's the most important part. Signing Barnabas McQueen's name to a telegram and leaving Rutledge Jackman alive would condemn Barnabas to death. He expected to get away with the horses by murdering the McQueens. If he's left alive, he won't fail a second time. I won't leave Barnabas and Bess with such a threat hanging over their heads."

The sun had dipped below the horizon, feathering the western sky with crimson, and somewhere a night bird chirped. Vivian had paused, and when Nathan turned to her, tears were on her cheeks. When she finally spoke, the words came softly, and he had to lean close to hear.

"I've never known a man like you, Nathan Stone. For something—or someone—you believe in, you would die, wouldn't you?"

"Yes," said Nathan. "Can a man do any less and go on callin' himself a man?"

Words were inadequate. She threw her arms around him, kissing him long and hard. With Nathan's arm around her, they walked on toward the boardinghouse, Empty trotting along beside them.

Fort Worth, Texas
June 23, 1877

"I didn't expect to see you again so soon," Captain Ferguson said when Nathan and Vivian stepped into his office.

"I must admit there's a selfish motive," said Nathan. "I need the use of your telegraph for a private talk with Byron Silver in Washington. I know it's asking a lot, and I didn't feel comfortable asking anyone but you."

Ferguson laughed. "I'm flattered, my friend. I'll arrange for the telegrapher to take off as much time as you need."

Vivian accompanied Nathan to the telegrapher's shack. Nathan began with twenty-one, Silver's code, following it with the Washington address. When he was given permission to send, he tapped out a short message:

Request twenty-one be present.

"We may have to wait awhile," said Nathan. "I'm asking that Silver be present. This could get him in trouble with

his superiors if they know what I'm about to ask of him.
I want him on the other end of the wire before I send
any details."

"If it can get him in trouble," Vivian said, "he may not
agree to it."

"Silver's a Texan," said Nathan. "He's bent or broken
enough rules to be sent to the federal pen for life. Why
should he stop now?"

While they waited for Silver to respond, there were several messages of a military nature. Nathan telegraphed permission to send, received each message, and set them aside.

"I hope he's there," Vivian said when they had waited
almost an hour.

"So do I," said Nathan.

Finally the instrument rattled a message and Nathan took
it down. The brief message read:

Twenty-one here stop. Identify yourself.

Nathan replied:

*Stone stop. Whiskey ring stop. Saint Louis.**

It referred to a government mission in which Nathan had
assisted Silver and it drew an immediate response. Nathan
laughed and began sending. It took time to convey his request, and more time for Silver's response, which proved
to be a series of questions.

"It's taking a long time," said Vivian. "Is he going to
help us?"

"Yes," Nathan said, "but he's offering too much help.
All I need from him is to have that telegram sent from
New Orleans, with Barnabas McQueen's name signed to
it."

After Nathan had telegraphed his answer to Silver, it was
a while before the telegraph key again rattled a request to
receive. Frowning, Nathan read the message.

"What is it?" Vivian asked.

"He doesn't like the idea of signing McQueen's name to
a telegram without Barnabas knowing about it," said Nathan. "He wants to send Captain Powers to alert Barnabas

*The Killing Season (Book 2)

to the plan. If Barnabas agrees, *then* the telegram will be sent."

"That's smart," Vivian said. "For all we know, when Jackman learns of the telegram signed by Barnabas, he might send his killers after the McQueens to finish the job. It's the least we can do, warning Barnabas. Who is Captain Powers?"

"Part of a federal force stationed in New Orleans. Once, after Silver and I had been ambushed—the day Eulie was shot—the McQueens took Silver in and patched him up. It was then that Captain Powers became friends with Barnabas and Bess."*

"You have powerful friends, Nathan. I'd like to meet this Byron Silver."

"You may have the opportunity," said Nathan. "One way or another, we seem to come together every few months."

The telegraph again chattered for permission to send, and Nathan granted it. Quickly he took down the brief incoming message. It said:

Powers being contacted stop. Fort Smith being contacted stop. Stand by.

"I don't doubt Barnabas will go along with us," Nathan said, "but why is he contacting Fort Smith? If the McQueens have left the hospital, Powers will have to ride out to the McQueen place. We could be here awhile. I'd better tell Captain Ferguson."

Taking the messages he had received pertaining to military business, Nathan knocked on Captain Ferguson's door.

"Silver's going to be a while getting back to me," Nathan said. "I don't want to take advantage of your generosity."

"You aren't," said Ferguson. "Stay with the instrument if you like. You can receive any messages intended for me."

Nathan returned to the telegrapher's shack, taking down several messages for Captain Ferguson while he waited for a response from Silver. Three hours later it came.

Barnabas approves stop. Message three days stop. Marshal from Fort Smith.

The Dawn of Fury (Book 1)

"Damn it," said Nathan, "I didn't ask for help from Fort Smith. Why couldn't he just send the telegram and leave the rest to me?"

"I'm glad he's sending help from Fort Smith," Vivian said. "I have a pistol, but I've never shot anyone. You could be up against four of Jackman's gunman, as well as Jackman himself. But how will the marshal find us?"

"He'll know we're returning from Fort Worth," said Nathan. "He'll intercept us before we reach Shreveport. I've spent considerable time at Fort Smith, and I'm not unknown."

Nathan and Vivian stayed the night in Fort Worth, and at first light said goodbye to Captain Ferguson. Their second day on the trail, a few miles west of Shreveport, Empty turned back to meet them, growling a warning.

"Somebody up ahead," said Nathan. "Rein up."

Another hundred yards and they would have entered dense woods. Nathan shouted a challenge.

"Come on out, keepin' your hands up."

Hands shoulder high, the rider trotted his horse into the open, and the westering sun glinted off the badge pinned to his vest. He laughed.

"Nathan Stone, it's good to see you again. Is it all right if I put my hands down?"

"I reckon," said Nathan. "Come on."

"You know him, then," Vivian said.

"Yes," said Nathan. "It's Mel Holt. Him and me stood off a bunch of killers once."*

Holt reined up, put out his hand, and Nathan took it.

"Mel," Nathan said, "this is Vivian Stafford, sister to a friend of mine."

"Pardner," said Holt, his eyes on Vivian, "I purely admire your judgement. Has this friend of yours got another sister like her?"

Vivian blushed and Nathan laughed.

"There's a spring up ahead," Holt said. "Let's make camp and cook some supper. Then we got some talkin' to do."

Holt listened while Nathan unfolded the story, concluding with his plan to force the gambler, Rutledge Jackman, to lead them to the stolen McQueen horses.

*The Killing Season (Book 2)

"If he leads us to the stolen horses," said Holt, "that's all the proof I'd need or want. You realize, of course, that we must call on them to surrender and take them alive if we can."

"Yeah," Nathan said. "I've been behind the badge myself. But don't go gettin' your hopes up. This bunch will have four horses, no bills of sale, and two witnesses alive and able to identify them."

"Whatever happens," said Vivian, "I feel better having you here. Nathan would have gone after them alone."

"I'm known in Shreveport," Holt said. "I'll have to remain outside of town until it's time to take Jackman's trail. When he rides out, look for me to the south, along the Red."

"Be there at first light," said Nathan. "We don't know when that telegram will reach Jackman's friend, the sheriff."

"I'll be ready," Holt said.

Nathan and Vivian rode on toward Shreveport.

"You didn't plan to take them alive, did you?" Vivian asked.

"No," said Nathan. "I reckon I can't blame Silver, keepin' me within the law. He once went to court in Kansas City to defend me against a charge of murder."*

Shreveport
June 28, 1877

"I'm going back to the Five Aces Saloon," Nathan said. "The telegram from New Orleans should arrive sometime tomorrow, and I want to be sure Jackman's there to get word of it."

Empty remained with Vivian at the boardinghouse while Nathan made his way to the saloon. For a Thursday night, business seemed exceptionally good, and there were three poker games in progress. Nathan went to the bar and ordered a beer, waiting for his eyes to become accustomed to the gloom. Looking around, he recognized none of the men at the tables. Several newcomers bellied up to the bar, and one of them said something that caught Nathan's attention.

"My money's on that big black gelding of Jackman's. It should be some race."

"Yeah," said his companion, "but it's near two hunnert miles to Little Rock."

"Gents," Nathan said, "I couldn't help overhearin' talk about a race in Little Rock, and I'd admire to know when it's goin' to be."

"July fourth," said one of the men. "Quarter mile. Five-thousand-dollar purse."

"Thanks," Nathan said.

Finishing his beer, he was about to leave when one of the house dealers knocked on a door beyond the farthest end of the bar. Jackman opened the door, the dealer entered, and the door was closed. Jackman was in town to receive word of the telegram being sent to the sheriff, and that answered another of Nathan's questions. He returned to the boarding house.

"That didn't take long," said Vivian.

"Mostly, I wanted to be sure Jackman's in town," Nathan said, "and he is. But while I was in the saloon, I learned there's going to be a big race at Little Rock on July fourth, and it seems Jackman's planning to enter McQueen's Diablo."

"Unless he gets slapped in the face with a good reason not to," said Vivian. "Like the telegram from New Orleans."

"That's goin' to leave him in an almighty embarrassin' position," Nathan said. "I overheard two men discussing Jackman's big black, and that's how I learned about the race. I'd say, from their conversation, the black is a recently acquired horse. It almost has to be McQueen's Diablo."

"If he's committed himself to entering Diablo in that race," said Vivian, "how's he to know that Barnabas didn't send that same telegram to every sheriff in half a dozen states? What's he going to do?"

"Being a gambler myself," said Nathan, "I'm counting on him backing out of that race in Little Rock. It's all he can do, and now he's got to come up with some way of disposing of the four horses taken from the McQueens."

"Without bills of sale, what can he do, except turn them loose?"

"He might sell them in Mexico with no questions asked," Nathan said, "but that's a long drive with no proof of ownership. Tomorrow I expect Jackman to lead us to the four horses and the four varmints that took them."

"You don't think they're at his stable?"

"No," said Nathan. "I think he's cautious enough to keep them hidden for a while, so he'll have to assign men to watch them. Who would be more likely than the four varmints that took them from McQueen?"

"I don't know," Vivian said. "It's hard to disagree with a man who's right as often as you are."

"Tomorrow, then," said Nathan, "we'll keep our horses saddled and ready to ride. We don't know when that telegram's coming, so we'll have to be prepared at first light. We'll attract too much attention if we stake out Jackman's saloon, but I reckon we can keep an eye on the sheriff's office and learn what we need to know. If he's aware of Jackman's shady dealings, when he gets that telegram he should head for the Five Aces at a fast gallop."

"There's a cafe and a mercantile across the street from the sheriff's office," Vivian said. "Between the two, we should be able to spend some time without arousing anybody's curiosity."

Nathan and Vivian had breakfast at the cafe across the street from the jail. It was still early, and there were no other patrons. The cook fed Empty in the kitchen.

"We can prolong breakfast until the mercantile opens," Nathan said. "Then one of us can browse in the store, while the other takes a rest on the bench out front."

"I hope that telegram comes early," said Vivian. "Waiting makes me nervous. I want this to be over and done."

"We won't be waiting too long," Nathan replied. "If I know Silver, that telegram will arrive within two hours."

Nathan's prediction was accurate almost to the minute. The clock in the courthouse tower was striking nine when the telegrapher reached the sheriff's office.

"We'll soon know," said Nathan. "Now I'm nervous. If I've guessed wrong, Silver may put me down for a damn fool, and Holt will have ridden from Fort Smith for nothing."

They had been in the cafe having coffee, while Empty waited with the horses. Nathan paid their bill and they exited just in time to see the sheriff step out the door. He set out afoot, since the Five Aces was only two blocks away.

"We'll walk, leading our horses," said Nathan. "We want to be just near enough to be sure he's actually going to the saloon. If he is, after receiving that telegram, it can only mean one thing."

It was still early and the saloon wouldn't open for another hour. The sheriff pounded on the door until it was opened. He then went inside and the door was closed.

"We still don't know if Jackman's there or not," said Vivian.

"Likely it was Jackman that opened the door," Nathan said. "Otherwise, I doubt the sheriff would have gone inside. He wouldn't likely reveal the contents of that telegram to anyone else."

"If he does ride out," said Vivian, "I just hope we can follow without being seen."

"Not likely we'll be seen," Nathan said. "There's some wild country to the north of here. Mostly deep canyons and brakes along the river. When I was a deputy U.S. marshal, working out of Fort Smith, I chased outlaws through there."

"Nathan Stone, is there anything you haven't done?"

Nathan laughed. "Not much. A few miles west of here— along the Red, after it swings into Texas—I had a shootout with the Cullen Baker gang. I rode all the way back to Fort Smith, full of outlaw lead and raging fever."*

"My God, you're lucky to be alive."

"I know," said Nathan. "Escape death often enough and you become fatalistic. I know that someday there'll be a slug with my name on it. Until then, I'm invincible."

Vivian shuddered. "Dear God, don't talk like that!"

It took only a few minutes for all their suspicions to be confirmed. When the saloon door again opened, Rutledge Jackman stepped out, followed by the sheriff. Jackman said something to the sheriff and he started back the way he had come. Jackman turned down the boardwalk in the other direction.

"He's going to send a rider, or he's going himself," Nathan said. "My guess is that he's on his way to a livery."

*The Dawn of Fury (Book 1)

That proved to be the case. After Jackman had ridden away, Nathan and Vivian mounted their horses and followed. Once Empty knew they were trailing the distant rider, he loped on ahead.

"We don't have to keep him in sight," said Nathan. "Empty will guide us. Hold back, while I ride downriver for Mel Holt."

Vivian rode on while Nathan turned south. He found Holt waiting, almost within sight of the town.

"Jackman's on his way," Nathan said.

Without a word, Holt trotted his horse beside Nathan and they rode north. Within minutes they caught up to Vivian, and Holt tipped his hat.

"Jackman's headed toward the river," said Vivian. "I've lost sight of Empty."

"He'll double back," Nathan said, "when he realizes we've fallen behind."

They rode on in silence, and the terrain became more rugged as they progressed. Empty loped back to meet them and Nathan reined up.

"Maybe he's found their camp," said Holt.

"No," Nathan said. "He's just making sure he hasn't lost us."

Empty again took the trail, turning northeast toward the river.

"The camp's somewhere north of here, along the Red," said Nathan. "Likely some dry canyon, with a runoff for water."

The next time Empty doubled back, he growled deep in his throat.

"He knows where they are," Nathan said. "We'll leave the horses here and continue on foot. Silver wanted you here representing the law, Mel. Take charge from here on."

"Oh, hell," said Holt, "with or without a badge, you think like a lawman. You know the rules. We'll cover them from two directions, and then we'll order them to drop their guns and show bills of sale for the horses. Besides horse stealing, there's a charge of attempted murder. I don't expect them to surrender."

Empty led them to the lower end of an arroyo that angled away from the river. There was abundant mud where the runoff from the Red had been swallowed by sand. Leading into the arroyo were many horse tracks.

"You take one side and I'll take the other," said Holt.
"We'll try and catch them in a cross fire from the rim. Wait
for my challenge. If they come up shooting, then I reckon
I don't have to tell you how to answer them."

Nathan crept along the rim, Vivian following. At first the
willows and undergrowth along the canyon floor kept them
from seeing anything, but eventually they could see a clearing in which nine horses grazed. One of them—a big
black—Nathan recognized as Barnabas McQueen's Diablo.
Five men stood in the clearing, and while Nathan was unable to understand Jackman's words, the anger in his voice
was unmistakable. Suddenly, Holt challenged them.

"Deputy U.S. Marshal! You're under arrest!"

Just for a heartbeat they froze, and then every man went
for his gun. But there was swift thunder from the rims as
the deadly cross fire took its toll. One man cut loose with
a Winchester, and was the first to die. Jackman's horse was
still saddled. He mounted, still throwing lead at Nathan's
position, and Nathan shot him out of the saddle. As suddenly as it had begun, it was over. Empty trotted out of
the brush and stood there looking at the carnage.

"Come on," Holt shouted. "I'll need you to identify
those horses."

"You first," Nathan shouted back. "McQueen's four are
branded with a small crown on the left hip."

Nathan and Vivian remained on the rim until Holt
reached the horses and examined the brands.

"You called it straight, *amigo*," Holt shouted. "Crown
brands on four of them. Come on. We'll ride back to town
and have the sheriff send a wagon for the bodies. I'm going
to demand an inquest, call the two of you as witnesses, and
establish the guilt of this bunch."

CHAPTER 4

Led by Mel Holt, Nathan and Vivian reined up before the sheriff's office with the four McQueen horses on lead ropes. The sheriff stepped out the door, his hand on the butt of his Colt.

"Sheriff?" Holt inquired.

"Yep," said the lawman. "Webb Haddock. What can I do fer you?"

"Maybe fifteen miles north of here, there's five dead men in an arroyo on the west bank of the Red. One of them is Rutledge Jackman. The other four coyotes stole these horses in New Orleans, leaving their owners for dead. I called on them to surrender and they came out shooting."

"Why . . . why, you can't do . . ." Haddock stammered.

"I can, and I have," said Holt. "I'm a deputy U.S. marshal from Fort Smith and my authority overrides yours. I'll want an inquest. For the record, I have witnesses who will testify to attempted murder. The stolen horses speak for themselves."

"Damn it," Haddock shouted, "Mr. Jackman is—"

"Dead," said Holt, "and he had you to thank. After you showed him that telegram a while ago, he led us to these horses and the four skunks that took 'em."

"I don't know nothin' about no telegram," Haddock snarled.

"I aim to visit the telegraph office," said Holt. "The telegrapher should be able to help you remember. Now, you set up that inquest for nine o'clock in the morning. I'm going to report this incident when I return to Fort Smith."

With that, Holt turned away. Nathan and Vivian followed him down the street, leading the McQueen horses and seeking a livery. Holt put up the horses, cautioning the liveryman that the animals were recovered stolen property, the responsibility of the U.S. government.

"We have a room at a boardinghouse," said Nathan.

"I'll try and get one there myself," Holt replied.

Holt had no trouble getting a room for the night, and

after stabling their horses, the three of them went to a nearby cafe to eat.

"If the dog's a problem," said Nathan, "he's a paying customer."

"He's welcome, long as he minds his manners," the cook replied. "What's he havin'?"

"He's a hound, and not picky," Nathan said, "just as long as there's plenty of it."

They were down to final cups of coffee when Holt had a suggestion.

"You have to get those horses back to New Orleans; why don't you just drive them to Memphis and buy passage on a steamboat?"

"Tarnation," said Nathan, "it's as far from here to Memphis as it is from here to New Orleans. That wouldn't make any sense."

"It would if you enter Diablo in that quarter-mile race on July fourth. I can help you with these horses as far as Little Rock, and from there, it's not more than a hundred miles to Memphis. I don't know how often the packets travel the Arkansas, but you might get a steamboat from Little Rock to New Orleans."

Nathan laughed. "You're just trying to parlay this law business into a horse race."

"You've rode behind this badge," said Holt. "Do you blame me? It's all shoot-or-be-shot, and no time for anything else."

"I couldn't agree more," Nathan said, "but who would ride Diablo? Certainly not you or me."

"Why not Vivian?" Holt asked.

"Vivian?" said Nathan. "She doesn't—"

"Ride that well," Vivian finished.

"I was about to say that you don't know the horse, and he doesn't know you," said Nathan.

"It's a good two hundred miles from here to Little Rock," Holt said. "When we ride out, swap her horse to a lead rope and let her ride Diablo. If she can ride him that far without him biting off a hand or foot, he'll be safe enough."

It was Vivian's turn to laugh. "You're generous with my hands and feet."

"I don't think so," Nathan said. "It hasn't been that long since she had saddle sores all over her—"

"Nathan," Vivian interrupted, "I'd like to try it. Let me at least attempt to become friends with Diablo. If it turns out that he hates me, I promise not to go through with it."

"We'll try it," said Nathan. "It's the least we can do, to bring a little pleasure to the dismal life of Deputy U.S. Marshal Mel Holt."

Sheriff Haddock arranged the inquest, Nathan and Vivian testified, and the case was officially closed. News of the killings had spread, drawing a crowd to the courthouse. The sheriff was nervous, and it seemed he wanted to speak in his own defense, but he kept his silence. When the procedure was done, Holt elbowed his way through the crowd without answering any questions from the curious. Nathan and Vivian followed his example, and with the McQueen horses on lead ropes, the trio rode north.

"Haddock was uneasy as a coyote among lobo wolves," said Nathan. "Do you reckon he can keep the lid on all this?"

Holt laughed. "Not a chance. Rutledge Jackman was a big man in town, and while he was alive, who would have questioned a friendship between him and Sheriff Haddock? But now, all the little people who didn't exactly revere Jackman won't be thinking kindly of Sheriff Haddock. I doubt he'll run for reelection."

"The telegrapher knows what was in that telegram he delivered to Sheriff Haddock," said Vivian. "He should be able to add that to what was taken down at the inquest and come up with some answers."

"Yes," Holt said. "If he has the brains God gave a goose he ought to be ropin' free drinks for at least a year."

"Now that we're away from town," said Vivian, "I want to make friends with Diablo, if I can."

They reined up and Vivian dismounted.

"We'll see how well he receives you before we swap your saddle," Nathan said.

"If he accepts me," said Vivian, "I'll ride him bareback. I've never ridden in a race before, but I've seen it done. The last thing we'll want is the added weight of a saddle."

"She's got savvy," Holt said admiringly.

As Vivian approached, Diablo snorted and flattened his ears, but the girl didn't hesitate. She spoke softly and hummed a tune, and Diablo's ears perked. The horse stood his ground, and when Vivian began stroking him, he nickered.

"He hasn't forgotten Eulie," said Nathan. "You remind him of her."

"To win over an animal like this," Vivian said, "she must have been a special person."

"She was," said Nathan. "She trained him and was the first to ride him."

"What became of her?" Holt asked.

"She was shot by a bushwhacker who didn't want Diablo to win the race," Nathan said, "but she died a winner. Diablo beat them all."*

"It'll be a tribute to her memory if he can do it again," said Holt.

"He can," Nathan said. "Look at her."

Vivian had her arms around the sleek neck of the big black, and when she vaulted on to his broad back, he only snaked his head around and looked at her. Leaning forward, she spoke to him, and the horse lit out in a fast gallop.

"My God," said Nathan, "she doesn't even have a bridle."

"I have an idea she not goin' to need one," Holt said. "If she knows what she's doing, she can turn him with knee pressure."

Suddenly, from a fast gallop, Diablo wheeled and came pounding back.

"By God," Holt shouted, "she took that turn like she was part of the horse, and I never seen a horse run and wheel like that."

Nathan said nothing, for there was a lump in his throat. His mind drifted back over ten years, and again he was seeing Eulie astride the big black as Diablo thundered toward the finish line. Again he heard the deadly bark of Winchesters, and Eulie was gone . . .

"Vivian," Holt shouted, "they'll all eat your dust."

But Vivian said nothing. Diablo drew up without a command, and Vivian threw her arms around his neck. She wept, and the two men stood there uneasily, not knowing what to say. Finally she righted herself and slid to the ground, as Diablo snaked his head around, watching her.

*The Dawn of Fury (Book 1)

"I have never, in all my life, experienced anything like that," Vivian said. "Let's get on to Little Rock."

They rode on, Vivian astride Diablo, her saddled horse on a lead rope. Nathan watched the girl in silent admiration, and there were times when Deputy U.S. Marshal Mel Holt laughed for no reason at all.

Little Rock, Arkansas
July 2, 1877

"Let's stable these horses, find us a place to stay, and get us a mess of town grub," Nathan said. "Then we'd better see about gettin' Diablo into that race."

They had no trouble learning about the race, for it seemed to have totally captured the imagination of the town. Posters had been printed in black and red, and it seemed that no wall, tree, or store window in town had escaped. Every poster shouted in brilliant red that "the track is on the north bank of the Arkansas."

"She's gonna be some race," the friendly cook told them while they were eating.

"We have a horse to enter," said Nathan. "Who do we see?"

"Sam Adderly, at Adderly's Mercantile," the cook said. "You can place your bets at any saloon. Already fourteen hosses entered, some of 'em at good odds. There's a practice track, if you hanker to show off your hoss."

"I think we ought to keep Diablo out of sight until time for the race," said Vivian when they had left the cafe.

"We're going to," Nathan said. "I've seen what big-time gamblers will do to win. We want Diablo to come as a surprise."

"You'll have at least one lawman on your side," said Holt.

Reaching Adderly's Mercantile, they found a huge chart posted on the wall beside the counter. Listed on it were all the entries, some from as far away as Kansas City and St. Louis. At the far right was the owner's name, and Rutledge Jackman's didn't appear there.

"Entry fee's a hundred dollars," Adderly told them. "We

aim to keep out folks that ain't serious. You can place your bets here, too."

"Later," said Nathan.

"How much are we going to bet on Diablo?" Vivian asked, when they had left the store.

"A thousand," said Nathan. "Maybe more, depending on the odds."

"I can manage fifty," said Holt. "That's a month's pay."

"Tarnation," Nathan said, "make it five hundred. You'll never again get a chance like this. I'll loan you the difference, and you can repay me from your winnings."

"But suppose something goes wrong and we lose?" said Holt. "My God, I'd owe you a year's pay."

"We aren't going to lose," Vivian said.

"No," said Nathan. "Besides, we owe you for helping us recover McQueen's horses. If we hadn't found Diablo, we wouldn't be entering him in this race, so you deserve a chance at some of the winnings."

"You're a *muy bueno amigo,*" Holt said. "My God, I've never seen more than a hundred dollars all at once, in my life."

Nathan laughed. "What would you do if you suddenly had five thousand dollars in your hands?"

"God," said Holt, "I'd drop this badge like it was hot and ride like hell for southwest Texas. I'd buy me a spread, a bull, some seed cows . . ."

The morning of July fourth, Nathan, Holt, and Vivian returned to the mercantile. Now it was time to place their bets.

"Thunderation," said Holt, looking at the chart on the wall, "they got Diablo down at twenty-to-one odds."

"That's because he's unknown in these parts, and nobody's seen him run," Nathan said, "and precisely why we didn't put him through any trial runs."

"Westwind is the horse we have to beat," said Vivian, studying the chart.

There was considerable excitement when Nathan, Holt, and Vivian placed their bets, for Nathan had advanced both Holt and Vivian five hundred.

"You folks must know somethin' the rest of us don't," Adderly said as he wrote out their receipts.

"We just like long odds," said Nathan. "Will you have enough *pesos* to pay us if we win?"

"Ten times over," Adderly said. "You wouldn't believe the money that's been laid on old Westwind."

"That good, is he?" Holt asked.

"He's never lost a race," said Adderly.

It was a sobering thought as the three of them left the mercantile. They went directly to the livery, for they must have Diablo at the starting line an hour and a half before the start of the race.

"Sixteen horses in the lineup," Nathan said. "With that many horses, there'll be some pushing and shoving. Viv, try to get Diablo off to a fast start and into an early lead."

"I intend to," said Vivian.

It was all the advice they could give her, for Diablo's fifteen opponents proved to be a formidable bunch. Westwind pranced about, draped in a fancy blanket embroidered with his name. The rest of the horses were no less impressive. Diablo was assigned the ninth position, clearly a disadvantage unless he took an early lead. Nathan's eyes met Holt's; they said nothing lest Vivian become more nervous than she already appeared to be.

"Diablo's the only horse without some kind of saddle," Vivian observed.

"You have a definite edge," said Nathan. "Except for Indians, not many can ride without a saddle."

It came time for horses and riders to take their positions, and no sooner had they done so than to Vivian's immediate left, a roan nipped at Diablo. Diablo did some nipping of his own, and the roan reared, unseating his rider.

"Ma'am," said one of the judges, "if your horse doesn't behave, he'll be disqualified."

Furious as Vivian was, she bit her tongue and said nothing. Diablo would show up the troublesome roan, along with all the others. Westwind was in third position, and his rider was having trouble holding him. He seemed to know he was favored because the many who had put their money on him shouted his name. Westwind pranced to the side just as the starting gun sounded, and the favorite started the race a stride behind. Before the echo of the starting gun had died, Diablo had taken the lead, and he never lost it. He thundered across the finish line three lengths ahead of Westwind. There was total chaos, as shouting, cursing men surrounded the judges.

"The black jumped the starting gun!" Westwind's owner bawled. "Disqualify him!"

Nathan and Holt fought their way to Vivian and Diablo. Suddenly there was the roar of a Colt, and the shouting and cursing ceased.

"This is Sheriff McCarty," a voice bawled. "The decision is up to the judges."

There was an uneasy silence as the three judges conferred; after a few minutes, one of the trio announced their decision.

"We saw nothing amiss. We are declaring the black the winner."

Again the crowd broke loose, and when the sheriff finally quieted them Nathan Stone spoke.

"Sheriff, the lady riding Diablo is unwilling that there be any doubt her horse won and demands that the race be run again."

Men cheered and shouted, and when silence finally reigned, one of the judges spoke.

"This is highly irregular, and although we've never seen it done before, we do not believe it's illegal. The young lady riding Diablo is to be commended for her sense of fairness. Riders, take your positions and prepare to run the race again."

There were no distractions, and when the starting gun sounded all horses got off to an equal start. Westwind and Diablo surged ahead of the rest; Westwind's rider applied the quirt while Vivian depended on her voice. Calling on a reserve that seemed lacking in Westwind, Diablo gained a length. They thundered on, with Diablo gaining, and crossed the finish line three lengths ahead. It was a glorious thing, the testimony of a rider's consummate faith in her horse, and even those who had lost their money cheered.

"My God," said Holt. "My God." He seized Vivian, kissing her long and hard.

Men gathered around with questions about Diablo, and there was no escape. Nathan, Holt, Vivian, and Diablo were there for more than two hours. When they finally reached Adderly's Mercantile to collect their winnings, there were more well-wishers.

"Except for winners of a few dollars, we're paying by

bank draft," Adderly told them. "We had word the James gang might ride down here and rob us."

"Diablo's purse goes to Barnabas McQueen," said Nathan

The ten-thousand-dollar draft was written to McQueen, while Nathan, Holt, and Vivian were paid individually.

"I've heard of things like this," Holt said, "but I never dreamed it could happen to me. Let's get to the bank before it closes so I can repay your five hundred."

"Yes," said Vivian, "I owe you, too. I never dreamed there was this much money in the whole world."

"I think we should take some of it in cash, and a bank draft for the balance," Nathan said. "You'd need a packhorse to carry it in gold, and a company of cavalry to keep the outlaws away."

"Lord, yes," Holt agreed. "I still don't trust Texas banks. I may leave mine in a bank in St. Louis."

"Is that spread in Texas still on your mind?" Nathan asked.

"Yeah," said Holt, "but now that I actually have the money, I'm wonderin' if maybe I won't come out better in Wyoming or Montana Territories. There's so much more land to be had, and I hear the grass is stirrup-high."

"I don't know about Montana," Nathan said, "but I hear the big ranchers are gobblin' up most of the land in Wyoming's Powder River Basin."

"Well, I got time to think," said Holt. "I might just take it easy for a while after I ride back to Fort Smith and turn in my badge. When will you and Vivian be leaving for New Orleans?"

"Tomorrow," Nathan said. "Barnabas will be wondering what became of us. I reckon we'll have to ride on to Memphis. We've been here three days, and I haven't heard the first steamboat whistle."

"Occasionally there's one in Fort Smith," said Holt, "but I think they're government packets. It used to be the jumping-off place, but no more. The railroads—the AT & SF and the Union Pacific—ended that."

When it was time for Nathan and Vivian to part company with the genial Mel Holt, it proved more awkward than any of them had expected.

"Too bad you aren't going on to New Orleans with us," Nathan said. "I've gotten used to you."

"So have I," said Vivian.

Holt laughed. "I feel like the real loser. I'll likely end up talking to myself. I hope our trails cross again. *Vaya con Dios*."

They watched Holt ride away. Then, with four horses on lead ropes and Vivian riding Diablo, they crossed the Arkansas and set out eastward, toward Memphis. Empty ranged on ahead, and they made the journey in two days.

Memphis, Tennessee
July 7, 1877

"Tomorrow's Sunday," Nathan said. "If my memory serves me right, there should be a southbound steamboat through here sometime tomorrow."

Stopping at the dock, they learned there would be a steamboat at three o'clock Sunday afternoon. Nathan bought passage for Vivian and himself, and made arrangements for their horses and the four animals belonging to McQueen to travel on the lower deck.

"Now," said Nathan, "we have the rest of the day, tonight, and all tomorrow morning to see St. Louis."

"What is there to see and do?"

"Frankly," Nathan said, "I'm not sure. All the times I've been here, except for the last time, I was in some kind of trouble and left in a hurry."

"What happened the last time?"

"Some distilleries—two of them here—were cheating the government out of whiskey tax, and Silver brought me here to help trap the distillery owners."*

"And you did?"

"Yes," said Nathan. "The owners went to prison, and their wives wanted me to stay and run the distilleries for them, among other things."

Vivian laughed. "You could have run the distilleries during the day, and taken care of the 'other things' at night."

"I'm smarter than I look, thank God," Nathan said.

The Killing Season (Book 2)

"Being of fairly sound mind, I saddled up and rode away, not daring to look back."

"When we leave the McQueens, why don't we go to Washington?"

"My God," said Nathan. "Why?"

"I'd like to meet this Byron Silver. He sounds interesting."

"Oh, he is," said Nathan, "but he's got a woman. Maybe more than one, by now."

"Damn it, I wasn't going to throw myself at him."

Nathan laughed. "You might. He's a handsome brute, with more scars than me."

"Is that all you have going for you, your scars?"

"Just about," said Nathan. "Oh, I'm a fair-to-middlin' gambler, too."

"What are you going to do with the money you won on Diablo?"

"Eventually, I'll use some of it to win more," Nathan said. "I reckon we can spend Christmas with the McQueens."

"My God," said Vivian, "that's six months."

"I know," Nathan said, "but I doubt they'll allow us to leave any sooner. After all, we have a ten-thousand-dollar check for Barnabas, and we're returning four horses he might never have seen again. Besides, when he learns you can ride Diablo, he may never let you leave at all."

"You really think he'll be that impressed?"

"I certainly do," said Nathan. "I've never seen anybody ride any better than you did."

"Not even Eulie?"

"Not even Eulie," Nathan said. "I'm reluctant for Barnabas to learn what you've done, because he'll never want you to leave."

"You wouldn't stay in New Orleans?"

"No," said Nathan, "for several reasons. One of the most important is that there are people in New Orleans who would like to see me dead."

"I'm beginning to wonder if that isn't the case just about everywhere."

"It is," Nathan replied. "I told you that's why I didn't want you with me. I draw lead like a lightning rod pulls lightning."

"But you think you can last until Christmas in New Orleans?"

"As long as I stay out of saloons and gambling houses," said Nathan.

"But can you?"

"I don't know," Nathan said. "I can last only so long, settin' on my hunkers, eating, and sleeping."

"There'll be horse races."

"I expect there will be," said Nathan. "Diablo's a four-legged gold mine."

"He'll need someone to guard Diablo from thieves."

"You're suggesting that I become bodyguard to a horse?"

"It might be the safest thing you've ever done," Vivian said.

"And the most boring," said Nathan. "Do me a favor; don't suggest it to Barnabas and Bess McQueen."

Contrary to his nature, Nathan took a room in the elegant Pioneer Hotel. With Empty at the livery with the horses, Nathan and Vivian had supper in the hotel dining room and then attended the theatre.

"I've never lived this fancy before," said Vivian, "but I believe I'd tire of it if I did it every day."

"I know I would," Nathan said. "After I've been on the trail for a while, I can't wait to get a bath, a soft bed, and a bait of town grub. But after a few days, I'm missing the bacon, beans, and coffee cooked over an open fire."

Vivian laughed. "And sleeping on the ground."

"Especially that," said Nathan.

With a blast of its whistle, the big stern wheeler eased up to the dock. Nathan saw to the boarding of the horses, and made sure they were secure in their stalls on the first deck. Then he and Vivian boarded, with Empty cautiously following.

"God," said Nathan, "I'd forgotten how small these cabins are," after they had entered their assigned quarters.

Empty sat there looking uneasily from Nathan to Vivian. He had been on steamboats before, but like saloons, he didn't care for them. There were two bunks, nothing more.

"With so little room," Vivian said, "what do we *do* during this trip?"

"Set here and look at one another, I reckon," said Nathan. "For sure, we won't be wrasslin' around."

CHAPTER 5

New Orleans
July 11, 1877

Nathan, Vivian, and Empty were more than weary of the steamboat when the craft finally eased up to the landing at New Orleans.

"Lord," said Vivian, "solid ground never felt so good."

It took a while to bring the horses from the first deck, but finally Nathan and Vivian had the animals on lead ropes and were on their way to the McQueen place. Empty knew where they were bound and ran on ahead, barking in great anticipation. Barnabas and Bess McQueen were waiting to greet them.

"Let's stable the horses," Nathan said, "and then we have a story to tell."

It was near suppertime when Barnabas and Nathan returned to the house, and the meal was on the table. Bess and Vivian were already acquainted, and Nathan introduced the girl to Barnabas.

"I already know her," said Barnabas. "I was layin' there with lead and fever in me, and I reckoned I'd died and gone to heaven."

"You owe her plenty," Nathan said, taking the bank draft from his shirt pocket. "After we recovered the horses, we stopped in Little Rock for a July fourth horse race. Vivian rode Diablo and took the purse."

"Then some of the money belongs to her," said Barnabas.

"No," Nathan said. "We each bet five hundred on Diablo, at twenty-to-one odds. That money belongs to you and Bess."

"My God," said Barnabas, "I'd give it all to have seen that race."

"Diablo ran it twice," Vivian added.

It took a while to tell the story, and when Nathan was

finished, the McQueens looked at Vivian, and it was Barnabas who spoke.

"Young lady, if you don't have other plans, I'd like for you to stay with us through the end of this year. There are five races comin' up, and Diablo can take 'em all. Will you ride him?"

"I'd love to," said Vivian.

"What about me?" Nathan asked. "If I pay board, will I be allowed to stay?"

Barnabas laughed. "We'll consider it. Actually, in October I'd like you to ride to San Antonio for a pair of Indian-gentled horses. Are you familiar with the Lipan Apaches?"

"Yes," said Nathan. "Eulie told me about them. They're settled along the Medina River, south of San Antonio. That's how Eulie gentled Diablo, with what she had learned from the Lipans."

"I had a friend of mine in San Antonio arrange for the Lipans to train these horses for me," Barnabas said. "Will you ride there and get them?"

"I reckon," said Nathan. "Just promise me that when Diablo wins, Vivian won't be shot out of the saddle."

"That sort of thing ended when you and Silver destroyed French Stumberg's gambling empire," Barnabas said.*

There was a race in Beaumont, Texas in August, and another in Natchez, Mississippi in September, and Diablo easily won both. In mid-October, Nathan prepared to ride to San Antonio.

"I wish I were going with you," Vivian said wistfully, "but I promised ..."

Nathan laughed. "I know you did. Barnabas has a winning horse and a winning rider. I'll likely have to steal you away from him in the middle of the night."

With Empty trotting ahead, Nathan rode west.

Houston, Texas
October 22, 1877

Lonzo Prinz, Rufe Collins, and Tobe Schorp rode into town, dismounted, and left their horses behind a saloon,

*The Dawn of Fury (Book 1)

across the street from the bank they intended to rob. The Cattleman's Bank wouldn't open for another hour. Who would expect a robbery at eight o'clock on Monday morning?

"Remember," said Lonzo Prinz, "no shooting. If nobody's hurt, they ain't likely to run us too far."

But Prinz was dead wrong. When the outlaws escaped with ten thousand dollars, within minutes a sheriff's posse was on their trail. Collins and Schorp were wounded, and near sundown, the exhausted trio was forced to hole up and rest. Lonzo Prinz had taken his Winchester and gone to a rise to study their backtrail. Instead, he discovered a rider who was approaching from the east. He rode toward the willows that surrounded the spring, and there was no way he could miss the wounded Collins and Schorp. There was no time for Prinz to warn his comrades. He bellied down with his Winchester and waited.

Before Empty reached the willows, he doubled back, growling. It was all the warning Nathan Stone needed. Dismounting, he crept toward the willows. Near the spring, Nathan could see two men, their heads on their saddles. But there were three horses! Nathan hit the ground as a Winchester barked, the slug nipping the crown of his hat. He fired twice but had no target. One of the men at the spring was on his feet, his Colt roaring, and Nathan shot him. The Winchester roared again, and the slug tore into Nathan's back, just below his right shoulder blade. Not knowing where the man with the Winchester was, he dared not move. Eventually the bushwhacker would have to return to the spring for his horse. But Nathan didn't last that long. He blacked out. Lonzo Prinz returned to the spring.

"Schorp's dead," said Collins.

"He might not of been," Prinz said. "What'n hell was you doin' while he was killin' Schorp?"

"I got two slugs in me already," said Collins sourly, "and one of 'em in my gun arm. You had a Winchester; why didn't you ventilate the varmint before he cut down on us?"

"He was no shorthorn," Prinz said. "I had him dead center, and he hit the dirt. But I cut him down while he was gettin' Schorp. We'd better mount up and ride all night. I'll go get the stranger's horse, and you saddle Schorp's. That'll give both of us an extra mount, and that posse won't never catch up to us."

"I been wounded," said Collins, "an' the one in my hip's still bleedin'. I can feel the blood squishin' in my boot."

"That ain't near as bad as feelin' a noose around your neck," Prinz said. "Now get them horses saddled an' let's ride."

Empty growled as Prinz approached Nathan's horse, and Prinz fired at the dog. Empty faded into the brush, for he well understood the deadliness of a gun.

When Nathan regained consciousness, darkness had draped its velvet mantle over the land, and the only sound was the chirp of crickets. The numbness had worn off, and there was only pain. Empty was near, anxiously awaiting some sign of life. Nathan got painfully to his knees, and using his Winchester for support, struggled to his feet. He was all but consumed with burning thirst; somehow he had to reach the spring. Weak from loss of blood, he fell to his knees, forced himself to stand, and fell again. When he reached the runoff from the spring, he fell belly down, burying his feverish face in the cold water. He drank deep, and then drank again. He moved just enough to get his face out of the water and again lost consciousness ...

Contrary to Sheriff Oscar Littlefield's wishes, the weary posse refused to continue the hunt for the three bank robbers without food and rest.

"Damn it," said Littlefield, "all they got to do is ride all night, and we've lost them."

"Hell," said one of the men, "they're bound to be as wore out and hungry as we are, and we know we got lead in two of 'em."

There was unanimous agreement from the rest of the posse, and Littlefield gave in. He would roust them out before first light and prod the hell out of them.

With first light, Empty nuzzled Nathan's feverish face but drew no response. There was a patch of dried blood on the back of Nathan's shirt, and the hound sniffed it. All he could do was remain near until mid-morning, when he heard riders coming. He loped up the rise and took refuge in a thicket overlooking the spring. He watched ten riders approach. Might these strangers not help the fallen Nathan Stone? He would watch and wait . . .

"There's the two of the varmints we shot," one of the riders shouted as the sheriff and his posse reined up on a rise overlooking the spring below.

"Don't go getting excited about them," said Sheriff Littlefield in disgust. "They purely ain't goin' nowhere. The third one's took the money and high-tailed it, likely been ridin' all night. Couple of you see if either of them two's still alive. The rest of us will look for the trail of the one that's still somewhere ahead."

Lonzo Prinz and Rufe Collins had made no effort to conceal their trail. Sheriff Littlefield dismounted, studied the tracks, and swore.

"What is it?" one of the men asked.

"Just as I expected," Littlefield said, "the varmint with the money rode out some time last night. What I didn't expect was the tracks of four horses."

"Sheriff," the man shouted who had examined Nathan, "one of these coyotes is alive."

Sheriff Littlefield had to make a decision. Either they continue following a trail that was growing colder by the minute, or they take the wounded man and return to Houston. The wind, out of the southwest, had freshened. Somewhere in the Gulf, a storm was brewing, and within a matter of hours there would be rain.

"Mount up," said Littlefield. "There's rain on the way, and it'll wash out the trail. Simpkins, you and Jarvis double up so's we got a horse for that wounded hombre. Maybe we can get back to town ahead of the storm."

While Sheriff Littlefield regretted not recovering the stolen money, he did have one of the thieves. The man who had escaped was well beyond Littlefield's jurisdiction, and he felt justified in leaving further pursuit to the Rangers.

"Sheriff," one of the riders said, "I thought you said somethin' about the tracks of four hosses."

"I was mistaken," Littlefield said cautiously. "One of them was an old trail. That outlaw who escaped with the money took the two extra horses with him."

The men rode away, taking the wounded Nathan Stone with them. Far behind, Empty followed. There was nothing more he could do.

*   *   *

When Nathan awoke, he could barely move, for a heavy bandage encircled his upper body. He had no doubt as to where he was, for before him were the iron bars and heavy barred door of a jail cell. The last thing he remembered was returning the fire of a man who was shooting at him, and in turn being shot from behind. Listening, he heard nothing, and he lay there for more than an hour before someone entered the cell block. With some effort he turned to face the cell door; he might as well learn why he was in jail.

"So you're awake, are you?"

"Yes," said Nathan. "Are you the sheriff?"

"That I am. Sheriff Littlefield."

"Then I have two questions for you, Sheriff. Where am I, and why am I in jail?"

"You're in Houston, Texas," said Littlefield, "and you're in jail for bank robbery."

"Sheriff," Nathan said, "I've never been in Houston in my life, until now."

"You're innocent of all charges, then," said Littlefield.

"I am," Nathan replied.

Littlefield laughed. "I been sheriff here goin' on fifteen years, and I never yet locked up a coyote that admitted to bein' guilty."

"What evidence are you using against me?" Nathan asked.

"Three outlaws robbed the bank," said Littlefield, "and we wounded two of them. We trailed the varmints and found two men. One of 'em was you, and the other was dead. We got all the evidence we need."

"I shot the dead man you found," Nathan said. "He was shooting at me, and I had to shoot him. Then somebody plugged me from behind."

"But you can't prove that," said Littlefield.

"No," Nathan said, "but you could have. I rode in from the east, and you could have backtrailed me. I've been nowhere near Houston, and you could have proven it beyond the shadow of a doubt. Why didn't you?"

"Because I believe in circumstantial evidence," said Littlefield, "and we found you in an outlaw camp, wounded. As for follerin' trails, there wasn't no way. There was rain, and we couldn't track your pardner. The varmint escaped with the bank's money, but they're all feelin' better, with one varmint dead and you behind bars."

"I want a trial," Nathan said, "and I want to send a telegram."

"Oh, you'll get a trial," said Littlefield, "but no telegrams."

With that, he was gone, leaving Nathan to ponder his situation. Obviously, while he had been defending himself against one of the bank robbers, one of the others had gunned him down. The remaining outlaws had fled with the money, leaving Nathan a scapegoat. He believed Sheriff Littlefield was using him as a pawn, to compensate for having failed to recover the stolen money. McQueen wouldn't be expecting him to return with the horses for several weeks, and he had been denied the opportunity to seek help. He lay back on the bunk, closed his eyes, and tried to think.

"All rise," said the bailiff as the judge entered the courtroom.

Judge McClendon was a stern old man who listened to Nathan's impassioned plea without a change of expression. The trial was a nightmare, and the crowning blow came when one of the bank tellers swore that Nathan had been one of the three men who had robbed the bank.

"That's a damn lie!" Nathan shouted desperately.

"You're out of order," said the judge. "Bailiff, bring him forward for sentencing."

His mind a mixture of dread and fury, Nathan was forced to approach the bench.

"Nathan Stone," Judge McClendon said, "this court sentences you to five years in the state prison at Huntsville, Texas."

Five days following his arrest, his wound still paining him, Nathan straddled a horse between two sheriff's deputies bound for Huntsville, sixty miles to the north. When the terrain grew rough and the thickets plentiful, Nathan occasionally caught sight of Empty. The dog was following him, but he couldn't follow beyond the formidable walls of Huntsville prison. All too soon they reached the prison and the gate was swung open. Nathan was then handed over to the prison guards, taken into the depths of the prison, and locked in a cell. There was a hard bunk with a straw tick, an earthen slop jar, and nothing else. On a wall outside the cell a bracket lamp burned. But for that, there was perpetual gloom, for there wasn't even a window. With a clang of finality, the iron-barred door was slammed shut and locked. Somewhere down the cell block, there was a cackle of insane laughter that faded to an anguished moan. Then there was only eerie silence.

For five days and nights, Empty never left the vicinity of the prison. Three times he tried to gain entry, only to be chased away by guards. During his third attempt, he narrowly missed being hit when the guards fired at him. At the start of the sixth day, half-starved, the hound walked slowly toward the rising sun. Uncertain, he paused, looking back at the distant prison. It was a cold, forbidding place, and with Nathan Stone lost to him, he longed for the only home he had ever known. He set out in a determined lope for New Orleans and the McQueen place, more than three hundred and fifty miles to the east.

The ride from Houston had aggravated Nathan's wound, and after the prison doctor had examined him, he was left alone for almost a week. At the start of the sixth day, after breakfast, one of the guards unlocked the heavy, iron-barred door.

"Stone, you've been assigned to the prison laundry. That is, if you got no objections."

The guard laughed uproariously, and Nathan said nothing. It was boring, tedious work, and whatever the weather outside, inmates assigned to the laundry were perpetually drenched with sweat. Nathan had no doubt that when he had been missing for a sufficient length of time, Barnabas McQueen would begin searching for him. Until then, he could only wait.

New Orleans
November 15, 1877

"Nathan should have returned a week ago," said Barnabas McQueen. "If he isn't here by tomorrow, and we have no word, I'll telegraph my friend in San Antonio."

"After the experience we had," Bess said, "I'm afraid someone may have stolen—or tried to steal—the horses from him. Perhaps he's hurt."

"We ought to go looking for him," said Vivian, "but we're only six days away from the race in Vicksburg."

"Damn the race," McQueen said. "I haven't paid the entry fee. Tomorrow I'll ride into town and telegraph San Antonio. At least we'll know whether he got there. If he was able pick up the horses, then there could have been foul play on the return trip."

But the situation didn't wait until morning. During supper there was frantic barking at the back door. When Barnabas opened the door, Empty came bounding into the kitchen.

"Nathan must be coming," said Vivian excitedly.

"No," said Barnabas. "Empty looks near starved; he's had to have been without food for maybe two weeks. That's how long ago something happened to Nathan Stone."

Hungry as he was, Empty turned back toward the door, bidding them follow.

"He wants us to follow him," Vivian said.

"I wish it was that simple," said Barnabas. "On good horses, we're a week away from San Antonio. If Nathan's in trouble or hurt, we may not have that much time."

"Then what are we going to do?" Vivian cried.

"I'm riding to town today," said Barnabas. "I'll wire Byron Silver in Washington. He has the necessary connections to contact the authorities in San Antonio, as well as the Texas Rangers in Austin."

"It's late in the day," Bess said. "Washington will likely be shut down until tomorrow morning."

"Maybe," said Barnabas, "but I know Silver. Where his friends are concerned, he'll be there, day or night."

When Barnabas reached the telegraph office, it was past seven o'clock in the evening. Addressing the telegram to twenty-one, Office of the Attorney General, Washington, D.C., he quickly wrote a short message requesting Silver's personal attention before he supplied any details. His message read:

Stone missing stop. Need help stop. Respond for details.

He signed his name, paid for the telegram, and settled down to wait.

"I ain't meanin' to be nosey," said the telegrapher, "but I expect Washington's closed up for the day. You likely won't get an answer till sometime tomorrow."

"You may be right," Barnabas said, "but I'll wait awhile."

Forty-five minutes later the instrument began to chatter and the telegrapher took the brief message. It read:

Twenty-one awaiting details.

Barnabas wrote rapidly, telling the little he knew and much he suspected, asking Silver to investigate the possibility of foul play by contacting Texas authorities. Silver responded in a matter of minutes. Brief and to the point, the telegram said:

Response late tomorrow.

The telegram was unsigned. Barnabas mounted and rode out, satisfied that he had done all he could do. If Silver could learn nothing through Texas authorities, Barnabas had but one other possibility. He would have to ride to Texas on his own, depending on Empty to lead him to Nathan. He found Bess and Vivian anxiously awaiting his return. Quickly he told them of Silver's response.

"I believe you did the right thing," Vivian said. "Nathan's called on Silver before, and since he hasn't this time I fear that for some reason he's unable to."

"That's what's bothering me," said Barnabas. "It's a hell of a temptation not to saddle up and follow Empty back to wherever he left Nathan, but we don't know what's happened to him, or the circumstances. With the telegraph, Silver can accomplish more in a day than I could in a week. Chances are, he'll have some answers by tomorrow, and he may be in a position to get Nathan some immediate help."

Washington, D.C.
November 16, 1877

Byron Silver was in his office two hours early. Quickly he composed telegrams to the Texas Ranger outposts at

Austin, San Antonio, and Houston. There wasn't a Ranger in south Texas who didn't know of Nathan Stone. When Ranger Captain Sage Jennings was gunned down from ambush, it was Nathan Stone who tracked the killer all the way to New Mexico, taking revenge for the fallen Ranger. The Rangers had never forgotten, and never would.*

Silver remained in his office, watching the clock. The Ranger outposts in Austin and San Antonio responded first. They had no word, but offered help should there be a need for it. Silver cursed under his breath as he read the response from the Ranger outpost in Houston:

Stone in Huntsville stop. Five years for bank robbery stop. Suspicious circumstances stop. If you do not investigate we will.

Silver wrote an immediate response:

Joining you for investigation stop. Arriving November twenty-four.

Silver then prepared a telegram to be sent to Barnabas McQueen. It said:

Stone in Huntsville prison stop. Suspicious circumstances stop. Meet me at Ranger outpost Houston November twenty-fourth stop. Investigation pending.

After the telegrams had been sent to the Rangers at Houston and to McQueen in New Orleans, Byron Silver requested and received permission to absent himself from his office for a month. He then booked passage on a sailing ship that would depart for Corpus Christi, Texas the following morning.

New Orleans
November 16, 1877

"It's two o'clock," said Barnabas. "I'm riding to town. If there's no answer, I'll wait at the telegraph office."

The Killing Season (Book 2)

"He's not a patient man," Bess said when Barnabas had gone.

"I know exactly how he feels," said Vivian. "I'm afraid of what that telegram will say, afraid something's happened to Nathan."

The telegram from Silver was there when Barnabas arrived. He read it twice, not believing what it said. He mounted and rode out at a fast gallop. When he reached the house, Bess and Vivian met him before he could dismount. Without a word he passed them the flimsy yellow paper with its shocking message.

"My God," said Bess when she had read the message, "how could anything so terrible happen so quickly? It must have happened within a week of the time he left here, before he ever reached San Antonio."

"Silver calls the circumstances mysterious," Barnabas said, "and I can believe they are, with him coming all the way from Washington."

"Nathan's been a friend to the Rangers for years," said Vivian. "There's bound to be a Ranger outpost in Houston. How could Nathan have been tried and convicted without them knowing?"

"If there's a county sheriff or city marshal," Barnabas said, "he would be more likely to take the trail of bank robbers. Texas Rangers would have bent over backward to avoid sending Nathan Stone to prison. That's reason enough for calling the circumstances suspicious."

"I'm riding with you to Houston," said Vivian.

"So am I," Bess said. "I'm not staying here, biting my nails and worrying."

"We'll close up the house, then," said Barnabas, "and leave the four horses at old man Guthrie's livery. He'll charge us twice what it's worth, but the horses will be safe there. We can leave in the morning and still reach Houston ahead of Silver."

Huntsville, Texas
November 17, 1877

With one weary day stretching into another, Nathan couldn't believe *somebody* hadn't learned of his predicament. His dreary job in the prison laundry was a six-day-a-week affair. It was late Saturday afternoon, and he had paused to wipe the sweat from his face when a guard approached.

"You have a visitor, Stone. This is not visiting hours, but we're making an exception this once. You have ten minutes."

Nathan was taken to a small room where there was a barred window and one chair. A visitor could speak through the barred window, and Nathan quickly learned why the prison had allowed him to see this particular visitor. While he didn't know the man, he was very familiar with the famous star-in-a-circle of the Texas Rangers.

"Stone," said the Ranger, "you don't know me, but I know of you. I'm Captain Dillard from the Ranger outpost in Houston. Yesterday, we received a telegram from a friend of yours in Washington, wanting a report on your whereabouts and circumstances."

"That would be Byron Silver," Nathan said.

"Yes," said Captain Dillard. "We were shocked to learn you had been sent here and I wired Silver that the circumstances were suspicious. I informed him that if he did not conduct an investigation, we would. Here's his response."

His heart pounding, Nathan read the short message.

"Now," Captain Dillard said, "I want you to tell me as quickly as you can how all this came about."

Nathan did so.

"I'm inclined to believe you," said the Ranger. "Sheriff Littlefield doesn't want to talk about you. He's been commended for delivering a pair of bank robbers, and he wants to leave it that way. We're going to appeal your conviction, and if that's denied, we'll ask for a new trial. I'm sure Silver will want to talk to you."

CHAPTER 6

New Orleans
November 16, 1877

After leaving the extra horses with the livery in town, Barnabas, Bess, and Vivian rode out, bound for Houston. Empty trotted ahead, pausing occasionally to be sure they still followed.

"I hope Silver got word to Nathan that we're coming," Vivian said.

"We don't know that he didn't," said Barnabas. "The situation must be serious for Silver to be coming from Washington."

"I'm just glad he's going to be there," Bess said. "We're going into a town where nobody will know us. The authorities will listen to Silver, where they might ignore us."

Houston, Texas
November 19, 1877

"Come in," said Captain Dillard, responding to a knock on his door.

Sheriff Oscar Littlefield entered, closed the door, and stood there looking at Dillard. When he finally spoke, there was an edge to his voice.

"Captain," said Littlefield, "I understand that you and other parties intend to appeal the conviction of Nathan Stone, who is doing time at Huntsville for bank robbery. May I ask why?"

"We don't believe justice has been done," Captain Dillard replied. "We believe you and the State of Texas have sent an innocent man to prison. We intend to appeal his conviction."

"I don't happen to agree with you, Captain," said Littlefield, "and I intend to see that your appeal is denied."

Captain Dillard stood up, placed the palms of his hands on his desk, and leaned across it. His eyes were cold, his voice colder.

"Sheriff, I'm going to give you some advice. Do not interfere with Stone's appeal. I am asking you to back off."

"And I'm refusing," said Littlefield.

"Have it your way," Captain Dillard said. "We can't make you, but by the Eternal, we can make you wish you had."

Littlefield said no more. He left the office, closing the door behind him.

Beaumont, Texas
November 22, 1877

"We can easily reach Houston tomorrow," Barnabas said. "We'll bed down in a hotel and get us some town grub and a night's sleep."

Barnabas took a room for Bess and himself, and another for Vivian. Then they found a cafe, and Barnabas arranged to have Empty fed.

"I feel guilty eating good food, when Nathan may have only bread and water," said Vivian. "Should we go to the prison and try to see him?"

"I don't think so," Barnabas said. "Silver will be here the day after tomorrow and we should let him take the lead. Silver believes Nathan was railroaded into prison, and unless I'm reading him wrong, he'll have some plan. I'm sure we'll be allowed to see Nathan while we're here."

"Then he won't be released any time soon," said Vivian, disappointed.

"I fear that he won't," Barnabas said. "An appeal can take weeks or months, and there is a chance it will be denied. In that case, the court will have to be petitioned for a new trial. God only knows how long that will take."

The trio reached Houston the following day and went immediately to the Ranger outpost. Captain Dillard told them as much as he knew about Nathan's situation, avoiding mention of his confrontation with Sheriff Littlefield. That information would be confidential until Byron Silver arrived.

"Captain," said Vivian, "I'm glad you rode to the prison and spoke to Nathan. Now he knows that we know where he is, and that something is being done toward his release."

"I don't know who was the most surprised to see me, Nathan or the prison officials," Captain Dillard said. "Stone had not been mistreated, and after my visit I don't think he will be."

"I'm sure you'll want to talk to Silver first," said Barnabas, "but unless he has some objection, we'd like to know how the investigation will proceed and what it will seek to prove."

"I can't see Silver having any objection to you being here," Captain Dillard said, "since he asked you to come. I can tell you this much: First we'll appeal the conviction. Should it be refused, we'll demand a new trial."

"And if that's refused?" Vivian asked.

"It won't be," said Captain Dillard. "You have my word."

Slowly Nathan became acquainted with the three prisoners who worked beside him in the prison laundry. Borg was the only survivor of a four-man gang that had attempted to steal a military payroll. Hez and Staggs were convicted killers. It wasn't difficult avoiding the trio during duty hours, for conversation was forbidden. But they soon became Nathan's uninvited companions in the mess hall.

"How long are you in for, Stone?" Borg asked.

"Five years," said Nathan, "for a robbery I had nothing to do with."

"Haw, haw, haw," Borg said. "That's near 'bout the way it was with me, I didn't git my hands on a *peso*. They just plumb shot the hell out of us, an' now I'm stuck here in this stinkin' hole."

Hez and Staggs looked at him; it was Staggs who spoke.

"My heart pumps rainwater for you, bucko. Me an' Hez, we're here for life."

"Speak for yourself," said Hez quietly. "I ain't aimin' to stick around that long."

Nathan said nothing, but he could see what was coming. The next time the three men approached Nathan, they were again in the mess hall, for it was their only opportunity to speak to one another.

"Stone," said Hez under his breath, "we're bustin' out of here."

"I'm not," Nathan said. "I'll stay here and do my time."

"No," said Staggs, "you're goin' with us."

"How and when?" Nathan asked.

"Saturday," said Staggs, "at the end of the shift. We'll take both guards hostage, usin' them to get us out the gate."

"We'll never make it," Nathan said. "Count me out."

"You're in, damn it, whether you like it or not," said Staggs. "If word of this gets out, we'll know it come from you. You'll be a dead man."

Nathan lay on his hard bunk considering Staggs's ultimatum. The two killers—Staggs and Hex—had little to lose, for they were serving life sentences. Borg, however, despite his present circumstances, could see an end to his five-year sentence. After some thought, Nathan believed he had the answer. There were two guards, a hostage for Staggs, and a hostage for Hez. The two killers were prepared to use Nathan and Borg as pawns. There was no other answer, and Borg was a damn fool to consider such a scheme. Nathan had to speak to Borg somehow, before Saturday.

Houston, Texas
November 24, 1877

Byron Silver reached the Ranger outpost astride a bay horse he had hired at a livery. He was dressed like the cowboy he had once been, and a Colt was thonged down on his right hip. He introduced himself as he met Vivian and Captain Dillard for the first time. He then turned to Barnabas and Bess McQueen and greeted them warmly.

"The first and last time I was with you folks, I'd been shot," said Silver, "and I'm not sure the present circumstances are much better. I reckon we'd better make ourselves as comfortable as we can while Captain Dillard tells us what he has learned."

"Howell," Captain Dillard said to another Ranger, "I'll be in my office for a while, and I'm not to be disturbed."

"Yes, sir," said Howell.

Captain Dillard was last to enter the small office. He

closed the door behind him and then took a seat behind his desk, while his four companions settled into chairs facing him.

"Based upon what I have learned," Captain Dillard said, "I have every reason to believe Nathan Stone has been wrongly imprisoned for a crime he didn't commit. I talked to him at length, and his story has a ring of truth. First, I'll tell you what Nathan told me, and then I'll tell you how they rushed him through a trial without presenting a shred of proof, just flimsy circumstantial evidence."

Captain Dillard talked for three-quarters of an hour. When he ceased speaking his companions remained silent for a moment. Barnabas McQueen was first to speak.

"My God, anybody who knows Nathan Stone can see this for the lie that it is. Nathan and Vivian have been working with me, racing horses. He was going to San Antonio to get a pair of Indian-gentled horses I bought."

"This is all so foolish," Vivian said. "Why would Nathan risk his life and reputation stealing ten thousand dollars he would have to split with two other men? He has twenty thousand dollars on deposit in a New Orleans bank. Honest money."

"I've known Nathan for ten years," said Silver, "and while his fast gun has forced him into some situations he would have avoided if he could, he would never take a dishonest dollar. I'd stake my life on that."

"So would I," Bess McQueen said.

"I can add little to that," said Captain Dillard. "The Rangers know and respect him, and based on what I've learned, I believe we should appeal his conviction immediately."

"Prepare the necessary papers," Silver said, "and I'll file them."

"Here they are," said Captain Dillard. "They've been ready for three days."

"We'll be here until a decision has been reached," Barnabas said. "How long do these things take?"

"Unfortunately," said Captain Dillard, "with Sheriff Littlefield opposing it, and with Judge McClendon siding him, it could take months."

"And all that time Nathan has to remain in prison," Vivian said. "Mr. Silver, is there no way he can be released while his case is being appealed?"

"None that I know of," said Silver. "The first step toward freeing him is to appeal his conviction, and unless the appeals court overturns it, the conviction will stand. Should his conviction be upheld, then we can demand a new trial."

"I don't mean to sound ungrateful," Barnabas said, "but how long will that take?"

"As long or longer than the appeal," said Captain Dillard. "Once a man is behind bars, the courts move slowly."

"I can't remain here more than a month," Silver said. "Captain Dillard, I'll have to depend on you and the telegraph to keep me informed. I'll arrange to be here if and when his appeal is heard, and for a new trial if there is one."

"I may have given Nathan false hopes," said Captain Dillard. "I believe you should go to Huntsville and tell him we're appealing his conviction, and that it's going to be long and drawn out."

"I intend to," Silver said. "He also needs to know that if the appeal is unsuccessful, a new trial may take even longer."

"Vivian, Bess, and me will go with you," said Barnabas.

Huntsville, Texas
December 1, 1877

Nathan's three companions were silent as to their intentions, but as their day began in the laundry, the trio's eyes were on him. With his conviction being appealed, the last thing he wanted was to become involved in a prison break. It could only hurt his chance of a successful appeal and perhaps lengthen his sentence. Since he had no idea what Borg, Hez, and Staggs had in mind, he must wait for them to make their move and then somehow foil their plan.

As the end of the day drew near, Nathan found Borg constantly at his side, so it was no surprise that, when the time came, Borg made the first move. In an attempt to distract the two guards, cursing loudly, Borg seized Nathan in a bear hug. But he wasn't quick enough. Nathan drove his right knee into Borg's groin, twisted free, and slammed a right to Borg's jaw. Borg collapsed like an empty sack. The two prison guards hadn't fallen for the trick. They

remained where they were, their Winchesters covering
Staggs and Hez. One of the guards pulled an alarm chain,
bringing a prison official and two more armed guards. Nathan couldn't hear what was being said, but one of the
original guards pointed to Borg, who sat up, rubbing his
jaw.

The prison official, whose name was Corrigan, spoke to
the pair of guards who had accompanied him.

"Take him to solitary." He then turned and spoke to
Nathan. "He jumped you. Why?"

"I don't know," said Nathan. "He took me by surprise."

"Starting Monday," Corrigan said, his eyes on Staggs and
Hez, "you will be assigned to kitchen duty. Guards, escort
these men to the mess hall, keep an eye on them until they
have eaten, and then take them to their cells."

When Staggs and Hez had been taken away, Corrigan
spoke to Nathan.

"Stone, that was fast thinking. You prevented what I
suspect might have become a nasty incident. Such an act
will not go unnoticed."

Nathan said nothing. While he had won Corrigan's approval, his three former companions would regard what he
had done as nothing less than betrayal. If he remained in
the prison for any length of time, he had no doubt the trio
would find a time and place to come after him with vengeance on their minds.

Houston, Texas
December 3, 1877

Byron Silver, Vivian, and the McQueens set out for
Huntsville, with Empty running ahead of them. The hound
seemed aware that they were going to the place where he
had been forced to leave Nathan. They arrived an hour
past noon, and Silver arranged for them to see and talk to
Nathan. While he obviously was glad to see them, he
seemed subdued and said little.

"Captain Dillard told us what you've told him," Silver
said. "Now why don't you tell us in your own words?
Maybe you'll remember something you didn't tell him."

"I doubt it," said Nathan. He repeated what he had told

Captain Dillard. "What I don't understand is what became of my horse."

"Grulla, wasn't it?" said Silver.

"Yes," Nathan replied. "Not the only one, by any means, but those fancy saddlebags had silver buckles, and were made in Mexico. King Fisher gave them to me."

"That's something," said Silver. "From what Captain Dillard has learned, the sheriff's posse found no horses, and that means they must have been taken away by the pair of outlaws who escaped. I'll have the captain pass the word along to the Rangers, and they'll all be watching for those saddlebags."

"I appreciate everything that all of you are doing for me," Nathan said, "but I've been dealt a bad hand. Sheriff Littlefield accepted me as one of the bank robbers, no questions asked. The man who fired at me, that I had to kill, was shot at close range and from the front. Sheriff Littlefield testified that the two robbers who had been wounded were shot from behind. Two men escaped, taking two extra horses with them, one of which was mine. I can't believe Littlefield didn't find the tracks of four horses and couldn't see that only two of them were being ridden."

"That's just some of the things that don't add up," said Silver. "Captain Dillard thinks these and other things Sheriff Littlefield overlooked or dismissed may be used to overturn your conviction. If your appeal is denied, we're going to petition the court for a new trial, and we're going to destroy Sheriff Oscar Littlefield."

"It couldn't happen to a more deserving old *busardo*," Nathan said, "but petitions and appeals take time. How long am I likely to be stuck here?"

"I won't give you any false hope," said Silver. "Appealing your conviction can take as long as six months, with Sheriff Littlefield and Judge McClendon opposing it. If that falls through, it could take as long or longer to win you a new trial."

"Damn," Nathan said. "You can't stay here that long, can you?"

"No," said Silver. "I took a month's leave. However, I'll be in touch with Captain Dillard by telegraph, and he or some of the other Rangers will be here to talk with you as often as they can. You won't be alone, and you won't be forgotten."

"I'll stay here until you're free, Nathan," Vivian said, "however long it takes."

"I appreciate that," said Nathan, "but it would serve no good purpose. Barnabas, I want you and Bess to go home, taking Vivian and Empty with you. Since I never made it to San Antonio, you can go there and get the horses I was supposed to bring you."

"No," Vivian said, "I'm staying with you."

"I don't want you out here alone," said Nathan. "There'll be horse races all over Arkansas, Louisiana, and Mississippi, and Barnabas had plans to enter Diablo in all of them. Didn't you, Barnabas?"

"Well . . ." Barnabas said.

"Vivian, Barnabas, Bess," said Silver, "you can arrange for Captain Dillard to wire you information, just as he has promised to do for me. Nathan has the Texas Rangers on his side, and if anything should happen to him, the Rangers will raise hell and kick a chunk under it. None of you can do more than that."

"He's talking sense," Nathan said. "It's bad enough, me being stuck here without the rest of you having to hunker around, waitin' for something to happen. If we have to go for a new trial, that'll be soon enough for you to return here."

It was a telling argument, and after handshakes with Silver and Barnabas, and tearful goodbyes from Vivian and Bess, the four departed. Nathan returned to his duties in the laundry, feeling dejected and more lonely than he'd ever felt in his life.

Staggs and Hez avoided Nathan in the mess hall, but when they looked at him, the hate in their eyes was obvious. While Nathan wasn't unfriendly, he didn't go out of his way to make friends. It came as a surprise one Sunday morning in the mess hall, when a slender man with dark hair, a horse face, and a lopsided grin sat down on the bench across the table.

"You look like a gent that keeps his mouth shut and minds his business," the stranger said.

"I try," Nathan replied.

"So do I. My name's Hardin. John Wesley Hardin. You must have heard of me, but nothin' good, I reckon."

Nathan grinned, in spite of himself. "Not a single word. I'm Nathan Stone."

"I've heard of you," said Hardin. "*Muy bueno* with the *pistola.*"

Nathan said nothing and Hardin continued.

"How long you in for, if I ain't bein' nosey?"

"You are," Nathan said. "I got five years for bank robbery."

"I'll likely be here the rest of my life," said Hardin. "My daddy named me after John Wesley, the preacher. He had hopes of me bein' a sky pilot, but I ended up workin' for the other side."*

Nathan didn't like the turn the conversation was taking, and changed the subject.

"After the day's work is done, what does a man do with himself in a place like this?"

"Speakin' for myself," said Hardin, "I generally head for my bunk after supper. I'm in the field from sunup to sundown, part of a maximum security detail, every man of us in leg irons. Every guard's equipped with a shotgun and orders that if shooting becomes necessary, shoot to kill."

He looked at Nathan, a lopsided grin on his haggard face, no trace of humor in his eyes. He was difficult to talk to, and when Nathan said nothing, Hardin continued, this time on a lighter note.

"Sundays, now, I generally go to the library after dinner."

"What kind of books do you read?" Nathan asked.

"Law."

Nathan found that amusing and hardly knew how to respond. Hardin laughed.

"I been raisin' hell since I was ten, on the outs with the law since I was eleven, and now I'm twenty-four. I aim to learn something about the law. Hell, if I ever get out of here, maybe I'll open me a law office."†

Nathan had heard much about John Wesley Hardin. The man had a reputation as a cold-blooded killer. In 1874, the State of Texas had posted a four-thousand-dollar bounty

---

*John Wesley Hardin was arrested August 23, 1877, in Pensacola, Florida.

†John Wesley Hardin opened his law office in February 1894 in Gonzales, Texas.

on his head, dead or alive. Having met the man, it wasn't easy matching him to a killer who, at twenty-four, had become a legend. To satisfy his curiosity, Nathan went to the prison library that Sunday afternoon. Hardin was there, engrossed in a heavy, leatherbound book.

"You just might end up with that law office, after all," said Nathan.

Hardin looked up, flashed his lopsided grin, and went back to his reading.

Houston, Texas
December 7, 1877

Vivian and the McQueens were preparing to return to New Orleans.

"I'll stay on top of the situation here," said Captain Dillard, "and as soon as there is any change, I'll telegraph you."

"I'll be here a while, yet," Silver said. "After you shake the tree, it's interesting to step back and see what falls. I aim to see that Nathan's appeal makes it through the proper channels without delay."

"I'm so glad," said Vivian. "I don't feel so bad about us leaving, with you and Captain Dillard in charge."

"If I'm needed," Silver said, "all of you know how to reach me. Should I be away from Washington, any messages will be forwarded, and I'll get back to you."

"Twice a month," said Captain Dillard, "I'll either visit Nathan or send someone else. I will see that he knows we're working toward his release."

Huntsville, Texas
December 14, 1877

The only time the prison inmates came together, except for work details, was in the mess hall. By the time Borg had been released from solitary, Staggs and Hez had begun a campaign to ostracize Nathan. When he sat down at a table to eat, others who were seated there got up and moved. Nathan countered their rejection by seating himself at an empty table. At the start of his third day of eating alone, John Wesley Hardin placed his tin tray on the table across from Nathan and sat down to breakfast.

"I don't know what you got," said Hardin, "but it must be contagious as hell."

"It is," Nathan said. "Borg, Staggs, and Hez tried to drag me into a jail break, and I didn't go along."

Hardin laughed. "I heard about that. They're callin' you a Judas to your own kind."

"My kind, hell," said Nathan, in disgust. "If I wasn't trapped in here, I wouldn't squat and eat within a hundred miles of any of this bunch."

Hardin laughed again, his hard blue eyes twinkling. "My feelings exactly, *amigo,* and if I'm any judge of yellow coyotes, this bunch is workin' their way into a killin' mood. I'd not be surprised if they all jump you sometime soon."

"You're not making any friends," said Nathan.

"Considerin' what I got to choose from," Hardin said, "then maybe I don't want any. Present company excepted, of course."

It was Nathan's turn to laugh, and his laugh was bitter. "My luck's taken such a rotten turn, they'll stomp hell out of me, and it'll be *me* that goes to solitary."

Nathan had heard of prison riots where men like him had been singled out for retribution. The mess hall was the obvious place, for nowhere else did all the inmates come together at the same time. Should the brawl become serious enough, one of his adversaries—Borg, Hez, or Staggs—could kill Nathan without being caught in the act. It was a cowardly method of destroying an enemy—the killers hiding among a surging mass of struggling men and preventing prison officials from fixing individual responsibility for any deaths. It all came together at suppertime, the day before Christmas. Hardin, who had continued taking his meals with Nathan, spoke.

"This is it, *amigo.* Borg, Hez, and Staggs ain't got the sand to take their seats at our table, but every day they've been workin' their way closer. They're at the table next to us, and they'll try to take you in the thick of the fight. They're likely armed with makeshift knives."

"Hardin, this is not your fight," said Nathan. "There are other tables."

Hardin laughed. "But none as interesting as this one.

Somebody in the back of the hall will start the dance, but don't look for Borg, Hez, and Staggs to jump in immediately. We don't make our move until the whole bunch rushes us. Then we flip this table on its side and force them three bastards to come after us."

Nathan said nothing, for it seemed the convicted killer at the table with him wanted this anticipated conflict. Hardin's cold blue eyes seemed to sparkle, and on his lean, horsey face was that lopsided, don't-give-a-damn grin. Suddenly, near the front of the mess hall, there was a shouted curse. Men surged to their feet, shouting and began throwing tin trays and cups.

"It's time, *amigo*," Hardin shouted.

Nathan leaped to his feet and the two of them overturned the table, its top toward the sea of men who surged forward. Then the unexpected happened. The two guards from the front of the mess hall dropped behind the overturned table, one at each end. Facing the ugly snouts of two shotguns, the surging men dropped back. Even Borg hesitated, but Hez and Staggs leaped the table. Each man had in his hand a piece of kitchen cutlery he had hidden and honed for the occasion.

Stepping aside, Nathan avoided Hez, seized his upraised arm, and slammed him to the hard floor, face down. Nathan was on him in an instant, twisting his arm, forcing him to drop the knife. But Hardin hadn't been so fortunate, for Staggs had a weight advantage and the two were locked in a death struggle. The prison guards had the rest of the inmates under control and the eyes of every man were on Hardin and Staggs. Suddenly it was all over and Hardin got shakily to his knees. Staggs lay on his back, his own knife driven into his chest. One of the guards had Hez on his feet, his hands manacled behind him, as one of the other guards went after Borg.

"I didn't do nothin'," Borg shouted.

Like Hez, his hands were manacled behind him, and the two were led away by prison guards.

CHAPTER 7

Huntsville, Texas
April 5, 1878

True to his word, Captain Dillard had kept in touch with Nathan Stone, taking him newspapers and occasional word from Byron Silver and the McQueens. This day, however, the Ranger didn't relish the task that lay ahead. As soon as the prison guard led Nathan into the little room with its barred window, he sensed something was wrong. The Ranger always greeted him with a smile, but this time it seemed forced.

"Bad news, Captain?" Nathan asked.

"I'm afraid so," said the Ranger. "Your appeal has been denied. I have petitioned the court for a new trial, and Silver's demanding a change of venue. He's going to act as your counsel before the court, and if he has his way, the trial will take place in Austin."

"I have all the confidence in the world in Byron Silver," Nathan said, "but do you really believe a change of venue will make any difference?"

"I most certainly do," said Captain Dillard. "Remember that bank teller who swore you were one of the bank robbers? At Silver's insistence, I backtrailed that young man. He is the son of a woman Sheriff Oscar Littlefield was more than a little fond of a few years back, and it was our friend Sheriff Littlefield who got the boy a job at the bank."

"So the bank teller might have helped Sheriff Littlefield look good at my expense."

"Silver thinks so and I agree," said Captain Dillard. "It's one of those things we can't prove beyond the shadow of a doubt, but we don't have to. It's enough to blow Sheriff Littlefield's credibility to hell and gone. We're demanding a trial by jury, too. So that's the good news. You will definitely be granted a new trial. The bad news is, of course, that we don't know how long you'll have to wait. It may take longer if we're granted a change of venue, but I believe it'll be worth the wait."

"So do I," Nathan said.

"Damn it," Barnabas McQueen said, after receiving a telegram from Captain Dillard, "I don't see how they can do this to a man and get away with it."

"They haven't gotten away with it," said Bess. "Captain Dillard said we would soon be hearing from Byron Silver with more information."

"I have confidence in Mr. Silver," Vivian said. "I know a new trial will take longer, but I want Nathan free of all charges and I believe it's the best way."

A week later, Captain Powers—in charge of the federal outpost in New Orleans—rode out to the McQueen place with a lengthy letter from Byron Silver. It explained much of what Captain Dillard had told Nathan, and ended by assuring them that Silver would be Nathan's counsel when he again went to trial.

St. Louis, Missouri
September 2, 1878

It was a dreary Sunday afternoon and the rain came down in gray sheets, slashing at the windows of the little church Anna Tremayne had attended all her life. Now she lay in a coffin before the altar, soon to be lowered into a grave in the little churchyard, beside her husband, John. As the minister droned on, young John Wesley Tremayne—not quite twelve years old—gritted his teeth and gripped the back of a pew with his hands. While he mourned the loss of Grandma Anna, his grief had been all but swallowed up by his anger. While his life without mother or father hadn't been ideal, it was about to become infinitely worse. He had been temporarily taken in by the minister and his wife, but only until arrangements could be made to send him to an orphanage.

Finally the service was over, and he was led into the drizzling rain, among mourners who followed the coffin to the old graveyard behind the church. He watched them lower the coffin into the grave with no outward emotion, and as though from far away, he could hear the shocked whispers of some of the female mourners.

". . . alone in this world, and not a tear."

"A cold-hearted little devil he is, and if I'm any judge, he'll come to a bad end."

But to young John Wesley Tremayne, tears were a sign of weakness, and in a world where he had continually fought for the dubious honor of a mother he had never known, he had dared not show anything but strength. He fought those stronger than he, and when he arose, bruised and bloody, it was without a whimper. Now he took fierce pride in not having allowed them to see him weep, and he silently vowed that no orphanage was going to hold him for long. Somewhere he had a father, an elusive being who could supply those answers his mother and grandparents had taken with them to the grave.

Except for the one time John Wesley Hardin had sided Nathan in the mess hall fight, Hardin had become a model prisoner. He remained friendly to Nathan, and the little free time that he had was spent in the prison library with the law books.

"Point me toward some of those law books you're finished with," Nathan said. "A man can do worse than study law, I reckon."

Denied access to newspapers, Nathan began reading law, and for him, too, the study soon became an antidote to the tedium of prison life. He and Hardin bothered nobody, and even the prison guards seemed to respect their dedication. Time passed, and with the regular letters Vivian had begun writing, Nathan kept his spirits up. Each time Nathan stepped into the little visitor's room with its barred window, he studied Captain Dillard's face. Finally, on the first day of March 1879, the Ranger brought welcome news.

"You've been granted a new trial, Nathan, along with a change of venue. It's set for July fourteenth in Austin. Every Ranger within riding distance will be there. I've already telegraphed Silver and the McQueens. You'll be leaving here on July tenth. Silver will be there ahead of you."

"I want you there," said Nathan. "You've kept me alive all these months."

"God willing, I'll be there," Captain Dillard said.

"I can never thank you enough for all you've done," said Nathan.

"You once did for Captain Sage Jennings what he was unable to do for himself," said Captain Dillard. "That's enough."

"There's a horse race in Beaumont, Texas on July fourth," Barnabas McQueen said. "I see no reason why we can't let Diablo win that race before we ride on to Houston."

"It might be a way of cheering Nathan," said Vivian, "and it is on the way."

"Barnabas McQueen," Bess said, "you ought to share Diablo's winnings with Nathan. I believe Eulie would have gone on to great things had she lived, and now Vivian's never lost a race, riding Diablo. You have Nathan to thank for bringing them to you."

"I've never denied that," said Barnabas, "but he wouldn't have it. He can win plenty, just as he did in Little Rock."

"Not on Diablo," Vivian said. "He's made a name for himself, and there are no more twenty-to-one odds."

"I reckon not," said Barnabas, "but that pair we brought from San Antonio should be ready by the time Nathan's free. We'll begin racing them when you think they're ready."

"They're ready now," Vivian said, "but I can't bring myself to leave Diablo for them."

"Vivian," said Bess, "why don't you invite your brother for a visit? He's never seen you ride, has he?"

"No," Vivian said, "and I am going to invite him. He wants to be there for Nathan's trial. He can take the train to Kansas City or St. Louis, and a steamboat to New Orleans."

Houston, Texas
July 5, 1879

Again Byron Silver took a sailing ship bound for Corpus Christi, and when he left the ship at the Houston port, he secured himself a horse at a livery. He then rode immediately to the Texas Ranger outpost.

"I'm glad you got here a few days early," said Captain Dillard. "Are you ready with your defense?"

"Pretty much," Silver replied. "We only have to convince the jury there's reasonable doubt, that no effort was made to prove or disprove what Nathan told the court actually happened. I'm prepared to go considerably beyond that."

"Then you've learned something I don't know," said Captain Dillard.

Silver laughed. "Count on it, pardner."

An hour before sundown, Harley and Vivian Stafford and the McQueens arrived. They rode to the Ranger station, where Silver and Captain Dillard were about to go to an early supper.

"I'm buying the steaks," said Barnabas McQueen. "Vivian rode Diablo to another big one, and we're all flush."

"My God," Harley said, "the last thing I ever expected was to win two thousand pesos on a horse, with my sister ridin' him. Why, I can remember her havin' saddle sores all the way from her knees to her—"

"Harley," said Vivian, interrupting, "can't we talk about something else?"

"Let's go eat," Silver suggested. "When I'm offered a steak, I just purely can't keep anything else on my mind."

When the meal was done, they spent some time over coffee, talking.

"I don't even like to suggest this," said Vivian, "but is there a chance we could lose, that Nathan won't go free?"

"There's always a chance," Silver replied, "but in light of what I've learned, I'd call it slight."

"Who are you going to question, besides Sheriff Littlefield and the bank teller?" Bess McQueen asked.

"Except for one that's dead," said Silver, "I'll call every man that rode in that posse, if I have to. But I don't expect it to come to that."

"I haven't seen Nathan in more than two years," Harley said. "I'd like to ride to the prison and talk to him."

"I'll go with you," said Silver. "Vivian, do you want to come?"

"Yes, please," Vivian said.

"You can tell him Bess and me will see him in Austin," Barnabas said. "Do you want to take Empty with you?"

"Not unless he particularly wants to go," said Silver. "We'd have a hell of a time trying to smuggle him in to see Nathan."

Barnabas had arranged for the hound to be fed steak trimmings, and having had his fill, Empty was waiting with the horses.

On July 9, Silver prepared to ride to Austin. With him rode Captain Dillard, Bess and Barnabas McQueen, and Vivian and Harley Stafford. It was a festive occasion, and in his enthusiasm, Empty ran on ahead.

"We'll take rooms near the courthouse," Silver said. "One of the hotels has a livery, and there are plenty of cafes. It's about a hundred and twenty miles, so we'll be arriving after dark. Not much between here and there, and I reckon I'm gettin' soft. I don't sleep on the ground, if I can get out of it."

The day before Nathan was to depart for Austin, John Wesley Hardin joined him for supper for the last time. While the man had the name of a killer, he had been Nathan's only friend.

"I wish you were gettin' another chance," Nathan said.

"No way," said Hardin, flashing his lopsided grin. "I was guilty as hell, and I count myself lucky that I didn't get the rope. I'll have time to read the rest of those law books, and if you ever see me outside these walls, I'll be wearin' a top hat and a swallowtail coat, and carrying a briefcase in my hand. Good luck."

Two prison guards escorted Nathan to Austin, and it was well after dark when they arrived. There were holding cells in the basement of the three-story brick courthouse, and Nathan was taken to one of them. Compared with the quarters at Huntsville, the cell was luxurious. A guard brought Nathan his supper, and he was barely through eating when the guard returned.

"You have a visitor. They're usually not permitted at night, but he's your counsel. I'll have to lock you in, Mr. Silver."

"Perfectly all right," said Silver. "Is there a limit?"

"No," the guard replied. "Take as long as you like."

He locked the door, leaving Silver and Nathan alone.

"Well," Silver said, "it's been a long time coming. Sorry we couldn't do it sooner."

"I have no complaints," said Nathan. "You did the best you could. If we win this, can it be removed from my record? I reckon I ought to be satisfied, just gettin' out, but—"

"I know how you feel," Silver replied, "and if I can prove you were wrongly convicted, then the State of Texas will owe you. The very least they can do is clean the slate. My God, if they need character references, you have every Ranger in Texas on your side."

"Don't sell yourself short," said Nathan. "Your influence means a lot."

Silver laughed. "I'm not sure the courts take me seriously. I'm a Texan, and we have a reputation for standing by our friends, even when they're guilty as hell."

"Strange you should mention that," Nathan said. "The only friend I had in Huntsville was John Wesley Hardin. He's reading all the law books in the prison library, and claims he'll open a law office when he gets out."

"He might just do that," said Silver. "Any time you want a Texan out of the game, you'd better kill him. If you don't, he'll come after you with a club, if he can't get his hands on anything more lethal."

Nathan laughed. "I guess all we can do now is wait until Monday."

"That's it," said Silver. "I had no real reason for coming by tonight, except that I just wanted you to know we're all here. I doubt there'll be any visitors allowed over the weekend. I really don't expect the trial to take more than a day, unless there's something I've overlooked."

Austin, Texas
July 14, 1879

With Byron Silver beside him, Nathan sat at the table for the defense. Twisting around in his chair, he surveyed the courtroom. Tears came to his eyes when he found three entire rows of seats occupied by men who wore the symbol of the Texas Rangers, the silver star-in-a-circle. There were others he had met in his checkered career, and one of them was the infamous Ben Thompson. Another was King Fisher. He almost laughed aloud as he recalled accompanying Fisher on a wild horse hunt into Mexico. An untamable stallion had demolished Fisher's corral and reclaimed his herd.

"Everybody stand," said the bailiff as the judge took his seat on the bench.

The judge waited until everybody had been seated. Then he spoke.

"I am Judge Warnell Travis. This is a new trial with change of venue, with counsel for the defense seeking to overturn the prior conviction of Nathan Stone. The defense has requested trial by jury. Since this is a change of venue, the court is seeking to dispense with some of the formalities. Eighteen potential jurors are present. Does counsel for the defense or the prosecution have cause to strike any of these potential jurors?"

"None for the defense," said Silver, rising.

"None for the prosecution," Sterling Ackerman said. He had been the prosecutor when Nathan had been convicted.

"Bailiff," said Judge Travis, "seat the first twelve men from the list of potential jurors."

"Now," said Judge Travis, when the jurors had been seated, "the bailiff will read the original charges against Nathan Stone, the testimonies, and the sentence imposed."

"Objection," Ackerman shouted. "The original witnesses are present, and prosecution believes they should, for the sake of accuracy, testify again."

"Denied," said Judge Travis. "This court has the right to hear the testimonies that sent this man to prison. Is the prosecution implying that the original testimonies might have been in error?"

"Of course not," Ackerman said nervously.

"Very well," said Judge Travis. "The bailiff will read as so instructed."

The bailiff read the transcript, ending with the sentence imposed.

"Now," Judge Travis said, "read the testimony of the defendant, Nathan Stone."

Nathan's brief testimony was read; it included repeated objections of the prosecution.

"I am hearing objections by the prosecution," said Judge Travis, "but not a word from Mr. Stone's counsel seeking to deny those objections. Why?"

"Judge," Silver said, rising, "why don't you allow Nathan Stone to answer that?"

"Objection," said Ackerman.

"Overruled," Judge Travis said. "Mr. Stone, approach the bench."

Nathan did so, looking Judge Travis in the eye.

"Where was your counsel, Mr. Stone?" Judge Ackerman asked.

"You're looking at him, Judge," said Nathan.

"Did you choose to speak in your own defense, or were you denied counsel?"

"I was denied counsel, Judge," Nathan said. "I asked to send a telegram, and I was denied that as well."

"You may be seated," said Judge Travis. He then fixed stern eyes on the prosecutor, and Ackerman got hastily to his feet.

"Judge," Ackerman said, "the evidence was overwhelming. We didn't think—"

"You are exactly right," said Judge Travis, in a dangerously low tone. "You certainly did not think. Be seated. We're going to hear from the defense. Mr. Silver, approach the bench."

Silver got up, approached the bench, and stood facing the judge.

"Mr. Silver," Judge Travis said, "in a brief opening statement, tell this court what you expect to prove. You may then present any new evidence or call witnesses."

Instead of speaking to the judge, Silver turned to face the jury.

"Gentlemen of the jury," said Silver, "I can prove that Nathan Stone had nothing to do with that bank robbery, that he was riding west and stumbled onto their camp. Two of the robbers were in camp, one of them wounded. Stone traded shots with the men, killing one. The other escaped, and from somewhere behind Stone, the third robber shot him in the back. Two of the robbers then escaped, one of them leading the dead man's horse. The other man led Stone's horse, and the two rode away with the money stolen from the bank."

"Objection," Ackerman shouted. "Counsel for the defense is speculating."

"Overruled," said Judge Travis.

"Judge," Silver said, "I have used these preliminary remarks to set the stage for an accusation I am about to make. According to the testimony of Sheriff Oscar Littlefield, two of the bank robbers were wounded in the chase, having been shot from behind. However, Nathan Stone is prepared to testify that he was facing the man who fired at him, that he returned the fire, killing the man. What kind of lawman looks at a dead man and doesn't bother to determine if he was shot from front or back?"

"Does the prosecution care to comment on that?" Judge Travis asked.

There was just a hint of sarcasm in his voice, and one of the jurors laughed.

"Judge," said Ackerman, "both men had been wounded in the chase. I'm sure Sheriff Littlefield just assumed—"

"You don't send a man to prison based on anybody's assumption," Travis snapped. "You may continue, Mr. Silver."

"When Stone was found wounded near the outlaw camp," said Silver, "the sheriff and his posse apparently made no further effort to trail the robbers who escaped. If they had, it wouldn't have been too difficult to find the tracks of *four* horses, one of them belonging to Nathan Stone."

"Your honor," Ackerman cut in, "there was a storm, and the trail was—"

"Mr. Ackerman," said Judge Travis, slamming the podium with his gavel, "you are out of order. Another such outburst and I'll declare you in contempt of court."

"Your honor," Silver continued, "the storm in question didn't wash out the trail until well after dark. In fact, the sheriff and his posse had returned to town well before the rain began. While Sheriff Littlefield seems to have forgotten that, most of the men who rode in that posse are here. I believe we can jog their memories, under oath."

"Do you have anything to say to that, Mr. Ackerman?" Judge Travis asked.

"There was little use in pursuing a trail soon to be lost," Ackerman said. "The sheriff had two of the bank robbers, one of them dead. There were three to start with, and it was safe to assume—"

"It's never safe to assume anything, Mr. Ackerman," said Judge Travis, "when false assumptions send a man to prison unjustly."

"An eyewitness—one of the tellers—testified that Stone was in the bank," Ackerman said. "Are you calling *that* an assumption too?"

"No," said Silver, "I'm calling that a carefully calculated lie to save Sheriff Littlefield's reputation, to justify sending an innocent man to Huntsville prison."

"That's a damned lie," Ackerman bawled. "You can't prove it."

"Order in the court!" Judge Travis shouted. "Mr. Prosecutor, I am declaring you in contempt of this court and fining you fifty dollars. You will pay before you depart, and if I am forced to declare you in contempt a second time, I'll have you jailed. Mr. Silver, you may continue."

"I had hoped this wouldn't be necessary," said Silver, "but since it is, then I'll make it easy as I can on the parties involved. Twenty-three years ago, Oscar Littlefield had an affair with a woman whose name was Eva Montgomery. She's long dead, and I mention her only to prove the truth of what I am about to say. Eva had a son. Oscar Littlefield's son. To Littlefield's credit, he helped with the boy as best he could. When the boy was barely eighteen, Oscar Littlefield got him a job as a bank teller. This son of Littlefield's—Stewart Montgomery—is the teller who identified Nathan Stone as one of the bank robbers. If I must, I can call Stewart to the stand, put him under oath . . ."

But the truth of Silver's accusation was immediately evident. White-faced, the young man in question leaped to his feet and ran for the door. Two men caught him, dragging him back into the court room.

"Mr. Ackerman," Judge Travis said, "have you anything to say?"

"Your honor," said Ackerman, sweating, "I knew nothing of this. I . . . I don't know what to say . . . I . . ."

"Then take your seat," Judge Travis said. "Gentlemen of the jury, it's time to retire and reach a verdict. Shall this man be returned to prison, based on original evidence, or should the court set him free?"

"Set him free!" shouted the jury in a single voice, rising to their feet.

"Nathan Stone," said Judge Travis, "you are free to go. I regret that I can offer you nothing on behalf of the State of Texas but an apology."

Judge Travis left the bench, seeming not to notice the stomping and shouting that prevailed in the courtroom. People Nathan didn't know wrung his hand and slapped him on the back. Texas Rangers, their faith in him vindicated, surrounded him. Finally he was able to speak to Ben Thompson and King Fisher.

"God," said Fisher. "Ben and me would of busted you out if we'd knew you was in there."

"Damn right," Thompson agreed, obviously more than a little drunk.

"Thanks," said Nathan, "but you hombres are generally in enough trouble without jumping into mine."

Nathan didn't get a chance to speak to Silver, Harley, Vivian, or the McQueens until he finally escaped the courtroom. He was barely down the courthouse steps when Empty came romping toward him, yipping his excitement. Nathan knelt, ruffling the dog's ears, and when he eventually got loose, he kissed Vivian long and hard. That done, he turned to Bess McQueen with the same treatment.

"I won't hold it against you," said Harley, "if we just shake hands."

Silver laughed. "That's kind of how I feel."

"Nathan, now that you're free," said Barnabas, "what's the first thing you'd like to do?"

"Order me some grub that I don't have to eat off a tin tray," Nathan said, "but I'll need to get out of these prison clothes."

"I thought of that," said Captain Dillard. "I have the clothes you were wearing when you went to Huntsville. They're in my saddlebag. Your Winchester and Colts are in my office in Houston."

"I'm obliged," Nathan said. "I can get another horse, but those weapons were given to me by Captain Sage Jennings. I wouldn't part with them for any price."

"I don't blame you," said Captain Dillard. "I'll get your clothes from my saddlebag. I think there's a cloakroom in the courthouse where you can change."

Nathan changed into his familiar clothing, leaving the

prison clothes in a trash can. As he was about to leave the courthouse, a door—probably to a closet—opened, and Oscar Littlefield stepped out. He froze when he saw Nathan. He seemed much older, for he had his hat in his hand and his hair was snow white.

"I'm sorry that ... had to come out," Nathan said.

"You got nothin' to be sorry for," said Littlefield. "A man does wrong, and it catches up to him. A lie always needs a bigger lie to cover it, until you can't hide it no more."

He went on out the door, and Nathan waited a few minutes before he followed.

"Sheriff Littlefield just came out," Captain Dillard said. "What was he doing in there?"

"Facing up to his past," said Nathan. "I feel sorry for him."

"Nathan," Silver said, "don't waste your sympathy on him. To cover his own carcass, he sent you to prison, for God's sake."

"I came out of it without any scars," said Nathan, "but Littlefield's hurting, and he's just been sentenced to life."

CHAPTER 8

Nathan bought another horse and saddle in Austin. A grulla, it was much like the one he had lost to the bank robbers. Reaching the Ranger outpost in Houston, Nathan belted on his twin Colts and secured his Winchester in the saddle boot.

"You're lookin' like Nathan Stone again," Harley said approvingly.

"I'm startin' to feel a little like him," said Nathan.

"I want you to spend Christmas with us in New Orleans," Barnabas said.

"Maybe I will," said Nathan. "Silver, why don't you join us?"

"I can never plan that far ahead," Silver replied. "We'll have to wait and see. I'd like to watch that black horse run, though."

Silver departed for Washington the next morning, and after saying their goodbyes to Captain Dillard, Nathan, Harley, Vivian, and the McQueens set out for New Orleans. Empty trotted ahead, often looking back to be sure Nathan was still there.

New Orleans
July 25, 1879

Back at the McQueen place, roaming the woods with Empty and enjoying plenty of good food, Nathan put all thought of Huntsville prison behind him. He began practicing with his Colts, quickly recovering his skill and speed. But as much as he thought of the McQueens, and despite the fact that Vivian seemed to have found a home, Nathan became restless. While he consistently won money on Diablo, he became weary of horse racing and seldom shared Vivian's excitement. When Barnabas began making plans for races in the spring of the next year, Nathan made up his mind. One day when they were alone, he spoke to Barnabas.

"Barnabas, there's nowhere I'd rather be than right here, for a while. But come the first of the year, I'll be ridin' on."

"I understand," said Barnabas. "What about Vivian?"

"I want her to stay here with you and continue to do what she's doing," Nathan said.

"Have you spoke to her about it?"

"No," said Nathan, "and I don't know exactly how to suggest it. Do you?"

"Maybe," Barnabas said. "I took a liking to Harley and suggested that he leave the railroad and throw in with us. Neither of us said anything to Vivian. No point in it, until he's made up his mind."

"That might be the answer," said Nathan. "Working for the railroad, Harley's gone a lot, and Vivian isn't comfortable in a railroad town. That's why I've kept her with me."

The last day of August, Harley Stafford rode into the McQueen place. At the supper table, he explained what he had in mind.

"While we were in Houston, Barnabas invited me to get into horse racing," Harley said, "and I've decided to do it. I've resigned from the railroad, and I have enough money saved to buy a couple more horses."

"You won't need any more horses," said Vivian. "Use the money to hire yourselves a rider. When Nathan goes, I'm going with him."

Harley looked helplessly at Barnabas, while Vivian turned questioning eyes on Nathan. Bess wisely retired to the kitchen. Supper ended on a sour note, and when they retired to their quarters for the night, Nathan expected a tirade from Vivian. She didn't disappoint him.

"Just whose idea was this? If you don't want me riding with you, then you could have just said so. You didn't have to drag Harley into it."

"Damn it," said Nathan, "Barnabas told me he had suggested this to Harley, but never once did I think Harley would actually do it. When he rode in today, it was as much a surprise to me as it was to you. I told you, once Barnabas learned you could ride Diablo, he wouldn't want you to leave."

"Yes," she admitted, "you did. But I didn't expect him to go this far. Now what are we going to do?"

"I believe you should talk to Harley," said Nathan. "Despite what you think of Barnabas, I doubt he could have talked Harley into it if Harley wasn't interested. One thing that I'm sure of, where Harley's concerned. He's still carrying a load of guilt for having left you in Virginia when he came west. I'm not sure that isn't part of his reason for accepting this proposal from Barnabas. Harley's concern for you is genuine, and even if that's his purpose for accepting McQueen's offer, you shouldn't be too hard on him."

She sat down on the bed, burying her face in her hands. "I know he feels guilty, and if I thought Barnabas really wanted him here . . ."

"You think Barnabas is luring Harley here so you'll stay," said Nathan.

"Yes," Vivian said. "I can't help it. How do *you* feel?"

"Barnabas McQueen's one of the best friends I have in this world," said Nathan, "but I'd have to agree with you. I've only been out of prison six weeks, and I'm already restless. Barnabas knows I'll be riding out, and it's not in his best interest for you to ride with me."

"But it's not fair to me, and it's not fair to Harley. It's not fair to me because he's using Harley to try and keep me here, and it's not fair to Harley because Barnabas doesn't really need Harley. I believe Harley's being used to keep me here, and I don't like thinking of what it may do to him when he figures it out."

"Whether you stay or not," said Nathan, "suppose Barnabas really wants Harley here? Suppose he has plans for Harley? Would that change the way you feel?"

"Perhaps," she admitted, "but how are we to know?"

"I'll talk to Barnabas," said Nathan, "and tell him how you feel. He'll understand and respect your feelings. If Harley's gone to bed, I'll talk to Barnabas tonight."

Nathan found Barnabas and Bess still at the kitchen table. Harley was absent. Nathan sat down and repeated to Barnabas what Vivian had told him. Barnabas laughed.

"Is that all that's bothering her? Harley made me promise not to say anything to her until he's had a chance to talk to her, and he's going to do that in the morning."

"Just to satisfy my curiosity," Nathan said, "what *are* your plans for Harley?"

"Harley's going to ride those two horses we brought back

from San Antonio," said Barnabas. "He's tall and lanky enough to ride without a saddle, and he only weighs a hundred and fifty pounds. Harley rode with us to Houston for your trial, and I learned something about him that I don't believe you and Vivian have noticed. Harley has that same touch with horses that Vivian does. By the time we reached Houston, Harley had made friends with Diablo. You know how long I've had that horse, and he just tolerates me. Give Harley Stafford a week or so, and he'll be riding Diablo. I don't know what the man has, but he's a natural with horses. I think the world of Vivian, but if she doesn't want to stay, then I believe Harley can take up the slack. I aim to prove it to her. On the fourth and fifth of October there are races in Beaumont. I'm planning for Vivian to ride Diablo in the Saturday race, but on Sunday, Harley will be riding Petalo, one of the horses we bought back from San Antonio."

"And this is what Harley aims to tell Vivian?"

"Yes," said Barnabas, "among other things. By the time you're ready to ride out, I'll have convinced Vivian that my invitation to Harley is honest, and I expect she will have learned something about him that she didn't know."

"And something I didn't know," Nathan said. "Vivian showed up in Dodge, broke and half starved, and I promised to help her find Harley. When we finally did—in Deadwood—Harley was on the bottle, bitter, and hating everybody. Not until he was shot up in a stage robbery did he begin to change."*

"I don't care what he was," said Barnabas. "He has a feel for horses, and if I'm any judge, he's going to make a name for himself as a rider."

"I appreciate you telling me this," Nathan said. "I won't repeat any of it to Vivian, unless Harley has trouble convincing her."

Nathan found Vivian sitting on the bed, where he had left her.

"Barnabas has convinced me," Nathan said, "and Harley's going to talk to you in the morning. I think you're in for a pleasant surprise. Now will you go to bed or do you aim to set there and sulk?"

"Maybe I'll just set here and sulk," said Vivian. "If you

ride out without me, you'll be sleeping by yourself, so you might as well get used to it."

Nathan laughed and blew out the lamp.

The next morning after breakfast, Nathan and the McQueens left Harley and Vivian at the table.

"I hope they can reach some agreement," said Bess. "I hate seeing them on the outs with one another, us being the cause of it."

"You're not the cause of it," Nathan said. "Harley's doing what he wants to do, and from what Barnabas told me, he's fully justified. But I'm not sure Vivian will believe him."

"She'll believe her own eyes," said Barnabas. "After dinner, Harley's going to prove to her he can ride."

"He's going to ride Petalo, then," Nathan said.

"Petalo and Modelo," said Barnabas. "But first, he's going to ride Diablo."

Nathan laughed in anticipation, but Harley didn't look all that confident when he came into the parlor.

"Well?" Barnabas said.

"She still has her doubts," said Harley. "I'm going to have to prove myself."

After dinner, they went to the horse barn for the horses. Vivian led Diablo, Barnabas led Petalo, and Harley led Modelo. Nathan and Bess followed. The horses were led to an open field, to a cleared stretch where Vivian often rode Diablo. Without a word, Harley passed Modelo's reins to Barnabas and turned to Vivian.

"I told you what I aim to do," said Harley. "You still haven't told me what you think."

"I think you're going to break your neck," Vivian said.

Harley took Diablo's reins from Vivian, and the horse looked at him, laying back his ears. Harley whistled a strange little tune, barely audible, and Diablo's ears came up. Very slowly Harley approached the horse, and Diablo didn't move, even when Harley placed his hand on the horse's lean neck. Suddenly, Harley vaulted onto Diablo's back, and before the horse could react, Harley leaned forward and spoke to Diablo. The horse broke into a fast gallop as Harley leaned forward, his lanky legs keeping him upright and steady. Just before reaching the woods, Harley wheeled the horse and Diablo came galloping back. Harley slid off, his arm around Diablo's neck, grinning at Vivian.

"Riding him across a field is one thing," said Vivian. "Winning a race with him might not be so easy."

"Oh, I don't intend to ride Diablo as long as you're here," Harley said. "I just want you to know that I can, and that I'm not here to help Barnabas hold on to you. October fifth, at Beaumont, I'll be riding Petalo, and we're going to win. Do you want to see me ride him now?"

"No," said Vivian. "I've had enough of your showing off for one day."

She took Diablo's reins and went stomping back toward the horse barn. Barnabas winked at Harley, and Harley laughed.

"Shame on the two of you," Bess said, "baiting her like that."

"When it comes to women," said Nathan, "there's just a thin line between heaven and hell, and from one day to the next a man never knows which side of the line he's likely to be on."

Barnabas and Harley laughed uproariously, while Bess tried mightily not to.

"I feel a little guilty," Harley said. "She's found something she enjoys, something she can do well, and now I'm horning in. She resents that. I won't be surprised if she leaves with Nathan, just to spite me."

"If she does, so be it," said Barnabas. "There's room for both of you. Horse racing is becoming so popular, there's going to be more and more two-day events. Perhaps Vivian will better understand that after the races at Beaumont."

Beaumont, Texas
October 4, 1879

Vivian said very little in the days that followed. Barnabas insisted on arriving early on Thursday, although the first race wasn't scheduled until two o'clock Saturday afternoon. To escape the silent Vivian for a while, Nathan and Harley visited some of the town's saloons. They were about to enter a place called The Blue Moon when Nathan turned away.

"What is it?" Harley asked.

"The grulla there at the hitch rail," said Nathan. "That's the horse I was riding when I stumbled on to those bank robbers."

"How can you be sure? There's plenty of grullas around. You're riding one."

"Those saddlebags," Nathan said. "They have silver buckles, and they came from old Mexico. King Fisher gave them to me. King's brand—a K inside a crown—is burned into the leather beneath one of the flaps. Let's have a look."

Nathan unbuckled one of the flaps, revealing King Fisher's brand.

"Well, by God," said Harley, "all we got to do is wait until that coyote heads for the horse, and you've got one of them."

"They could still be together," Nathan said. "I'd like to take them alive, wire Captain Dillard, and have the bastards sent to Huntsville."

"Given a choice, they ain't likely to give up without a fight," said Harley. "Maybe if we both throw down on them, it won't end up in a shoot-out."

"This is not your fight, Harley," Nathan said.

"Maybe not," said Harley, "but if there's two of them, I'm buying in."

They waited three-quarters of an hour, and Nathan grew impatient.

"I'm going inside and challenge the varmint ridin' that grulla," Nathan said. "He could have left the horse here and gone somewhere else."

"Then I'm goin' with you," said Harley.

"If you're going," Nathan said, "go in first. Go to the bar and order a beer. I'll call out the man ridin' the grulla. If there's two of them, and they both decide to fight, then one of them is yours. If there's just the one man, stay out of it."

"You're callin' the shots," said Harley, heading for the swinging doors.

Nathan waited, counting slowly to a hundred. He then entered the saloon, allowing his eyes to adjust to the lamplit interior before making his move. He counted nine men. Four of them sat at a table playing poker, two were at a table in the corner, and three—one of them Harley—stood at the bar facing the door.

"I want some talk with the gent ridin' the grulla," said Nathan. "The one totin' fancy saddlebags with silver buckles."

One of the two men at the corner table stood up. "What might you be wantin' with him?"

"I'd be wantin' him to show me a bill of sale," Nathan said. "That's my horse."

"I'll meet you outside, then," said the stranger, kicking back his chair.

"Go ahead," said Nathan. "I'll be right behind you."

He headed for the door—a little too readily, Nathan thought, as he stepped in behind him. Suddenly a Colt roared behind them, and the man ahead of Nathan turned on him, his hand streaking for his Colt. Nathan seized the wrist with his left hand and slammed his right fist into his antagonist's jaw. Only then did he turn to see what had happened behind him. The second man at the table stood beside it, blood soaking the right shoulder of his shirt.

"He was about to shoot you in the back," said Harley, his Colt still cocked and ready.

"I'd appreciate you gents takin' your trouble somewheres else," the barkeep said.

"We aim to," said Nathan. "Where can we find the sheriff?"

"Him or his deputies will find you," the barkeep said. "He's hired extra men because of the races Saturday an' Sunday."

Within minutes, a man with a star on his shirt and a shotgun in the crook of his arm entered the saloon. Nathan didn't wait for him to speak.

"These hombres—the one on the floor and the one drippin' blood—are wanted for bank robbery in Houston. I want them locked up and a telegram sent to Captain Dillard at the Ranger outpost."

"I'm Lytle Hays," said the lawman. "I'm just a deputy. You'll have to talk to Waddy McLean, the sheriff."

"I'll talk to him," Nathan said, "but I'm takin' this pair of coyotes with me."

Hays led the way to the sheriff's office as Nathan and Harley, their Colts drawn, marched the two captured men ahead of them. The sheriff saw them coming and swung the door back for them to enter.

"Waddy," said the deputy, "these hombres with Colts drawn have a story for you. The jaspers they're coverin' started some gunplay in the Blue Moon. Somethin' having to do with a bank robbery in Houston."

"For the time being," the sheriff said, "until I get some facts, lock those two in a cell and fetch a doc for the one that's bleeding."

When the two men had been locked in a cell and Hays had gone for a doctor, Nathan told his story, leaving out nothing.

"I don't remember the robbery or the original trial," said Sheriff McLean, "but I do recall the new trial in Austin. So you're the gent that was railroaded into Huntsville."

"Yes," Nathan said, "and that's why I didn't just shoot those two varmints we just marched in here. I want them to take their turn in Huntsville."

McLean laughed. "I can't say I blame you, but there's a matter of proof."

"That's why I want you to telegraph Captain Dillard at the Ranger outpost," Nathan said. "I want this pair taken back to Houston so those bank tellers can have a look at them."

"I can't hold them, even overnight," said McLean, "without some charges. Suspicion of a two-year-old bank robbery won't be enough."

"Well, hell," Harley said, "hold them for attempted murder. If I hadn't plugged the one that's bleedin', he'd have shot Nathan in the back."

"I can do that," said McLean. "I won't bother questioning them. If they're guilty, as you say, the crime is out of my jurisdiction. It's a job for the Rangers. I'll send that telegram to Houston."

Nathan and Harley waited, and while McLean was gone, Deputy Hays returned with a doctor to attend the wounded man. The sheriff was gone for an hour, but when he returned, he had a reply from Captain Dillard.

"There's a something in here for you," McLean said, passing the message to Nathan.

Quickly Nathan read the few words, and then read them again.

Hold suspects on suspicion of bank robbery stop. Rangers coming for them October sixth stop. Suggest Stone return to Houston.

"Are you answering this telegram, sheriff?" Nathan asked.

"Already did," said McLean. "Told him I'll hold these gents for the Rangers."

"Then I'll telegraph him," Nathan said. "Come on, Harley."

Nathan and Harley found the telegraph office and sent the telegram.

"I reckon we'd better find Barnabas and tell him we'll be riding on to Houston," said Harley.

"You don't have to go," Nathan said.

"I reckon I do," said Harley. "I can testify that both them varmints was ready to fill you full of lead. Why would they have tried that if they wasn't guilty as hell?"

"You have a point," Nathan said. "Reason enough for you to ride along."

Harley laughed. "I got a better reason than that. Me and old Petalo's goin' to win that race on Sunday, and Vivian will likely sulk all the way back to New Orleans."

There were only nine entries in Saturday's race, and the favored horse was a dun whose name was Jack Rabbit. Vivian seemed preoccupied and had little to say.

"Vivian, are you all right?" Barnabas asked.

"Of course I'm all right," said Vivian shortly. "Why wouldn't I be?"

"She ain't all right," Harley said, under his breath. "She's still on the prod, and if I'm any judge, Diablo's goin' to pick up on her mood. Don't bet your money on this one."

Diablo came in a poor third. Vivian sat there white-faced, as though in shock, and as Nathan tried to help her dismount, she fought free of him. Harley led Diablo away to be rubbed down. Nathan glared at Vivian in disgust.

"So I lost," she shouted. "Why don't you shoot me?"

"That would be too easy on you," said Nathan mildly. "You've had a burr under your tail entirely too long. You might as well get used to losing until you improve your rotten disposition. The horse senses your mood, and as long as you don't give a damn, neither will he."

Vivian refused supper and went to bed. The McQueens were in a somber mood, and to escape them, Nathan and Harley made the rounds of the saloons in Beaumont. They sat in on a poker game and came out winners, Nathan with two hundred and Harley with a hundred and twenty-five.

"Maybe we ought to just play poker all night," said Nathan.

"I wouldn't blame you in the slightest," Harley said. "You're bunking with sourpuss."

"Don't be too hard on her," said Nathan. "She knows she's being unreasonable as hell, but her pride won't let her back down."

"That's where I was when you found me in Deadwood, drinkin' myself into an early grave," Harley said. "Wrapped in pride, I was a pitiful package, ridin' shotgun for grub and a place to sleep. Then I was gunned down in a stage holdup, and layin' there more dead than alive, I changed my mind about a lot of things."

"I think Vivian's being pulled in two different directions," said Nathan. "Her pride is telling her she belongs with me, while her common sense disagrees. Deep down, she knows, just as I do, that someday I'm going to run headlong into a slug with my name on it. She has a future with Barnabas, none with me."

"So if she loses enough races for Barnabas, she reckons he'll run her off, forcing her to ride with you," Harley said.

"I'm guessing," said Nathan, "but that's how it looks to me. I reckon it's got to reach the point where she no longer seems to have a choice, that Barnabas might show her the gate whether she wants to go or not. You need to win that race tomorrow, and as many more as you can, within the next few weeks."

There were ten horses in the race and Petalo, an unknown, would be running against long odds. An hour before the race started, they were fifteen-to-one.

"I've got a thousand dollars on him," said Barnabas.

"It being his first race," Bess said, "do you think that's wise?"

"Maybe not," said Barnabas, "but not for reasons you suggest. You know Petalo can win, but you have doubts about Harley."

"Oh, I don't know who I doubt," Bess said. "Whether

it's Harley, Petalo, or the both of them. Mostly, if they win, I fear what it may do to Vivian."

The favorite was a gray whose name was Caliente. The Horse took the lead quickly, with intentions of widening it, but Petalo was only a length behind. Harley leaned forward on the horse's neck and Petalo began gaining. The two went into the final stretch neck-and-neck, but Petalo slowly but surely pulled ahead, winning by half a length. Afterward, McQueen had one arm draped over Petalo's lean neck and the other about Harley's shoulders. Nathan looked for Vivian, but she was nowhere in sight. Neither was Bess McQueen, and Nathan hoped they were together. When Petalo had been rubbed down and stabled, Nathan, Harley, and McQueen went to collect their winnings. When they returned to their hotel, Nathan found Bess in the room he shared with Vivian.

"I was just leaving," said Bess.

She went out, closing the door, leaving Nathan and Vivian alone.

"I reckon Harley's satisfied any doubts you've had about him being here," Nathan said.

"Yes," Vivian said, so softly he almost didn't hear her.

"Then you have no reason for being angry with Barnabas and Harley, do you?"

"No," she replied, her voice trembling.

"Vivian, come here," said Nathan.

When she finally faced him, tears were creeping down her cheeks. Slowly she came to him, buried her face on his shoulder, and wept long and hard. Removing only her hat, he stretched her out on the bed and lay down beside her.

"Now talk, damn it. What's *really* biting you?"

"I . . . I can't tell you."

"Then I'll tell you," said Nathan. "You want to go with me, yet you want to say here and ride Diablo, but you want someone else to make up your mind for you. You want to be forced into one or the other, don't you?"

"Yes," she said, in a small voice. "I've never wanted anything as much as I want to continue racing, but I don't want to lose you."

"You won't lose me," said Nathan. "I'm never away more than a few months. I always come here to heal and lick my wounds."

"Until that day," she said, her voice breaking, "when you'll never . . . come back to me."

"When that day comes," said Nathan, "there'll be nothing anyone can do, for destiny deals the cards. If I never ride back, then you'll know that I'm resting easy, knowin' you are with Harley and among friends. Can't you accept that?"

"Perhaps someday, but not . . . not now . . ."

Breakfast was a happy affair, as Vivian attempted to get back on the good side of everybody.

"I've been behaving like a selfish, spoiled brat, and I—"

"You sure as hell have," Harley cut in. "Try that again and I'll take a switch to you."

"I can't say that I won't ever do it again," said Vivian, "but I'm apologizing for this time. I just hope Diablo will forgive me."

"You'll find horses more forgiving than people," Barnabas said. "Ride him with a kind hand, confidence, and determination, and he'll run his heart out for you."

CHAPTER 9

Houston
October 7, 1879

"Their names are Lonzo Prinz and Rufe Collins," Captain Dillard said. "While neither has a record, they were once arrested on suspicion of bank robbery and released for lack of evidence. It was Collins who tried to back-shoot you, Nathan."

"I realize them having my horse and saddlebags won't be enough to convict them," said Nathan. "There must be some way of forcing them to talk."

"So far, nothing beyond their names," Captain Dillard said. "In the morning, the bank tellers who were on duty at the time of the robbery will have a look at these two."

"Does that include Sheriff Littlefield's son, who identified me?"

"No," said the Ranger. "After his relationship to Littlefield came to light in Austin, he left the bank and nobody knows where he is. We could have tracked him down and maybe convicted him of perjury, but you were set free and we believed justice had been done."

When Nathan and Harley reached the jail the following morning, Captain Dillard was already there. Sheriff Littlefield nodded to Nathan and Harley. When the tellers arrived—McDaniel, Terrel, and Wilkerson—Captain Dillard questioned them.

"Before you see these men, do any of you recall anything about them, such as color of hair, eyes, and possible scars?"

"Only two of them came into the bank," said Terrel.

"That's true," Captain Dillard said. "The third man stayed with the horses."

"They were masked," McDaniel said, "but the man who came to my window had a mole just above his right eyebrow, and his nose was crooked, like it had been broken."

"I can't help you," said Wilkerson. "The man who took money from me had no marks I can recall. He had dark hair, down to the collar of his shirt."

"We're going to ask the three of you to look at these men," Captain Dillard said. "I'd advise you not to make any claims unless you're willing to swear to them in court."

Prinz and Collins sat on their bunks, staring at the men in the jail corridor.

"The man with the bandaged arm," said McDaniel. "I'd like a closer look at him."

"Collins," Captain Dillard said, "come over here."

Collins got up and shambled over to the cell's barred door.

"He has the broken nose," said McDaniel, "and the mole above his left eyebrow. I'd say this is the man who took money from me during the robbery."

"You'd swear to that in court?" Captain Dillard asked.

"Yes," said McDaniel.

"Collins," Captain Dillard said, "you've been identified as one of the men who held up a Houston bank two years ago. What do you have to say for yourself?"

"I didn't do it," said Collins.

"We have evidence enough to hold you," Captain Dillard said. "It'll be up to you to convince a judge and jury that you're innocent."

"You got nothin' against me," said Prinz. "Let me out of here."

Too late he realized his mistake. Collins turned on him, his face a mask of fury.

"Damn you," Collins bawled, "you was right there with me, just like in Waco."

Prinz came off his bunk swinging, and his fists slammed Collins against the bars of the cell.

"Back off, Prinz," said Captain Dillard, drawing his Colt.

Prinz returned to his bunk and sat down.

"Sheriff," Captain Dillard said, "take Collins out of there and lock him in another cell. I believe he'll be a valuable witness, and we don't want Prinz trying to influence him."

The next morning, preparing to return to New Orleans, Nathan and Harley stopped to talk to Captain Dillard.

"Collins refused to take the rap by himself," said Captain Dillard. "He implicated Prinz as well as Schorp, the man you shot, Nathan. In fact, Collins sang loud enough to convict the two of them for a similar bank robbery in Waco three years ago. We lost them there for lack of evidence, so this promises to be a particularly sweet victory. On behalf of the Rangers, I want to commend the both of you for capturing this pair."

"I reckon I had a selfish motive," Nathan said. "There was a time when I'd have been content to gut-shoot the pair of them, but that would have been too sudden. I reckon I'll get more satisfaction out of them doing five years in Huntsville prison."

"If they're convicted of robberies in Houston *and* Waco," said Captain Dillard, "they'll be lucky to get off with ten years."

New Orleans
October 17, 1879

With Empty trotting ahead of them, Nathan and Harley rode into the McQueen place. Vivian seemed to have settled down, and during supper Nathan and Harley recounted their success in Houston.

"I'm glad we can finally close the door on that infamous experience in Houston," said Barnabas. "We have two more big weekends between now and Christmas. Both are two-day events, with races on Saturday and Sunday. Vivian will be riding Diablo. Harley, I want you to ride Petalo in the first event and Modelo in the second."

"Just win me two more races with long odds," Nathan said, "and I'll be a rich man."

The events were held at Natchez and Vicksburg, and all the McQueen horses were big winners. Because of his loss in Beaumont, Diablo ran against longer odds but redeemed himself gloriously.

"That's enough," said McQueen. "Let's enjoy the holidays and let the horses rest."

But they were in for a surprise. A week before Christmas, looking like a down-and-out Texas cowboy, Byron Silver rode in. Tied behind his saddle was a sheepskin-lined long coat, and thonged down on his right hip was a Colt revolver.

"Tarnation," said Nathan suspiciously, "when you show up, there's usually trouble on your heels, like a pack of lobo wolves."

Silver laughed. "You should talk. Every time you wander off on your own, you end up in somebody's *juzgado.* There's Missouri, Texas, and God knows how many others from which you somehow managed to escape without my help. You owe me, big time."

"And you're here to collect," said Nathan.

"Amigo," Silver said, adopting a hangdog look, "you misjudge me, and I am deeply wounded. Fortunately, I heal *rapido.*"

"Well, get down and come in," said Barnabas. "You and Nathan can pick at one another later. Bess will have supper on the table by the time you stable your horse and wash up."

"Go on in the house," Harley said. "I'll rub down and stable your horse."

"He hasn't even worked up a good sweat," said Silver. "I just bought him in town."

"By God, I knew it," Nathan said. "You wouldn't buy a horse if you didn't have plans that involve considerable travel, and you won't be needin' that heavy sheepskin coat around here."

"Damn," said Silver, "a man can't come south for a little vacation without having his motives questioned by the Pinkertons."

"You insult me," Nathan said. "Draw, you varmint."

They were on the back porch, digging at one another, when Bess came to the door.

"Supper's ready," said Bess.

"Then let's eat," Silver said. "If he don't mend his ways, I can shoot him anytime."

They were finished with supper and enjoying extra cups of hot coffee when Silver got around to revealing the true nature of his visit.

"A couple of years back," said Silver, "Congress passed what they called a Desert Land Act. Supposedly, it was intended to help small ranchers by making available desert land at twenty-five cents an acre, for a hundred and sixty acres. A man could then irrigate the land and eventually, for a dollar an acre, own it."

"Captain Ferguson at Fort Worth told me about that," Nathan said.

"Then you have some idea as to what went wrong, and why," said Silver.

"Yes," Nathan replied. "The whole thing is a legalized land-grab, ramrodded through Congress by wealthy ranchers. They'll buy up thousands of acres of land for a dollar and twenty-five cents an acre."

"Exactly," said Silver. "A man with money can hire several dozen cowboys, with the stipulation they are to each file on a quarter section, eventually signing it over to the big rancher who's paying them thirty dollars a month."

"That sounds illegal," Barnabas said.

"Not unless there's conclusive proof," said Silver, "and by that, I mean proof that the wealthy ranchers are paying men to file on land they have no intention of improving. Land that is later to be handed over to a man who isn't legally entitled to it."

"And how do you aim to prove that?" Nathan asked.

"I thought you and me might mosey up to Wyoming's Powder River Basin," said Silver. "It shouldn't be too hard to hire on with one of these big guns and pick up some solid evidence."

"Or a good dose of lead poisoning," Nathan said.

"That may very well go with the territory," said Silver. "If you go, it will be strictly as a volunteer. Washington hasn't authorized me any help."

"I'll go with you," Harley said.

"Barnabas needs you here," said Nathan. "I'm forty pounds heavier than you and not able to ride those horses."

"He's right," Vivian said. "Besides, they've worked together before."

"Indeed we have," said Silver. "Nathan took over and finished an assignment for me when I was wounded. If it hadn't been for him, two years of important undercover work would have been wasted."

Nathan laughed. "You see how he is. He builds me up until I can't refuse. That's why I'm always calling on him for help, because he owes me."

"When are you planning to go?" Barnabas asked.

"I thought we'd wait until after Christmas," said Silver. "I have enough pull to get us and our horses steamboat passage to St. Louis, and from there to Cheyenne on the

Union Pacific. From Cheyenne, we'll be maybe two hundred miles from where the Powder forks to the south."

"I reckon you know who these wealthy ranchers are," Nathan said.

"Yes," said Silver. "I only had to determine who within the territory had contributed the most money to help reelect various senators and congressmen. A man with a ten-cow spread can't afford such generosity."

"Once you've gathered evidence," Vivian asked, "what can be done?"

"I've been told his land-grab can be reversed," said Silver, "but we must prove to the federal government's satisfaction that wealthy ranchers are taking over these lands through fraud. Naturally, we can't get proof against them all, but once we can prove one's doing it, then I can demand an investigation of the others. I aim to force them to give up the land they've taken illegally."

"I have to admire your dedication to truth and justice," Barnabas said. "I must admit I haven't thought too highly of the Congress since that Yankee congressman swindled us out of twenty million dollars buildin' the Union Pacific."*

Silver laughed. "I'm sorry I can't counter all the sins of the United States Congress, but I'll do what I can."

Two days after Christmas, Nathan and Silver rode to New Orleans, where they boarded a steamboat for St. Louis. Their horses were stalled on a lower deck, while Empty went with Nathan and Silver to their small cabin. The dog sat there between the bunks, looking uneasy.

"He's never cared much for steamboats," said Nathan.

"Neither have I," Silver said, "but they're handy, getting from one place to another. I reckon we'll get our fill of the saddle after we reach Cheyenne."

"When we reach Wyoming Territory, are we going to use our own names?"

"I reckon we'll be safe enough," said Silver. "Our comin' out of this alive depends on us looking and acting like a pair of not-too-well-off, drifting cowboys."

"Which brings another question to mind," Nathan said.

---

*Oakes Ames, a wealthy congressman from Massachusetts, was instrumental in creating Credit Mobilier, which defrauded the nation of twenty-three million dollars.

"Cowboys looking for work don't often show up in the dead of winter. How do we account for that?"

"We don't go looking for work," said Silver. "I've learned something about these high rollers, and they have their own waterhole in Cheyenne, the Cattleman's Club. With the wind whistlin' through the peaks and the mountain passes neck-deep in snow, I reckon this bunch will be settin' before the fire, passing the bottle and shufflin' the cards."

"That's not the kind of diggings where a pair of out-of-work cowboys are likely to fit in," Nathan said.

"I know that," said Silver. "It's up to us to devise some way of meetin' one of these hombres, to interest him in hirin' us. Haynes McCutcheon and Chad Buckalew are two of the most likely."

"Meaning they already own more than their share of range," Nathan said.

"Ain't it always that way? Like we say in Texas, all I want is the land that adjoins mine."

Reaching St. Louis, they found there wouldn't be a Union Pacific westbound until the next afternoon. After stabling the horses, they found a boardinghouse where Empty was welcome and took a room for the night.

"I'm almost afraid to suggest we go out on the town," said Nathan. "I still remember that night we stopped in that riverfront saloon for a few hands of poker. We were damn lucky to get out of there alive."

"If it's all the same to you," Silver replied, "I'd as soon have a steak and then bed down for the night. I never sleep much on a steamboat."

Nathan and Silver took their time at breakfast, since the Union Pacific's westbound did not depart until two o'clock.

"Don't look now," said Silver, "but that hombre with the tied-down Colt has taken a damn strong interest in one of us. He's been watching us ever since we sat down."

"If he's still here, and still watching us when we're ready to leave," Nathan said, "I'll make it my business to introduce myself. When some ranny gets that interested in me, I become almighty curious. I don't have that many friends."

"Neither do I," said Silver. "Friends come and go, but enemies and back-shooters stack up like cord wood."

Finally, when Nathan had a chance to observe the

stranger, he didn't like the looks of the man. He was young, not more than twenty-one or -two. There was a half smirk on his face—the mark of many who considered themselves badmen—and he was dressed all in black, including his flat-crowned hat.

"I'll pay for breakfast," Silver said when they were ready to leave, "and I'll back your play if there's trouble."

Approaching the table, Nathan spoke.

"You've been taking my measure ever since I sat down. Do I know you?"

The stranger laughed. "I doubt it, but I know you. You're Nathan Stone, the killer."

"I'm Nathan Stone," Nathan replied coldly. "What do you want of me?"

"I'm Mitch Sowell, and I'm callin' you out. I'll meet you in the street."

"I have no fight with you," said Nathan.

"Oh, but you do," Sowell replied. "You have a reputation, and I aim to fight you for it."

"Please," said the nervous cook, sensing trouble, "no fighting in here."

"Nathan," Silver said, "go ahead. I'll follow him out and watch your back."

It was a deliberate insult, an implication that, given the chance, the cocky young gunman might shoot Nathan in the back. Nathan nodded, heading for the door. Empty had already been fed and was waiting outside. Once Nathan was through the door, Sowell got to his feet.

"Hold it," Silver said. "You'll go out when he's facing you."

Nathan halted a dozen yards down the boardwalk, facing the cafe, his back toward the morning sun. As he awaited the inevitable, his shoulders seemed to sag with weariness. As Sowell left the cafe, men paused, while others quickly removed themselves from the line of fire. Nathan tried one more time.

"Sowell, I have no fight with you. Back off while you still can."

Sowell laughed. "You got to fight. There ain't no way out."

"When you're ready, then," Nathan said.

Nathan wanted nobody contesting his claim of self-defense. He waited until Sowell had his Colt free of the holster, before making his move. He then drew and fired once. Sowell stumbled back against a hitch rail, dropping his weapon without firing a shot. Finally his knees buckled, and he fell face down. There was only the whisper of the wind, as the echo of the single shot died away. Other men came on the run, and there was talk, as those who had seen the event related it to those who had not.

"... chain lightning. I never seen his hand move ..."

"He's a natural-born killer, if I ever saw one ..."

"One of you fetch the sheriff," Silver ordered.

The sheriff's office was in the next block, and the lawman arrived quickly. Nathan had holstered his Colt, saying nothing until the sheriff asked the inevitable question.

"Who shot this man, and why?"

"I shot him," said Nathan, "and I'm claiming self-defense."

The sheriff turned to the onlookers. "Did any of you see it?"

Half a dozen men responded, Silver among them. After an unpleasant hour, the killing was declared self-defense, and Nathan was allowed to go.

"Damn it," Nathan said, "I'm going to hide out somewhere until train time."

"No point in that," said Silver. "You were justified."

"I'm always justified," Nathan replied, "but that doesn't make it any easier."

An hour before train time, Nathan and Silver saw their horses and saddles loaded into a boxcar. Empty disliked locomotives as intensely as he did steamboats, and Nathan had to force him aboard a passenger coach. A well-dressed woman whose hat was festooned with an ostrich feather glared at Empty with obvious distaste, and Empty growled at her.

Cheyenne, Wyoming
January 3, 1880

Before leaving the train, Nathan and Silver donned their sheepskin-lined coats. There was snow on the ground and even more falling, and the west wind chilled them to the marrow of their bones.

"I don't like to question the government's judgement,"
said Nathan, "but why in hell couldn't this investigation
have been done in warm weather?"

"My boy," Silver said, "the wheels of government turn
slowly. The powers that be have known about this problem
for two years. I have long since ceased to question orders
handed down by my superiors. Let's get the horses to a
livery and ourselves to a hotel."

"I reckon we'd better," said Nathan. "It'll be dark in an
hour and then, by God, it'll *really* get cold."

"I've never been here before," Silver said. "Do you
know the town?"

"I know you can see the lights of the Plains Hotel from
here," said Nathan, "and as I recall there's a livery across
the street from the hotel."

"Then let's head for that hotel and the livery," Silver
said. "If I'm any judge, there's a blue norther on the way."

Quickly they saddled their horses and, with Nathan leading, they following the railroad track eastward for a ways,
before cutting back to the south. Through blowing snow,
they could see the bulk of the Plains Hotel ahead of them.
The horses picked their way through deep snow that blan-
keted the street, veering away from the hotel and toward
the welcome warmth of the livery. Inside, Empty shook
himself, creating a snow shower. In the office was a glowing
red stove, which the liveryman seemed reluctant to leave.

"Grain our horses," Silver said, "and store our saddles."

"Saddles in the tackroom," the liveryman said.

"Thanks," Silver said. "We'll see you when the storm
blows itself out."

The storm seemed to have grown in intensity as they
fought their way back to the hotel. Stomping the snow off
their boots, they entered the lobby. Hanging lamps cast
their cheerful glow, while a fire roared in an enormous
fireplace. A bar stretched along one wall, and there were
a few tables and chairs for those who wished to sit and
drink or engage in various games of chance. In the very
back of the room were two billiard tables, the balls racked
and ready.

"Tarnation," said Silver, "I've never seen a better
equipped hotel. Is there a good place to eat close by?"

"Across the street, behind the hotel," Nathan said.

When they reached the registration desk, Empty remained well behind Nathan.

"Pardner," said Nathan, "I reckon we'll be here as long as this storm lasts. This is my dog, and he's never bit anybody that wasn't needful of it. Is he allowed to go with us?"

"As long as you're responsible for him," the clerk replied. "Better make it pronto, if you aim to eat. The cafe sent word they'll be closin' early because of the storm."

"It does appear to be gettin' worse," said Silver.

"We have only two kinds of winters," the clerk replied. "Worse and worser."

"What about summer?" Nathan asked.

"Usually the first two weeks in August," said the clerk, with a straight face. "There's a monthly rate, if you want to wait for warm weather."

Nathan and Silver left the lobby, stepping into a corridor that, minus the wind, was almost as cold as outside. They ignored the stairs, for their room was on the first floor. Silver unlocked the door, and by the light of a bracket lamp in the corridor, Nathan found and lighted a lamp on the dresser. There was a whiff of wood smoke as the fierce wind whipped the smoke back down the flue, stirring to life coals within the stove that sat next to the room's only window.

"Thank God there's still some fire in the stove," said Nathan, "but where's the stove wood?"

"No stove wood," Silver replied. "Coal is replacing wood back east, and I reckon the coming of the railroad has brought it west. I'd say that's the purpose of those big wooden kegs in the corridor. Take that coal bucket and fetch some in."

Nathan brought in a bucket of coal and they coaxed the fire into life.

"Now," said Silver, "we'd better fight our way over yonder for some grub, before the cafe closes for the day. By the time we return, it should be warm in here."

Except for the cook, the cafe proved to be deserted.

"Another hour," the disgruntled cook said, "and I'm hangin' it up for the night."

"Hope you don't have far to go," Silver said. "Way the snow's comin' down, it'll be neck deep on a tall Indian pretty soon."

"I got a room at the hotel," the cook said. "They own

this place, an' part of my deal includes room an' board. It's their way of bein' sure folks that stay at the Plains always got a place to eat."

"We'll be seein' you at breakfast, then," said Nathan, "unless it's so deep none of us can get here."

"Oh, I'll be here. Snow's my name. Actually, it's Snowden, but I been here so long, all the handle I got is Snow."

"Then maybe you can tell us somethin' about this territory," Silver said. "We're on our way west, and we're needin' a place to earn some bacon and beans before movin' on."

"It's almighty slim pickings around here, even when the weather's decent," said Snow. "Only two possibilities is the McCutcheon and Buckalew spreads, up yonder in the Powder River basin. I hear they're hirin' riders."

"That's hard to believe, in the dead of winter," Nathan said. "That's contrary to the ways of every cattleman I ever heard of."

"I reckon," said Snow, "and if I said anything more it'd be gossip, and I got to go on livin' here."

"You're right," Silver said. "It ain't smart, second-guessing other folks. It's purely none of our business *why* a man's hiring, as long as he pays decent wages. When this blue norther let's up, I reckon we'll just ride up to the basin and see if these hombres can use a couple more riders."

"I reckon I can tell you this," said Snow. "Mr. McCutcheon and Mr. Buckalew ain't at their ranches in the basin durin' the winter months. They live at the Cattlemen's Club on Prairie Avenue. But if anybody asks, you didn't hear it from me."

"Nobody will get anything out of us," Silver replied. "Do you know if the Cattleman's Club is for members only, or will we be allowed to enter?"

"The Longhorn Saloon's downstairs," said Snow, "and you'll be allowed in there. The drinks are a mite high, I hear."

It was time to take their steaks off the fire, and the genial cook got busy preparing their meal. He fed Empty in the kitchen, watching with appreciation as the hound wolfed down every morsel of the food. Finished with their meal, Nathan and Silver left the cafe and slogged through knee-deep snow back to the Plains Hotel. Only when they were safely in their room did they discuss what they had learned.

"We've learned three things," said Silver. "We know the McCutcheon and Buckalew spreads are run by *segundos* in winter, that both these hombres have rooms upstairs at the Cattleman's Club, and that any proof of their guilt in this land-grab is likely right here in town."

"Then we're going to play hell gathering any evidence at either ranch," Nathan said, "even if they're of a mind to hire us."

"I doubt we'll be riding to either ranch," said Silver. "Even if one of them takes us on, he won't know whether we're there or not until spring. If we're hired, and are asked to sign for a hundred and sixty acres of government land, that will be sufficient proof that where there's smoke, there's also fire."

"But we'll still have only our suspicions," Nathan said. "You know damn well we'll not be given copies of anything we're asked to sign."

Silver laughed. "That's where the fun begins. We'll have to learn where those records are kept, get our hands on them, and escape without being shot dead as last year's Christmas goose."

CHAPTER 10

The snow continued until almost dark of the following day. By the time Nathan and Silver had finished supper, wind had swept the clouds away and the first stars twinkled in a meadow of purple velvet.

"I reckon we might as well mosey over to the Cattleman's Club," Silver said.

"Empty," said Nathan, "knowing how you feel about saloons, I'm leaving you here."

Silver locked the door to their room, and, hunching into their heavy coats, they went out into the gathering darkness. Mercifully, the wind had died down and the snow had not begun to freeze, so they had only to take their time. When they led their saddled horses out into the cold, the animals snorted their displeasure.

"They're smarter than we are," said Nathan.

"If you know where Prairie Avenue is," Silver said, "lead out."

Nathan led the way, turning east on Prairie Avenue. The many places of business along the street were closed, and only in the two-story brick building several blocks ahead was there any sign of life. Lights glowed from second-floor windows and smoke billowed from many chimneys.

"That's got to be the place we're lookin' for," Silver said.

"It reminds me of the Cattleman's Emporium in Austin," said Nathan when they had reined up before the canopied entrance. To their surprise, a doorman came forth to greet them.

"There's a livery in back," the doorman said. "Shall I stable your horses?"

"I reckon not," Silver replied. "We don't aim to be that long."

Nathan and Silver entered and found the cook at the cafe had told it straight. All the first floor was a saloon, and compared to most, it was elegant. A long mirror, in four sections, stretched the length of the bar, and the lofty beamed ceiling was a veritable sea of hanging lamps. The floor was of polished wood, and from the tops of the high oval windows, drapes brushed the floor. The tables were of heavy oak, flanked by quartets of high-backed chairs. A carpeted stairway led to the second floor. There was just one bartender on duty, for it was early. Not another soul was in the place as Nathan and Silver headed for the bar.

"A beer," Silver said.

"Same here," said Nathan.

The beer was brought, and the mugs were unusually large.

"One dollar," the bartender said. "Each."

"Let's find us a table," Silver said. "We've paid the rent."

They took a table near the center, their backs to the bar, where they could see the front door to their left and the stairs to their right.

"This is some high-falutin place," said Nathan. "Now how do we get to McCutcheon or Buckalew?"

"I can't think of a better way than approaching the bartender and lettin' it be known we'd like to hire on," Silver said.

"I'll let you do the talking, then," said Nathan. "I don't like that stiff-necked varmint. He acts like there's royal blood somewhere along his backtrail."

Silver laughed. "I don't aim to ask about McCutcheon or Buckalew at first. I'll ask if anybody's hirin' riders, and see if he volunteers any information."

"Pardner," Silver said, as they again approached the bar, "we're lookin' to maybe hire on as line riders. You know of anybody in these parts that's hiring?"

"Not much hiring done after snow flies," said the bartender cautiously.

"We know that," Silver persisted, "and that's why we're askin' you. We've heard there are some big ranches north of here, and this bein' the Cattleman's Club, we was hopin' you might know if we got a chance."

"The McCutcheon and Buckalew spreads sometimes hire extra riders," said the bartender. "I'll be seeing both these gentlemen sometime in the morning, and I can tell them you are looking for work. See me at two o'clock tomorrow afternoon, and maybe I can tell you yes or no."

"We're obliged," Nathan said.

Nathan and Silver were silent until they reached their horses, and it was Nathan who spoke.

"Suppose the answer is no?"

"Then we'll have to try something else," said Silver, "but I believe we'll be told what we need to hear."

"There's one possibility we haven't considered," Nathan said. "The very fact that we're trying to hire on in the dead of winter is enough to make these hombres suspicious. They could play along with us and then have us shot in the back at the first opportunity."

"All the more reason you should relish these outings with me," Silver said cheerfully. "There's never a dull moment. But you could be right. That's why, as Shakespeare put it, if 'tis to be done, it must be done quickly. We must gather our evidence and get the hell out of here."

The next afternoon, a few minutes before two o'clock, Nathan and Silver returned to the Cattleman's Club.

"I'm not promising you anything," said the bartender. "Mr. McCutcheon will see you. He's in suite five, on the second floor."

Silver knocked on the door, and a voice bade them enter. They stepped into the room and Nathan closed the door behind them. McCutcheon looked more like a banker or lawyer than a rancher. He wore slippers and a navy blue robe over pale blue pajamas, and he sat in an overstuffed chair before a crackling fire. There was a matching leather sofa to his left, and he nodded toward it. Nathan and Silver sat down. Without a word, McCutcheon got up and stood facing them. He was a big man, probably in his fifties, with thinning hair. He spoke.

"You have the advantage, knowing my name. I don't know yours."

"I'm Nathan Stone," said Nathan.

"I'm Byron Silver," Silver said.

"Unusual," said McCutcheon. "Not many riders looking for work when the snow's already knee deep and the temperature near zero."

"Our reasons for being here at this particular time should be of no concern to you," Silver replied. "Wherever he is, a man has to eat. We're asking for work, not charity."

McCutcheon laughed, and it wasn't a pleasant sound.

"Spoken like a Texan, born and bred. Forever neck deep in pride, even when he's running from the law."

"We're not running from the law," said Silver. "Would it matter to you if we were?"

"No," McCutcheon replied. "It might work in your favor. A man on the bad side of the law ain't likely to cross me, although a few have."

"And what became of them?" Nathan asked.

Again McCutcheon laughed, and it was uglier than before. "They're all dead, and they all died hard. Do you still want to work for me?"

"On one condition," said Silver. "Stay off our backtrail. Anybody comes lookin' for us with the smell of law about him, then we'll come lookin' for you. And it won't be to renew old friendships."

"I'll respect your privacy," McCutcheon said, "if you'll respect mine. I am a power in the Powder River basin, and as such, I have powerful enemies. Before going to work for me, you will sign a nondisclosure agreement, wherein you swear not to talk to anybody about me or my affairs. Violate that agreement, and you will be terminated immediately."

Silver laughed. "I thought you were going to say eliminated."

"There is more than one kind of termination," said McCutcheon. "You may draw your own conclusions."

"We'll sign your agreement," Silver said, "after you've told us where we'll be going, what we'll be doing, and how much we're to be paid."

"That's not unreasonable," said McCutcheon. "You'll be going to one of my line camps along the Powder River. You'll keep snow cleared from the hay sheds and, when necessary, break the ice in the shallows along the river. Pay is forty and found. If you prove satisfactory, after three months you'll receive a fifty-dollar bonus."

"Then let's get on with it," Silver said. "Bring on the nondisclosure forms."

"Very well," said McCutcheon. "Have a seat at the desk by the window."

Nathan and Silver moved to the desk, but stood behind their chairs, watching Haynes McCutcheon. He eyed them for a moment and then knelt before a safe. Only when he had closed the safe and approached the desk did Nathan and Silver take their seats before the desk.

"These are in triplicate," said McCutcheon, "and you must sign all three copies at the bottom. All are the same. Read the first copy, and you will see that it's nothing more than your pledge of silence, insofar as I am concerned. There's a pen and an inkwell in the desk drawer." He put the forms before them.

Nathan placed the pen on the desk. Removing the lid from the inkwell, he clumsily dropped it, spilling the ink.

"Never mind," said McCutcheon, striving to contain his exasperation, "I'm sure I have another."

He went to a cabinet in the corner, opened the door, and eventually came out with a second inkwell. This he opened and placed on the desk. Without hesitation, Silver took the pen and dipped it into the inkwell. He signed the first page in the designated place at the bottom, lifted it just enough to sign the second page, and then lifted the second page to sign the third. He kept the pages separated just enough for the ink to dry, passing the pen to Nathan, who quickly followed Silver's example. McCutcheon then took the signed forms and turned toward the safe. Kneeling before it, he placed the signed papers inside, closed the door of the safe, and turned the dial. When he again faced Nathan and Silver, he spoke.

"You'll find the home ranch at the south fork of the Powder, about two hundred miles north of here. Snide Cordier is *segundo*. He'll assign you to a line cabin and see that you have a pack horse with sufficient grub. You'd best allow the sun a couple of days to melt some snow. The drifts will be deep."

It was all the dismissal Nathan and Silver needed. They left, closing the door behind them. Mounting their horses, they rode back toward the Plains Hotel.

Silver laughed. "That was slick, dropping the inkwell."

"I bought you all the time I could," said Nathan. "What did we sign?"

"The first two pages were harmless," Silver said. "They were what he said they were. The third page began exactly like the first two, but only for a paragraph. Clip away that paragraph, and the rest of the page becomes a request to the federal government for one quarter section of land, at twenty-five cents an acre. After three years and payment of an additional dollar an acre, Mr. McCutcheon has himself another quarter section."

"How the hell can he do that? We'd have to sign a quit-claim deed, giving possession of it to him. I learned that much law while I was at Huntsville."

"A slick lawyer can copy the original signature well enough to get it through court," said Silver. "He can legalize those papers if he never lays eyes on us again."

"Not if we take them off his hands," Nathan said. "All we have to do is figure out how to break into that safe. Thoughtful of him, suggesting we stay in town a couple more days, until the snow begins to melt. That allows us some time to get to that safe."

"That couple of days in town can work in McCutcheon's favor," said Silver. "If he's the least bit suspicious, there'll be time to have us gunned down."

After Nathan and Silver had departed, McCutcheon again read the recent letter he had received from Washington. The envelope bore the address of a prominent senator to whom he had contributed thousands of dollars. The letter had served its purpose. He threw it into the fire and watched the flames consume it. Less than an hour later, there was a knock at the door. After a pause, the knock was repeated, and McCutcheon opened the door just enough to permit entry. The visitor wore range clothes, including a heavy coat, and a revolver was thonged down on his right hip. Having said nothing by way of greeting, he stood with his back to the fire, warming his hands. McCutcheon spoke.

"Grimes, have you gathered the men?"

"Yeah," said Grimes, "but why four of us? I think me and Elkie—"

"Damn it," McCutcheon exploded, "I'm not paying you to think. I'm paying four of you to do a job that must not be bungled. This is no pair of shorthorns. One of them is a federal man, and the other is a gunman of some reputation. I want them eliminated and I don't want it done on my range. They're staying at the Plains Hotel, and one of them has a dog. Five hundred for each of you when the job's done to my satisfaction."

"Half now, and the rest when the job's done," Grimes countered. "That's so you don't get picky over details."

"Half now," said McCutcheon, "and I'm going to be damned picky before you get the rest. This had better be clean."

*   *   *

"The more I think about it," Silver said, "the less I like McCutcheon's idea of us bein' here in town a couple more days. I think we'll make our move tonight."

"I hope you've had some experience cracking a safe," said Nathan. "I haven't."

"I'm fair-to-middlin' good at it," Silver said, "but the quickest, least complicated way is to pull a gun on McCutcheon and have him open it for us."

"I hope you've given some thought to us getting out of there alive," said Nathan.

"You're only looking at half of it," Silver replied. "There may be as much hell goin' in as comin' out. You can count on a crusty old pelican like McCutcheon havin' a few killers on his payroll."

"After supper, then," said Nathan, "let's open the ball."

They waited under after dark before leaving the hotel. Empty, knowing they were going to the cafe, normally loped on ahead, but this time he did not. He crouched, his hackles rising. Nathan leaped forward and, taking Silver with him, they went belly down in the snow. There was the deadly bark of rifles, and like a swarm of angry bees, slugs ripped the air where they had been standing just seconds before. The nearest cover was the hotel, half a dozen yards away and, lizard-like, they scuttled toward it.

"What the hell?" somebody shouted, flinging open the front door of the hotel. Lead ripped into it, slamming it shut. In an instant, Nathan and Silver were on their feet, running toward the side of the building. Empty ahead of them, they ducked into the shadow of the hotel, and the firing ended as suddenly as it had begun.

"By God," Silver panted, "that was close. If somebody hadn't opened that door—"

"If it hadn't been for Empty's warning," said Nathan, "the door wouldn't have made any difference. They'd have got us with the first volley."

"You're right," Silver agreed. "If we get out of this alive, remind me to get myself a hound."

Nathan laughed, but there was no humor in it. "If we get out of this alive, I'll likely be tempted to remind you to get yourself another pardner. There's at least four of the bastards, and none of those were warning shots. Unless they're thinkin' ahead of us, we'd better get to the livery and grab our horses."

"I doubt they'll be coverin' the livery," said Silver. "It's too close to the hotel, and if I'm any judge, the law will be comin' to investigate all that shooting. Right now, one bunch is as unwelcome as the other."

They reached the livery only to be met by questions from the liveryman.

"What was the shootin' about? Was somebody kilt?"

"No," said Silver. "Just some drunks blowin' off steam."

Quickly they saddled their horses, leading the animals a ways before mounting.

"Now," Nathan said, "I reckon it's time we decide what we're going to do, and how."

"We're going after those papers in McCutcheon's safe," said Silver, "but because of recent developments, the how of it has been changed somewhat. We definitely won't be going through the lobby and up the stairs."

"Through the window, then," Nathan said.

"Yes," said Silver. "We can rope one of the chimneys and reach the roof. Then a rope tied to McCutcheon's chimney should get me down to the window."

"A lighted window," Nathan said. "You'll be a perfect target. All McCutcheon will have to do is shoot you."

"He won't be there," said Silver. "You're going to cover the chimney with a blanket long enough to fill the room with smoke. While McCutcheon's gone to raise hell with somebody, you remove the blanket and I'll enter through the window. When he returns, the smoke will have cleared, and I'll be waiting for him. *Comprende?*"

"It's just crazy enough that it might work," Nathan said.

"Not only will it work," said Silver, "McCutcheon will open the window for me."

"I'm to keep the chimney covered until he leaves the room," Nathan said, "but how am I to know when he leaves the room?"

"I'll be to one side of the window, where I can see into the room," Silver said. "When he leaves the room, I'll tug hard on the rope."

"You're comin' out the window and back up the rope?"

"Yes," said Silver. "I'll tie the free end of the rope until I'm done with McCutcheon."

"You'd better bind and gag McCutcheon, or he'll be bawling like a cut bull before we can get off that roof," Nathan said.

"I don't think so," said Silver. "I'll buffalo him with the muzzle of my Colt."

"We'll have to get the hell out of this town pronto," Nathan said. "I hope you're not planning to wait for the next train."

"Oh, we'll take the train," said Silver, "but not from here. I reckon we'd better hightail it to Denver, and take a Kansas-Pacific eastbound from there."

"I feel some better about that," Nathan said. "Now we'd better get over yonder to the Cattleman's Club before McCutcheon decides to surround it with gunmen."

"We can't be sure they haven't already," said Silver, "since their ambush failed. Before we try to scale the roof, we'll ride around the building and see if we draw any fire."

"There are trees behind the place," Nathan said, "and that side of it should be pretty much in shadow. We can leave our horses there, mounting the roof from that side."

Silver was first to mount the roof. Nathan, a blanket slung over his shoulder, waited a moment, then followed. Silver loosed the rope from the chimney and they crossed the roof to McCutcheon's side. Quickly, Silver looped one end of the rope over the chimney and looped the other end under his arms.

"Give me time to get over the edge," said Silver softly, "and then cover that chimney with the blanket. When I tug the rope, remove the blanket. That'll mean McCutcheon has opened the window or the door, or has left the room. Stand by, and when you feel the rope go taut, haul me up. We may have to get out of here in one hell of a hurry, and if the horses are discovered, we're in big trouble."

Nathan waited until Silver was over the edge before he covered the chimney with the blanket. He grinned in the darkness when he heard violent cursing below. Within seconds there was a tug on the rope, and Nathan removed the blanket from the chimney.

Silver was far enough to the side of the window that he couldn't be seen, and as he had expected, the first thing McCutcheon did was open the window. Coughing and choking, he flung open the door and stomped off down the corridor, bawling for attention. Leaving the rope hang loose where he could reach it, Silver stepped into the room, taking refuge behind the door. Already, with the door and window open, the smoke had begun to clear. Silver tensed as he heard footsteps and voices.

"It's cleared up some," said McCutcheon, "but by God, the room was full of it."

"I believe you," another voice replied. "Probably just a strong gust of wind forced it back down into the room. If it happens again, I'll have someone get on the roof and have a look at the chimney."

McCutcheon closed the door and then froze, for the sound seemed inordinately loud as Silver cocked his Colt.

"Turn around," said Silver, "and do it slow. Don't make any funny moves with your hands."

"You!" McCutcheon snarled. "What do you want?"

"I think you know," said Silver. "You're going to open the safe, pronto."

"And if I refuse?"

"Then I'll bash your skull and open it myself," Silver said. "Your choice."

"You'll pay for this," McCutcheon said. "I have powerful friends in Washington."

"Not any more," said Silver. "We know who sent you the letter, and a senate investigating committee is about to give him a choice. He can resign, or he'll be censured and booted out. Now open that safe."

McCutcheon knelt before the safe, fumbling with the dial. Slowly the heavy door was swung back.

"Now get up and stand back," Silver ordered.

But McCutcheon rolled to one side, a pistol roared, and a slug whipped through the sleeve of Silver's coat. He fired once and McCutcheon dropped the Colt. Quickly, Silver knelt before the safe. Seconds counted, for he could hear the thump of boots on the stairs and in the hall. Having no time to sort them, he seized all the papers in the safe, stuffing them into his coat pocket. Holstering his Colt, he ran to the door and shot the deadbolt. By the time he reached the window, there was shouting in the corridor and pounding on the door. Quickly, Silver looped the rope under his arms and swung free of the windowsill. When he reached the roof's edge, Nathan seized his hand.

"There's hell to pay," Silver said. "McCutcheon had a Colt in the safe, and I had to shoot him. Once they break in there and find the window open, they'll be after us like hell wouldn't have it."

"Did you get the papers?"

"If they were in the safe, I did," said Silver. "No time to go through them, so I took them all."

Reaching the backside of the building, Nathan looped the rope over the chimney and swung over the edge of the roof. He dropped into his saddle just as a man rounded the corner of the building. Nathan snapped a shot at him and he went belly down, either hit or taking cover. But he was very much alive, for he began shouting, alerting the others.

"Let's ride," said Silver.

Nathan led out. Reaching the Union Pacific tracks, where much of the snow had begun to melt, he rode eastward, Silver right behind him. They followed the tracks for several miles until they reached a creek. There they left the tracks, following the creek. Ahead of them, Empty yipped once.

"We'd better rest the horses and head for Denver," said Nathan. "For all the people in Cheyenne know, McCutcheon has been robbed and murdered. With the telegraph, the sheriff in Cheyenne could have dead-or-alive warrants out on us everywhere by morning."

"Not if I can reach the telegraph first," Silver replied. "I can justify what we've done by proving McCutcheon was involved in a land grab. He has a friend in the Senate, and I'm expecting that gentleman to sing like a mockingbird when he learns McCutcheon's dead. We have him to thank for telling McCutcheon we were on the way."

"So that's why we used our own names," said Nathan. "By God, it was a trap. You *knew* it was a trap, and we were the bait!"

"Well, yes," Silver admitted. "I had to get in a position to get my hands on these papers, and there was no other way. But I'll be honest with you. The ambush near the hotel took me by surprise. I believed McCutcheon would wait until we were out of town, and he did give us directions to his ranch. If you had known all the facts—all the risks involved—would you have come with me?"

"I reckon," said Nathan. "There's no accounting for the fool things a man will do in the name of friendship."

They rode on, resting the horses at hourly intervals, and when the first rays of the rising sun fanned out across the eastern horizon, they looked down from a rise upon the growing city of Denver.

"We never did get supper last night," said Nathan. "I'm

hungry enough to chomp down on a grizzly, hide, hair, and claws."

"So am I," Silver replied, "but first I'm going to get that message off to Washington and kill any warrants the law in Cheyenne may be preparing. There are ranchers all over the frontier who won't see anything wrong with McCutcheon's land-grab, and we have to discredit this story before it's allowed to take hold."

"Let's go to the Kansas-Pacific railroad terminal," said Nathan. "They'll remember me there, and you should get immediate use of the telegraph."

Nathan was remembered and he spent an enjoyable hour with the dispatcher, as Silver went through McCutcheon's papers and telegraphed Washington. They were out of the railroad terminal, looking for a place to eat, before Silver spoke.

"I have all the necessary papers to expose McCutcheon's land-grab, and all the land he has illegally claimed will revert back to government ownership. Details are being wired to the law in Cheyenne, as well as to the newspaper there. We're cleared."

"I'm glad to hear that," said Nathan, "but what about Chad Buckalew and his grab?"

"He's being investigated," Silver replied, "and if his scheme is like McCutcheon's in any way, then every acre he's falsely claiming will be disallowed. The newspaper there in Cheyenne will give him hell."

"What do you aim to do now?" Nathan asked.

"I'm going back to Washington," said Silver. "This Yankee senator McCutcheon's been buying off is about to be investigated by the Senate. I don't want to miss that."

"What do you reckon will happen to him?"

"Oh, he'll be disgraced and kicked out," Silver said. "He'll be forced to find honest work, if he's capable of it. Where are you going?"

"I reckon I'll ride to south Texas and visit my old friend, King Fisher. Last time I was there, he had stolen away Molly, one of the Horrell girls, and the Horrells were about to give him hell."

"If you get in neck deep, don't send for me," Silver said. "Even the United States government can't settle that Horrell–Higgins feud."

CHAPTER 11

St. Louis, Missouri
January 5, 1880

A little more than three months past his fourteenth birthday, John Wesley Tremayne had made good his resolution and escaped the hated orphanage. Life there hadn't been all that bad, although he had been compelled to attend church every Sunday. He was quick with his hands and had been constantly punished for fighting. He had become an enigma, astounding and confounding his teachers, absorbing their most difficult assignments with ease. He spoke fluent Spanish, and at the end of his second year, stood at the head of all his classes. But there had been a method to his madness, and by the time he was ready to leave, it was the last thing they expected of him. On a Monday night, just after bed check, he had slipped away into the darkness with only the clothes on his back. Reaching the railroad yards, he had climbed aboard a boxcar, part of a string that made up a westbound freight.

Near midnight, the train chuffed into the Kansas City yards, pausing just long enough to take on fuel and water. As it departed, picking up speed, a shadowy figure climbed into the boxcar. Soon the new arrival was snoring, but John Wesley Tremayne dared not sleep. In the bitter cold, huddling into his heavy coat, he listened to the clicking of wheels on the coupling joints and awaited the dawn.

"Well, now," said the stranger, when it was light enough to see, "I didn't know I had comp'ny. Ye should of spoke up. Ye got a name?"

"Wes Tremayne."

The man was dressed in flannel shirt, dirty trousers, and runover boots. He stood up and stretched, and he stood only about six or seven inches above five feet. After several attempts at what obviously was false joviality, he became surly.

"You ain't much of a talker, are you, kid?"

Wes said nothing but he fixed his cold blue eyes on those of the stranger, and the man saw no fear in them. Suddenly he seized the haft of a knife, removing it from his left boot. With a wolf grin, he faced Wes.

"I've always thought them that's got more ought to share with them that ain't got near enough. Shuck out of that coat, kid."

"You can have it," said Wes, "only if you're man enough to take it." He got to his feet, waiting.

"Leander O'Malley don't take that kind of talk from nobody."

"I don't want to hurt you, O'Malley," Wes said. "Back off while you can."

"You? Hurt me?"

O'Malley lunged with the knife, but Wes wasn't there. Before O'Malley could recover from the thrust, Wes seized his arm and slammed him headlong into the side of the boxcar. He lay there catching his wind while Wes waited for him to get to his feet. But when he got to his hands and knees, he charged from that position. Wes caught his wrist, halting the course of the knife, and they fought for the weapon. While Wes had tremendous strength in hands, arms, and shoulders, his antagonist had a weight advantage, and they fell to the floor. Slowly, Wes turned the deadly blade away, and against the wall of the car he got enough leverage to roll O'Malley off. Throwing all his weight on the hand that gripped the knife, he drove it down, into O'Malley's chest. As suddenly as it had begun, the fight was over. Wes lay there gasping for breath, his mind flooded with conflicting emotions. His elation over having beaten a bigger, stronger adversary was tempered with the sobering realization that he had killed a man. Weaponless, he had been forced to defend himself with his bare hands. He withdrew the knife, cleaning its blade on the leg of the dead man's dirty trousers. He slipped the blade of the knife under his belt, got to his feet, and slid open the boxcar's door. He dragged the lifeless O'Malley to the aperture, rolled him out, and closed the boxcar door.

Pueblo, Colorado
January 8, 1880

Silver had taken a Kansas-Pacific train east, while Nathan had ridden a hundred and fifty miles south, to Pueblo. There he could take an AT & SF train as far as Dodge City, on his way to south Texas. Nathan spent the night in Dodge and had supper with Foster Hagerman of the AT & SF.

"I hated to lose Harley Stafford," Hagerman said, "but I'm glad for him. Did you know your old friend Wyatt Earp has moved on?"

"No," said Nathan. "Somebody else's loss is your gain, I reckon."

"He left last year, ridin' south. Got in some trouble in Mobeetie, according to one of the stage drivers. Mobeetie's got a sheriff now."*

Mobeetie, Texas
January 12, 1880

Nathan was amazed to find Mobeetie had doubled in size, though most of the growth, he noted wryly, consisted of three more saloons. He rode on to Fort Elliot, where the post commander, Captain Selman, welcomed him.

"Where's the missus?"

"In New Orleans," Nathan said. He then told Selman of Vivian's numerous victories astride Diablo.

"I've heard of the horse," said Selman, "but I didn't know she was riding him. These events, when published in the newspaper, read like the horse did it all. The rider is seldom mentioned."

"I hear Mobeetie has a sheriff," Nathan said.

"Yes, thank God," said Selman with a sigh. "Him and me are on a first-name basis, with four saloons. Will you stay the night with us?"

---

*Wyatt Earp left Dodge City in September 1879, bound for Las Vegas, New Mexico. He stopped in Mobeetie, Texas long enough to be run out of town by Deputy Sheriff Jim McIntire. Earp and Mysterious Dave Mather had tried to work a "gold brick" swindle.

"Yes," said Nathan, "and I'm obliged for your hospitality. I think Empty's already at the mess hall."

Austin, Texas
January 21, 1880

Having found a room for the night, Nathan visited the Texas Ranger outpost, where he found Bodie West on duty. Bodie had taken the place of Captain Sage Jennings, one of Nathan's long-time friends. The old Ranger had been gunned down in an ambush, and the killer had escaped to New Mexico, where Nathan had caught up to him.

"I heard about your trouble in Houston," said West, "but I couldn't get away. Some of us had to keep the lid on around here. I was stuck in San Antonio when your trial was held here. Soon afterward, I ran into Captain Dillard here. He told me the entire story."

"If one man ever owed another his life," Nathan said, "I owe Captain Dillard. When I went before the judge here in Austin, I couldn't believe my eyes. In three rows of seats near the front of the court room, there were only Rangers. There were so many stars, my God, it was like lookin' at the Texas sky on a clear night."

"You rode the long trail for one of us," said West simply, "and we didn't forget. Nor will we ever."

"I'm forever obliged," Nathan said. "I've been away for a while. When I was last here, King Fisher had stolen away Molly Horrell, and the Horrells were hell bent on taking her back. Did they?"

West laughed. "They did not. Molly refused to return, and when the Horrells rode into Fisher's place after her, King just shot the hell out of them."

"Any of them killed?"

"No," said West, "but the whole damn bunch rode out with lead in 'em, and their tails between their legs. King and Molly were married in Uvalde, and you won't believe how it's changed him. Except for the Horrells, he hasn't shot anybody but himself. A year or so back, he shot himself in the leg."

Nathan laughed. "I can't imagine that. Sounds like you're enjoying peace and quiet for a change."

West sighed. "That may be coming to an end. Ben Thompson's here."

"Billy too?"

"No, thank God," said West. "One Thompson at a time is enough. He's been peaceful so far, since he's been winning at the poker table. But that can change any time. The man's got a devil inside, and nothing unleashes him any quicker than a night of hard drinking."

"It's been a while since I've seen him," Nathan said. "Maybe if I track him down, I can keep him at least partly sober."

"Good luck," said West.

Nathan found Ben Thompson at the Cattleman's Emporium, at a downstairs table with a bottle before him. Dragging back a chair, Nathan sat down. Thompson glared at him without any friendliness.

"Howdy, Ben."

Ignoring the glass, Thompson seized the bottle, upended it, and emptied it. He set it down with a crash that shattered it.

"Bartender," Thompson bawled, " 'nother bottle."

"Ben," said Nathan, "you've had enough. Let's get something to eat."

Thompson sprang to his feet, toppling his chair. The bartender hit the floor, and just a split second ahead of Thompson, Nathan drew his Colt. He laid the muzzle of the weapon just above Thompson's left ear, and he sprawled face down across the table.

"That was slick, mister," the bartender said, "but there's goin' to be hell to pay when he wakes up."

"Maybe not," Nathan replied. "Make some hot, black coffee."

The bartender did so, bringing two steaming cups to the table. He hurried away, for Thompson was stirring. Quickly, Nathan put Thompson's chair in place, and he slid off the table onto it. He looked at Nathan through slitted eyes and spoke in a slurred voice.

"My God . . . my head . . . hurts."

"We were about to have some coffee," Nathan said, "and you passed out. You need the coffee, Ben. Drink up."

"Yeah . . . need coffee," Thompson mumbled. He seized the cup with both hands, gulping the coffee. Nathan took the empty cup from him, passing him the other full one.

Thompson emptied the second cup and sat there shaking his head.

"Ben," said Nathan, "you need food. How long since you've eaten?"

"I . . . dunno," Thompson said.

"It's time to eat," said Nathan. "Let's get a steak."

"No . . ." said Thompson. "Sick . . ."

"You'll feel better when you get to your feet, when you've eaten something," Nathan said. "Come on. I'll help you."

Nathan got Thompson to his feet, walked him to the door, and managed to get him outside. The sun was down, and a cool west wind had sprung up. It seemed to revive Ben Thompson, and he steadied himself. Nathan led him to the nearest cafe, and they took a table near the door. Empty had remained at the livery with Nathan's horse, and Nathan was thankful for that. He had no idea how long it might take for Thompson to become fully sober. But to Nathan's surprise, Thompson drank more coffee and began to eat.

"Ben," said Nathan, "a good night's sleep will do wonders for you. Do you have a room?"

"Yeah," Thompson said. "The Alamo Hotel."

"Let's go there," said Nathan, "and I'll meet you for breakfast in the morning."

Having seen Thompson to his hotel room, Nathan waited a few minutes to be sure the little gambler didn't slip out and head for a saloon. Was he a fool, concerning himself with the well-being of Ben Thompson, who seemed not to care a damn for himself? Nathan returned to the livery for Empty, and the two of them returned to the out-of-the-way hotel where Nathan had taken a room. He had eaten little, focusing his attention on Ben Thompson. He and Empty would have a more leisurely supper later.

The next morning, when Nathan knocked on the door to Ben Thompson's room, there was no answer. The door was locked.

"Mr. Thompson left an hour ago," the desk clerk informed Nathan.

Only in Cow Alley, the least desirable section of town, did the saloons open before noon. There, in a joint called Frog's Place, sat Ben Thompson, a bottle on the table before him.

"I thought you were going to have breakfast with me," said Nathan.

"Hell," Thompson said, "this *is* breakfast. Drag up a chair."

"Ben," said Nathan, taking a chair, "I'm riding to King Fisher's ranch. Why don't you come with me?"

"Just come from there," Thompson said. "King's got himself a woman and by God, she's defanged and declawed him. He didn't have a drop of whiskey, and I near died of thirst before I could get away. I'm meetin' Billy in Dodge, and who knows where we'll go from there. Why don't you come along?"

"I just came from Dodge," said Nathan. "I'm past due for a visit with King. I reckon I'll mosey on down there."

"You'd better take your whiskey with you, then," Thompson said.

They left the saloon together. At the corner, they encountered a pair of drunks, one of whom pointed to Ben and laughed.

"By God," he shouted, "a genuine dude. One of them remittance men, I reckon."*

To Nathan's surprise, Thompson grinned at the pair, playing the part of a foppish and inexperienced easterner. He coughed, as one with lung fever who had been sent west for his health. Encouraged, one of the men took a swipe at Thompson's top hat, and it rolled into the gutter. Thompson's temper took flame like a prairie fire, and he drew his pistol.

"Damn you," he roared. "You are a scoundrel and a coward. Is this how you would treat a stranger and a sick man? I am Ben Thompson, and equal to a dozen of the likes of you."

The stranger drew his gun, leaped behind an awning post, and fired at Thompson. The little gambler returned fire, grazing the drunk's ear. As the frightened man ran away, lead from Thompson's pistol burned a furrow along his side.

"Ben," Nathan said, "that's enough. You'll have the law on you."

But the man with a bloodied ear and a crease in his side returned with a sheriff's deputy before Nathan could get Thompson off the street.

---

*A "black sheep," sent money from home. Banished lest he tarnish the family name.

"Who started this?" the lawman demanded.

"He did," Thompson snarled. "I defended myself."

"That's true," said Nathan. "The other man's gun has been fired."

"Hand over the weapon," the deputy demanded.

He examined the revolver, found it had been fired, and returned it. Then he spoke to the man who had complained.

"Looks like a Mexican standoff to me. You can file a complaint and take it before a judge, if you like, but there's no evidence you were assaulted. It'll be your word against his."

Something in Thompson's cold stare got to the stranger. Followed by his companion, he turned and stomped away. The deputy shrugged his shoulders and went on about his business.

"I reckon I'll saddle up and ride north," said Thompson. That was as close to goodbye as he ever got.

Nathan checked out of his hotel room, took his horse from the livery, and rode south.

South Texas, near the Rio Grande
January 24, 1880

"Get down and come in," said King Fisher when Nathan rode up.

Empty was already on the porch, being greeted by Shaniqua, Fisher's Mexican housekeeper, for she had fed him well. Molly stood on the porch, smiling a welcome.

"Where's Vivian?" Fisher inquired. "Has she already sent you packing?"

"Not exactly," said Nathan. "Let me unsaddle my horse, and I'll come in and tell you all about it."

When Nathan returned to the house, Shaniqua had coffee ready, and Nathan spent the next hour telling them of Diablo's victories, with Vivian in the saddle.

"Thunderation," Fisher exclaimed, "what are you doin' here? With your brand on a woman like her, ridin' a hoss that can't lose, you must of been grazin' on loco weed, just lettin' her out of your sight."

"I reckon that kind of life is just too tame for me," said Nathan. "I miss the shootin' and being shot at."

"By God, I don't," Fisher said.

"That's what I hear," said Nathan. "I saw Ben Thompson in Austin, and he said you'd been defanged and declawed. Said you didn't have a drop of whiskey on the ranch, and if what he says means anything, you're a disgrace to Texas."

"He's an evil little man," Molly said, speaking for the first time. "I hope he's gone for good."

"Ah, hell," said Fisher, "Ben's a little strange, but he ain't no worse than your kin."

"I can't deny that," Molly said hotly, "but it's not something I'm proud of. Since I was born a Horrell, I can't change that, but at least I had the good sense to rid myself of them. If that little villain, Ben Thompson, shows up here again, I'm leaving."

With that, she stomped away from the table. Fisher flung up his hands in frustration while Shaniqua, renewing her friendship with Empty, ignored them all.

"I've never been one to buy into a family feud," said Nathan. "I reckon I'll ride on and come back another time."

"Stay," Fisher said. "She's had a burr under her tail ever since Ben left. Just try not to mention him again. She'll sulk her way out of it."

"I don't fault a man for his friends," said Nathan, "and I reckon—in his own way—Thompson's a friend of mine. Being honest, I'd have to tell you Vivian doesn't like Ben. He can be a gentleman when he chooses, but there's another side to him that just purely scares hell out of the ladies."

"Well, I won't throw down a friend on a woman's whim," Fisher said.

"Not even if that woman's your wife?" Nathan asked.

"Not even then," said Fisher.

"King," Nathan said, "I'm not one to talk down a man's friends, but Ben Thompson's headed for hell on greased skids. Molly fears he'll take you with him. While I like Ben, I'm seein' him in the same light."*

"Maybe you're right," said Fisher grimly, "but a man who won't go to hell for a pard ain't much of a friend."

Nathan slid back his chair, put on his hat, and stepped

---

*On March 11, 1884, Ben Thompson and King Fisher were ambushed in San Antonio.

out on the porch. Uncertain as to what was taking place, Empty followed. Nathan went on to the barn, fully expecting his host to call to him, but Fisher did not. Nathan saddled the grulla and rode out, following the Rio Grande westward.

Dodge City, Kansas
February 2, 1880

The westbound had just pulled out, and there was a knock on Foster Hagerman's office door.

"Come on in," Hagerman said.

The door opened, and Harley Stafford stood there grinning. Hagerman got to his feet, extended his hand, and Harley took it.

"Pull up a chair," said Hagerman. "If you're looking for work, or if you just came in to say howdy, I'm glad to see you."

"Some of both," Harley said. "I've given up racing."

"I can't say I'm sorry," said Hagerman. "Our chief of security was wounded last week during an attempted robbery. It's doubtful that he'll ever walk again. When can you start?"

"Today," Harley said. "It wasn't meant for a man to set on his hunkers, working just two days a month."

"Sounds pretty good to me," said Hagerman. "Since you left, I've had maybe two days I could call my own. What about your sister?"

"She can easily take up the slack," Harley said, "and it'll be better for both of us. For the lack of anything better to do, I'd taken to hanging around the saloons and gambling houses in New Orleans, and a man can't do that without drinking and gambling. Gamblers knew I was riding for Barnabas McQueen, and I was faced with bribes on every hand, all wanting me to lose an occasional race."

"I can safely say you'll never be faced with that, working for the AT & SF," said Hagerman. "The worst that can happen is that you may be shot dead, but you already know that. Nothing's changed. When you're in town, we'll pick up the tab for your room at the Dodge House and your meals at Delmonico's. Oh, there is one difference. I'll ask for a raise in pay, taking you up to two hundred a month."

"I'm obliged," Harley said, "but the job would be enough. I've won money on every McQueen race except one, so I'm not hurting."

"Good," said Hagerman, "but I'm paying you for the risk involved. The James gang has made a fine art of train robbery, and others have begun to follow their example."

Hungry, Wes Tremayne had left the train in Kansas City. Big for his age, able to do the work of a man, he had survived on a poorly paid job at a livery, mucking out stalls. He had slept in the hayloft, often half-frozen, as the bitterly cold wind whipped through the cracks. Worse, there were drifters seeking shelter, and he often fought them for the little money he had, or for his clothing. One night he climbed into a partially loaded boxcar in the AT & SF railroad yards. A string of cars waited on a side track while an engine with tender backed toward them. When the tender bumped into the first of the cars, the brakeman completed the coupling and signaled the engineer with his lantern. The big locomotive lurched into motion, gathering speed, bound for Colorado. But the destination of several of the boxcars was Dodge City, Kansas, and in the small hours of the morning the cars were shuttled onto a side track and left there. Wes Tremayne slipped out. The sliding doors had not been locked, for the car was carrying heavy machinery. Dawn was several hours away, and the cold west wind had the feel of snow. While the railroad depot was closed, a small waiting room was unlocked, and it was there that Wes sought refuge. He had the price of a meal, and he suspected the prospects of work here would be as bad or worse than in Kansas City. With the first light of dawn, Wes left the depot seeking a cafe. He'd eaten nothing since the previous morning, and was sorely in need of food and hot coffee. It was early, and there were few on the streets, and when Wes found a cafe that was open, there was nobody but the cook.

"Mister," said Wes, after paying for his meal, "I'm traveling west and I need work. I can do just about anything. Do you know of anybody needing a man?"

"Well," the cook said, "you might try the Alhambra Saloon. Talk to Vic Irwin. He's forever needin' a swamper.

It's the kind of work most men shy away from, because it pays just about enough to keep you in grub. But if Vic likes you, he'll fix you a bunk in the storeroom.''

"Thanks," said Wes. "I'll talk to him."

"You'll have to wait. The Alhambra don't open until ten o'clock."

Wes walked the streets, pausing in an occasional doorway to escape the wind. Already there was sleet rattling off the boardwalk, an almost certain sign of snow to follow. Somewhere a clock—probably in a church or courthouse tower—struck nine. When it finally struck ten, the snow had already started, but Wes knew where the Alhambra Saloon was. He found a single bartender on duty.

"I need to talk to Mr. Irwin," Wes said.

"Set down," said the bartender. "I'll get him."

Vic Irwin prided himself on knowing and understanding men. He had operated saloons all his adult years, and he had opened in Dodge while it was still a tent city. The moment he entered the saloon, the young man got to his feet, and not once did his ice-blue eyes leave those of Irwin.

"Mr. Irwin," he said, extending his hand, "I'm Wes Tremayne, and I need work. I've been told you need a swamper, and I'm asking for the job."

Impressed, Irwin took the extended hand. Finally he spoke.

"Yes, I am needing a swamper, and I'll be honest with you. It's a trying, thankless job. Whiskey generally brings out the worst in men."

"I understand," said Wes. "I can take care of myself, and I still want the job."

"You have it," Irwin said, "and you can begin today. You start at two o'clock in the afternoon, and you're here until two in the morning. Your wages are a dollar fifty a day, and there's a bunk for you in the storeroom. I haven't had breakfast. Will you join me?"

"Thanks," said Wes, "but I've already had breakfast."

"Come on," Irwin said. "You can stand some more coffee, and I'm buying. You don't start work for another four hours."

They left the saloon. As the bartender watched them go, he spoke aloud.

"Geez, I can't figger the old man. He's never paid a swamper more'n a dollar a day in all the years I've knowed him."

CHAPTER 12

South Texas
February 10, 1880

Nathan rode west, bound for El Paso, his mind awash with conflicting emotions. Had it been more than six years since he had left El Paso, with a price on his head and a band of bloodthirsty bounty hunters on his trail? He allowed his mind to drift back to December 1874, when he had ridden to New Mexico to kill a man. The eventual showdown had left him wounded, out of his head, riding where his horse had taken him. Myra Haight, her son Jamie, and her daughter Ellie had found him near their barn. When he had been well enough to ride, he had taken the Haights with him to El Paso. There he had bought for Myra a half interest in Granny Boudleaux's struggling boardinghouse. This he had done for Myra, but he had been able to remain with her only a few days. Young Arlie Stewart, seeking a reputation as a fast gun, had forced Nathan into a gunfight. Seeking revenge for the death of his only son, wealthy Artemus Stewart had put a bounty on Nathan's head and had hired a pack of bounty hunters sworn to gun him down. Promising Myra Haight he would return, Nathan had left for San Antonio, riding for his life. But the bounty hunters had caught up to him, and wounded, he had played out his hand, when King Fisher had come to his rescue. The two had become friends.

Now Nathan was struck by the irony of it all. He had left in El Paso Myra Haight, a woman who had been more than just a friend and who had promised to wait for him. Reaching south Texas, he had encountered King Fisher, who had not only saved his life but had become his friend. Six years later, as he was leaving south Texas, his friendship with Fisher was questionable, and he knew not what awaited him in El Paso. He knew Artemus Stewart had increased the price on his head, but what of Myra? She had been an attractive woman but older than Nathan, and he couldn't believe she had waited six years for a rambling, gambling man she might never see again. Empty ranging ahead, Nathan rode on, his troubled mind immersed in unanswered questions.*

Dodge City, Kansas
February 12, 1880

Vic Irwin had been so impressed with Wes Tremayne that he had advanced the boy a week's pay, so that he might have money for food. And Wes hadn't disappointed him. Not only did he work his twelve-hour shift without complaining, he often stayed later without being asked. When he was ribbed and hoorawed by the Alhambra's drunken patrons, he gave as good as he got, and soon they became his friends. Except for Burt Savage. A womanizer, riding shotgun for the stage from Dodge to Fort Griffin, Burt never missed an opportunity to put Wes down. It all came to a head one Tuesday night when Wes was mopping up spilled beer from the hardwood floor. Burt Savage deliberately kicked over the scrub bucket, with its soapy, dirty water.

"Sorry, scrub woman," he said.

More than a dozen men, including Vic Irwin, witnessed the sorry spectacle, and for a moment there was stunned silence. Irwin almost intervened, but thought better of it. Wes Tremayne, if he were to survive in the West, would have to fend for himself. Swiftly he did so. He swung the wet mop, slopping the business end of it into Burt Savage's face. Before Savage could respond to that indignity, Wes dropped the mop and slammed a hard-driven right into Savage's jaw. Savage was flung over a table and into a wall. He slid to the floor and sat there looking foolish as men began to laugh. But the laughter dribbled off as Savage went for his gun.

"Pull that gun, and I'll kill you," said Harley Stafford. His own Colt was in his hand, cocked and steady.

Savage got unsteadily to his feet, his eyes sparking with hate, and he spoke to Wes in a cold, deadly voice.

The Killing Season (Book 2)

"Next time we meet, kid, you'd better have a gun, because I aim to kill you."

Without another word, he elbowed through the swinging doors and was gone.

"You done right, Wes," a man shouted, "but you watch your back. He's a killer."

Wes Tremayne said nothing. Just for a moment, his eyes met those of Harley Stafford and, retrieving the mop, he continued mopping the floor. The hour was late, and men began drifting out of the saloon. Soon only Vic Irwin, Harley Stafford, and Wes Tremayne were left.

"Vic, I could use some coffee," said Harley.

"So could I," Irwin said. "I'll make some."

They sat at a table drinking coffee while Wes continued his swamping.

"For my sake, I hate to admit it," said Irwin, "but that young man is destined for something better than swamping saloons. That is, if he can stay alive."

"I've never seen a man that good with his hands who couldn't handle a gun," Harley said. "He'll need time and practice, though."

"If you can figure a way, get him a gun and teach him to use it," said Irwin. "He has more than his share of pride. When I hired him, he was dead broke, and I had the devil's own time, advancing him a week's wages so's he could eat."

"Go on about your business," Harley said. "When he's done cleanin' up, I'll invite him to have some coffee. He needs a friend. Besides you, I mean."

Harley had no trouble getting Wes to join him for coffee once he had finished his nightly chore of swamping the saloon.

"You're mighty handy with your fists," said Harley. "Have you considered becoming a professional fighter?"

"No," Wes said. "I fight when I have to, like tonight."

"You handled yourself well," said Harley, "but you heard what he said. You must get yourself a gun and learn to use it."

"Will he shoot me if I have no gun?"

"He would have tonight," Harley said, "and by the time your trails cross again, he'll have had some time to feed on his hate."

"I appreciate what you did tonight," said Wes, "but why did you do it?"

"I like your style," Harley said. "Something about you reminds me of a friend who took an interest in me when I needed it most."

"And you're taking an interest in me?"

"Not unless you want it," said Harley. "I have an extra Colt you can use, and when I'm in town, I can maybe tell you a little about the use of it. But mostly, it's all up to you. A Colt has to become part of you, and firing it as natural as pointin' your finger."

"Do you believe I could ever handle a gun as well as you?" Wes asked.

"I do," said Harley. "But you'll never know unless you try."

"I'd like to try," Wes said.

Harley returned to the Dodge House, got the extra Colt, and returned to the Alhambra Saloon. And thus began Wes Tremayne's education in the use of a revolver.

El Paso, Texas
February 15, 1880

Granny Boudleaux had been up in years and Nathan wasn't sure the old lady would still be alive, but he headed immediately for her boardinghouse. To his surprise, the place had been beautifully maintained, and when he knocked on the door, Granny answered. She looked not much older than the day he had last seen her, and she planted a kiss that all but took his breath away.

"Thank God," said the old Cajun, "I not know if you be alive or dead."

"I'd have returned sooner," Nathan said, "but I heard Artemus Stewart had raised the price on my head."

"That he do," said Granny, "but then he die. Two year now."

"Where's Myra, Jamie, and Ellie?" Nathan asked.

"California," said Granny. "I save money for you, like she say."

"Keep the money, Granny," Nathan said. "I'll keep my half interest in your place. I'll likely be needin' somewhere to hole up in my old age. Why did Myra leave?"

"I not like to tell you," said Granny. "She marry man

with rancho along the Colorado River. She be gone four year."

"I can't blame her," Nathan replied. His sense of loss was mingled with relief, and in an odd sort of way he was pleased. When he had thought of Myra, he had been plagued with guilt for having left her alone, for having been gone for so long. Now that he knew she had made a life for herself—even with another man—he felt better.

"What you do now?" Granny Boudleaux asked, invading his thoughts.

"I reckon I'll stay here a few days," said Nathan, "now that old Artemus Stewart's not around to hire bounty hunters."

"You half owner," Granny said. "Your room always ready."

"I'm obliged," said Nathan. "It's been a long ride, and a while since I've slept in a bed. I believe I can sleep the rest of today and tonight. Is my dog still welcome?"

"He always welcome," Granny said. "I wake you for supper."

The room was clean as ever, but there was newer furniture and a new, plush carpet on the floor. Granny had apparently done well, and Nathan was impressed.

Dodge City, Kansas
March 1, 1880

Harley Stafford sat in Foster Hagerman's office, while Hagerman pondered what had just been suggested to him. Finally Hagerman spoke.

"If you really believe this Wes Tremayne is the kind of man we need, then I'm willing to consider him. It's a long step from saloon swamper to a position with the AT & SF."

"I realize that," Harley said, "and so does he, but he was hungry, and took the only work he could find. Hell, that shouldn't doom a man to being a swamper for life."

Hagerman laughed. "I'd have to agree. Does Vic Irwin know you're about to lure his swamper away?"

"He does," said Harley. "This is as much his idea as mine. We believe Wes Tremayne is destined for something better than saloon swamping. He thinks on his feet, is quick with his hands, and he can use a gun. Give him a few more weeks, and he'll be outdrawing me."

"Those are strong qualifications," Hagerman said. "All that's left is learning the Morse code."

It was Harley's turn to laugh. "He already knows the code. I taught it to him there in the Alhambra, tapping a spoon against a beer mug."

"I'll talk to him in the morning," said Hagerman. "If he impresses me as much as he has you and Vic, then I'll make a place for him."

Harley didn't break the news to Wes until they were having breakfast the following morning. Wes carefully set down his coffee cup before he spoke.

"I'm obliged, but you haven't known me even two months. Besides, I feel like I'd be letting Mr. Irwin down."

"Wes," said Harley, "this was Vic's idea. You'll be letting him down if you don't give it a try."

"You had nothing to do with it?"

Harley laughed. "Maybe a little. But Foster Hagerman wants to talk to you, and the last word will be his."

Wes Tremayne knocked on the door to Hagerman's office, and was bid enter. He did so, closing the door behind him.

"Mr. Hagerman, I'm Wes Tremayne."

He offered his hand and Hagerman took it, nodding to a chair before his desk. Wes took the chair, never once losing eye contact with Hagerman. For a moment, the railroad man only looked at Wes, tapping his fingers on the desktop, and it was Wes who spoke.

"Yes, sir, I know the code. Harley taught me."

Hagerman laughed. "You know it very well. It isn't easy, sending Morse on a desktop. I can start you as a baggageman at fifty dollars a month. You'll work out of Dodge, with room and board provided when you're in town. You'll be riding to both ends of the line, wherever you're needed. On some of the western runs, you'll be in charge of military payrolls, and may be called upon to fight. That means using a gun. Any questions?"

"Just one," said Wes. "When do I start?"

"The day after tomorrow," Hagerman said. "March fifth."

"I won't let you down, sir," said Wes, getting to his feet.

His ice blue eyes softened just a little. He then stepped through the door and was gone.

"By God," Foster Hagerman said aloud, "he's going to be a man to ride the river with, but if he's a day past fifteen, I'll eat my hat."

After six weeks in El Paso, his only diversion an occasional poker game in one of the saloons, Nathan was seriously considering moving on. True, Granny Boudleaux had fussed over him and had fed him and Empty at any hour of the day or night they chose to eat, but the routine was getting to him. The stage from San Antonio came in twice a week, and Nathan was usually there for the newspapers from South Texas. He was half hoping there might be some word on King Fisher. But there was nothing, and when he eventually got some information, it was from a direct source. One of the passengers who stepped down from the stage was Molly.

"Molly," said Nathan, hurrying to her, "what are you doing here?"

"I'm getting as far from King Fisher and my damned, ornery kin as I possibly can," she said hotly.

"It's near suppertime," said Nathan. "Let's go somewhere and eat. Then we'll talk."

"I doubt you'll want to hear anything I have to say," Molly replied.

"Yes, I do," said Nathan. "I like you, and I thought you were the best thing that ever happened to King Fisher."

"I once thought so too," Molly replied, "but I've learned better."

"We'll talk after we eat," said Nathan. "Aren't you hungry?"

"Half starved," she admitted. "I had just enough money for stage fare."

"That won't do," said Nathan. "Where are you going from here?"

"I don't know," Molly said bitterly. "To hell, maybe. Isn't that where all the Horrells belong?"

"But I heard in Austin that you and King—"

"Were married?" she laughed. "That's a lie King spread around, hoping to prevent my hell-raising kin from coming after me. I shared his bed but not his life."

"Save the rest of it until we've had some grub," said Nathan.

"Where's your dog?"

"He's at Granny Boudleaux's boardinghouse," Nathan said. "She feeds him about six times a day and he's taken to staying there when I come into town."

They found a cafe, and Nathan ordered steak for them both. Molly ate all of hers and half of Nathan's.

"I'm ashamed of myself," she apologized, "but I've never been so hungry in my life."

"Nothing to be ashamed of," said Nathan. "You won't starve as long as I'm around."

Molly had seemed hard as nails, but she had found a sympathetic ear, and the barriers began to fall. She soaked Nathan's shirt with her tears, and it was a while before she was able to talk.

"Ben Thompson was the cause of it," Molly finally said.

"He's only temporary," said Nathan. "He shows up maybe once a year, and you're rid of him for a while."

"Oh, it wasn't just him," she cried. "It's all been festering like a sore, ever since King took me home with him. Thompson just brought it to a head. Nothing I wanted ever mattered. King still went to Uvalde or San Antonio on Friday, and I wouldn't see him until sometime Monday. He went right on drinking, gambling, and sleeping with other women as though I didn't exist."

"But if you weren't with him, how can you be sure? I knew he drank and gambled, but in all the time I've known him, he didn't seem like a womanizer."

"He told me," she cried. "He kept telling me he was going to find him a woman that knew how to please a man, that didn't spend all her time whining about his habits."

"So you can't go back," said Nathan.

"It isn't so much I can't," she replied. "I won't. I'll take a job in a whorehouse first. I already have the name, so why shouldn't I play the game?"

"Because you don't have to," said Nathan. "I own half of Granny Boudleaux's boardinghouse, and I want you to stay there and look after my half. She can use the help, and it'll be a home for you. There'll be money, too, because she's done well."

"Why would you do this for me?" she asked tearfully.

"Because you're a good woman and because I like you,"

said Nathan. "That, and I'd say you saw King as a means of ridding yourself of the Horrells. I had hoped it might go deeper than that, between you and him."

"So did I," she admitted. "I'd been slapped around all my life, and King was the first man who was ever kind to me. I took that for something stronger, deeper, and if he had given just a little ..."

The tears came again, and Nathan began to see the hopelessness of it all. While King Fisher was his friend, he was being forced to see the man through the eyes of this sobbing girl. Fisher, like Ben Thompson, was flawed. When they chose, each had the ways of a gentleman, but there was a dark side to them that bothered Nathan. With his fast gun, Nathan Stone fell into the same grisly mold as King Fisher and Ben Thompson, but beyond that, he wasn't like them at all. If he helped this unfortunate girl, he had no doubt that, learning of it, King Fisher would give him hell. So be it. He spoke.

"Come on, Molly. It's not far. We can ride double."

She came with him without argument, and he was a bit troubled by her ready smile. It wouldn't take a lot, he decided, for Molly to divert her affections from King Fisher to Nathan Stone. Reaching Granny Boudleaux's, Nathan didn't mention King Fisher. Instead, he introduced Molly as an unfortunate who had fled San Antonio to escape the hell-raising Horrells.

"So if it's all right with you, Granny," said Nathan, "I'd like for Molly to remain here with you, helping where she can."

"Is good," Granny said. "Just lak—"

She caught herself just shy of mentioning Myra Haight's name.

"Just like home," Nathan finished.

"Is home," said Granny. "No debt to bank. We make much money. Suppertime."

"We had a little somethin' in town, Granny," Nathan said, "but it's hard turnin' down one of your meals. Maybe we can hold some more."

It was more for Molly's sake than his own, and she didn't disappoint him. When the meal was finished, Granny led Molly to a room next to Nathan's, and he wondered if the old lady already knew something he did not. Later, far into the night, he was sure of it, for when he answered a knock on the door, Molly Horrell was there.

"I can't sleep," she said softly. "The ghosts won't leave me alone."

Nathan let her in and closed the door. Come the dawn, she was still there.

Dodge City, Kansas
March 15, 1880

Harley and Wes took the eastbound to Kansas City. The following morning, at six, they would depart for Pueblo, Colorado. There would be a military payroll bound for Fort Dodge and, after a turnaround in Pueblo, a shipment of gold ore back to Kansas City.

"You're about to cut your teeth on a big one," Harley said. "On the way west, we're subject to bein' shot between here and Dodge, and on the way back, between Pueblo and Kansas City."

"The only thing I don't like," said Wes, "is bein' locked in the baggage car. If we're hit, I can't be of much help to you. Can't we change that?"

"With good reason," Harley said. "What do you have in mind?"

"If you're ridin' the caboose," said Wes, "why not have a boxcar at the far end of the baggage car, behind the tender? I can ride the boxcar, where they won't be expecting me."

"I think that can be arranged," Harley said. "From Kansas City, I'll telegraph Hagerman in Dodge."

The six a.m. westbound left on schedule, Harley riding the caboose and Wes concealed in a boxcar between the tender and the baggage car. The thieves stopped the train a few miles west of Wichita. Harley climbed atop the caboose with a Winchester as six of the outlaws reined up just out of range. One of them shouted an order.

"You on the caboose and anybody inside, leave your guns and step out with your hands up."

"And if we don't?" Harley shouted.

"We'll shoot the engineer and fireman and dynamite the baggage car," the outlaw shouted back.

But when the train had begun slowing, Wes Tremayne had climbed through a hatch to the roof of the boxcar. Belly down, he made his way toward the tender, and by the time the four outlaws demanded the fireman and engineer step down, Wes was within range. It all depended on him. Swallowing hard, he cut down on them with his Colt. Two of the outlaws dropped, all the break the trainmen needed. Seizing their weapons, the engineer and fireman gunned down the remaining two outlaws. Leaping from the engine cab, they ran toward the rear of the train, their Winchesters ready. Wes ran along the tops of the cars, reloading as he ran. Harley saw him coming and opened up with his Winchester. Realizing their comrades at the head of the train were down, the six outlaws ran for their horses. The brakeman stepped out of the caboose, firing after them with his Winchester, but they were out of range, mounting their horses.

"They're gone," Harley shouted. "Let's get this train moving."

"Then we'll have to reverse it and back it to Wichita," said the engineer. "They ripped out a considerable piece of track."

"Do that," Harley said. "We can't set here on the prairie with a payroll aboard. Pile those dead owlhoots in the baggage car. Maybe the sheriff in Wichita can identify them."

Reaching Wichita, the engineer backed the train onto a side track and Harley sent a telegram to Kansas City, requesting a section crew to repair the track. The trainmen were loud in their praise of Wes, crediting him with gunning down two of the outlaws.

"Wes," said Harley, "you came through when it counted most."

"The first time I ever shot a man," Wes replied, "but there was no other way."

"There never is when you're dealing with outlaws," said Harley. "They'll kill you if they must and not give it a thought. I aim to talk to Hagerman and see if we can't rid ourselves of that baggage car. It's as good as telling outlaws there's a payroll aboard. How many times did Nathan tell them to secure the payroll in the caboose, in a bolted-down strongbox?"

"Who?"

"Nathan Stone," Harley said. "He got me on with the railroad after he left. "My God, he was good. He once trailed a band of outlaws into Indian Territory, and only two of them escaped. Singlehanded, he killed eleven men."*

"I'd like to meet him," Wes said.

"Eventually you will," said Harley, "and when you do, he's not the kind of man you'll soon forget."

The section crew took awhile repairing the track, and the westbound went on its way four hours behind schedule. Foster Hagerman was waiting for them when the train rolled into Dodge. Harley stepped down from the caboose, grinning.

"You made a good choice," Harley said. "Wes gunned down two of the outlaws, while the engineer and fireman got two more. I just sat in the caboose and watched the rest of them ride for their lives."

"From now on, I think we'll do what Nathan was forever suggesting," said Hagerman. "We'll bolt down that strongbox to the floor of the caboose and secure the payrolls there."

"What about the boxcar behind the tender?" Wes asked.

"I think we'll keep that," said Hagerman. "It made a difference when the outlaws tried to take the engineer and fireman hostage."

"Wes needs a rifle," Harley said. "Do you have a Winchester he can use until he can get one of his own?"

"Yes," said Hagerman, "and I'll see that he gets a new one, compliments of the railroad. Losing that payroll would have hurt us."

The train pulled out for Pueblo. Trainmen began talking about the quiet young man with the pale blue eyes and a fast gun.

El Paso, Texas
April 1, 1880

Nathan's relationship with Molly Horrell blossomed quickly and became so obvious that Nathan felt compelled

The Dawn of Fury (Book 1)

to speak to Granny Boudleaux. Finally, when he was alone with her, he did.

"Granny, I don't quite know how to say this, but Molly . . ."

"Molly need a man," Granny cackled, "and you a man. Why that bother you? Molly younger and more pretty than Myra was."

"It bothers me for the same reason my . . . my arrangement with Myra bothered me," said Nathan. "I'm a wanderer, needin' to ride on, and I don't know when I'll be returning to El Paso."

"You feel guilty," Granny said, "but why? She partners with me. She have home, food, and money. When you here, she have you. *Bueno*!"

"I only hope she sees it that way," said Nathan.

"I talk to her," Granny said. "I need her, you want her, she wait."

But Nathan had his misgivings. And when the time came, they would be justified.

CHAPTER 13

Dodge City, Kansas
April 16, 1880

As Wes Tremayne became more confident, he thonged down his Colt on his right hip and began wearing it regularly. True to his word, Foster Hagerman presented Wes with a new Winchester. With Harley's help, Wes bought a horse and saddle and learned to ride. Harley and Wes were usually in town on Friday night, and it became a custom for them to have supper at Delmonico's, where Vic Irwin usually joined them. Harley was amused, for it was difficult to tell whether Vic Irwin or Foster Hagerman was proudest of the progress Wes Tremayne had made in so short a time. Far into the night, Wes practiced drawing his Colt, until he could draw and fire with dazzling speed.

"My God," Harley told Foster Hagerman, "the kid can already outdraw me. Before he's done, he'll equal or better Nathan Stone."

"Something about him—maybe his eyes—makes me think of Nathan," said Hagerman.

It being Friday, Hagerman joined Harley, Wes, and Vic at Delmonico's for supper, and they had just left the cafe when trouble started. It was almost dark, and from across the street came a challenge.

"You, saloon swamper, I told you we'd meet again. Nobody slaps Burt Savage around and goes on livin'. I'm invitin' you to draw, unless you got a yellow stripe down your back."

The three men with Wes Tremayne were in no position to side Wes, as long as it was a fair fight. And though they had confidence in him, their misgivings were strong. While Wes had proven himself against train robbers, and could draw and fire with blinding speed, he had never faced another man in a shoot-out. It was a trial that had to come, and Wes Tremayne knew it. He stepped off the boardwalk and stood there waiting as his three companions got out of the line of fire.

"When you're ready, scrub bucket," Savage taunted.

Wes said nothing. He seemed totally relaxed, and his confidence had an adverse effect on his opponent. Burt Savage drew and fired, but he was no match for Wes Tremayne. The roar of Savage's Colt sounded as an echo, and his slug slammed into the ground at his feet. Wes holstered his Colt and waited as Savage stumbled backward into a hitch rail. His knees buckled and he fell face down in the dusty street.

"Great shootin', Wes," Harley shouted.

A sheriff's deputy arrived, and it took only a few minutes for him to declare that Wes had acted in self-defense. But men from within Delmonico's had witnessed the fast gun of Wes Tremayne, and it became a thing of which legends are made. For the next two days, Wes was embarrassed beyond words as men slapped him on the back and insisted on shaking his hand. It was with considerable relief that he boarded the eastbound for Kansas City on Monday.

"How long is this likely to go on?" he asked Harley.

"Kid," said Harley, "it's just started. When word of it gets around, there'll be others, all wantin' to prove they can beat you."

"But why?" Wes persisted. "I only defended myself."

"That's how it always begins," said Harley, "and it'll go on as long as men try to look taller than they are by pulling a gun."

El Paso, Texas
May 1, 1880

The longer Nathan remained in El Paso, the more difficult it became for him to leave. Molly's first night in his bed—to Granny Boudleaux's amusement—became an unabashed nightly ritual, and if Molly Horrell ever thought of King Fisher, she concealed it well. On Monday, Nathan always took Granny Boudleaux's money to the bank for deposit, and it was on such an occasion that he became involved in a holdup. He was about to present his deposit to the teller when the robbers made their presence known.

"Down on the floor, all of you," a masked man shouted. There were four of them, all with guns drawn. Nathan dropped to one knee and fired, dropping one of the robbers, and before the others could overcome their surprise, he cut down a second man. Encouraged, one of the tellers opened fire, and the remaining two outlaws broke for the door.

"My God," exclaimed an elderly man who proved to be the bank's president, "that was a remarkable thing!"

To Nathan's dismay, the rest of the bank's personnel and the customers who had seen his reaction gathered around him, and that's how it was when Sheriff McCormick arrived. He examined the two dead men, whistled long and low, and then set about asking questions of the bank's patrons and personnel. When he reached Nathan, there was admiration in his eyes.

"That was a slick piece of work," he said. "Do you know who those men are?"

"No," said Nathan, "I've never seen them before."

"They're part of the Sandlin gang," McCormick said. "They're wanted on both sides of the border, and there's bound to be a reward."

"I don't want it," said Nathan. "I have my own reasons for disliking bank robbers."

But the harder Nathan tried to escape the limelight, the more difficult it became. While he refused to talk to newspaper reporters, others who had witnessed the shooting seemed to glory in the repeating of it. As a result, he eventually was forced to accept a thousand-dollar reward, and that fired public interest to even greater heights. But one evening, near dark, as Nathan rode out of town, a hidden rifleman cut down on him. He barely escaped with his life, and attempts to trail the bushwhacker were futile.

"It's likely the Sandlin gang, bent on revenge," Sheriff McCormick said.

"I'm obliged to the town for making them aware of me," said Nathan. "Why did you think I didn't want your rewards and newspaper stories?"

"Well," McCormick said, "it's the first time anybody ever interrupted a holdup and gunned down some of the gang. We had no idea—"

"Now you do," said Nathan, "and what would you suggest that I do?"

"Was I you," McCormick said, "I'd ride on. This bunch is dug in solid, wanted on both sides of the border. I hear there may be more than two dozen of them. They got a regular border empire, and if they want you, they'll get you."

Nathan rode back to Granny Boudleaux's, considering what Sheriff McCormick had told him. It was reason enough for him to leave El Paso. He didn't consider it his responsibility, bringing the Sandlin gang to justice, but what choice did he have if he allowed himself to be sucked into a grudge fight? It was time to talk to Molly, and he planned to do so immediately after supper. But his enemies didn't wait. They allowed him to stable his horse and reach the house, and from the darkness, half a dozen Winchesters cut loose. Lead shattered windows with a tinkling crash, and soot rained down as a slug struck a stovepipe.

"On the floor!" Nathan shouted.

But the onslaught ended as suddenly as it had begun.

"My God," Molly cried, "what was that all about?"

"The Sandlin gang's after me," said Nathan. "They're out to get even for the owlhoots I gunned down in the bank last week. They tried to backshoot me in town a while ago."

"You talk to sheriff," Granny Boudleaux said.

"I have," said Nathan. "He suggested I ride on."

"No," Molly cried.

"There's more than two dozen of the varmints, and they're holed up on both sides of the border," said Nathan. "You want a daily dose of what you had tonight?"

"Cost hundred dollar, fix windows," Granny Boudleaux said.

"If you go, I'm going with you," said Molly.

"Molly," Nathan said, "there are men all over the frontier who would like to see me dead, and they'll kill anybody standin' in the way. That includes you."

"If you ride away," said Molly, "I may never see you again."

"If I stay here and ride into El Paso, you may never see me again," Nathan said. "I'll ride back when this settles down, but I don't aim to stay here, where lead meant for me can kill you or Granny. Surely you can understand that."

"I can understand your reasoning," said Molly, "but I don't like it."

"He smart hombre," Granny said. "You listen."

Assured by Nathan that he would return, Molly made the best of it, and Nathan rode north the next morning at dawn.

Las Vegas, New Mexico
June 1, 1880

It was still early, but Nathan and Empty sought a cafe for supper. As they entered, it came as a surprise to Nathan when he found himself face to face with the notorious Doc Holliday. Nathan hadn't seen Holliday since the temperamental little gambler had shot up a saloon in Dallas. Ignoring Nathan, Holliday left the cafe.

"My God," said the cook in awe, "that's Doc Holliday."

"Yes," Nathan said, "I've seen him before."

"The word is, he's here to get Charlie White," said the cook.

"Who's Charlie White?"

"Bartender over to the Tumbleweed Saloon," the cook said. "A grudge on Holliday's part, I reckon."*

"If you got no objection to my dog, he's a payin' customer," said Nathan.

"He's welcome," the cook said. "It's been a slow day."

After supper, Nathan found a livery and stabled his horse. He then went looking for a hotel and a room for the night. It was still early, and since Nathan had never been in Las Vegas before, he decided to see the town.

"Empty," said Nathan, "I may visit a saloon or two, so I'm leavin' you here with my bedroll and saddlebags."

Nathan locked the door, unconcerned with leaving Empty behind, for he didn't know which the hound hated more—steamboats, locomotives, or saloons. Las Vegas didn't seem much more than a village, and when Nathan reached the Tumbleweed Saloon, it appeared the most likely place to spend some time. It was still the supper

*A few months before, Doc Holliday had run Charlie White out of Dodge City. There is no known reason for Holliday's grudge, nor did he ever confront White again.

hour, and there were only five men in the saloon. One of them was the bartender, and the remaining four were at a table, playing poker. Nathan ordered a beer and wandered over to the game in progress.

"Mind if I sit in?" he asked.

"Table stakes," said one of the men. "Dollar a game."

Nathan dragged out a chair and sat down. He promptly lost three hands and was about to fold when the bat wings swung open and Doc Holliday stood there.

"I ain't wantin' trouble, Doc," the bartender said, his hands shoulder high.

"You're damn well about to get it," Holliday shouted.

Charlie White ducked behind the bar and came up with a sawed-off shotgun, but he had no chance to use it. Holliday had drawn his pistol and fired twice. The scatter-gun clattered to the floor, and the hapless bartender fell across it. Holliday turned and walked out the door. Only then did one of the poker players venture behind the bar, and he shouted to the others.

"Charlie's alive! Somebody get the doc!"

By the time the doctor arrived, two of the tables had been shoved together, and the wounded Charlie White was stretched out on them.

"He was shot twice," one of the poker players volunteered.

"I don't think so," said the doctor. "His head's been creased, and that's the extent of his injury. He'll have a fierce headache for a while, but he'll live."

The owner of the saloon was sent for, and Charlie White was sent home. The poker game broke up, amid speculation that Doc Holliday might return. Nathan left the saloon and returned to his hotel, wondering why no lawman had shown up to investigate the shooting. He was unimpressed with Doc Holliday. Twice he had encountered the man; both times he had been engaged in a saloon shooting.

Caldwell, Kansas
June 19, 1880

Nathan had spent an unusually pleasant Saturday night in the Sunflower Saloon. There had been a six-hour poker game that had broken up at midnight. Suddenly a fight broke out near the bar, and it took half a dozen men to separate the combatants. One of the men—the drunker of the two—wore a brace of twin pistols.

"Who's the gent with the *buscadera* rig?" Nathan asked a bystander.

"George Flatt. Used to be a marshal, but his hard drinkin' and quick guns got him in trouble. The gent that just tangled with him is Frank Hunt, a new deputy marshal that's been appointed by Mayor Mike Meagher. Flatt gives Hunt hell ever' chance he gets."

Apparently, some of Flatt's friends had persuaded him to leave the saloon, and Nathan left right behind them.

"George," said one of the men accompanying Flatt, "let's go to Segerman's Restaurant for some grub."

After some persuading, Flatt agreed to go, and the trio started across the street to the restaurant. Suddenly there was a shot, and Flatt lurched forward, shot through the back of his skull. Before he fell, three more slugs ripped into his body.

"Frank Hunt's killed him," somebody shouted. "I seen him."*

Ogallala, Nebraska
June 26, 1880

Ogallala proved to be a lively town stretched along the Union Pacific Railroad tracks. There was an abundance of saloons and boardinghouses catering to railroad men, and again Nathan left Empty behind while he visited the saloons. He had won more than three hundred dollars since leaving El Paso, and not once had he been forced to pull a gun. But the saloons in this Nebraska town interested him. One of them—the Cementario—had a crimson death's head painted above the door. It was the rowdiest of the lot, and Nathan was surprised to find the house dealer was none other than the unpredictable Billy Thompson. Nathan bought a beer, leaned against the bar, and searched the

*On October 11, 1880, Frank Hunt sat before an open window in the Red Light Saloon and dance hall. An unknown assassin fired through the window, mortally wounding Hunt.

crowd, fully expecting to see Ben. But this time, it seemed Billy was on his own, for Ben was nowhere in sight. Nathan moved closer and it soon became obvious that Billy Thompson had continued his relationship with the bottle. He was just drunk enough to have unbounded confidence in himself, which proved to be his undoing. One of the men dropped his cards, slid back his chair, and stood up.

"Billy Thompson," he shouted, "you're a cheatin', tin-horn bastard!"

"Damn you, Jim Tucker," Billy snarled. "Draw."

But Texan Jim Tucker had an edge, for he hadn't been drinking. Both reached for their guns as onlookers fought to get out of the line of fire. Billy Thompson didn't get off a shot. He stumbled back and sat down in his chair, bleeding from five wounds.

"Here comes Sheriff Naylor," somebody shouted.

Sheriff Ollie Naylor looked from Jim Tucker to the bleeding Billy Thompson. Despite his wounds, Billy still gripped his Colt.

"Even break, Sheriff," said Tucker. "He was cheating."

"He sure as hell was," another man agreed. "If he ain't dead, let's string him up."

"Nobody's gettin' strung up," said the sheriff. "Some of you tote him to the doc's place."

Thompson was taken away, but there was angry talk as Jim Tucker spread out the cards from which Billy had been dealing. Nathan remained in the saloon after the sheriff had departed, and there was more talk about lynching Billy Thompson.

"Wait till the little varmint's healed some," a man said. "Then we'll introduce him to the business end of a rope."

Ben Thompson always seemed to be around when Billy got in over his head, but for once, it seemed Billy was on his own. Nathan found the doctor's office and went in. Since he considered himself a friend to Ben Thompson, he could at least telegraph Ben and tell him of Billy's predicament—if only he knew where Ben was. Nathan waited in the outer office until the doctor came out.

"I'm Dr. Summers. What can I do for you?"

"I'm Nathan Stone, a friend of Ben Thompson, brother to the man that was brought over from the saloon. I reckon I can telegraph Ben, if Billy knows where he is."

"Billy Thompson is in no condition to talk to you," said

Dr. Summers. "As soon as I'm finished with him, the sheriff is having him moved to the hotel, under guard."

There was little Nathan could do except leave, and he did. Many a man on the frontier had been shot dead for cheating at cards, and it seemed Billy Thompson had been in town long enough to accumulate some enemies. Nathan found Sheriff Ollie Naylor.

"Sheriff," said Nathan, "I know Ben Thompson, Billy's brother. As a favor, I'm willing to telegraph the news to Ben, if you know or can learn where he is."

"Friend," Sheriff Naylor replied, "do *yourself* a favor and stay out of this. If Ben Thompson shows up in this town, he'll likely be strung up alongside his hell-raising little brother."

"Bein' sheriff," said Nathan, "you seem almighty certain Billy's goin' to be strung up."

"I've never lost a prisoner to vigilantes yet," Naylor said, "but there's always a first time. I'm just one man. After the doc's had him moved to the hotel, I'll post a guard at his door. Beyond that, I'm makin' no promises."

While Nathan had no intention of taking on a lynch mob to save the troublesome Billy Thompson, he decided to remain in town another day or two. He still wasn't convinced that Ben wouldn't show up.

The next afternoon, Nathan returned to the saloon where Billy Thompson had been shot, and to his surprise, he encountered Bat Masterson.

"Been here long?" Bat inquired.

"Couple of days," said Nathan. "I was here when Billy Thompson was shot."

"I heard about that," Masterson said. "Let's find us a table and talk."

They took chairs at a corner table, and Masterson called for a bottle and glasses. He drew the cork with his teeth and filled their glasses. Masterson spoke.

"I am assuming Billy isn't dead. Where is he?"

"At the hotel," said Nathan. "I would have telegraphed Ben, but I have no idea where he is. I've been warned to stay out of this by none other than Sheriff Naylor himself."

Masterson laughed. "That's good advice. Ben's about as welcome here as a Comanche war party at a sodbuster barn raising. He's in Dodge. Somebody from the saloon where

Billy was shot telegraphed Ben, and he talked me into comin' here and saving Billy's hide if I can. I came in on the Union Pacific westbound."

"Tarnation," said Nathan, "he was hit five times. He won't be able to move for maybe a week, and then he'll likely be moved to the jail. You aim to take him out on the train?"

"Yes," Masterson said. "He'll be in no condition to ride."

"I'm not fond of Billy Thompson," said Nathan, "but I consider Ben a friend. I'll help you if I can."

"You'd best keep your nose clean," Masterson said. "I have a plan, and if it fails, I see no reason for you being hanged from the same limb as Billy and me."

Taking Bat's advice, Nathan didn't involve himself in the rescue. Instead, he went to the Union Pacific terminal and learned that there was an eastbound every night at eleven. It almost had to be the train Masterson had in mind. Every night, half an hour before the train arrived, Nathan was in the shadows across the street from the hotel. Four days after Masterson had reached town, the escape took place. At ten-thirty, a surrey with curtains drawn rolled up before the hotel. Ten minutes before eleven, a fusillade of gunfire ripped the night. Not surprisingly, the furor took place at the farthest point from the railroad terminal. Billy Thompson was lowered out a second-floor hotel window with a rope, and Masterson was waiting for him. As the two of them entered the waiting surrey, there was the whistle of the approaching eastbound.*

"My hat's off to you, Bat Masterson," Nathan said aloud as the surrey vanished into the night. He slipped away, returning to his room, where Empty waited.

Dodge City, Kansas
July 1, 1880

While Wes Tremayne had won the respect of all who knew him, there was a dark side that began to trouble him. He was pointed out in Kansas City and Pueblo as a fast

*Bat Masterson and Billy Thompson reached Dodge in mid-July. Billy had recovered.

gun who had accounted for two train robbers on his first run, and papers in other towns had picked up the account of his fight with Burt Savage in Dodge. Newspapers in Kansas City, having gotten his schedule, had begun sending reporters to meet the train.

"Harley," said Wes, "I'm tired of newspaper people following me around. What can I do about them?"

"Not much, kid," Harley said. "Sometimes I think the railroad encourages them. It's a way of letting train robbers know they're likely to catch hell."

But the stalking turned deadly. Wes had just stepped down from the baggage coach in Dodge when he was challenged.

"Tremayne, I'm callin' you out. Draw."

"I don't know you," Wes replied, "and I have no fight with you."

"The hell you don't! I'm Ivan Curry. I'm faster than you, and you ain't gonna deny me the chance to prove it."

The engineer and fireman had left the cab, and Harley had stepped down from the caboose. They were out of range, waiting. Wes sighed. It was his fight, and he waited for Curry to draw. His first shot was wide, and only then did Wes draw. He fired once, and Curry stumbled back into the wall of the depot. He dropped the Colt, his knees buckled, and he fell facedown in the ballast along the track. Wes ejected the spent shell, thumbed in a live one, and holstered the Colt. Drawn by the shots, a crowd was gathering.

"Damn it, Wes," Harley scolded, "never hold back when you know you have to fight. He could have killed you."

"But he didn't," said Wes. "I didn't want to fight him."

The arrival of the train in Dodge was still an exciting event, for there were current newspapers from Kansas City and St. Louis, as well as mail and goods not readily available in Dodge. All those who waited, whatever their reason, were drawn to the shooting. One of them was the editor of the local newspaper.

"I was forced to draw," said Wes, "and I don't want to talk about it. Please leave me alone."

But his plea fell on deaf ears and he was forced to take refuge in Foster Hagerman's office. He found Hagerman unsympathetic.

"Hell, Wes, you did what you had to do. Besides, it will add to your reputation."

"A reputation I don't want," said Wes. "Why can't I just do my job and be left alone?"

But the curious, including the newspaper editor, found willing witnesses who told of Wes Tremayne allowing Ivan Curry to shoot first, and then killing him with a single shot. Wes Tremayne was forced to accept the terrible truth. As much as he appreciated his position with the railroad, the very nature of it was creating for him a deadly reputation as a killer. Supper at Delmonico's became a gala event, with Harley, Foster Hagerman, and Vic Irwin praising him. But when darkness crept over the land and distant stars became pools of silver in a purple meadow, Wes Tremayne reached a decision. Four months shy of his fifteenth birthday, taking his few belongings, he saddled his horse and rode away.

Nathan considered riding to Cheyenne but thought better of it. While he didn't doubt Byron Silver's ability to undo the turbulent events that had resulted from their recent visit, he didn't believe in kicking sleeping dogs. He considered riding back to Dodge, but came up with two good reasons for avoiding it. Trouble stalked Ben and Billy Thompson like their shadows, and he had little doubt the unpredictable pair would be in Dodge. So he rode south, toward Denver.

Nathan reined up. They were nearing the South Platte River when Empty came trotting back, his hackles up. Dismounting, leading his grulla, Nathan continued on foot. There was something or somebody ahead of them. Suddenly a horse nickered and Nathan's grulla answered. Nathan threw himself belly down, and slugs ripped the air where he had been standing. One of them creased the grulla, and the animal galloped away. His Winchester in the crook of his arms, Nathan moved ahead, and the very instant he spotted his antagonist, the man saw him. Nathan cut loose with the Winchester, and the lead slammed into the other man, taking him down the bank and into the river. Only then did Nathan see the girl who crouched in the underbrush.

"Come on out," Nathan said, "and if you have a gun, leave it there."

"I don't have a gun," she cried. "He robbed a bank and took me captive."

She crept out, and Nathan doubted she was more than nineteen. He also doubted she had been taken captive, for she was dressed for riding. Her boots, Levi's, and red-checked shirt looked new.

"He took you from the bank, I reckon," said Nathan.

"Yes," she replied. "I-I'm hurt. He kicked me in the belly—"

She had unbuttoned her shirt near the belt line, and almost caught Nathan off guard. He still held the Winchester, and he flung it as hard as he could. The muzzle of it struck her wrist, and she dropped the deadly little derringer.

"Damn you," she shouted, "you've broken my arm."

"I'm ready to forget you're a woman, and break your neck," said Nathan grimly. "Now you're goin' to talk, and talk straight, or you'll be sorry you ever laid eyes on me."

"You can't make me talk," she snarled.

"Maybe not," said Nathan, "but I can make you wish you had."

CHAPTER 14

Seeking to get as far from the railroad as possible, Wes Tremayne rode south. While in Dodge, he had learned something about the territory to the south. Within a day's ride, there was Mobeetie, Texas, and nearby Fort Elliott. Beyond that, Fort Griffin, Fort Worth and all of south Texas. He was drifting, with no destination in mind, not knowing what he wanted to do. He thought of Vic Irwin, Harley Stafford, and Foster Hagerman, the men in Dodge who had befriended him, and suffered pangs of guilt. He had taken the coward's way out, riding away without a word to any of them. With the railroad providing his room and board in Dodge, he had saved almost all his money, so he wasn't broke. He rode into Mobeetie well before midnight, checked his horse into the livery, and took a room at the newly constructed hotel. With so much on his mind, he wasn't sure he could sleep, so he left the hotel and visited one of the saloons. He had never had more than an occasional beer, so he avoided the bar. While poker interested him, he had avoided it, not wanting to risk his money. Now he had cut loose from the railroad, was in a strange town, and he felt a little reckless. A poker game was in progress. One of the men folded, leaving a house dealer and three soldiers who seemed more drunk than sober. Wes dragged out a chair and sat down.

"Table stakes," the house man said. "Dollar a game."

Wes remained in the game long enough to win ten dollars. By the time he kicked back his chair and stood up, one of the saloon women had taken his arm.

"There's more action upstairs," she said.

"Thanks," said Wes, "but I reckon not."

She laughed. "Come back, kid, when you have some hair on your chest."

Wes left the saloon and returned to the hotel.

"What's your name?" Nathan asked the sullen girl.

"Kate McDowell."

"Who was the man I shot?" Nathan asked.

"Will Blackburn."

"There was nobody else involved in the robbery?" Nathan asked.

She laughed. "There are four others. Will double-crossed them and took all the gold. They would have killed him. Now they will kill you."

"They can try," said Nathan. "Now why don't you tell me where you fit into this?"

"I told you I was taken captive. Will wanted me to go with him, and when I refused he took me anyway."

"You're lying," Nathan said, "and you're not very good at it. I freed you from Blackburn, and you thanked me by tryin' to gut-shoot me with a sleeve gun."

"At least I knew Will," she snapped. "I don't know you. For all I know, you're just another outlaw after the gold."

"For a town woman taken against your will," said Nathan, "it was mighty convenient, you bein' all decked out in a man's shirt, Levi's, and boots. Explain that."

"Will brought the clothes and made me change. Now are you satisfied?" she said.

"No," said Nathan. "I aim to have a look in Blackburn's saddlebags, but I reckon I'd better pull your fangs first. Get belly down; I'm goin' to tie your hands behind you."

"Is that necessary? You took my gun."

"All right," Nathan said, against his better judgement. "Don't try anything foolish."

But no sooner had he turned toward Blackburn's horse than she sprang into the saddle of her own mount, kicking it into a gallop. Nathan's grulla grazed a hundred yards away, and he had but one option. Mounting Blackburn's horse, with intentions of riding after her, he made an alarming discovery. The horse was lame, reason enough for Blackburn attempting to gun him down. Having lost Kate McDowell—if that had been her real name—he turned his attention back to the saddlebags the lame horse carried. But to his dismay, there was nothing but personal items, leading him to wonder if the elusive girl had told him the truth about the bank robbery. But why had he been forced to kill a man who might not have been what the girl claimed he was? Empty growled, alerting Nathan to a new danger. Seven horsemen approached, and the lead rider wore a lawman's star on the left lapel of his vest. Some of the men held Winchesters at the ready, and the others were prepared to draw their Colts. Nathan waited as they approached. They reined up, and it was the badge-toter who spoke.

"Lift them irons slow an' easy, usin' your thumb an' finger, and them let 'em drop."

"Sheriff," said Nathan, "don't I get a chance to tell you who I am and to explain why I'm not who you think I am?"

"That bay hoss pretty well explains who you are," the sheriff replied. "Now where's the woman and the money?"

"I don't have the answers you're lookin' for," Nathan said, "because I'm not the man you're lookin' for. Now, damn it, you're going to listen to me."

"Then you keep your hands shoulder high," said the sheriff, "and do some talking."

"For starters," Nathan said, "this is not my horse. You'll find my grulla grazing down the river a ways. My name is Nathan Stone."

Quickly he explained what had happened and what the girl had told him, and of her eventual escape.

"I've heard that name somewhere," said one of the men in the posse.

"So have I," the sheriff said. "Mister, do you have any proof you're who you claim to be?"

"Yes," Nathan said. From the pocket of his shirt, he removed the pocket watch given him almost ten years before by Byron Silver. He snapped open the case before passing it to the sheriff, revealing the great seal of the United States and the address of the attorney general in Washington.*

"Why, hell, I know you," the sheriff exclaimed. "You was one of the hombres that busted up that land grab in Wyoming Territory. It was in the Denver papers. I'm Sheriff Handy Green from Denver."

He offered his hand and Nathan took it.

"Sheriff," one of his riders said, "if Blackburn went into the river, maybe we can fish him out downstream."

"Good thinking," said the sheriff. "Wash, you and Tull see if you can find him."

The two men rode away, and Nathan again turned to the sheriff.

*The Dawn of Fury (Book 1)

"Sheriff, all I know about this is what the girl told me, so I don't know if it's true or not. She told me her name was Kate McDowell, and that she had been taken captive by the man I shot. She said his name was Will Blackburn and that he had robbed a Denver bank."

"He robbed a bank, all right," said Sheriff Green, "but he wasn't alone. How was this woman dressed?"

"Like a man," Nathan said. "Her hair was short, and her hat was down over her ears, like it was a mite big for her."

"The second man might have been a woman," the sheriff said. "Which way did she ride out?"

"Upstream," Nathan said.

"Pegram," said the sheriff, "that trail oughta be plenty fresh. Have a look."

They waited. Wash and Tull returned after a few minutes, and it was Tull who spoke.

"He told it straight, Sheriff. He was downstream, maybe half a mile, caught up in a drift. We hauled him out on the bank, if you want him."

"We'll have to tote him back to town for positive identification," the sheriff said, "but if Pegram finds a trail, we're goin' after that woman first."

Pegram returned at a fast gallop. "Hoss headed upstream," he said, "pickin' 'em up an' a-layin' 'em down."

"Stone," the sheriff asked, "was the woman's horse carryin' saddlebags?"

"No," said Nathan.

"I was afraid of that," said the sheriff. "Damn it, Blackburn likely hid the loot when his hoss went lame. We'll never recover the money unless we catch her. Let's ride."

They rode out at a fast gallop, upriver.

"Empty," Nathan said, "we're in no hurry to get to Denver. I reckon we'll find us a place to hole up and wait a spell. I got a gut feeling me and that slippery little filly will meet again."

Nathan led the grulla across the river, picketing the animal where it couldn't be seen from the farthest bank. He then found a thicket that would conceal both himself and Empty and allow him to see for half a mile beyond the paint where he had shot Blackburn. The sun was warm and Nathan dozed, unaware of the passing of time. But when Empty growled, Nathan was instantly awake. Just beyond the clearing on the farthest bank there was some movement

in the brush. Kate McDowell stepped out, looked carefully
all around, and then hurried downstream. On the opposite
bank, keeping out of sight, Nathan followed. Reaching the
dead body of Will Blackburn, she ignored it and went on.
Eventually she paused, looked around, and then dropped to
her knees. Brushing away dead leaves, she began scooping
handfuls of dirt from what had been a stump hole. Nathan
crossed the river where there were sand bars and the water
was shallow, and saw the girl triumphantly lift a canvas bag
from the hole. Only then did she notice Nathan standing a
few yards away. She fought the fury and hate that threatened to engulf her and forced a weak smile. Finally she
spoke.

"There's enough for us both. Come with me."

"Thanks," said Nathan, "but I reckon not. The sheriff
and his posse will be returning directly, and I'll be turning
you and the money over to them. I owe you that for trying
to kill me."

She ran back the way she had come, but Nathan was
prepared for that. He had built a loop in his lariat, and he
dropped it over her shoulders, pinning her arms. Hauling
her up short, he slammed her to the ground on her backside. She then employed a weapon women have relied on
since time began. She wept.

"Save it," Nathan said. "You can get up if you want, but
the rope stays where it is."

By the time she got to her feet, the tears had vanished
and she began cursing Nathan in as vile a manner as the
lowest bullwhacker.

"I'm within a gnat's eyelash of takin' the other end of
this rope and horse whipping you," said Nathan. "Open
your mouth one more time, and I'll forget you're a female."

Something in Nathan Stone's eyes got to her, and she
became silent. The sheriff and the posse returned an hour
later.

"She's all yours, Sheriff," said Nathan. "I watched her
dig up that canvas sack, and I reckon it's the missing
bank money."

"It's the money, all right," Sheriff Green said, after opening the sack.

"I never saw that sack in my life," the girl shouted. "It's
his word against mine."

"Maybe not," Sheriff Green said. "There were witnesses

who saw you in the bank. Do you know where her horse is, Stone?"

"I think so," said Nathan. "I'll get it."

The horse had been tethered beyond the thicket from which the girl had emerged, and Nathan led the animal back to where Sheriff Green and the posse waited.

"Wash, you and Tull double up on the ride back to town. We'll need an extra horse to carry Blackburn's remains."

The ride to Denver was uneventful, and when they reached the outskirts of town, the sheriff spoke to Nathan.

"We're obliged for your help, Stone. It ain't often, when they get away with a head start, that we bring back the robbers and the money. Will you be around for a day or so in case we need your testimony."

"Yes," Nathan said. "I'll see you again before I leave town."

Denver, Colorado
July 3, 1880

Nathan's recollections of Denver were bittersweet. It was here that he had met and become friends with Wild Bill Hickok. Had it been almost four years since Bill had been murdered in Deadwood?*

"Empty," said Nathan, "if we're to spend a couple of days here, we got to find us a way of spendin' the time."

There was snow on the distant peaks of the Rockies, and the westering sun appeared to be resting there before continuing its journey to the farthest side of the earth. There was a distant crackle that Nathan recognized as fireworks, and Empty became skittish, seeking the safety of some trees. Reaching a hotel where he and Empty had stayed before, Nathan took a room for the night.

"Why the fireworks?" Nathan asked.

"Tomorrow's July fourth," said the desk clerk. "I reckon somebody's started the celebration early."

Leaving his horse at a nearby livery, Nathan and Empty had supper. Darkness was near when they returned to the hotel, and the popping of fireworks had become almost continuous.

The Killing Season (Book 2)

"Empty," Nathan said, "you're so jumpy, I reckon you'd better stay right here at the hotel. I may visit a saloon or two."

Nathan left the hotel, bound for a saloon called the Casa Verde. It was a secluded, two-story affair, with gambling twenty-four hours a day. But the gambling didn't interest Nathan. His interest was on the second floor, where "pretty girls" who wore little or nothing catered to high rollers. It was a blatant attempt to take a man's mind off how much and how often he had lost. It had been here, in September 1876, that Nathan had rediscovered Melanie Gavin. Nathan had been so infatuated with Melanie that he would have married her, but the girl had run away from Dodge while Nathan had been chasing train robbers in New Mexico. Would she still be at Casa Verde after four years? Nathan entered the building, finding it hadn't changed. The downstairs had a bar, a kitchen, tables for dining, some poker tables, and a roulette wheel. As before, one of the waiters met him in the foyer.

"The first floor is reserved for dining or gambling for table stakes, sir. All the high-stakes tables and the pretty girls are on the second floor."

"The second floor, then," said Nathan.

The upstairs seemed as plush as ever, and the "pretty girls" moved from table to table, deftly avoiding groping hands. They still wore pink slippers, pink bows in their hair, and short pink jackets that covered only their shoulders and their arms to the elbow. Four of the near-naked pretty girls worked the floor, but Melanie wasn't among them, so Nathan went directly to the bar. He got the attention of one of the three bartenders, and the man raised his eyebrows questioningly.

"I'm looking for Melanie Gavin," Nathan said. "She's a longtime friend. I last saw her four years ago when she was working here."

"She no longer works here," said the bartender with some disapproval. "She is part owner. I will ask if she wishes to see you. Your name?"

"Nathan Stone."

He stalked to the far end of the gambling hall and knocked on a door that had a glass pane in the upper half. The door opened just a little, allowing him to speak, and it was then closed.

"She'll see you," the bartender said, when he returned. "Knock on the door."

Nathan knocked, and when Melanie opened it, he had the surprise of his life. Her dark hair still cascaded to her shoulders, reminding him all the more of Molly Tremayne and that brief but stormy affair of fourteen years ago. She wore a low-cut green gown that all but swept the floor. But she didn't seem all that excited at seeing him again.

"Well, don't just stand there with your mouth hung open," she said. "Come on in."

"Sorry," said Nathan, closing the door behind him. "I wasn't sure it was you, decked out in all that finery."

"Make up your mind," she said curtly. "Last time, you jumped all over me because I was naked in a saloon."

"I'm not sure I didn't like you better that way," said Nathan. "Something's missing."

"It was all there, the last time I looked," she said sarcastically. "Do you expect me to stand naked in the same place for four years until you show up for another roll in the hay?"

"I don't know what I expected," said Nathan, "but not this. When I was here before, you said I was welcome anytime, and I sure as hell don't see any welcome. As for the roll in the hay, I don't have to come to Denver for that. There are other women equipped just as well as you, but without your high-toned, prissy attitude."

He had his hand on the knob of the door when she took hold of his cartridge belt. He turned around, prepared for he knew not what, and she threw her arms around him. Before he could utter a word, she kissed him on the lips, long and hard.

"Melanie Gavin," he said, when she finally let him go, "I purely don't understand you."

"I meant what I said about you being welcome," she said. "I just had the foolish idea I'd see you a little more often than once every four years."

"I've been to hell and back since I was here," said Nathan, "and it was a long, hard ride. I see you put the time to better use than I did."

"You said you'd prefer that I didn't prance around naked in a saloon," Melanie said, "and I got to thinking about that. I saved every dollar I could, and six months ago I was able to buy a half interest in this place."

"Who owns the other half?"

"Bella DeCarlo," said Melanie. "She inherited it from her husband, Anton. He was shot last year, after he was caught slickdealing."

"He deserved it," Nathan said. "Hell, the odds always favor the house. You don't have to cheat."

"That's what Bella believes," said Melanie. "We have a standing offer of fifty dollars to anyone who can prove our house dealers are cheating."

"That being the case," Nathan said, "I reckon I'll set in on one of your high-stakes games. That'll give me plenty of time for a look at those naked women."

"Look but don't touch," said Melanie. "Bella takes over at nine o'clock. If you're still around, you can escort me to my boardinghouse and we'll talk about old times."

"I'll be here," Nathan said, "but if we get too deep in those old times, there'll be a lot more than just talk."

"There'd better be," said Melanie, "after a four-year wait."

Nathan sat in on several games of five-card stud and saw no evidence of cheating. He consistently won more than he lost, and by the time Melanie was ready to leave, he was ahead more than three hundred dollars.

"I've improved my living conditions," Melanie said as they walked to the nearby boardinghouse. "I now have a kitchen and I can make breakfast in the morning."

"It's tempting," said Nathan, "but I've already rented a room, and Empty's there. He's skittish with all the fireworks going. They remind him of gunshots, and he's learned that generally means somebody gets hurt."

"After midnight, it'll be July fourth," Melanie said, "and there'll really be some noise, so why don't we get the poor dog and bring him to my place? Then you can stay the night, and I promise I can feed both of you better than any cafe."

"You've convinced me," said Nathan. "With that kind of offer, we'll stay tomorrow night as well. I want some more of that high-stakes poker. I came out three hundred ahead tonight."

"Damn it, I share my bed with you, feed you, and then you take my money. All men are selfish brutes, taking advantage of women."

"Usually with an almighty lot of cooperation from the women," Nathan said.

She laughed as he took her hand, and they headed for Nathan's hotel room, where Empty waited.

Indian Territory
July 5, 1880

Leaving Mobeetie, Wes Tremayne watched his backtrail. Soon there would be a stage from Dodge bound for Fort Griffin, and Wes didn't wish to be recognized by the driver or the man riding shotgun. Having seen a map of the Southwest in Foster Hagerman's office, he rode eastward, knowing he would eventually reach Dallas or Fort Worth. He soon became aware of wagon tracks leading in the same general direction as he was riding. There were other tracks as well, for six horsemen—three on each side—accompanied the wagon. The terrain became more rugged and Wes wasn't surprised when he came upon the abandoned wagon. There were no teams, and apparently the occupants of the hapless wagon had mounted the mules or horses and had ridden away. But beyond the wagon, a man lay face down, the back of his homespun shirt a mass of blood. Wes dismounted, and seeking a pulse, found none. The man was dead, and from his brogan shoes, Wes believed he had been at the reins of the animals drawing the wagon. That explained why the wagon had left the level plain and entered the dense woods. The mounted riders had taken it, probably at gunpoint. Had the dead man been alone, or had others—perhaps a woman with children—been taken captive by the killers? Wes Tremayne was faced with a dilemma. While this was none of his business, could he in good conscience ride away? Despite his hating to attend church, much of its teaching had remained with him, and he recalled the parable of the Good Samaritan. If innocent people were being held captive by thieves and killers, he could not in good conscience leave them to their fate. He checked his Winchester and then his Colt, thumbing a sixth shell into the empty chamber. He then rode cautiously on, unable to see more than an occasional track to assure him he hadn't lost the trail. Suddenly a horse nickered, and Wes leaned forward, seizing the muzzle of his own mount before it could respond. He dismounted, leading his horse back the way he had come. There he tied it, hoping it wasn't close enough to betray him. He carried the Winchester in his left hand, and kept his right near his thonged-down Colt. The camp, when he found it, was next to a spring, and as he had feared, there were two women captives. Wes decided they were probably mother and daughter, and they apparently hadn't been harmed. Yet. He moved closer but couldn't see all the men. He counted five. Where was the sixth?

"Drop the rifle," said a cold, deadly voice from behind him, "and then, with finger and thumb, ease that Colt out and let it fall."

Denver, Colorado
July 5, 1880

Nathan remained with Melanie Gavin two nights, and then, difficult as it was, managed to say goodbye. He rode on to the sheriff's office, where he found Sheriff Green about to ride away.

"I'm ready to ride out," Nathan said, "and I promised I'd talk to you first."

"I'm obliged," said Sheriff Green, "but we won't be needing your testimony."

"What about the girl, Kate McDowell?"

"Oh, hell," the sheriff said, "I don't want to talk about it. With Will Blackburn dead, and the bank's money recovered, the judge turned the girl loose. She lit out this morning, soon as I let her out of jail."

"Well," Nathan said, "maybe our luck will hold, and we'll never see her again."

Nathan rode south toward New Mexico. El Paso, as he recalled, would be something more than five hundred miles. He had hopes that he might take up residence in some small New Mexican town, allowing him to slip into El Paso occasionally without having to fight the Sandlin gang. Riding late, he reached Pueblo. He knew the dispatcher from his days with the AT & SF, so he and Empty were allowed to spend the night in the bunkhouse at the railroad terminal. After an early breakfast, Nathan rode slightly southwest, knowing he would soon reach the Rio Grande and that he could follow the river directly to Santa Fe. He reached the river early in the day, as the sun bore down with a vengeance. It was hot, even for Colorado.

"Empty," said Nathan, "I'm goin' to picket this horse, strip, and dunk myself in that old river."

Empty lit out downstream, and Nathan waded into the water. It wasn't even waist deep, and it was far from cold. He leaned over and ducked his head under the water, and was knuckling it from his eyes when he saw the girl. Kate McDowell had gathered up his hat, boots, and clothes, and stood there grinning at him.

"Damn you," Nathan shouted, "leave my clothes alone."

"Make me," she shouted back.

But Nathan had an ace in the hole. Snarling like a rabid lobo, Empty sprang at Kate, tumbling her down the bank and into the river. Nathan wasted no time getting to her, and she came after him like a spitting, clawing devil. She was unbelievably strong, and Nathan was at a disadvantage because he was stark naked. She raked him with her fingernails, and in the shallow water, managed to drive a knee into his groin. He seized the front of her shirt, and her attempts to break loose ripped all the buttons off. Taking a wild swing, she drove her right fist into Nathan's nose, and for a moment the pain and the blood all but blinded him. Stumbling backward he fell and his head went under. Seizing his hair, she lifted his head clear of the water. He came up sputtering and choking and glared at her, and she let go of him. When he managed to get to his knees, she laughed.

"Damn it," he choked, "why didn't you just go ahead and drown me?"

"You wouldn't have been much use to me dead," she replied.

"By God," he snarled, "you've got more brass than a whorehouse bed. I don't aim to be of any use to you, alive or dead."

Ignoring her, he fished around in the water until he found his boots. Pouring the water from them, he threw them out on the river bank. His hat, trousers, and shirt were floating downstream, and he went after them. When he neared the river bank, exhausted, he couldn't believe his eyes. She had removed her boots and her mutilated shirt, and was stepping out of her dripping Levi's.

"Let's call a truce," she said. "At least until we dry out."

Too angry for words, Nathan just glared at her. He seized his sodden trousers, shook the clinging leaves and grass from them, and began getting dressed.

CHAPTER 15

Wes Tremayne was fully aware of his precarious position. Whatever else these six men were, they were obviously killers. He dropped his Winchester and slowly lifted his Colt from the holster and let it fall.

"Now," said his captor, "walk straight ahead and don't do nothin' foolish."

Wes walked into the outlaw camp, and the five outlaws got to their feet.

"Found this varmint spyin' on the camp," said the man behind Wes. "I would of shot him, but he don't look old enough to be the law."

"Hell, Carlyle," one of the men said, "he ain't old enough to shave. You should of looked around some. His mama may be out there lookin' for him."

The outlaw who appeared to be the leader of the band carried two Colts in a tied-down *buscadera* rig, with a third under his belt. It was he who spoke.

"Moody, you and Carlyle thong his hands and feet until we decide what to do with him. Doak, you and Sellers find his horse and backtrail him. He may not be alone."

"He ain't of no use to us, Pierce," said one of the outlaws. "Why not just shoot him and be done with it?"

"By God, Burris, I'm givin' the orders," Pierce said.

One of the other outlaws, Moody, joined Carlyle, and Wes soon had his hands bound behind him. Carlyle shoved him down on the ground near the two women, and then bound his ankles. He was left there with nothing to do but study the captive women. They had not been bound. One of them was no more than a girl, perhaps in her late teens. Her eyes were on Wes, while the older woman appeared not to see him. Her bonnet hung to one side, and the front of her dress had been ripped to the waist. Embarrassed, Wes tried to turn away, but he couldn't ignore the woman.

"Ma'am," he said, speaking to the older woman, "have either of you been hurt?"

The distraught woman stared ahead, saying nothing. In a trembling voice, it was the girl who finally spoke.

"They ... they murdered my father, right before our eyes. Mother fought them and they ... beat her ... humiliated her ..."

"Did they ...?"

Wes couldn't bring himself to say the word, but the girl understood. She blushed, but she was game.

"No, but ... they ... you can see what ... they did ... but ... something happened. She can't .. won't talk ... not even to me ..."

Wes thought he understood. While at the orphanage, he had witnessed a brutal fight between two older boys. One of them had been armed with a knife and had mutilated his opponent to the extent that a female teacher had fainted. For many days she had remained in shock, unable to speak.

"She's in shock," said Wes. "The mind kind of closes, shuttin' out the painful things we wish we had never seen."

"I ... I didn't know," the girl said. "I didn't know ... what to do ... what I should do ..."

"Nothing," said Wes, "as long as it's light, and they're watching. But we must escape or they'll kill us, and I don't aim for that to happen. I'm Wes Tremayne."

"We're the Tuttles," the girl replied. "My mother's name is Emily, and I'm Rebecca."

"Rebecca," said Wes, "if they let us live until dark—if you can free my hands—I'll get us out of this."

"Oh, if you only could," she whispered. "They have whiskey, and I ... I heard them say they have plans for ... Mother and me."

"I reckon they'll have to be close to drunk to do ... what they got in mind," said Wes. "Get me loose ... let me get my hands on a gun ... and I'll see that you come to no harm."

"I will," Rebecca whispered. "Oh, somehow I will."

Doak and Sellers returned, and Wes sighed. They had found his horse.

"We backtrailed him all the way back into Texas," said Doak. "Nobody's with him."

"Well, now," Pierce said, "it's time he answered some questions. Who are you, kid, and why was you follerin' us?"

"I'm Wes Tremayne, and I wasn't followin' you. I was

ridin' this way when I found I was near your camp. I wanted to see where you were, so I could pass you by and keep on riding."

"Haw, haw, haw," said Carlyle. "This just ain't your day. You should of knowed, when you seen that dead hombre, you was gettin' in over your head. Now there ain't but one way to silence you permanent."

"Carlyle," Pierce snapped, "shut your mouth."

Wes didn't know what to make of the situation. Four of the outlaws mounted up and rode out, leaving Sellers and Carlyle in camp.

"This could be our chance," said Wes quietly.

"No talkin'," Carlyle shouted.

The two outlaws fixed their eyes on their three captives, and Wes was forced to keep his silence lest he arouse their suspicions. Rebecca dared not attempt to free his hands as long as their captors watched them so closely. Then Wes had an idea.

"Hey," he shouted, "I'm thirsty. One of you bring me some water."

"Go to hell," said Carlyle. "You got your hands tied behind you, and I ain't about to hold the cup while you drink. I ain't your mama."

"Tie my hands in front of me, so I can hold the cup myself," Wes said. "Unless both of you are afraid I'll escape, with you lookin' at me."

"Carlyle," said Sellers, "keep the mouthy bastard covered. I'll tie his hands in front long enough for him to wet his whistle."

Sellers loosed the rawhide thongs. Wes allowed his wrists to be bound in front of him and Sellers brought him a tin cup of water. Wes made no move to drink the water until Sellers had backed away and joined Carlyle. He then raised the cup to his lips, pretending to drink, while spilling most of the water on his rawhide bonds. When the cup was empty, he set it down and rolled over on his side, his back to the outlaws.

"Git up, Sellers," said Carlyle, "and tie his hands behind him. This was your idea."

"He ain't goin' nowhere," Sellers said.

But Wes was working his wrists against the wet rawhide, and it began to give. There was a chance the rest of the outlaws would return before dark and simply shoot him. If he managed to free himself from his bonds, there was still the women to consider, and his odds against six armed men were impossibly high. While Rebecca was willing to help him, she was being watched. He must free himself and get possession of a gun. Time was running out.

"Sellers," said Carlyle, "you better tie that hombre's hands behind his back. If Pierce comes back and finds him like that, he'll skin you."

"I'm gettin' damned tired of Pierce orderin' me around," Sellers said. "You'd think this is the army and he's got all the brass."

But Wes could hear him coming, and he managed to free his hands of the stretched rawhide. Wes moved like a striking rattler, seizing Sellers's legs and slamming him to the ground. Sellers had the wind knocked out of him, allowing Wes time to grab his revolver. He swung the weapon as hard as he could against the outlaw's head, and Sellers went limp. Carlyle fired, but he had a poor target, for Sellers's limp body was between him and Wes. Though Carlyle missed, when Wes Tremayne fired, the slug went true. Carlyle dropped his gun and, stumbling back against a tree, clung to it for support. But he had been hard hit, and he slid to the ground, where he lay unmoving. Wes was working frantically at the thongs that bound his ankles.

"Oh, what can I do to help?" Rebecca cried frantically.

"Try to get through to your mother," said Wes. "We have to make a run for it. You have only as long as it takes me to saddle the horses."

"But she . . . she doesn't ride," Rebecca said.

"She's going to, this once," said Wes. "Both of you will ride one horse, and it'll be up to you to see that she doesn't fall off. I'll have to be free to watch our backtrail."

Sellers was beginning to stir, so, using the thongs that had bound his own ankles, Wes tied the outlaw's hands behind his back. Quickly Wes retrieved his own Colt and Winchester and saddled his horse. To his dismay, he found Emily Tuttle unchanged, despite all of Rebecca's pleading.

"Leave her be," said Wes. "I'll saddle a horse, and when you're mounted, I'll lift her up. You'll have to hold her in place so she won't fall."

Rebecca Tuttle said nothing, but she was game. There were no tears, and she didn't seem afraid. When Wes had the horse saddled, he helped Rebecca to mount, but when he took Emily's arm, all hell broke loose. The woman fought him like a crazed animal; having no choice, he knocked her unconscious.

"Did you have to do that?" Rebecca asked angrily.

"No," said Wes. "I could have left her to the outlaws. Help me get her astraddle of the horse. We may not have much time."

Neither of the women were dressed for riding, and their long skirts were hiked well above their knees.

"Just hold her in place," Wes said. "I'll take the reins of the horse."

Wes led out, riding south. He believed the four outlaws had business in Mobeetie, and he dared not ride in that direction, lest he meet them returning. He quickly learned his fears were well founded. There was a thud of horses' hooves and shouting close behind them.

"They're coming after us!" Rebecca cried fearfully.

"Here," said Wes. "Take the reins of the horse and keep going. Maybe I can slow 'em down. I'll catch up to you."

"Oh, please be careful," she said. "There are so many of them."

"Maybe not for long," said Wes. Swiftly he drew the Winchester from the saddle boot and led his horse into a concealing thicket.

"We're gainin' on 'em," Pierce shouted. "Spread out."

Just for a second, Pierce was visible, and Wes fired. As the outlaw slid over the rump of the horse, Wes fired at the next rider.

"Hell's fire," one of the outlaws shouted. "He's shot Pierce and Moody. Get him!"

"Get him yourself," came an answering shout. "He's kilt two men with two shots."

There was the sound of retreating hoofbeats, and Wes couldn't believe his good fortune. Leading his horse, he continued in the direction the two women had gone. He was about to mount when the animal nickered, and from somewhere ahead, there was an answer. Groaning inwardly, he had his suspicions confirmed when he came upon the two women, neither of whom were on the horse.

"I tried to hold her," Rebecca said, "but she took to fighting me and slid off. I just couldn't get her back on the horse. She's too much for me."

Emily Tuttle lay on the ground, her volumnous skirt up to her armpits, her mad eyes on Wes.

"It's ... it's like she's lost her mind," said Rebecca. "What are we going to do?"

"I'm goin' to tie her hands and feet," Wes said, "and tote her belly down in front of me. Then we'll circle around and try to get back to Mobeetie without another fight with what's left of that bunch of outlaws."

"I heard the shooting," said Rebecca. "Did you ... ?"

"I got two of them," Wes said. "The others may have given up on us."

"That was the bravest thing I ever saw," she said. "How can I ever thank you?"

"You don't owe me any thanks," said Wes. "They were aimin' to kill me and I saved my own hide. We still have to get you and Miss Emily to the sheriff at Mobeetie, or to Fort Elliott. If nothing else, the army can see that you're taken back to ..."

"Ohio," the girl finished. "But we have nothing there. My father's family disowned him when he sold everything we owned to come west."

"Your mother—"

"Is an orphan," said Rebecca. "Her parents are dead, and I've never heard her speak of anyone else. I'm afraid she's lost her mind. What am I going to do with her?"

"I don't know," Wes said. "You said your father sold out in Ohio. Didn't he leave you *something?*"

"Why do you think those men killed him?" she snapped, exasperated. "He had all our funds sent to the bank in Dodge City. We took the train that far, and after he closed out our account with the bank, he bought the wagon, teams, and supplies."

"The outlaws took your measure and followed you from there," said Wes. "If all this hadn't happened, where were you going?"

"South Texas. Father had dreams of owning a cattle ranch."

Emily Tuttle had calmed down, the madness having gone out of her eyes. They now seemed dull, uncaring.

"Ma'am," said Wes, his hand on Emily Tuttle's arm, "you'll have to ride the horse."

"No," she said. "Albert will bring the wagon."

"My father's name was Albert," Rebecca whispered.

"Ma'am," said Wes, as kindly as he could, "Albert's dead."

"No," she screamed, "no!"

She threw herself at him, but he got out of her way. She lay face down, sobbing with an intensity that shocked Wes. Chills crept up his spine, and when he looked at Rebecca, it seemed she was about to break from the strain. Tears crept down her cheeks, leaving the look in her eyes as forlorn as that in the distraught Emily's.

"Ma'am," said Wes, "if you won't ride the horse, we'll have to leave you here alone."

While he was unable to explain to Rebecca what he had in mind, she quickly caught on and did her part. Wes helped her to mount the horse, and he then mounted his own. Not looking back, they rode away, quickly losing themselves in surrounding brush.

"No," Emily Tuttle cried, struggling to her feet, "don't leave me!"

Wes reined up and dismounted. When the frightened woman reached them, he helped her up onto his horse. He then mounted behind her and they began their roundabout journey back to Mobeetie.

Ignoring the brazen woman who had just removed her sodden clothes, Nathan dragged on his still dripping boots. Without fully turning his back on her, he cautiously made his way to his horse, mounted, and rode away. Kate Mc-Dowell—if that was her name—had tried to kill him. It seemed that, with Will Blackburn dead, she had illusions about some kind of relationship between herself and Nathan Stone. He shuddered and rode south along the Rio Grande as Empty trotted along behind.

Santa Fe, New Mexico
July 8, 1880

Nathan found a room for the night and then went looking for a mercantile. There he bought several pair of Levi's, new shirts and socks, and a tin of grease. Thanks to the vengeful woman who threw his clothes into the river, his boots must be thoroughly greased lest they stiffen beyond endurance. Nathan sat on the hotel bed, working the grease into the leather of the stiffened boots, while Empty sat near the window watching.

"Thank God you jumped her, old son," said Nathan, speaking to the dog. "I believe she was about to ride away with my boots and clothes, leavin' my jaybird naked out there on the plains."

But the more he thought of Kate McDowell, the more of an enigma she became, for within his saddlebags there had been hundreds of dollars in double eagles. If she had really wanted to cause him grief, why hadn't she simply taken his horse, leaving him afoot and virtually broke? Of course, she hadn't known about the money, and if she had, Nathan was inclined to believe her interest was in him. He thought of her without the rough clothing and decided that with a bit of finery she would be an attractive woman.

"Damn it," he said aloud, "that's what she wanted me to think."

Empty canted his head, lolling his tongue as though laughing at Nathan's dilemma. Nathan continued in silence until he had worked most of the grease into his boots, then stomped his feet into them and donned his hat.

"Come on, pard," he said to the dog, "and let's get some town grub. Maybe a slab of apple pie will sweeten my disposition."

Nathan did feel better after eating, and he bought a copy of the town's twice-weekly newspaper and headed back to his room. The entire front page had been devoted to a single story, headlined "The Lincoln County War." Nathan had heard of it and of its most prominent participant, a young hellion known as Billy the Kid. Removing his hat, gunbelt, and boots, he stretched out on the bed while Empty curled up on the throw rug.

According to the newspaper, the "war" was actually a deeply rooted feud that had arisen from cattle rustling, rivalry over choice grazing, litigation over the settling of an estate, and the meddling of unscrupulous politicians seeking to use the Tunstall-McSween-Murphy feud for their own ends.

Nathan read the story with interest, for he wondered how Billy the Kid—no more than a young boy—had come to play so prominent a part in the conflict. The violence had begun early in 1878 with the killing of John Tunstall, an

English-born rancher. Unarmed, Tunstall had been gunned down by members of a deputy sheriff's posse. At least four known outlaws had ridden with the posse, and they had been more interested in killing the unarmed victim than in enforcing the law. One of those with Tunstall when he had been shot had been the youth who had made himself a reputation as Billy the Kid. The Kid, a slender, buck-toothed boy of about eighteen, had already been a fugitive from the law. He had hired on as a range hand and had been with Tunstall only a short time. Tunstall had given the kid a good horse, a saddle, and a new gun. Billy had been quick to learn, and had been genuinely fond of his employer.

As the newspaper pointed out, little was known of the Kid's early life. The time and place of his birth were uncertain, and his original name appeared to have been Henry McCarty. The earliest record of his family had been the remarriage of his mother, Mrs. Catherine McCarty, to William Antrim. The wedding had taken place on March 1, 1873, at Santa Fe. The Antrims and the two McCarty boys, Henry and Joe, went to live in Silver City, New Mexico. But less than a year after her remarriage, Mrs. Antrim died from a lung ailment. After her death, Henry—then known as the Kid—ran wild, and near Fort Grant, Pima County, Arizona, he shot and killed his first man. A coroner's jury called the shooting "criminal and unjustifiable," forcing the Kid to skip the county. Reaching Lincoln County, New Mexico, the young gunman had assumed the name of William Bonney and had gone to work for John Tunstall.

As the story unfolded, Nathan found himself more and more in sympathy with the boy known as William Bonney, alias Billy the Kid. After the murder of Tunstall, Billy had set out to take vengeance on the killers, who, having been in the sheriff's posse, had not been prosecuted. On the morning of April 1, 1878, Sheriff William Brady and his deputy, George Hindman, had been shot and killed in broad daylight while walking on the main street of Lincoln. Billy the Kid had been one of several accused of the crime, and Lincoln County had offered a reward of two hundred dollars for each of the killers.

Three days after the killing of the lawmen, Andrew Roberts, a member of the posse that had killed Tunstall, rode into town. Hearing of the rewards, the heavily armed man had set out for Blazer's Mill, where he was told the killers of Brady and Hindman might be. As he neared the mill, he met a party of riders that included Billy the Kid. The men ordered Roberts to surrender, but he refused, and Charles Bowdre—one of Billy's companions—shot Roberts. Dying, Roberts shot three of his assailants. George Coe and John Middleton were wounded, while Richard Brewer, the young man who had been foreman on Tunstall's ranch, was killed.

On April 18, a grand jury indicted Bowdre, Billy the Kid, and several others for the killing of Andrew Roberts. The indictment also charged Billy and two others for the killing of Brady and Hindman. The following day, the Kid appeared in court and pleaded not guilty. Following his appearance, a minor revolution rocked Lincoln County, and not until April 14, 1879, did the Kid come to trial. Sheriff Brady had been a member of the Murphy faction, and following Murphy's death, the McSween followers had held an unauthorized election and installed a new sheriff sympathetic to their interests. But the Murphy bunch appealed to the governor of the territory, who appointed a Murphy man to the position. Returned to power, the Murphy faction set out to arrest Billy the Kid and crush the McSween group. The newly appointed Murphy sheriff and his posse— aided by hired gunmen brought in from other counties— found Billy in July 1878 with his McSween followers in Lincoln. The showdown came for the Murphy and the Tunstall–McSween riders, who had been led by McSween since Tunstall's death.

"My God," said Nathan aloud, "it beats all I ever heard."

But there was much more. After two days of ineffectual shooting in town, Billy and his friends had been driven into and trapped in the McSween residence. Late in the afternoon of the third day—July nineteenth—the Murphy posse set fire to one wing of the adobe house. As the fire crept toward them, the defenders blazed away with their guns while Mrs. McSween played the piano. During the fight, Deputy Sheriff Robert Beckwith of the Murphy clan was killed, and four of the embattled defenders, including McSween himself, met similar fates. As darkness settled over Lincoln, Billy the Kid ran from the house and escaped into the night. Later that night, the posse became part of a mob that broke into the Tunstall–McSween store and robbed it of some six thousand dollars worth of goods.

With both Tunstall and McSween dead, the Murphy faction was victorious, and Billy the Kid had become an outlaw on several murder charges. But news of the bloody vendetta reached Washington, and President Rutherford B. Hayes appointed General Lew Wallace as acting governor of New Mexico, with instructions to bring peace. Wallace immediately issued an amnesty proclamation, and Billy, gun in hand, had met the general alone in a designated place. A reconciliation failed because two of Billy's deadly enemies—aided my Murphy sympathizers—had broken jail. Protecting himself, Billy the Kid rode away.

"Damn them," Nathan said, "They'll never let him out of it alive. He'll be murdered in the name of the law."

Acting Governor Wallace had appointed Oden Wilder as sheriff of Lincoln County, with authority to deputize as many men as he needed to arrest those who had participated in the feud. Every man so deputized would be paid a hundred dollars a month and provided with ammunition for Winchester and Colt. There was a hand-drawn map of Lincoln County, and Nathan was struck with its nearness to El Paso.

"Empty," said Nathan, "Sheriff Wilder needs some hombres in that posse that don't kill without cause. I reckon we'll ride down there and lend a hand for a while."

His horse carrying double, Wes Tremayne took his time. Thankfully, Rebecca Tuttle rode well, and Wes had only to concern himself with Emily. Hoping to avoid the remaining three outlaws, Wes rode south for what he believed was ten miles. He then veered west, and they soon were out of Indian Territory. Rebecca trotted her horse abreast of his.

"I'm glad we're back on the open plains," Rebecca said. "It seemed so gloomy and kind of forbidding back there, like something was ... waiting ..."

"Indian Territory," said Wes. "I've heard a lot about it, but nothing good."

Little was said during the ride back to Mobeetie, Texas. James McIntire, the little town's new sheriff, listened attentively while Wes explained what had happened.

"My God," McIntire said, "you tangled with the Eck Pierce gang and killed Pierce?"

"He saved Mother and me," said Rebecca.

"Four of the bunch rode out," Wes said. "I reckoned they had business here."

"They did," said McIntire. "I rode over to Fort Elliott, and while I was there they robbed a saloon and killed a man."

"You didn't try to catch them?" Rebecca asked.

"Ma'am," said McIntire, "besides me, there's eight men in Mobeetie, and not one of them would follow me into Indian Territory."

"No help from the army, I reckon," Wes said.

"None," said McIntire. "Half a dozen men with Winchesters could hole up down there in the territory and gun down a whole company of soldiers."

"Sheriff," Wes said, "freeing these ladies from Pierce and his outlaws might have been the easy part. Mr. Tuttle is dead, they have no place to go, and Miss Emily is clean out of her head."

"I fully agree with you," said McIntire, "and it's more than I can handle. I suggest you ride to Fort Elliott and talk to the post commander, Captain Selman."

Wes could understand McIntire's reluctance to become involved in the situation. It wouldn't be any easier for the post commander, but he wouldn't have much choice. They rode on to Fort Elliott, and Wes asked for a meeting with Captain Selman.

"Captain Selman will see you now," said Sergeant Willard.

The three of them were shown into Selman's office, and the captain listened as Wes told him what had happened. He concluded with an explanation of Emily Tuttle's condition.

"We have no facilities for treatment here," Captain Selman said. "I can have the post doctor examine her."

"How is that goin' to help," Wes asked.

"I don't know that it will," said Captain Selman. "I'm at as much a loss as you are, and I'm suggesting this because I don't know what else to do. There's a comfortable sofa in the next room. I'll send for the doctor."

Rebecca led Mrs. Tuttle into the adjoining room and had her lie down on the sofa. A table and chairs completed the furnishings. Hanging from a peg on the wall was a gunbelt and holster, and within the holster was a revolver. Closing the door behind her, Rebecca returned to Captain Selman's office. Within a few minutes, Sergeant Dillard returned with the post doctor.

"This is our post doctor, Lieutenant Carlton," Captain Selman said. "Miss Tuttle, if you'll tell him—"

But Selman was interrupted by a shot from the next room, and when he flung the door open, Rebecca screamed. Emily Tuttle still lay on the sofa, but her face was gone. In a pool of blood on the floor lay the revolver.

CHAPTER 16

Lincoln County, New Mexico
July 10, 1880

Sheriff Oden Wilder eyed Nathan with suspicion. Finally he spoke.

"You're not from around here, and you're not partial to the Tunstall, McSween, or Murphy factions."

"No," Nathan replied.

"Then what's your interest?"

"A hundred dollars a month," said Nathan. "That, and the fact that I have some time on my hands."

"Not wanted by the law?"

"No," Nathan replied. "I've had some experience working for the law. I rode for the court out of Fort Smith, Arkansas for a few months, and you're welcome to telegraph the Texas Ranger outposts at San Antonio, Austin, or Houston. They know me well. And if that's not enough, telegraph Captain Ferguson, the post commander at Fort Worth."

"I reckon that won't be necessary," said Wilder. "Part of the problem here is that we have had men riding under the authority of the law who were sympathetic to the Tunstall, McSween, or Murphy bunch. The acting governor has demanded that the killing stop, and that means enforcing the law against any of the three hell-raising elements involved."

"All three factions are still active?" Nathan asked.

"Yes and no," said Sheriff Wilder. "The Murphy bunch is pretty well intact, but with Tunstall and McSween dead, their followers seem to have banded together under the leadership of William Bonney, also known as Billy the Kid."

"Those who are still alive are fugitives, then," Nathan said.

"Not necessarily," said Sheriff Wilder. "We intend to

prosecute those who robbed the Tunstall–McSween store, provided there's sufficient evidence. This bunch, we believe, are part of the Murphy outfit. The remnants of the Tunstall and McSween factions are pretty well united behind Billy, and they're supporting themselves by stealing horses and cattle. They're all subject to arrest by whatever means may be necessary."

"I hope you haven't issued John Doe execution warrants," said Nathan. "I won't ride under the kind of law that permits killing a man for the sake of a reward, without proper identification."

"Neither will I," Sheriff Wilder said, "and I'm pleased you feel that strongly. There's been entirely too much killing in the name of the law. I'll swear you in."

Wilder administered the brief oath, and from a desk drawer took a silver star.

"I'll need a hotel or boardinghouse where my dog's welcome," said Nathan.

"We have an arrangement with the Santa Fe House," Sheriff Wilder said. "You'll get room and board for a single price. Here's a letter identifying you as a legal representative of this office. Use it to secure your room at the hotel, and to requisition your shells at Elmo's Mercantile."

The Santa Fe House, a two-story structure, proved to be a better-than-average hotel, with its own restaurant. Across the street was a livery and an all-night cafe. Nathan was assigned a room on the first floor, and as he and Empty were about to enter the room, a door opened across the hall. A man stepped out, and Empty growled, his hackles rising.

"I don't like dogs," the stranger said, his hand near the butt of his revolver.

"I reckon it balances out, then," said Nathan mildly. "My dog doesn't like you."

"I'm Slack Tarno, deputy sheriff, part of Sheriff Wilder's posse, and I'm sayin' that damn scruffy hound don't belong in this hotel."

"I'm Nathan Stone, deputy sheriff, part of Sheriff's Wilder's posse, and the dog goes where I go. My temper's on a short rein. Any hostility toward my dog, and I'll be takin' it personal."

Tarno stomped on down the hall toward the lobby, and

Nathan noted he carried twin Colts in a *buscadera* rig, both holsters thonged down.

Half an hour before suppertime, in an arrangement with the hotel, Nathan took Empty to the kitchen, where the cooks fed him.

"Sorry, pardner," said Nathan to the dog, "but we won't be takin' our meals together for a while."

The men Sheriff Wilder had deputized were on call twenty-four hours a day, requiring them to remain in a single location so they could be mounted and on the trail in a matter of minutes. So for the sake of unity, Nathan would take his meals in the hotel's restaurant, something he seldom did. He returned Empty to their room, washed up, and made his way to the hotel's dining room.

"You deputies have been assigned those two big round tables, over yonder next to the wall," one of the cooks told Nathan. "Your order will be taken immediately."

There were eight chairs at each of the round tables. Five men were already seated at one, while three were seated at the other. Nathan took a chair at the table with the trio, for Slack Tarno was seated at the other. Nathan's companions seemed amiable enough, and they introduced themselves.

"I'm Tuck McFadden," said one.

"I'm Bib Driscoll," said the second.

"I'm Warren Hinderman," said the third.

"I'm Nathan Stone," Nathan said, shaking their hands.

Within minutes, three more men took chairs at the table. They were Tobe Crump, Beal Pryor, and Stub Byler. Nathan introduced himself and shook their hands. A sixth man had taken a chair at the second table.

"My God," said Tuck McFadden, "there's thirteen of us. An unlucky number."

"Sorry," Nathan said. "Does anybody know how many deputies will be hired?"

"Nobody's told us," said Bib Driscoll. "There was a dozen of us ahead of you, and we heard rumors that Wilder's been given permission to hire as many as twenty men."

"That's one hell of a big posse," Nathan said.

"This is one hell of a big county," said Driscoll, "and it's in one hell of a big mess. I won't be surprised if we have to split into two or three groups."

Conversation ceased while the waiters took orders. That done, men from the second table, with the exception of Slack Tarno, got up and introduced themselves to Nathan. There was Bode Watts, Peavy Burris, Neil Sutton, Rand Dismukes, and Simpson Dumont. They all seemed friendly enough, and Nathan didn't foresee any trouble, but Slack Tarno wasn't one to leave well enough alone. When he spoke, it was loud enough for everybody in the restaurant to hear.

"Stone's got this ugly hound dog that lives with him. I'm surprised he ain't got the varmint in a chair, hiked up to the table."

"I considered it," said Nathan, "but I reckoned you'd be here. He's almighty picky about who he sets down to eat with."

"That's sound thinkin'," McFadden said. "Set him down next to Tarno, and he's likely to get fleas."

"Yeah," said Driscoll, "an' God only knows what else he might catch."

Except for Tarno, everybody within hearing roared with laughter, and there was more fun at Tarno's expense. Tarno tried to ignore them, his smoldering eyes concentrating all their hatred on Nathan. The rest of the men, seeing and understanding Tarno's reaction, said no more, and conversation lagged. When the waiters brought the food, the meal was eaten in silence. Tarno was the first to finish and the first to leave the dining room.

"I reckon we shouldn't of baited him," said McFadden. "He purely don't like you, Stone, and if looks could kill, this would be your buryin' day."

"He'd already decided he didn't like me," Nathan said, "and none of you had anything to do with that. We had words in the hall after my dog growled at him."

"Hell, you can't blame the dog," said Tobe Crump. "Nobody else likes him, either. If what he says means anything, he used to be a bounty hunter, and I never knowed one that had any feelin' for anything or anybody."

"He seems like the wrong kind of man for a sheriff's posse," Nathan said. "From the little I know about the situation here, most of the violence started after some known outlaws in a sheriff's posse shot and killed John McSween."

"You got the straight of it," said Bib Driscoll, "and I

won't be surprised if this Slack Tarno is of the same stripe. There's already been word that the governor's goin' to raise the price on the heads of Billy and them ridin' with him."

"Somebody should talk to Sheriff Wilder about Tarno," Nathan said. "He didn't strike me as the kind of man who'd hire bounty hunters."

"I reckon he personally don't favor it," said Driscoll, "but Tarno ain't from around here, and Sheriff Wilder ain't had that many men to choose from. As I understand it, the governor warned him against hirin' anybody from these parts, lest we end up with some grudge killers like them four that gunned down John Tunstall."

"There's an election in November," Warren Hinderman said. "After that, Wilder will be out, and somebody else will be in."

"Who's favored to win?" Nathan asked.

"Unless things change," said Tobe Crump, "a gent name of Pat Garrett will take it by default. Lincoln County's in such a godawful mess, I reckon nobody else wants it."*

"Yeah," Tuck McFadden said, "and from what I hear, Garrett and Billy the Kid used to be friendly toward one another. Garrett could disband the posse, sendin' us all on our way."

"So a sheriff friendly to Billy could be elected," said Nathan.

"It's possible," Tuck McFadden said. "Tunstall and McSween had a lot of friends here in Lincoln County. Probably enough of them to elect a sheriff, and likely all or most of them sympathetic to the Kid."

Fort Elliott, Texas
July 10, 1880

The post doctor entered the room and closed the door. Rebecca Tuttle threw her arms around Wes and wept with great soul-wrenching sobs. Captain Selman took a seat in his big leather chair, rested his elbows on his desk, and waited. Slowly Rebecca's sobs trailed off into sniffles and she stepped back, knuckling tears from her eyes.

*Pat Garrett was elected sheriff of Lincoln County, New Mexico in November 1880.

"I-I'm sorry," she said. "It-was-such a shock."

"It was," Selman agreed. "What happened out there . . . that could have led her to do . . . this? Did those men . . . abuse her?"

"No," said Rebecca. "They ripped the front of her dress, but it . . . wasn't that. All her life, she's been close to my father. She saw him shot to death before her eyes and she . . . just seemed to . . . lose her mind."

At that point, the post doctor stepped back into the room, closing the door behind him. When he spoke, it was to Captain Selman.

"Sir, in her obviously distraught condition, it was a mistake, leaving her alone in that room with a loaded weapon."

"Lieutenant," Captain Selman snapped, "I am now fully aware of that. I am sorry that I failed to understand the extent of the damage to her mind. That's why I sent for you."

"Please," said Rebecca. "If this is anybody's fault, it's mine. I should have stayed in there with her, but I never thought . . . I had no way of knowing . . . she would do . . . this."

There came a knock at the door and when Captain Selman granted permission to enter, Sergeant Willard stepped in.

"Sir," Willard said, "there was a shot—"

"Yes, Sergeant," said Captain Selman. "Mrs. Tuttle is dead by her own hand. We must file a report on this. Doctor, will you return with him to the orderly room and help him to prepare the necessary papers?"

"Yes, sir," the lieutenant said, and he departed with Sergeant Willard.

"Miss Tuttle," said Captain Selman, "unless you wish otherwise, I'll see that she is prepared for burial in the post cemetery. I recommend a closed coffin."

"I'd be grateful, Captain," Rebecca said.

"It's late," said Selman. "I think we should wait until morning for burial. I'll arrange quarters for you for the night."

"Thank you," Rebecca said.

Captain Selman sent a corporal to escort Rebecca to the small cabin. Wes accompanied them and the corporal left them at the door. The cabin was sparsely furnished with a single bunk.

"What about you?" Rebecca asked.

"I'll spread my blankets somewhere outside," said Wes.

"Please ... come in for a while," she begged. "I don't want to be alone."

"I will," said Wes, "but leave the door open."

She looked at him in a strange way, and Wes had a gut feeling she had expected him to stay the night with her. Nervously he sat down in the only chair, while she sat on the narrow bed.

"Wes," she said.

He was forced to look at her, and big silent tears had began rolling down her cheeks.

Wes said nothing, waiting for her to continue. She swallowed hard and continued.

"Wes, I have nowhere to go. What am I going to do?"

"I don't know," said Wes. "Maybe an orphanage ..."

He knew immediately he had said the wrong thing. Her tears increased tenfold, and she threw herself face down on the bed. Quickly Wes closed the door, lest someone passing by think he was mistreating her. Finally she sat up, rubbed her eyes, and looked at him.

"Rebecca," said Wes, "I'm sorry."

"It's not what you think," she said. "It's just that ... it seems to be hopeless. I'd welcome even an orphanage, but I can't have even that. I was eighteen years old just three weeks ago. I'm supposed to be a grown woman, but I ... I don't feel that way. I just feel ... well ... lost. I have nowhere to go and there's little I can do, except cook, wash, and keep house."

"What can I do?" Wes asked. "I'm not even—"

He bit his tongue just shy of saying "fifteen years old," but she caught on.

"Wes, how old are you?"

"Old enough," he said uncomfortably. "You saw me kill three men, and they weren't the first."

"I know," she said, "but you're so ... young. Why, you don't even ... shave."

Wes turned nine shades of red, but before he could open his mouth, she laughed.

"I-I'm sorry," she said, not sounding sorry at all. "It's none of my business."

"You're right," said Wes, choking back his anger, "it's none of your business. I fill a man's boots, I do a man's work, and I can handle a gun. This is the frontier, and anything a man's called on to do, I can do. If you're so damned smart, how old am I?"

"Twelve," she said, with just the hint of a smile.

"Twelve?" he shouted. "Why, I'll be fifteen—"

He got up from the chair and she got up off the bed, and when they met, she kissed him hard on the mouth. He stumbled back and sat down in the chair, lost somewhere between astonishment and embarrassment. Again she laughed, and he shook his head, saying nothing.

"In many ways, you are a man," she said. "I wasn't making fun of you. Actually, I was laughing at myself. I'm alone for the first time in my life, with nowhere to go and nobody to turn to, and I'm afraid. I was about to ask you to take me with you, when you're younger than I am. I have no right to ask you to take on that much responsibility."

"You're sayin' I'm not man enough," said Wes, becoming angry all over again.

"Oh, you're man enough," she replied, "but you're too much the gentleman. It would be asking too much, taking me with you—"

"What in tarnation are you talkin' about?" Wes demanded.

Again she laughed. "My God, are you that simple? You wouldn't come in here with me without leaving the door open, and when I kissed you, you acted like I'd hit you in the head with a sledgehammer. Day in and day out, on the trail, I suppose I could never be sure that, when you most needed to be a man, you'd be a fifteen-year-old boy."

Wes opened his mouth, but words failed him. He got up and stomped out the door, slamming it behind him. Rebecca smiled and, removing her clothes, stretched out on the narrow bunk.

Lincoln County, New Mexico
August 1, 1880

The first call for the sheriff's posse came at four o'clock on Sunday morning, three weeks following Nathan's arrival.

Bib Driscoll awakened the members of the posse. To Nathan's surprise, Sheriff Wilder had put Driscoll in charge.

"Horse thieves hit the Hitchfelt ranch," Driscoll said. "We ride in fifteen minutes."

Thirteen men rode out, Driscoll in the lead. They reached the Hitchfelt ranch to find the house ablaze with light. Hitchfelt met them, a Winchester under his arm.

"Nineteen of my best horses," Hitchfelt moaned, "and they shot one of my riders."

"Did you get a look at any of 'em?" Driscoll asked.

"How the hell would we of done that?" Hitchfelt demanded. "It was dark as the inside of a cow's gullet."

"Well," said Driscoll, "do you have any idea which way they went?"

"South, along the river," Hitchfelt said. "Four of my men was trailin' 'em."

"They're just beggin' for an ambush," said Driscoll. "Why didn't they wait for us?"

"Damn it," Hitchfelt said, "we didn't know how long it'd take you. The varmints is on the way to the border with my horses."

"They may bushwhack your riders and still reach the border," said Driscoll. "Let's ride, men."

Just as first light began to gray the eastern horizon, they rode south. The trail was plain enough and Bib Driscoll's prophecy became grim reality. Before they'd ridden ten miles, they met a riderless horse on its way to the home corral.

"Damn," said Peavy Burris, "they done it, for sure."

When they reached the scene of the ambush, one of the Hitchfelt riders was dead and the remaining three seriously wounded.

"Peavy Burris, Neil Sutton, Rand Dismukes, and Simpson Dumont," Bib Driscoll said. "Get these men back to the Hitchfelt ranch. The rest of us will go after the thieves."

But it soon became evident the posse wasn't going to catch up to the horse thieves. Driscoll reined up and the others gathered their horses around him.

"We ain't more than half a dozen miles from the border," said Driscoll, "and we been told not to cross it. Might as well turn back."

"Turn back, hell," Slack Tarno said. "Who's goin' to

know we crossed the border if we bring the varmints back roped across their saddles?"

"We've been told not to cross the border," said Driscoll quietly, "and we ain't goin' to. Ride on beyond this point, and I'll shoot you out of the saddle."

Tarno wheeled his horse, saying nothing, joining the other riders. Nobody spoke, for in their first foray with the long riders, the outlaws had been victorious. Nathan had seen enough to have his doubts about the effectiveness of the sheriff's posse. Long before the posse could be alerted, the thieves would be well on their way to the Mexican border.

Fort Elliott, Texas
July 11, 1880

Returning to the orderly room, Wes Tremayne spoke to Sergeant Willard.

"Sergeant, I'd like a few minutes with Captain Selman."

Willard nodded, knocked on Captain Selman's door, and received permission for Wes to enter. He did so, closing the door behind him. He spoke.

"I wouldn't bother you again, Captain, but I need some advice regarding Rebecca."

"I understand," Selman said. "You didn't feel comfortable in her presence."

"No, sir," said Wes, "because the questions I have involve her, and I need advice."

"Speak your mind," Selman said.

"I can't just ride away and leave Rebecca," said Wes, "but I don't see how I can take her with me. What am I goin' to do with her?"

Selman laughed. "She's an almighty pretty girl, and I can't imagine any man riding away and leaving her. Is she of age?"

"Eighteen, just last month, she says," Wes replied.

"She's old enough to make her own decision, then. What does she want to do?"

"I don't know," said Wes. "I wanted to talk to you, before I . . . say anything to her."

"I can't tell you what you *should* do," Captain Selman

said. "All I can do is present you with some choices. It will then be up to you to make your own decision."

"I understand," said Wes.

"Very well," Selman said. "There's a saying on the frontier that a woman alone must take in washing or take in men. Crude, but unfortunately true. To give you some idea, Indian squaws are paid ten dollars a month to do the post laundry. With that in mind, the alternative doesn't seem so bad, does it?"

"No," said Wes, "and if that's her two choices, then I'll have to take her with me."

"A commendable choice," Captain Selman said, "but the more difficult of the two. On the western frontier, women—especially the young, pretty ones—are scarce. There'll be times when you'll have to fight for her, and other times when you may be fighting *with* her. The best possible advice I can give you is this: If you take her with you, be sure you want her and that she wants to go. Don't be in a hurry to make up your mind."

"I feel like I should make a decision before the burying in the morning," said Wes.

"Perhaps," Captain Selman said. "It might be easier on her, knowing she's not to be left alone on the frontier. Just keep in mind that, while you're making it easier for her, you're making it a hundred fold more difficult on yourself."

With those ominous words of warning ringing in his ears, Wes walked back to the cabin where Rebecca waited. He knocked on the door, and when there was no answer, he knocked again. Still there was no response, and he reached a decision. If he was going to be responsible for this woman, he reasoned that such responsibility allowed him the right to return to this cabin where she waited. Taking a deep breath, he opened the door and stepped inside. The curtains had been drawn, but there was enough light to see, and he caught his breath. Stark naked, she was stretched out on the bed, apparently sleeping. He closed the door quickly, and she sat up.

"Where did you go?" she asked.

"To get you a job in the post laundry," he said coldly. "You start tomorrow."

"Well, I hope I'll be allowed to go to the burying," she replied, just as coldly.

He sat down in the chair and she slid over to the edge

of the bed, dropping her feet to the floor. He looked at her, but what she saw in his eyes didn't please her.

"Well," she snapped, "do I pass inspection?"

"Yes," said Wes, "but forget the post laundry. You're more suited to something else. With your mother lying dead in the post dispensary, I expected better of you."

"Mother's dead, and I can't change that," she said, "so I'm looking out for myself. I have decided I'm going with you, and I see no reason for any secrets between us."

"There's none left, as far as you're concerned," said Wes, "but don't it bother you, wastin' all this temptation on me? I'm only twelve, you know."

Her response was most unladylike, and Wes laughed. When her anger subsided, she spoke.

"I'm so impressed with what I've seen you do at twelve, I want to be around when you're grown up. You should really be something by then."

"Why wait?" said Wes, reaching a decision. "I reckon I'm as much a man as you are a woman."

She laughed, but only for as long as it took him to reach the bed.

Wes and Rebecca had been invited to eat at the officer's mess, and when they arrived Captain Selman greeted them. While Rebecca probably knew nothing of his conversation with Wes, there was something about her that suggested Wes had made his decision and that it had been the right one. After supper, Wes and Rebecca returned to the cabin.

"Are you still going to take your bedroll and sleep outside?" she asked.

"I reckon not," he replied. "There'll be enough of that after we leave here. Why? Do you think that bunk's a little narrow for the both of us?"

"I can manage if you can," she said.

Fort Elliott, Texas
July 12, 1880

When Wes and Rebecca reached the post cemetery, there were two wooden coffins, both closed. Captain Selman spoke to Rebecca.

"I took the liberty of sending a detail after your father's body. I believed it would be fitting and proper to lay them to rest side by side."

"Thank you, Captain," said Rebecca. "I had forgotten about that. There was just too much ... all in one day."

Wes had thought the worst of it was over, but when Rebecca saw the two coffins side by side, the enormity of her loss seemed to hit her all the harder. She wept and wailed until it seemed she might faint from the strain. Finally, after the chaplain read from the Bible, the service was over and Wes led Rebecca away. She clung to him fiercely, prompting Captain Selman to speak to Wes.

"You're welcome to stay another night if you think she needs more time to accept all this. Perhaps she should see the doctor before you go."

"No," said Wes. "I reckon we'll be on our way. She needs time, not a doctor."

"What about the horses on which you rode in?" Selman asked.

"The horse I rode is mine," said Wes. "I reckon the horse Rebecca rode belonged to one of the outlaws."

"Yes," Rebecca said, "it did belong to one of the outlaws. Father bought mules to draw the wagon, and after they shot him, they took the mules."

"It could mean trouble," said Selman. "The owner could accuse you of stealing the horse. If there's a problem, feel free to telegraph me and I'll stand behind you."

"We're obliged, Captain," Wes said.

"Where are we going?" Rebecca asked, as they rode away from the fort.

"We're going to track down those three outlaws that got away with your gold and your mules," said Wes. "We owe them, and I pay my debts."

CHAPTER 17

When the posse returned to the Hitchfelt ranch, Hitchfelt was waiting for them.

"Who's in charge of this ragtag outfit?" he snarled.

"I am," said Driscoll.

"I got two dead men, three others shot all to hell, and I'm missin' a hoss herd. What do you aim to do about it?"

"I aim to ride back to town and report to Sheriff Wilder," Driscoll said.

"We could of rode 'em down," said Slack Tarno, "but this chicken-livered bunch was afraid to cross the border."

"We had our orders, Tarno," Driscoll snapped, "and I aim to see that Sheriff Wilder knows you was all for disobeying 'em."

Driscoll led out, heading for town, and the rest of the posse fell in behind. Reaching town, they rode directly to the sheriff's office, and Wilder came out to meet them. Driscoll quickly told him what had happened, and before he could respond, Tarno cut in.

"We ain't never gonna catch that bunch until we ride into Mexico after 'em."

"The acting governor has been specifically warned that we are not to cross the border into Mexico," Sheriff Wilder said. "Mexican authorities are trying to stop the driving of stolen stock into and out of Mexico. To the Mexican border patrol, one gringo may look like another. They wouldn't know us from the horse thieves, and crossing the river could get us all shot dead."

It made sense, and Tarno said nothing more. The riders stabled their horses and made their way back to the hotel. Mostly because of Tarno, Nathan had left Empty behind, and the dog was hungry.

"We'll get your breakfast," said Nathan, "and then I'll get mine."

Empty was fed in the kitchen, and when he had finished, Nathan took him back to the hotel room. By the time Nathan got his order in for breakfast, most of the other deputies had finished eating.

"I thought I smelt dog stink," Tarno said.

"I don't know how you smell anything," said Nathan, "seein' as how you're surrounded by skunk stink."

"I been wonderin' about that myself," Tobe Crump said.

There was a roar of laughter as Tarno had his nasty humor flung back in his face. In a fury, he turned on Nathan.

"Damn you, ever since you showed up, you been rubbin' me the wrong way, an' now you got ever'body laughin' at me."

"Tarno," said Nathan, "you're bein' laughed at because you're always making a damn fool of yourself. You're so good at it, you don't need any help, so don't give me any of the credit."

"By God, that's the truth if I ever heard it," Driscoll said. "Tarno, you've been as mean as a stomped-on rattler ever since you got here. That badge don't stand you a damn bit taller than anybody else. You go on spoilin' for a fight, and somebody's goin' to oblige you."

"When that somebody gits ready," said Tarno, "let the varmint speak up."

"I generally don't dirty my hands with scum," Nathan said, "but I've been known to make exceptions. One more nasty remark about me or my dog, and I'd be tempted to show you the error of your ways."

"If you wasn't standin' on your hind legs," said Tarno, "I wouldn't know which was you an' which was the dog. I'll bet fifty dollars I can stomp hell out of you and take me a switch to your hound."

"Make that a hundred," Nathan said, "and you've got a bet."

"A hundred it is," said Tarno.

"There's a open field over yonder behind the Masonic hall," Rand Dismukes said. "All the room we'll need to bury Tarno when it's over."

They were a rough bunch of men, and none of them liked Tarno. So by the time they reached the field, excitement ran high.

"Shuck your guns," said Driscoll. "If this ends up in a shoot-out, Sheriff Wilder will fire the lot of us."

Nathan and Tarno unbuckled their gunbelts, and with

the August sun beating down, they removed their shirts as
well. Tarno was heavily muscled, and the hair on his chest
didn't stop there but covered the upper part of his body.
With bearded face and wolf grin, he seemed more beast
than human. He went after Nathan, the fingers on his big
hands working like talons, but Nathan was quicker. He
seized one arm and flung Tarno over his head. Tarno fell
like a lightning-struck oak, sending up a cloud of dust.

"Yeeeehaaa," Stub Byler shouted, "don't he look natural, layin' there like a hog?"

The taunt got to Tarno as nothing else could have, and
he surged to his feet. Nathan was waiting; stepping aside,
he tripped Tarno, who went face down in the dirt. There
was more laughter. The commotion had attracted other
people, one of them Sheriff Wilder.

"Break it up," Wilder bawled.

Tarno was on his hands and knees. Staggering to his feet,
he turned on Wilder.

"This is a private fight, Wilder, and it ain't none of
your business."

"As long as you wear the badge and I'm paying you, it
damn well *is* my business," Wilder roared.

Tarno grabbed his shirt, ripped off the badge, and flung
it at Wilder's feet.

"Now get out of town," said Wilder. "If I catch you here
again, I'll jail you."

Nathan was buttoning his shirt when Tarno turned on
him with a snarl.

"I ain't done with you, dog man. I'll settle with you another time."

"Thanks for the warning," Nathan said. "I'll watch my
back."

Sheriff Wilder waited until Tarno was gone, and then he
spoke to Nathan.

"What was that all about, Stone?"

"He kept pushing," said Nathan, "until I'd had enough."

"It's true, Sheriff," Driscoll said. "Tarno's been spoilin'
for a fight ever since he rode in. I nearly had to pull iron on
him to keep him from crossin' the border against orders."

"Good riddance, then," said Wilder.

Without another word, he walked away. Nathan and the
rest of the deputies returned to the hotel.

North Texas
July 15, 1880

"I'm so glad we're out of Indian Territory," Rebecca said. "I expected those outlaws to be laying in wait for us."

"They didn't expect to be followed," said Wes, "and they're drivin' your teams of mules. They're headed for Fort Worth or Dallas."

"I don't understand why we're following them," Rebecca said. "They're two days ahead of us. By the time we catch up to them, they'll have sold the mules, and it'll be my word against theirs they killed and robbed my father."

"Your word against theirs? Are you expecting to have them arrested?"

"I suppose," she said. "What else can we do?"

"I can shoot them," said Wes.

"What good will that do if they've sold the mules and spent all the money?"

"My God," Wes said, exasperated, "don't you understand anything?"

"Oh, I understand more than you think I do," she said angrily. "I understand that I'm just a foolish female from Ohio who doesn't know anything, while you're an experienced man of the West who knows everything."

"Oh, damn," he cried, "are we goin' through that again?"

She said nothing, and they rode on in silence. Harley Stafford had told him a little about tracking, and he believed the trail he followed was not more than a day old. But he lacked experience, and the ambush caught him unprepared. The roar of a Winchester ripped the stillness, and the lead flung Wes over the rump of his horse. Rebecca's horse reared, and that was all that saved her. She was thrown and she lay quietly, lest the bushwacker fire again. But there were no more shots, and hurrying to Wes, she knelt beside him. While she knew little about gunshot wounds, she could tell he had been hard hit. Blood welled from a wound high up, and his breathing was shallow.

"Oh, God," she cried, "what am I going to do?"

Wes had believed the outlaws had been headed toward Fort Worth. If he had been right, Rebecca had only to follow the tracks they had been following. But suppose the outlaws made camp shy of Fort Worth and she stumbled upon them? Having had no experience in such matters, she knew of nothing else to do. She caught up the spooked horse and led him back to where Wes lay. She examined his wound; the bleeding seemed to have stopped. Three times she tried getting Wes across his saddle, and three times she failed. The smell of blood had again spooked the horse and the animal backstepped as she approached him. She took turns pleading with him and cursing him, all to no avail. Then there came the distant, welcome rattle of a wagon, and she could have shouted her relief when she saw it approaching from the northwest. Two men rode ahead of it and two behind, all dressed in Union blue. She stood up, waving her hat, and the advance riders trotted their horses until they reached her. They dismounted, and a sergeant spoke.

"What happened, ma'am?"

"Outlaws," said Rebecca. "I'm Rebecca. That's Wes that's been shot." Quickly she told them how she and Wes had been trailing the rest of the gang and how Wes had suddenly been shot. "We followed them out of Indian Territory."

"Always a dangerous proposition, ma'am, when you're in or near Indian Territory," said the sergeant. "We're bound for Fort Worth. There'll be a doc there, and we're not more than thirty miles out. Privates Picket and Wilson, get the wounded man into the wagon. Hargis, ride on ahead and have a look at the trail they've been following."

"Oh, thank you," said Rebecca. "Wes believed they were going to Fort Worth."

The wagon moved out and Hargis rode ahead. The sergeant, trotting his horse alongside Rebecca's, spoke.

"I'm Sergeant Mullinax. If these men are at the fort, and you can identify them, you can bring charges and have them placed under military arrest. First we'll get the wounded man to a doctor, and then I'll go with you to talk to Captain Ferguson, the post commander."

Corporal Hargis returned, and his report verified what Rebecca had told them.

"Three of them, Sergeant," Hargis said, "and they've got four mules on lead ropes. I found the place where one of 'em fired the shot."

"What I don't understand," said Rebecca, "is why they didn't shoot me."

"They likely didn't consider you a threat, ma'am," Corporal Hargis said. "Getting a wounded man on his horse and to the fort would have been difficult for you."

"It's also possible," said Sergeant Mullinax, "that they don't intend to remain at the fort any longer than it takes to dispose of those mules."

"I'm not concerned with the mules or the outlaws," Rebecca said. "I just want to get Wes to a doctor. Trailing them was his idea."

"There's nothin' wrong with goin' after what belongs to you," said Sergeant Mullinax. "You just have to be careful you don't ride into an ambush. Those three had their eyes on their backtrail."

The surviving outlaws—Burris, Doak, and Sellers—reached Fort Worth and wasted no time calling on Sergeant Rainey, the post quartermaster.

"We got four mules to sell," said Doak. "Are you buying?"

"Maybe," Sergeant Rainey said cautiously. "You got bills of sale?"

"No," said Doak, "we ain't. We found 'em just north of here, driftin', and they ain't branded. We're claimin' 'em."

"Sorry," Sergeant Rainey said. "Buying stock without bills of sale is against government regulations."

"Anybody else around here that might be interested?" Doak asked.

"Civilian freighters, maybe," said Sergeant Rainey. "Bean's outfit is unloadin' at the sutler's now."

Roy Bean and his three teamsters had just rolled in from Corpus Christi, well over three hundred miles away, and were in no hurry to unload their freight. Burris, Doak, and Sellers found them in the saloon, inside the sutler's store.

"You're Roy Bean?" Doak asked.

"Depends on who's wantin' to know, an' why," said the teamster. He drank the rest of his whiskey and stood up. His bullwhacker boots were run over and his old hat clearly had battled the elements and lost, while his homespun trousers were held up with red suspenders and the sleeves of his old flannel shirt were rolled up to the elbows. Leaning against the table was a Winchester rifle.

"We got four mules we're needin' to sell," Doak said, "and we was told you might take them off our hands."

"Maybe," said Bean. "How much?"

"Fifty dollars apiece," Doak replied.

"See me tomorrow," said Bean, "an' I'll consider 'em."

"We need to sell 'em today," Doak said.

"Why?" Bean inquired. "Is the owner lookin' fer 'em?"

"Damn it," said Doak, exasperated, "we're ridin' out today, and we don't aim to take 'em with us."

"Then git off my case," Bean said. "Even if they're yours to sell an' they're prime, I won't have the money till tomorrow."

The trio was about to leave the saloon when the wagon with its soldier escort drove into the compound. Rebecca Tuttle rode behind it.

"We'd best leave them mules where they are," said Burris, "and get the hell away from here. Them soldiers know all about us by now, and I ain't riskin' military arrest for no two hundred dollars."

"I'm with you," Sellers said. "If Doak hadn't been so squeamish about bushwhacking the woman, it wouldn't have caught up to us like this."

"Shut up," said Doak, "and let's ride."

Lest they attract attention, they walked their horses until they were past the sentry's post, near the gate. Mounting, they rode south, leaving the troublesome mules tethered near the quartermaster's.

Sergeant Mullinax accompanied Rebecca to the office of Captain Ferguson, the post commander. Rebecca told her story.

"So you have reason to believe these three men are here," Ferguson said. "Have you spoken to the sentry on duty?"

"Yes, sir," said Sergeant Mullinax. "He went on duty at three o'clock, and he had not seen these men with the mules. That means they're somewhere on post, for they weren't that far ahead of us."

"Four mules shouldn't be hard to find," Captain Ferguson said. "I'll assign some men to look for them and warn the sentry at the gate. Miss Tuttle, can you identify these men you're accusing?"

"Yes," said Rebecca.

"Sergeant Mullinax," Captain Ferguson said, "since you are involved in this already, I'd like for you to ask around for the men in question, while keeping an eye out for the mules."

Mullinax went immediately to the sutler's, entered the saloon, and told the bartender what he was seeking.

"Three strangers was in here a little while ago," said the bartender, "and they had some words with that gent over yonder. The one with the red suspenders."

Sergeant Mullinax approached the table where Bean and his three teamsters sat.

"I'm looking for three men," Sergeant Mullinax began, "and—"

"They got four mules they're needin' to sell," Bean finished.

"You didn't buy them, then," said Sergeant Mullinax.

"No," Bean said. "They ain't been gone but maybe twenty minutes."

Since the newly arrived sentry hadn't seen the mules leave, that meant they had to be somewhere on post. Extra horses and mules were kept in the quartermaster's corral and Mullinax went there, to find four mules tethered to the fence. Sergeant Mullinax made his way to the quartermaster's and spoke to Sergeant Rainey.

"They were here," said Sergeant Rainey. "Four mules with no bills of sale. Claimed they found the animals wandering loose."

"I'll leave them where they are, for the time being," Sergeant Mullinax said. "I believe their owner will be claiming them."

When Sergeant Mullinax returned to the post commander's office, Rebecca Tuttle was gone.

"She's at the dispensary," said Captain Ferguson. "The doctor's working over the man who was shot."

"The four mules are at the quartermaster's corral, sir," Sergeant Mullinax said.

"What about the men who took them?"

"I suspect they saw us coming," said Sergeant Mullinax, "and rode out. I'd say they realized they were in trouble when they saw the girl ride in with us."

Rebecca waited nervously outside the room where Wes had been taken. She thought of the stormy days after they had come together, and smiled. By turns he had been silent, temperamental, and hostile, and it had taken her a while to understand him. Realizing he was inexperienced with women and unsure of himself, she had been careful not to say or do anything that might reveal her newly found insight. He had been neck deep in pride, having made his way in a man's world and met every challenge. Then he had been faced with the greatest challenge of all—a lonely, desperate female. Not knowing what else to do, she had thrown herself at him in the most brazen manner, and he had taken her willingly. They had just gotten used to one another, and now Wes lay wounded, perhaps mortally. If he survived, how would he respond to his having ridden into an ambush? She didn't doubt he would become a man in every sense of the word—if the learning experience wasn't the death of him. She'd been alone with her thoughts for more than an hour when the doctor, Lieutenant Burke, returned.

"He'll live," said Burke, "but he'll need rest. Are you his missus?"

"Not yet," Rebecca said. "He's Wes Tremayne, and I'm Rebecca Tuttle."

"I'll speak to Captain Ferguson," said Lieutenant Burke, "and arrange quarters for the two of you. Wherever you were headed, plan on delaying your journey for two weeks."

"Thank you," Rebecca said. "Please put us together."

Burke winked at her, and despite herself she blushed.

Lincoln County, New Mexico
August 2, 1880

The morning following their fruitless ride after the rustlers, Nathan met Pat Garrett, the man who was being urged to run for sheriff of Lincoln County. Garrett had joined the deputies for breakfast in the hotel dining room. He had questions regarding the rustling and the obvious difficulty in resolving the problem. Breakfast was over and the men were down to extra cups of coffee when Garrett spoke.

"Having chased these rustlers, do you men have any idea as to how they might best be captured?"

"I got an idea," said Bib Driscoll, "but I don't know how it could be done. Only way I can see, is maybe gettin' a man into their outfit that could pass us the word as to where they aim to strike next."

"An excellent idea," Garrett said, "but I doubt it can be done. It would take a man trusted by Billy and his bunch, and that kind of man wouldn't betray them to the law."

"Then the only other way," said Tuck McFadden, "is to ride them down, but not being allowed to follow 'em across the border kills that."

"We never know where they'll strike next," Warren Hinderman said. "Hell, there's no way we can stake out every ranch in Lincoln County. I think Acting Governor Wallace is barking up the wrong tree, not allowin' us to chase the varmints across the river."

"It's not Wallace's decision to make," said Garrett. "Washington has an agreement with the Mexican government, and President Hayes has specifically ordered that we honor that agreement. So we can't pursue the outlaws across the river."

"Where are these outlaws when they're not rustling horses and cattle?" Nathan asked. "They must have a place where they hole up."

"Not necessarily," said Garrett. "I believe some of them are small ranchers, using the Tunstall, McQueen, and Murphy feud to cover stealing from their neighbors."

"There's talk of you running for sheriff of Lincoln County," said Bode Watts. "If you was sheriff, what would you do? How would you bust up this gang?"

"I'd go after the leader," Garrett replied. "You kill a snake by cutting off its head. I'd go after Billy the Kid. This is still a grudge thing, and Billy's kept it alive."

"Hell, every friend of Tunstall and McSween is a friend to the Kid," said Neil Sutton. "You could ride over Lincoln County for a year and not root him out."

"I knew Billy before all this started," Garrett said. "I'm gambling that I can find him."

Fort Worth, Texas
July 16, 1880

Given laudanum, Wes slept around the clock. Rebecca had slept on a cot outside his room and was beside him when he awakened.

"Where am I?" he asked.

"Fort Worth," said Rebecca. "After you were shot, soldiers found us."

"I rode into an ambush," he said bitterly. "I'm just a damned tenderfoot, a shorthorn that's in over his head."

"I suppose it wasn't the smartest thing you've ever done," said Rebecca, "but how else do we learn without making mistakes?"

"A man don't go on livin', making that kind of mistake. I should be dead."

"Oh, stop acting like you're God Almighty," Rebecca said. "You were shot, but you're alive, and we got the mules. I sold them this morning."

"I reckon the outlaws escaped," he said.

"Yes," said Rebecca. "They'd been trying to sell the mules and must have seen us as we rode in. They slipped away while you were being brought here, before I had a chance to talk to Captain Ferguson, the post commander."

At that point, the doctor came in. "I'm Lieutenant Burke," he said.

"I'm obliged to you," said Wes. "How bad am I hurt?"

"Two weeks' worth," Burke replied. "I've arranged quarters for you, and I'm having you moved there."

"I got to lay in this bed for two weeks?"

"No," said Burke, "but you have to rest. That means staying out of the saddle. That slug narrowly missed a lung. You're young but not indestructible. You must have time to heal."

Wes said nothing. For the first time since escaping the orphanage in St. Louis, he felt helpless and vulnerable, and he hated it. By late afternoon, he had been moved to an available officer's cabin. Shortly before supper, Sergeant Mullinax stopped by.

"I'm owin' you," said Wes. "How was it you and your men happened along at just the right time?"

Mullinax laughed. "I suppose I can tell you that without violating regulations. We had picked up an army payroll at Fort Elliott. It comes by train as far as Dodge City, and by escorted patrol from there to Fort Elliott. From Fort Elliott, it's distributed to all other Texas forts."

"What do you know of those three outlaws that bushwhacked me?" Wes asked.

"Not much," said Mullinax. "I never laid eyes on them. I do know they rode south. I trailed them a ways, to get some idea as to where they might be headed. Captain Ferguson telegraphed their descriptions to Texas Ranger outposts to the south of us."

"What are the most likely towns?"

"Waco, Austin, and San Antonio," Mullinax said. "Of course, there's Corpus Christi, on the gulf, and Laredo, on the border. You're not thinking of pursuing them, are you?"

"My God, no," said Rebecca, who had been listening.

"Why not?" said Wes.

"They took less than five hundred dollars from my father," Rebecca said. "Is it worth getting shot again?"

She had said exactly the wrong thing. Wes reared up on his elbows, his eyes like twin daggers, and spoke through clenched teeth.

"The money has nothing to do with it. When they gunned me down, it became a personal thing. Despite what you think, just because they shot me once, it don't mean they'll manage it a second time."

"It's time I was leaving," said Sergeant Mullinax, and he departed.

"By the time you can ride," Rebecca said, "those men will be two weeks ahead of us. I don't think we should ride after them."

"Then *we* won't ride after them," said Wes. "I'll ride after them, and you'll stay here until I return."

"Oh?" Rebecca said. "Where would you be now if I'd stayed at Fort Elliott while you rode after them?"

"I owe you my life," he said, "and you're not going to let me forget it, are you?"

"Not if that's what it takes to keep you from getting yourself killed," said Rebecca. "Does that pride of yours run so deep, and are you so mule headed, that you can't see that I care what happens to you? If I did some foolish thing, risking my life, wouldn't you care enough to try and stop me?"

"Yeah," he said, sheepishly.

He extended his hand, and she came to sit beside him on the bed.

"I never knew my father or my mother," he said, "and I don't know what it's like, having somebody . . . care about me. I reckon that's the one part of bein' a man that don't come easy to me. How do you feel something for somebody else, when . . . when you've never experienced it yourself?"

"You're experiencing it now," said Rebecca, "and you're better at it than you think."

CHAPTER 18

Lincoln County, New Mexico
November 2, 1880

"The Kid and some of his bunch has been seen at Coyote Springs," Sheriff Wilder told the posse. "I want all of you to ride out there and lay low for a day or two. This may be our chance to jump them without waiting for them to raid another ranch."

"Good idea, up to a point," said Bib Driscoll. "I'm not sure any of us has ever seen the Kid. All we've been able to do is chase him in the dark, after him and his outfit had stole somebody's horses or cows."

"Then I'll ride with you," Sheriff Wilder said. "I'm catching seven kinds of hell for not running this bunch down. We'll ride at sundown."

Near Coyote Springs was the one-saloon village of White Oaks, and it was there that the Kid and his gang had their first encounter with the posse. But the outlaws had taken the precaution of posting a lookout, and they broke for their horses as the sheriff and his posse approached.

"Ride them down!" Wilder shouted.

But there was no moon, and when the posse began firing, they succeeded only in hitting several of the outlaws' horses. The unhorsed outlaws were given a hand up by companions, and, riding double, managed to escape. The next week, Pat Garrett became Lincoln County's new sheriff, while Billy and two companions again escaped by killing one of their pursuers. On December 15, Governor Wallace increased the reward to five hundred dollars for the Kid's delivery to the Lincoln County jail. Again Pat Garrett, who had not yet taken office, met with the Lincoln County posse.

"I was elected on a promise to put a stop to the rustling and the killing," said Garrett, "and that means bringing in the Kid. We're going to trample every thicket and fire every shack in Lincoln County, if that's what it takes."

Fort Sumner, New Mexico
December 19, 1880

"I have word that the Kid and some of his outfit will be in Fort Sumner this weekend," Garrett told the deputies. "We're going to be there waiting for them."

Accompanied by Rudabaugh, Wilson, Bowdre, O'Folliard, and Pickett, the Kid rode warily into Fort Sumner on Sunday night. Suddenly the lawmen emerged from where they had been hiding.

"Halt," Garrett shouted, "this is the law."

But the fugitives rode for their lives, and the posse opened fire. O'Folliard was shot out of the saddle. Rudabaugh lost his horse. Leaping from his dying mount, he was able to seize the reins of the dead O'Folliard's horse and escape with his companions.

"Rein up," Garrett ordered. "We'd never catch them in the dark, and they could cut us down from ambush."

Stinking Springs, New Mexico
December 23, 1880

More horses had been rustled the night before, and again the posse followed the outlaws as far as the border. Snow had begun falling around midnight, as they rode back to Lincoln. When they stopped to rest the horses, Nathan spoke to Garrett.

"How long do these hombres generally stay in Mexico?"

"Only long enough to dispose of the rustled stock," Garrett said. "I won't be a bit surprised if they're back in Lincoln County tomorrow night."

"I can't see ridin' all this way for nothing," said Nathan. "Why don't we hole up and wait for them to ride back?"

"Too much territory to cover," Garrett replied. "There's near two hundred miles of border west of El Paso, and that much and more to the east. They never cross at the same place twice."

"But when they do," said Nathan, "they always return to Lincoln County."

"Yes," Garrett replied.

"If I'm any judge," Nathan said, "there'll be a foot of

snow by morning. Suppose we ride back and hole up somewhere to the south of Lincoln County and wait? The snow
will cover our tracks, and we can ride a line along the
southern end of the county until we cross their trail. From
there, we can follow their tracks and maybe take 'em by
surprise."

"By God," said Bib Driscoll, "he's got somethin' there."

"I think he has, myself," Garrett said. "I know a place
where we can get in out of the weather until the storm
breaks. Sometime tomorrow afternoon we'll go looking for
their trail."

Bundled in their heavy coats and gloves, scarves shielding
their ears, and their hats thonged down against the wind,
they rode north. Within minutes, the deepening snow had
covered their tracks. Garrett led them to a box canyon with
a spring. The canyon rim shut out the merciless wind and
blowing snow, while a roaring fire kept the cold at bay.
There was hot coffee and hot food, and by feeding the fire
in shifts, they were comfortable. The snow continued, and
there was only a little difference between first light and the
darkness of the receding night.

"If we wait too long to go lookin' for their trail," said
Tuck McFadden, "we'll end up chasin' 'em in the dark, and
we've had nothin' but rotten luck doin' that."

"I'm keeping that in mind," Garrett said, "but we'll have
to give them time to bypass us. We'll be leaving tracks in
the snow, and if we ride out too soon, they'll cut our trail
and know we're after them."

The snow ceased before noon, but the big gray clouds
seemed only tree-top high, and the wind still howled out
of the northwest. The best light they'd had all day was no
better than twilight, and when Garrett gave the order to
saddle up, darkness seemed only minutes away.

"After all this," Neil Sutton said, "I hope the varmints
didn't decide to wait out the storm in Mexico."

"It's a chance we had to take," said Garrett. "If they're
ridin' back today, we should cut their trail in less than two
hours. If they've fooled us and laid up across the border,
we'll still reach town by suppertime. There'll be hot grub
and warm beds tonight."

Garrett and his posse rode eastward, and in less than an
hour they came upon the tracks of five horses headed
north.

"It's got to be them," Garrett said. "Let's ride."

To their dismay, sleet began rattling off their hat brims and stinging their faces. Nobody doubted there would be more snow, and success or failure depending on their catching up to the outlaws before the trail was lost. The going was hard and slow, forcing them to rest the horses often. During such a stop, almost shouting to be heard above the wind, Garrett gave them last-minute orders.

"If it gets any worse, they may hole up for the night. In any case, shoot to kill. It's the only way we'll ever take the Kid."

They soon reached an abandoned stone hut, and in an adjoining lean-to, there were three horses. Suddenly a shadowy figure emerged from the hut.

"Fire," Garrett shouted, believing it was the Kid.

The hard-hit outlaw staggered back inside, but was shoved out. The four desperate men tried to pull their remaining three mounts into the building, but Garrett killed one of the animals, blocking the doorway.

"Pour lead through the door," Garrett ordered. "They can't hide from ricochets."

It was the truth. The rock hut had become a death trap, as lead splattered against the stone walls. The desperate outlaws had but one choice.

"Don't shoot no more," came a shout from within the hut. "We're comin' out."

The four came out with their hands up. Nathan recognized Billy the Kid from the many wanted dodgers he had seen. He looked pitifully young as he and his companions had their hands bound. They were then mounted on their horses, while Nathan and Warren Hinderman brought out the dead man.

"Charlie Bowdre," said Garrett.

For a time, Billy the Kid was imprisoned at Las Vegas, New Mexico, and finally at Santa Fe. He would not be returned to Lincoln until time for his trial, lest his many friends and sympathizers attempt to break him out. Pat Garrett, by now the new sheriff, met with Lincoln County's deputies for the first time.

"Men," said Garrett, "the governor commends you for your service, and to that I am adding my thanks. With the Kid in jail awaiting trial, we believe we have broken the

back of this gang of rustlers and killers. As of today, this
posse is being disbanded. However, I can still use a couple
of you as deputies, but I must warn you, there'll be a considerable reduction in pay."

"Not me," Bib Driscoll said. "I done been spoilt."

Most of the others laughed, for they seemed of a similar
mind, leaving Garrett to seek deputies elsewhere. Nathan
returned to his hotel room, where Empty waited.

"Well, pard, we're footloose again, but I reckon we'll
stay here another day or two, until the weather breaks and
we get our bearings."

The new year—1881—had blown in with a blizzard on
its heels and temperatures of near zero. Lincoln was a fair-
sized town, and Nathan decided to see what it had to offer
now that his official duties were over—the deputies had
taken a pledge of sobriety and had been encouraged to
avoid the saloons. The town had several, and one of them—
the Silver Dollar—was nothing short of spectacular. The
region boasted some men of wealth, most of it from mining,
and Nathan learned that this prosperous saloon was owned
by four miners who had struck it rich. Rare among such
frontier establishments, it boasted a second floor, and there
were quarters for the owners when they chose to remain
in town for a few days. Leaving Empty at the hotel, Nathan
walked through the snow to the end of the block. In deference to the harsh winters, the Silver Dollar had its own
stable to the rear of the building, encouraging patrons to
stay as long as they wished. In the early afternoon, with
snow on the ground and more to come, Nathan was amazed
at the number of men who lined the bar or sat at the many
tables. Along one wall, the bar ran the entire length of the
building, and at each end an enormous fireplace occupied
two-thirds of a wall. Wind roared down the chimneys, causing the fires to spit and spew puffs of smoke that mingled
with tobacco smoke fogging the many hanging lamps. Men
lined the bar, while others were doing some serious drinking at the many tables. Directly beneath a hanging lamp, a
poker game was in progress. A participant threw down his
cards in disgust, kicked back his chair, and got up. Nathan
took the chair and bought in.

"Five-dollar limit," said the house dealer.

Nathan lost four pots, won a small one, and then lost
three more. Four of the other men all seemed affluent, but

the other—a grizzled old rancher—kicked back his chair and stood up. His eyes on the house dealer, he spoke.

"House man, I'm callin' fer a new deck. This damn deck you're dealin' from has got some cards missin'. I can't git nothin' but three of a kind. Where's them fourth draws?"

The house dealer placed the remainder of the deck face down on the table, and when he spoke his voice was dangerously low.

"Pilgrim, are you accusing me of cheating?"

"If he's not," Nathan said, "I am."

The house dealer was quick, but not quick enough. He froze, for Nathan Stone had him covered with a cocked Colt.

"Whatever's in your hand," said Nathan, "place it on the table."

Slowly the house dealer unclenched his right hand, revealing a deadly derringer.

"I think you owe us all some money." Nathan said. "Then, if you value your health, I reckon you'd better get out of here."

But the scene hadn't gone unnoticed. One of the three bartenders had a sawed-off shotgun, and a man wearing a frock coat and derby hat was rapidly approaching the table.

"I am Jess Delaney, one of the owners," he said. "What's the problem here?"

"Your house man," said Nathan. "Ever since I sat in, he's been slick dealing."

"Hell, he's been doin' it long 'fore that," said the old-timer who had first complained. "I dropped a bundle in here last night."

"Prove it," Delaney said, his eyes on Nathan.

"All of you show your hands," said Nathan.

The four men dropped their cards on the table, face up, and each man held three of a kind. With the rest of the deck face down on the table, Nathan dealt every man, including himself, the needed fourth card.

"Quay," Delaney said, his hard eyes on the house dealer, "you will return the money you have taken from these men, and then you'll get the hell out of here."

Sullenly, Quay did as ordered, and when he had gone, Delaney spoke.

"The rest of you belly up to the bar. Drinks are on the house."

When all the men had been served their drinks, Delaney spoke to Nathan.

"You know your cards, my friend. May I ask your name?"

"Nathan Stone."

"You used to house deal for old Judge Prater in Waco, didn't you?"

"For a short time," said Nathan, "but that's been more than ten years. I don't seem to remember you."

"I recall you being an honest dealer," Delaney said, "and I could use one. Would you be interested? I pay twenty percent."

"Maybe," said Nathan, "but no Sundays. What are the hours?"

"Six until closing," Delaney said. "We close at two in the morning."

"It's nowhere near six," said Nathan. "Why was Quay here so early?"

"His idea," Delaney said. "Normally, none of the owners are here before six. The four of us take turns staying until closing."

"Who are the other owners?"

"Hiram Kilgore, Ward Guthrie, and Cash Seaborn. This is my night, and I just came in early. Tomorrow it'll be Kilgore, then Guthrie, followed by Seaborn."

"Will I be the only house dealer?" Nathan asked.

"No," said Delaney, "there's a young lady, Katrina McGuire. She'll take off Mondays and work Sundays, when you're off. I'll need you both on Fridays and Saturdays."

"It's been a long time," Nathan said, "and I may be rusty, but I'll try it for a while."

"Good," said Delaney. "Since today is Saturday, I'll need you tonight."

"I'll be here," Nathan said, "and I'll have my guns. Any objection to that?"

"None," said Delaney, "as long as you don't use them without cause."

Fort Worth, Texas
August 3, 1880

"Where are we going from here?" Rebecca asked as she and Wes rode away from Fort Worth. "Please tell me you aren't going to try and find those three outlaws."

"Oh, all right," he said. "The trail's cold. They could be in Mexico by now."

"And that's the only reason you're not going after them."

She looked at him, concern in her gray eyes, and he laughed.

"You think I'm always lookin' for a fight?" he asked.

"I'm never sure. Just when I think you have a grip on that pride of yours—"

"I'm of a mind to ride all the way to the ocean," he said. "I've never seen the ocean."

"I believe it's called the Gulf of Mexico," she said with a smile.

"Damn it, whatever."

They reined up at a spring an hour before sundown, allowing the horses to rest prior to watering them.

"This is nice," said Rebecca. "We can't go much farther before dark. Why don't we just make camp here?"

"We can," he replied. "Are you tired?"

"Some. Aren't you?"

"Yeah," he admitted. "I'm sore as hell where I was shot. We'll have the time to cook some grub and douse the fire before dark."

The night passed uneventfully, and Wes was saddling the horses the next morning when they heard the gunfire somewhere to the south.

"That's the way we're going," Wes said. "Sounds like somebody's in trouble."

"Must we become involved?"

"We don't have to," said Wes, "but where would I be if Sergeant Mullinax and his patrol had felt that way? The shooting will be over before we get there. Come on."

Topping a rise, Wes reined up. Ahead of them, two horses grazed along the rim of an arroyo.

"Stay here," Wes said, dismounting.

"No," she said, "I'm going with you. The owners of those horses are hurt or dead."

One of the men lay on his back; he was very, very dead. He had been hit three times in the chest. Pinned to his vest was a lawman's star.

The second man lay face down. When Wes turned him over, he saw that he also wore a star. He had been shot once and his breathing was ragged. His eyelids fluttered as Wes felt for a pulse. He tried to speak.

"Who . . . are . . . ?"

"I'm not the hombre that shot you," said Wes. "Your partner's dead. Where can we take you? Where's the nearest town with a doc?"

"Lampasas," he muttered. "South . . ."

Quickly, Wes tied the dead man across his saddle, and then hoisted the wounded man over his saddle in a similar position.

"Can you lead the horse with the dead man?" Wes asked.

"Yes," said Rebecca.

Wes took the reins of the wounded man's horse and, riding as fast as they dared, they rode south. They had gone only a short distance when they reached a river.

"According to Captain Ferguson's map," Wes said, "this has to be the Colorado. The town must be downstream from here."

The little town of Lampasas had but a single street, and it was perched on the bank of the Colorado River. Somebody sounded the alarm, and by the time Wes and Rebecca had reined up before the sheriff's office, a small crowd had gathered. Several men had their hands on the butts of their Colts.

"One of these men is still alive," said Wes, "and he needs a doctor."

"Doc Coggin's place is down the street," a bystander said. "Come on."

Someone had taken the reins of the dead man's horse, and others were lifting him from the saddle. Rebecca rode on after Wes. Reaching the doctor's office, two men eased the wounded lawman from the saddle and carried him into the doctor's office. A balding man in a town suit approached Wes.

"I'm Mayor Patten. Where did you find them?"

"A few miles north of here," said Wes. "We heard shooting, but by the time we got there the fight was over. One man was already dead. We brought the other here as quick as we could."

"He's Sheriff Lyle Tidwell," Patten said. "He caught up to those damn rustlers. We're obliged to you for bringing them in. Will you and your missus stay until the sheriff's able to talk? The town will put you up at the hotel."

"I reckon we can stay," said Wes, "but I can't tell you any more than I already have."

"Please stay, then," Patten said. "There'll be an inquest for the dead man, and for the record we'll need a signed statement from you."

Wes and Rebecca were assigned a room at the local hotel. With little to do in the small town, in the late afternoon they returned to the doctor's office.

"We were wondering about Sheriff Tidwell," Wes told the doctor.

"He'll live," said Doctor Coggin, "but he'll be laid up for a while."

While they were there, Mayor Patten came in. He nodded to Wes and Rebecca and spoke to Dr. Coggin.

"How is he, Doc?"

"About as good as can be expected, under the circumstances," Coggin said.

"How long you figure he'll be laid up?" Patten inquired.

"At least two weeks," said the doctor.

"My God," Patten said, "we can't go that long without a sheriff. Ike Blocker and his gang will have this town for breakfast."

"Hire another deputy," said Dr. Coggin.

"Find me one," Patten said, "and I'll hire him. Deputy Hinkel was an ex-Ranger, and there's not another man in this town the equal of him. Ike Blocker's deadly with a gun, and there's not a man around here that can stand up to him."

"I can," said Wes.

"You?" Patten said, raising his eyebrows. "Why, you're—"

He never finished the sentence. Wes Tremayne had drawn his Colt with blinding speed, and Patten found himself staring into its deadly muzzle. Rebecca was more startled than the mayor. She had believed Wes had overcome the need to prove himself—and now this. Before she could respond, Mayor Patten spoke up.

"I'm prepared to pay you fifty dollars and put you up at the hotel if you'll take the deputy's badge until Sheriff Tidwell's back on his feet."

"I reckon I can handle that," said Wes.

"Come with me to the sheriff's office, then," Patten said, "and I'll swear you in."

Before they even reached the sheriff's office, Wes was having serious doubts about his hasty decision. He cut his eyes toward Rebecca, who refused to look at him. Her face was deathly white and she was biting her lower lip. The swearing-in took only a few seconds. Patten handed Wes his badge and the keys to the cell block.

"You needn't stay here at night," Patten said, "unless there are prisoners."

"One thing," said Wes. "How many men are in this Blocker gang?"

"Not more than five or six," Patten replied, "and from what I've heard, the others are not the equal of Blocker with a gun."

"Five or six against one," said Rebecca, "they don't have to be fast with a gun."

Patten appeared not to hear. He went out, leaving Wes to face Rebecca's fury. She wasted no time unleashing it.

"My God," she wailed, "have you lost your mind? You don't owe this town anything."

"I'm not doing it for the town. I just want to see if I have what it takes to become a lawman on the frontier. Besides, I might run into those three varmints that drygulched me. Sergeant Mullinax said they rode south."

"Oh, I can understand the need for that," she said sarcastically. "Six potential killers aren't enough. Just when I think you have some sense, some feeling—"

"You find out I ain't halter-broke," he said. "You want to lead me around on a rope, shoving me into a hole, protecting me. I can protect myself, damn it. There won't be any risk for you. Just hide out here in the hotel and I'll do what I have to."

"I will not hide out in the hotel," she said defiantly. "Just because I hate what you're doing doesn't mean I don't respect your right to do it. I still have the money from the sale of the mules. I'll buy myself a gun and ride with you."

"Oh, for God's sake," he groaned, "that's the quickest way to get me shot dead. How can I defend myself if I'm concerned about you?"

"If you are concerned about me," said Rebecca, "what I want would mean something to you. I've seen you shot down before my eyes once, and it's not the sort of thing I can get used to. Is that so hard to understand?"

"No," he admitted, "but why do I have to do all the changing? Part of being a man is giving as good as you get, and standin' your ground against other men. I don't aim to tuck my tail and run like a scared dog to avoid a fight. Not for you, not for anybody. If you can't take me like I am, I'd just as soon we split the blanket."

"I don't want that," she said. "I want you, but I want you alive. How far must you go to satisfy yourself that you're a man? How many more times must you be shot?"

"I don't know," said Wes. "I just know that when I've done what I believe I should have done, I don't want you jumpin' on me, talkin' down to me like I'm five years old."

"Then I won't say anything more," she said, "but I am going to buy myself a gun. If I'm with you and we're being shot at, then I'll shoot back."

He caught her up in a bear hug, and for the moment, everything was right between them.

Lincoln, New Mexico
January 8, 1881

Nathan returned to his hotel room and changed clothes. Since he was no longer one of Lincoln County's deputies, he and Empty had taken to eating at the cafe across the street from the hotel. Returning to the hotel, Nathan shucked his hat, his gunbelt, and his boots. He then stretched out on the bed until time for his first night at the Silver Dollar. When he got up to go, Empty waited at the door.

"Not this time, old son. You don't like saloons. I'll let you out for a run in the snow when I get back."

When Nathan reached the Silver Dollar, he got his first look at the female house dealer. She wore a green floor-length gown cut low and what might have been a diamond necklace, and her auburn hair down to her shoulders. If she was surprised to see Nathan, she concealed it well. He spoke.

"Kate, you've changed some."

"Oh, I wear clothes when the occasion calls for it," she said, "and the name is Katrina McGuire."

"I liked you better when you were Kate McDowell," said Nathan. "You seemed a little more honest."

"I'm more honest now than I've ever been," she replied. "At least I'm trying to earn an honest living. But I suppose you're going to ruin that."

"Not necessarily," said Nathan, "but let's be honest with one another. I'm Nathan Stone. Now who are you? Kate McDowell or Katrina McGuire?"

"Kate McDowell," she said with a sigh, "but please don't call me that. I'm Katrina."

"All right, Katrina," said Nathan, "but I don't aim to forget you throwing my clothes and boots in the river."

She laughed. "You were a sight. Mad as hell and jaybird naked. We'll get along, Nathan Stone. Play your cards right and you could see a lot of me."

It was Nathan's turn to laugh. "You mean there's more?"

"Maybe a little," she said with a sly smile. "It'll be up to you to seek it out."

CHAPTER 19

A week after Sheriff Lyle Tidwell had been shot, Wes and Rebecca were able to talk to the lawman. He was still pale, weak, almost apologetic.

"I'm obliged," Tidwell said, "but a mite surprised to find Patten hired you on as a deputy. Son, he ain't done you no favor. Soon as I'm on my feet, you'd be smart to just saddle up and ride on. Ike Blocker fancies himself the fastest gun around, and he'll be sure to test you."

"Leaving you to face him alone?" Wes asked.

"I was elected to wear the badge," said Tidwell. "I got no choice."

"In a way, neither do I," Wes said. "I've always had to fight just to stay alive, and I don't like men who bully others around. Maybe I just want to see if I have what it takes to be a lawman."

"Well, I reckon you've come to the right place," said Tidwell. "I'd give a year's wages to see Ike Blocker get a dose of his own medicine."

"How do I go about finding him?" Wes asked.

"He'll find you," said Tidwell, "once he knows you're here. He's insulted me just by ignorin' me, stealin' cattle and horses as it suited him. Then when I ride after him, there's a fight, with me on the losin' end. I've lost two deputies in six months. I believe he's left me alive just so he can taunt and humiliate me."

"Suppose I take Blocker out of the running," Wes said. "Will that bust up the gang?"

"It'd go a long way," said Tidwell.

Rebecca had kept her silence, but when they were alone her reaction was about what Wes had expected.

"I suppose you're going to nail printed dodgers on every tree in the county, informing Ike Blocker you're waiting for him," Rebecca said.

"That's not a bad idea," said Wes. "Do you think it'd be better if I just wait for them to rustle somebody's cattle, ride after them, and take on the whole gang at one time?"

"It makes no difference what I think," Rebecca said. "Do it your way."

"I aim to," said Wes. "I'll ride down every pig trail in this county. I want Ike Blocker to know I'll face up to him, that I think he's afraid to face me man to man."

"I understand what you're trying to do," Rebecca said, "but suppose Ike Blocker has no pride? Suppose he refuses to accept your challenge, and comes after you with his whole gang of outlaws?"

"According to you," said Wes, "I wrote the book on pride. I reckon I'm in a position to see that pride in other men, and I'm seein' it in Ike Blocker."

"You've never even met the man," Rebecca said.

"I don't have to," said Wes. "I'm judging from what I've heard."

Wes Tremayne rode from one village to another, letting it be known he represented the law. Though Rebecca said nothing, she followed through on her threat to buy a gun. Wes had agreed, knowing how determined she was, and she bought a Colt double-action .38. A little more than two weeks after he had been shot, Sheriff Lyle Tidwell was back on his feet.

"You only agreed to stay until I was up and about," Tidwell said, "and I reckon I'm as well as I'll ever be. I'd like for you to stay on awhile, but only if you're willing."

"I can't go now," said Wes. "Blocker would think I'd made big talk and wasn't man enough to live up to it. He'll be along, and I wouldn't want to disappoint him."

Rebecca had begun to breathe easier, for it seemed like Blocker wasn't going to accept Wes Tremayne's challenge. But on Saturday night, September third, what she dreaded most became reality. When Wes answered the knock on their door, Sheriff Tidwell stood there.

"Blocker's in the saloon across the street, Wes."

"Is he alone?"

"Yes," said the sheriff. "It's you and him. Some other gents and me will be backing your play."

Wes pulled on his boots, buckled on his gunbelt, and reached for his hat.

"I'm going with you," Rebecca said.

"No," said Wes.

"Yes," she insisted. "I'll stay out of the way."

She followed him out the door and down the stairs. True to her word, she waited in the hotel lobby, where she could see out the window. Wes paused on the boardwalk, and a shadowy figure stepped out of the saloon across the street. He laughed, and then he spoke.

"I been hearin' about you, bucko. You talk like a hombre that makes big tracks, but Ike Blocker thinks you're just a snot-nosed kid with a big mouth. You can take water and save your hide by skeedaddlin' back into that hotel. You got till the count of five."

Wes stood his ground, and Blocker began to count.

"One . . . two . . . three . . . four . . ."

Lincoln, New Mexico
January 15, 1881

During his first week at the Silver Dollar, Nathan was pleasant to Kate McDowell, and nothing unusual happened until the following Saturday night. Slack Tarno came in just before midnight and, pointedly ignoring Nathan, took a chair at Kate's table. There he sat, a bottle of whiskey before him, until a few minutes before closing. Finishing his whiskey, he got up and left the saloon. Before leaving, the dealers had to settle up with the house, and Kate finished first. When Nathan stepped out on the boardwalk, the town was completely deserted, with only an occasional light bleeding out into the street. The hotel was three blocks away, and Nathan could see Kate's shadowy form ahead of him. Suddenly there was a scream that was choked off, and the girl disappeared. Nathan lit out down the street, avoiding the noisy boardwalk, cocking one of his Colts as he ran. He was hampered by the snow, but it saved his life. In the pale moonlight, he could see boot tracks leading to the open space between two store buildings. He could hear cursing, and as he eased his head around the corner, a slug ripped splinters into his face.

"Let her go," Nathan commanded.

Slack Tarno laughed. "Why don't you come and get her, dog man?"

"Let her go," said Nathan, "and I'll spare your miserable life. Hurt her, and I promise you, you're a dead man."

"Maybe not," Tarno said. "Now you pull your irons slow and easy, and toss 'em out where I can see 'em. You don't, and I'll kill her."

But Kate began to struggle. While she couldn't free herself, she twisted around until she faced Tarno and drove her knee into his groin. With a grunt, he let her go, but he didn't drop the gun. For a few seconds Kate was between them, and when Tarno fired again, she fell. Nathan shot Tarno twice, and knelt beside Kate, who was on her hands and knees.

"How bad is it?" he asked.

"Bad enough," she groaned. "He shot me in the behind."

"Come on," he said, helping her to her feet. "The whole town will be wondering about those shots. We can follow this alley the rest of the way to the hotel. If you're hurt badly enough, I'll get the doc for you. With any luck, nobody will find this varmint until sometime tomorrow."

Keeping next to the buildings where there was no snow, they reached the hotel. There was a back door through which they entered.

"Which is your room?" Nathan asked quietly.

"Eleven," said Kate, from somewhere producing a key.

Nathan got her inside and locked the door before finding and lighting the lamp. Kate shucked her coat and skinned off her dress, then the little she wore beneath it.

"On your belly, across the bed," Nathan said.

The slug had burned a nasty furrow along the inside of her thigh, and it bled so that it looked more serious than it probably was.

"Is it bad enough for a doctor?" Kate asked.

"No," said Nathan. "I have disinfectant and salve in my saddlebags, unless you'd prefer a doctor."

"No," she said. "Go get your medicine."

Nathan unlocked his door, and Empty bounded out into the corridor.

"Come on," said Nathan. "It's time you romped in the snow for a while."

He let the hound out the back door and, returning to his room, got the necessary medicine from his saddlebags. Using Kate's key, he let himself into her room.

"I'll need to bathe that wound," Nathan said, "and the water in this pitcher is mighty cold. Are you ready?"

"Yes," she said. "Let's be done with it."

Nathan poured water into the basin and, soaking a towel, cleansed the bloody wound.

"God, that's cold," Kate groaned. "That's worse than being shot."

"I'll dry the wound and spread on some sulfur salve. Then you can get under those blankets and get warm."

"Nathan," she said, when he had applied the salve, "thank you."

"No thanks necessary," Nathan said. "That was Slack Tarno. He's had it in for me."

"Damn," she said, "and I thought he wanted to have his way with me."

"Maybe that, too," said Nathan, "but first, he aimed to kill me."

"Will you . . . stay with me tonight? Please?"

He thought of his first meeting with her, when she had tried to kill him, and the time at the river, where she had been about to take his clothes. What more could she do to him that she hadn't already attempted?

"I have to let my dog in," he said. "I'll be back."

Despite her pain, she smiled, and again he was amazed at how attractive she was.

Lampasas, Texas
September 3, 1880

Ike Blocker drew at the count of five, but Wes Tremayne hadn't moved, and the confidence of his young adversary unnerved the outlaw. His first shot went wide, and he had no chance for another. Wes drew and fired once. Blocker stumbled backward through the batwing doors of the saloon and died on the floor. Wes ejected the empty casing from his Colt and reloaded. Rebecca was the first to reach him. Seizing his arm, she just stood there trembling.

"Son," said Sheriff Tidwell, "that was the nerviest thing I ever saw. You're a natural-born lawman if I ever seen one."

"I seen John Wesley Hardin draw," said a bystander, "and this kid makes him look almighty slow."

The saloon was in no hurry to remove Blocker's dead body, for it had drawn a landslide business. By the time the outlaw was carried out, the entire town had gathered. But Wes had taken the trembling Rebecca and had disappeared into the hotel.

Sunday morning, Sheriff Tidwell joined Wes and Rebecca for breakfast at the cafe.

"The sheriff's job is yours, if you want it," Tidwell said. "You got more pure nerve than I ever had. I'll step down."

"Thanks," said Wes, "but I don't want it. I'll stay awhile, in case some of Blocker's outfit has ideas of gettin' even."

"I don't expect they will," Sheriff Tidwell said. "It's the way of most outlaw gangs to have one really bad actor, while the rest lean on his reputation."

"Oh, I hope you're right," said Rebecca. "I've been scared out of my wits, but now I believe Wes can defend himself in an honest fight. But it makes no difference how strong a man is if some coward shoots him in the back."

"That's the God's truth, ma'am," Tidwell replied. "That's the way Hickok got it, and I reckon it'll always be that way. But there'll always be a man who lives up to his destiny, even at the risk of havin' some two-legged varmint drill him from behind. I've heard it said a coward dies a thousand times, but a brave man only once."

"Somehow, that makes me feel better," said Rebecca. "Wes can face those who will face him, and I'll watch for the cowards who would shoot him in the back. I have a gun."

Sheriff Tidwell laughed. "That's the spirit, ma'am. A strong man needs him a strong woman, especially on the frontier."

Rebecca Tuttle had come to grips with her fear and experienced a peace she hadn't known since leaving Ohio. Wes Tremayne saw the difference in her and he sighed with relief.

Lincoln, New Mexico
April 27, 1881

Slack Tarno's passing wasn't mourned, and nobody ever learned who had shot him. He had been shot from the front, his own pistol had been fired, and the law dismissed it all as yet another case where a man's unsavory past had caught up with him. Since the episode with Tarno, and Nathan's rescue of Kate, there had been no more animosity. Nathan spent most of his nights with Kate, but for Empty's sake he had kept his room. The dog didn't like Kate. Nathan understood, for he still believed there was something false about the girl, but he would face up to that when it became a problem. That problem came along soon enough, and it began with Cash Seaborn, the youngest of the Silver Dollar's four partners.

"Cash Seaborn's spending a hell of a lot of time at your table," Nathan said one night after closing.

"So what?" Kate replied. "He's not sharing my bed."

"Not yet," said Nathan, "but he has ideas."

"What man doesn't? Don't you suppose I'll have something to say about that?"

"I don't know," Nathan replied. "It depends on how strong you are about keeping your position as a house dealer."

"He wouldn't dare force himself on me, holding that over my head," said Kate.

But Seaborn could and did. Early Tuesday morning, an hour after closing, he came to Kate's door. When she opened it, he wasted no time forcing his way inside, only to be greeted by Nathan's hard right. He stumbled back through the door, slammed into the corridor wall, and slid to the floor.

"You bastard," he said through gritted teeth, "you'll pay for this. Both of you."

"I don't think so," said Nathan. "You're trying to claim privileges that don't belong to you. You have three partners to answer to, and there's two of us to see that you do exactly that. Now get up and get out."

"You ain't heard the last of this," Seaborn snarled. "I'll see both of you dead or locked up."

Nathan closed and bolted the door, but it was a while before he or Kate slept. There was considerable excitement in town the next morning, for Billy the Kid was to be returned to await hanging.

"The Kid was convicted of murder on April 9," said Sheriff Pat Garrett, "and he'll be hanged on May 13, here in Lincoln."

A two-story adobe building, once a store, had been re-modeled as a makeshift courthouse, and it was there—to a room on the second floor—that Billy was taken. Garrett had assigned two deputies—Bob Olinger and J. W. Bell—to guard the Kid. Olinger, hating the Kid, wasted no oppor-tunity to taunt him, often shoving the muzzle of a shotgun in his face. When Deputy J. W. Bell removed the handcuff from Billy's left wrist to allow him to eat supper, the Kid made his move. He swung the empty handcuff at Bell's head, and with Bell on the floor, the Kid grabbed the depu-ty's six-gun and killed him. From across the street, Olinger heard the shot and came running. But the Kid was waiting for him, and from an upstairs window, fired both barrels of Olinger's own shotgun. It literally blew the deputy's head off, and the Kid dropped the shotgun out the window, across the deputy's body. Still shackled, but armed with two six-guns and a Winchester, he calmly hobbled down the stairs. Reaching a nearby blacksmith shop, he ordered the handcuff from his wrist and the shackles from his legs filed off. He then stole a horse and rode away. People in and around Lincoln were mostly friendly to the Kid, and there was no pursuit. The old courthouse was a block be-yond the Silver Dollar, and Nathan left early to see what had caused all the excitement. He arrived in time to see two men bringing J. W. Bell's body down the stairs. Oling-er's remains had been covered with a blanket.

"The Kid's escaped," Nathan was told.

"That ain't gonna help Garrett's reputation none," some-body said.

It was true. Garrett, who had been out of town at the time of the escape, vowed to track down the Kid.

"Garrett won't ever take him alive," Nathan told Kate.

But Nathan and Kate had problems of their own. While Cash Seaborn all but killed them with kindness, he hadn't forgotten. Prior to his coming to Lincoln, he had worked with a small-time criminal in Santa Fe. Saul Yeager had been a master counterfeiter and had been caught and sent to prison for two years. Only by a quirk of fate had Seaborn escaped a similar sentence, and he had fled to Lincoln. Now he believed Saul Yeager had done his time, and Seaborn began devising a plan. If he could find Yeager, he could yet safely become a rich man while destroying the duo he hated the most. Reaching Santa Fe, Cash Seaborn began making the rounds of saloons and cheap rooming houses. When he finally found Yeager, he was holed up in a squalid little room and in no mood to talk to Cash Seaborn.

"Damn you," said Yeager, "you let 'em send me up the river for two years and you didn't lift a finger. You could of at least hired me a lawyer."

"It wouldn't have done you any good," Seaborn said soothingly. "They got you with the goods. I got a foolproof system this time. You turn out the eagles, like before, and I'll buy them from you, half price. There'll be no risk for you, and you'll still earn half the profits, just like before."

"Yeah," said Yeager, "and when you get caught, you'll turn me in. No, thanks."

"Don't be a damn fool," Seaborn said. "How can I turn *you* in, when I'm circulating the phony pieces myself? I'm part owner of a saloon where I'll be passing the stuff, and if I'm caught, it'll be me doing time."

Yeager laughed. "I like the sound of that, havin' done two years while you went free. But I'm out of business. They took my equipment and my materials, and I ain't even got the money to eat regular."

"I'll pay for the necessary equipment and materials," said Seaborn. "Consider that an investment. What must you have?"

"For starters," Yeager said, "a ten-mold die and a small charcoal stove. Bring me two ingots of copper, two of gold, and one of silver."

"Damn," said Seaborn, "that'll cost a pile."

"Your choice," Yeager said. "You know of a cheaper way of gettin' your hands on ten thousand dollars in gold eagles?"

Seaborn laughed. "You got me there. I'll bring you the equipment and double all the metals. Turn me out as many eagles as you can as quick as you can. I'll pay you cash, no strings attached."

"Seaborn," said Yeager, "you got yourself a deal."

Lampasas, Texas
December 24, 1880

"We hate to see you folks go, Wes," said Sheriff Tidwell. "Won't you stay with us until after Christmas?"

"Please, Wes," Rebecca said, "can't we?"

"I reckon," said Wes.

The next several days were memorable ones for Wes and Rebecca. After a bountiful Christmas dinner in the hotel's dining room—an event attended by the entire town—Mayor Patten presented Wes with a silver-mounted Colt 44-40. Upon it was engraved his name, the year, and the town's name. Into each side of the walnut butt was an inlaid ivory replica of a lawman's star. Wes said nothing for a moment, his eyes on the toes of his boots. Finally, swallowing hard, he spoke.

"It's the finest thing anybody ever did for me. Thank you."

Removing his Colt, he slipped it under his belt, placing the new weapon in his holster. Rebecca said nothing until they had returned to their hotel room, and Wes wasn't prepared for her response.

"I'm so proud of you," she said, her voice breaking. She then flung her arms around him and wept.

"Hey, now," he said, "I didn't get shot. Why all the tears?"

"You still have a lot to learn about women," she sniffled. "They cry when their hearts are broken, and when they're so happy, nothing else will do."

"Tarnation," he said. "Somebody oughta write a book."

Santa Fe, New Mexico
June 28, 1881

When Cash Seaborn entered Saul Yeager's room, he eyed the four canvas bags on the table.

"Two thousand of them," said Yeager. "Have a look."

Seaborn took one of the eagles and dropped it on the table. It looked, weighed, and even rang like government issue. Each of the coins had been poured from molten copper, and then plated with a thin layer of an alloy of which nine parts were gold and one was one part silver-copper. It was the exact ratio used by the U.S. Mint in the manufacture of bona fide gold eagles. Seaborn grinned with delight.

"You owe me ten thousand dollars in genuine gold coin," said Yeager.

"I aim to pay you in full," Seaborn said.

He flicked his wrist, and suddenly Yeager's horrified eyes were fixed on the ugly snout of a double-barreled derringer. Seaborn fired once, then fired again. Saul Yeager slumped against a chair and then crumpled to the floor. Seaborn opened the second-floor window. Using the fire escape—a rope with one end tied to the bedstead—he lowered the four bags of coins to the ground, and slid down the rope after them. Already he heard pounding on Yeager's door. His death would go virtually unnoticed—a sleazy little man on the outs with the law whose past had caught up with him.

Lincoln, New Mexico
July 10, 1881

Nathan and Kate were having breakfast when they heard the news. Pat Garrett was on his way to Fort Sumner, having learned from an informant that Billy the Kid had a girl there.

"Where's Fort Sumner?" Nathan asked one of the cafe's cooks.

"Over east of here," said the cook. "It's an abandoned military post that's been took over by a gent name of Pete Maxwell. That's where he houses his ranch workers, and he's got a roadhouse there."

Fort Sumner, New Mexico
July 14, 1881

The Kid had been hiding near Fort Sumner, and after dark slipped into the old post to see Celsa Gutierrez. Feeling safe in the girl's bedroom, the kid relaxed until midnight. When he got hungry, he took his pistol and made his way to Maxwell's for something to eat. He reached Maxwell's porch, not knowing that Sheriff Pat Garrett was inside questioning Peter Maxwell as to the Kid's whereabouts. Deputies McKinney and Poe waited outside, and Billy saw their shadowy forms.

"Who is it?" the Kid asked softly.

McKinney and Poe said nothing. Drawing his gun, Billy stepped into the house. He entered one of Maxwell's unlighted bedrooms, where he could see Garrett's dim form on a bed.

"Who is it?" the Kid asked again.

It was the last he ever spoke. As he backed out the door, Garrett fired twice. One went wild, but the other struck Billy in the chest, killing him instantly. Two men built a wooden coffin, and the following day at noon the Kid was buried in the old post cemetery. He was barely twenty-one years old, laid to rest in a borrowed white shirt that was several sizes too large for his skinny frame.*

Lincoln, New Mexico
July 20, 1881

As rapidly as he could, Cash Seaborn began working the counterfeit eagles into the funds of the Silver Dollar. Every fourth night, he was in control until closing, and all the genuine gold coins reaching his hands were quickly exchanged for the counterfeit eagles. He had no doubt that the scheme would be discovered, but when it was, he was determined none of the evidence would be in his hands. As he paid Nathan and Kate their percentages, he gave them only the counterfeit eagles. Nathan became more and more suspicious, at a loss as to why Cash Seaborn hadn't made some move against them.

"Perhaps he hasn't thought of a way, without making a fool of himself," Kate said.

"He's too damn sneaky and devious to suit me," said Nathan. "I'm used to men who'll grab a gun and come looking for me, not some weasel that tries to get at me in a way I can't get my hands on him."

"We don't have to stay here," Kate replied. "We could just move on."

"We could," said Nathan, "but it purely rubs me the wrong way to run out on some varmint that's out to get

*Despite the legends, there is no recorded evidence that Billy the Kid killed more than five or six men in his short life. In a dispute over a tract of land, Pat Garrett was gunned down from ambush on February 29, 1908, near Las Cruces, New Mexico.

me. He always shows up at the wrong time, and I have to face him on his terms. That's how it was with Slack Tarno. Let's stick around a while until this rattler decides to strike."

It became a decision Nathan would regret. Just a week after Cash Seaborne had disposed of the last counterfeit eagles. Horton Goodner, president of the local bank, called on Jess Delaney, ranking partner in the Silver Dollar.

"Mr. Delaney," said Goodner, "we find ourselves in an ... ah ... delicate situation, and it involves the Silver Dollar."

"Then speak up," Delaney said. "What is it?"

"I'd prefer that you see for yourself," said Goodner, producing a gold eagle. Part of the surface had been scraped away, revealing the copper underneath.

"Why, that's copper," Delaney said. "It's counterfeit."

"Precisely," said Goodner, "and we have more than eighteen thousand dollars' worth on our hands. The Silver Dollar is our largest depositor, and only your deposits can justify such an accumulation so quickly."

"Have you spoken to Sheriff Garrett about this?" Delaney asked.

"No," said Goodner.

"Then don't," Delaney said. "We'll stand good for the loss, if there is one. I'll want to talk to my house dealers and possibly question your tellers."

"Very well," said Goodner. "I'll allow you one week."

CHAPTER 20

Lampasas, Texas
January 2, 1881

Before leaving, Wes had some questions about south Texas that Sheriff Tidwell tried to answer.

"It's mostly cow country," said Tidwell, "unless you're interested in freighting. There is a mighty lot of goods comin' in by sailing ship, with landings at Galveston, Port Lavaca, and Corpus Christi. Now that the Comanches has been took care of, it's likely the safest thing a man can do."

"What about ranching?"

"Learnin' cow is just day-in and day-out hard work," Tidwell said. "Horses, now, it's a mite more interesting. Frank Bell's got a horse ranch on the Medina River, a few miles east of San Antone. His breakers are Lipan Apache Indians, and they gentle their horses without ridin' 'em down. Frank's horses are winning races all over Texas, Louisiana, Arkansas, and Lord knows where else. As you'd expect, they're prime targets for rustlers. If you'll tell Frank I'm vouchin' for you, he might take you on to protect his stock."

"That does sound interesting," said Wes. "I reckon we'll ride down there and talk to him."

Medina, Texas
January 5, 1881

Wes and Rebecca, following Sheriff Tidwell's directions, reached what they believed was the Medina River. To their surprise, as they rode downstream, they came upon what seemed the beginning of a small town. Already there was a mercantile, a saloon, and a pair of other buildings whose log foundations had been laid. A crudely lettered sign across the front of the store read "Medina Mercantile."*

"Might as well stop at the store," Wes said.

Entering the mercantile, they found its merchandise limited. The owner was probably in his fifties, slightly bald, and over a boiled shirt and dark trousers, wore a white apron.

"Gib Watts, at your service," he said.

"I'm Wes Tremayne, and this is Rebecca," said Wes. "We're on our way to the Frank Bell ranch. We're headed the right way, I reckon."

"Indeed you are," Watts said. "Fact is, Mr. Bell's place is what give rise to the town. Without the business from him and the Lipans, wouldn't be no need for a store. We got more goods comin'. Another month or so, and they won't have nothin' in San Antone you can't find here."

"We'll take a couple of tins of peaches, for now," said Wes, "and we'll likely see you again before long."

"Do that," Watts said, collecting a dollar for the peaches.

"His prices seem a little high," said Rebecca after they'd left the store.

"Not from what I've heard," Wes replied. "There are parts of the frontier where these tins are a dollar each and more. From the maps I've seen, we can't be more than a hundred and fifty miles from Corpus Christi, and trade goods should be plentiful."

The Frank Bell ranch had a look of prosperity. Besides the ranch house, there proved to be numerous outbuildings. There were two long, low barns, each surrounded with six-pole-high corrals. There were horses in some of the corrals. The grounds were shaded by enormous oaks, and a line of cottonwoods bordered the Medina River. As they neared the house, a man stepped out on the porch. Wes and Rebecca reined up, and Wes spoke.

"I'm Wes Tremayne, and this is Rebecca. We'd like to talk to Mr. Frank Bell."

"You're lookin' at him," said the man on the porch. "You and the missus step down."

He was tall—over six feet—and his high-crowned Stetson made him seem taller. His dress consisted of dark trousers, a pale yellow shirt, and polished black riding boots. On his right hip was a thonged-down Colt.

*Medina, Texas came into existence in 1880.

"Sheriff Tidwell, at Lampasas, thought you might have a place for me here," Wes said.

"I know Tidwell," said the rancher. "Why would he be sendin' you to me?"

"I like horses," Wes said, "and Sheriff Tidwell thought maybe you could use a gent that's handy with a gun. That is, if you have rustlers interested in your horses."

"Entirely too many rustlers," said Bell. "How handy *are* you with that pistol?"

"Handy enough," Wes said.

Bell took a two-bit piece from his pocket and flung it into the air. With a swiftness the eye could scarcely follow, Wes drew and fired, plugging the coin.

"You'll do," said Bell. "See the house over yonder, to the left of that horse barn? It will be quarters for you and your missus. There's extra stalls in the barn for your horses. Come over to the house after you're settled, and we'll talk. Supper's at five o'clock."

The house, while small, was roomy enough. It had once been white, but the elements had taken their toll, and it, along with its shake roof, had weathered gray. The furnishings were modest but adequate.

"I like it," Rebecca said. "Hotels are nice, but there's nothing like having a house."

"Let's stable our horses and get back to Bell's place," said Wes. "I'd like to know more about his problems, and about those horses."

Lincoln, New Mexico
July 21, 1881

Jess Delaney said nothing to his partners about the distressing visit from the bank's president, Horton Goodner. Instead, he waited until the following day, when it would be his turn to remain at the Silver Dollar until closing. Business was always slow until after supper, and when Nathan and Kate reached the saloon, Delaney herded them to a table. He didn't beat around the bush, but told them exactly what Horton Goodner had told him. He still had the counterfeit eagle from which the gold plate had been scraped away, and this he placed on the table. Nathan took an eagle from his pocket, and with his knife started to scrape the surface. Seeing what he had in mind, Kate presented an eagle of her own. When Nathan had scraped away the thin gold plate from his coin, he took Kate's eagle and performed a similar operation. Only then did he speak to Delaney.

"Somebody's been workin' these counterfeit eagles into the saloon's take, and I reckon we're among the suspects. But there's somethin' I want you to consider. Once every four days, Katrina and me have been paid our percentage in eagles, and I think I can promise you that every one of those coins is counterfeit. Do you reckon we'd be settin' on a pile of these phony coins if we'd been slipping them into the Silver Dollar's daily take?"

"No," Delaney said. "That's why I wanted to talk to you and Katrina before going to the law. Or for that matter, even to my partners."

"I don't aim to accuse anybody without proof," said Nathan, "and if you'll go along with me, I can get that proof."

"What do you want me to do?"

"Have the bank's president question his tellers as to the day or days of the week most of these eagles have been deposited," Nathan said. "Then tally up the nights you, Kilgore, Guthrie, and Seaborn have closed. Get the idea?"

"Yes," Delaney said. "You're looking to link one of us to specific days when most of these counterfeit eagles were taken to the bank."

"I am," said Nathan. "Can you think of a better way? It has to be one of you, me, or Katrina. I believe we've been here long enough to have proven ourselves."

"I'll do as you suggest," Delaney said, "because we must do something. But even if it all points to one of us, it'll still be only circumstantial evidence."

"Just do as I've suggested," said Nathan, "and if it works out as I believe it will, I'll get you the evidence you need. These counterfeit coins are so near perfect, I'd never have known unless some of the plating had worn off. That means somebody, somewhere, is a master craftsman, and such perfection suggests he's done this before. If he has a record, I believe we can find him and learn how these counterfeit eagles ended up here at the Silver Dollar."

"You—or somebody—would have to telegraph every sheriff in the country to get information such as that," Delaney said. "We only have a week before Goodner turns this over to the law."

"Information on known counterfeiters should be on file with the Treasury in Washington," said Nathan.

"Probably," Delaney agreed, "but I doubt they'd release such information to us."

"I can find out with one telegram," said Nathan. "I'll send it in the morning."

"Good," Delaney said. "By then, I'll have written down our closing schedule for the past few weeks. Tomorrow, Goodner should have spoken to his tellers."

That ended the conversation. Delaney went about his business while Nathan and Kate took their places for the night's dealing. They didn't get a chance to discuss the situation until after closing.

"It's Seaborn," said Kate. "He's framing us."

"He's trying to," Nathan said, "but we're going to beat him at his own game."

When Jess Delaney reached the bank the following day, Horton Goodner, was waiting for him. Goodner had some papers spread out on his desk.

"There is some kind of pattern emerging here," said Goodner. "According to my tellers, virtually all these counterfeit eagles have been deposited on specific days. Every fourth deposit has been heavy with eagles, light on everything else. Is this information going to help you reach some conclusion?"

"Yes," Delaney said with a sigh. "It already has."

Carefully, Nathan prepared a telegram to be sent to Byron Silver in Washington.

Need name and whereabouts of counterfeiter capable of creating flawless gold coins.

"I'll be back for the answer," Nathan told the telegrapher. From there, he went to the Silver Dollar, where Jess Delaney was waiting.

"Here's the report from Horton Goodner at the bank," said Delaney, "and here's what I came up with, based on individual closings over the past couple of months."

It stacked up almost exactly as Nathan had expected. On days when large numbers of eagles had been deposited,

Cash Seaborn had been in charge of the till until closing the night before.

"Looks bad, doesn't it?" Delaney said.

"It all depends on who you want to believe," said Nathan. "You have every right to suspect Katrina or me—or both of us—unless there's evidence pointing to someone else. Whoever's responsible had to get the counterfeit coins somewhere, and I'm hoping the telegram I'm expecting will answer that question."

The answer to Nathan's telegram was brief and unsigned. It said:

Master counterfeiter Saul Yeager released from territorial prison April this year stop. Contact authorities in Santa Fe.

"This is where we'll have to let Sheriff Garrett in on the secret," said Nathan. "He'll be in a position to request information from the sheriff in Santa Fe."

Nathan and Delaney explained the purpose of their investigation to Sheriff Garrett, and he telegraphed the sheriff in Santa Fe. The answer, when it came, was shocking.

Saul Yeager murdered stop. Investigation incomplete stop. Suggest you come here.

"Now you've got my curiosity fired up," said Garrett. "Delaney, let's you and me ride up there and see what's behind all this. Stone, you want to come with us?"

"I'd like to," Nathan said, "but I'll be needed at the Silver Dollar. We're trying to keep the lid on this until we learn more about it. This wouldn't be a good time for me to disappear, for several reasons."

"That's sound thinking," said Delaney. "I promise you, we won't come back without some answers."

Medina, Texas
January 12, 1881

"Indian-gentled horses sell for as much as five hundred dollars," said Frank Bell.

Wes and Rebecca had spent a week at the ranch, and were having supper with Bell and his wife, Martha.

"I can appreciate that," Wes said, "after watching Tameka and Wovoka work. They've been talkin' to the same horses for a week. How long does that go on before they're tame enough for a saddle?"

"As far as Tameka and Wovoka are concerned," said Bell, "that day never comes. The horses are never introduced to a saddle. They're expensive for saddle horses, and most of them are bought for the track. Unless a rider is mighty small, he can't afford the luxury of a saddle. Barnabas McQueen, a gent from New Orleans, bought two horses from me. He has a lady rider who rides them bareback, and they've never lost a race."

"Where do these two horses go when they've been gentled?" Rebecca asked.

"You'll be meeting McQueen in Beaumont," said Bell. "As long as the buyer is in Texas, I think we'll deliver the horses. Several buyers had their horses stolen. It'll be up to you to get this pair to Beaumont."

"I'm going, too," Rebecca said. "I can lead one of them."

"There may be some danger," said Bell. "Outlaws from Indian Territory often drift into Arkansas and Louisiana, steal whatever they can get their hands on, and then hightail it back into the territory."

"There's a track at Beaumont?" Wes asked.

"Yes," said Bell, "and it draws horses and gamblers from everywhere."

"And outlaws, I reckon," Wes said.

"Yes," said Bell. "Sometimes there's as much as half a million dollars in that town. It depends on the race, and the horses in competition. I keep expecting a bunch of outlaws to ride in and take it all."

Bound for Beaumont
February 1, 1881

"This is exciting," said Rebecca as they made camp near a spring. "After we deliver the horses, why don't we stay for the race on Saturday? I've never been to a horse race before."

"Neither have I," Wes replied. "Since we're involved with Bell's horses, I reckon it'll be interesting to stay and see 'em run."

"Perhaps we can win some money," said Rebecca. "I still have most of the money from the sale of the mules."

"Fetch me a bucket of water from the spring," Wes said. "I need hot coffee."

But when Rebecca returned from the spring, she brought more than Wes expected. Behind her walked a trio of men, their weapons drawn. About to reach for his Colt, Wes froze when he recognized the trio.

"You always was a rotten shot with a Winchester, Doak," said Burris. "The varmint's alive, bright eyed and bushy tailed."

"No matter," Sellers said. "He's brung us a pair of prime hosses, and after he's dead, we can put the gal to good use."

Knowing what was coming, Wes drew, but the odds were impossibly long. Weapons roared, and a slug struck his head with the force of a sledge hammer. The world suddenly went black, and he knew no more.

Santa Fe, New Mexico
July 27, 1881

When Delaney and Garrett reached Santa Fe, they went immediately to the office of the sheriff.

"I'll tell you as much as I know," Sheriff Hollings said, "and show you what we found in the room where Saul Yeager was murdered."

"We're obliged," said Garrett.

"We know almost for a certainty that Yeager is the man who molded your coins," Hollings said, "because he's been convicted at least twice for that very crime. I'm especially interested in your case because Yeager had an accomplice, and we believe that's the man who murdered him. This hombre who circulates the counterfeit coins is a slippery coyote. There was never any evidence against him and nobody to testify. This time, however, we may have him cornered. The metals needed to mold those counterfeit eagles aren't cheap and they can only be had through certain sources. We contacted those sources when our friend Yeager was released from prison. If he bought any of those metals—anywhere in New Mexico—we were to be notified. Having gotten no word, we believed Yeager had at last decided to go straight, or had perhaps quit the territory. However, in the room where he was murdered, let me show you what we found."

Hollings opened a closet door and removed the items from a shelf. There was part of a bag of charcoal, a small charcoal stove, a ten-die mold, and parts of three bars of metal, one of which was gold.

"My God," said Delaney, "that's all it takes to create gold coins the equal of those coming from the U.S. Mint?"

"That," Hollings said, "and the skill to mix and mold the proper ratios. This may well be the key to capturing Yeager's accomplice, solving a murder, and nailing the culprit who is flooding your town with counterfeit coins."

"We're in over our heads," said Garrett. "We'll follow your lead."

"Then you brought the photograph of the man in question," Hollings said.

"Actually," said Delaney, "it's an etching. Four of us bought a saloon, and there was a story in the newspaper. The paper created the etching to go with the story."

"Here's what we believe happened," Hollings said, "and the etching may get us proof. We believe that Yeager, just out of prison and broke, would have been reluctant to get back into counterfeiting so quickly unless somebody provided some strong motivation. It's pretty obvious, from the amount of metals used, and from the accumulation of counterfeit eagles you've discovered, that Yeager must have molded at least twenty thousand dollars' worth."

"Enough for a pretty damn good stake," said Garrett, "or he wouldn't have shot the goose layin' the golden eggs."

"Exactly," Sheriff Hollings said. "We believe Yeager's accomplice bought the equipment and raw materials right here in Santa Fe. Armed with the etching you brought, we're going to knock on some doors and ask some questions."

The third shop they visited brought results. The proprietor studied the etching for a moment and immediately pointed to Cash Seaborn.

"He's the man you're looking for," said the merchant.

When the trio reached the street, it was Jess Delaney who spoke.

"I know what's comin' next, and it won't be pleasant."

"I reckon it won't be," Sheriff Hollings said. "It'll be up to the courts of Lincoln and Lincoln County to prosecute. As much as I'd like to try the varmint here, he committed his crime outside of my jurisdiction."

"We won't waste any time nailing his hide to the barn door," said Garrett.

"Before you do," Delaney cautioned, "we must try to recover the genuine gold coins he's replaced with counterfeit. The remaining three of us can't swallow such a loss."

"It's unlikely that they're in a bank in his name," said Sheriff Hollings. "You can count on him having hidden them somewhere. Much as I hate to suggest it, you might have to plea-bargain him a lighter sentence as a means of recovering the money."

Southeast Texas
February 1, 1881

When Wes Tremayne regained consciousness, he was alone. The outlaws had been too anxious. One slug had creased his head, while a second had struck the buckle of his gunbelt. His belly felt like he had been kicked by a mule. While his physical hurts were minor, his ego suffered mightily. For the second time, these three outlaws had gunned him down and had left him for dead. That in itself would have been a disgrace, but they had gone a step farther. They had taken his horse, his woman, and the two expensive Indian-gentled horses Frank Bell had trusted him to deliver. Thinking him dead, they hadn't bothered taking his gun. He reloaded the empty chambers, shoved the weapon into his holster, and set out walking. The trail led east, and he gloomily concluded they could be bound for Houston, Beaumont, or some distant point in Louisiana. But he had two powerful forces driving him: He knew the men he was trailing, and he wanted the three of them dead. Graveyard dead.

A few miles ahead, Burris, Doak, and Sellers took their time, scarcely able to believe their good fortune.

"These hosses ain't crowbaits," Burris said. "They ought to bring two hunnert apiece, easy."

"Burris," said Sellers, "you don't never think any farther than saddle broncs. This pair is considerable more than that."

Rebecca only half-listened to them. While she had seen Wes fall and lay unmoving, she couldn't believe he was dead. She was thankful they hadn't searched her, for she still had her Colt under the waistband of her Levi's. Her shirttail concealed the butt of the weapon, for she had pulled the shirt out against the heat. Burris had her horse on a lead rope, while Doak and Sellers each led one of Bell's horses. Rebecca realized she couldn't defend herself against the three of them, but when they came for her—to strip her, use her—she vowed she would kill at least one of them.

Wes struggled on, his head pounding. The sun seemed hotter than it probably was, and when he reached a small stream, he bellied down and ducked his head under the water. The outlaws had jumped him at breakfast time, before he'd even had coffee, and he felt the worse for it. When Wes again took the trail, he studied the tracks. The horses were walking, proof enough the outlaws were in no hurry. Wes lengthened his stride, believing that he could catch up to them before the inevitable happened. Before they mistreated Rebecca.

Lincoln, New Mexico
August 1, 1881

Jess Delaney and Sheriff Garrett reined up before riding into town.

"I got nothin' against you trying to force Seaborn to tell what he's done with your money," Garrett said, "but don't lose sight of the fact he's a criminal. As such, he could pull a gun and start shooting."

"Give all of us time to reach the Silver Dollar," said Delaney, "and then move in next to a window. It'll be after six o'clock and dark by then. I want Cash to get the idea that he might squirm out of this by giving us back our money. But he'll know better if he happens to see you."

Jess Delaney said nothing about what he had learned, or about his plans. Naturally, the house dealers would be there, and so would Cash Seaborn, for this would be his night to remain until closing. However, when Hiram Kilgore and Ward Guthrie showed up, there might be trouble with Seaborn. Two bartenders had charge of the saloon until six o'clock, and Seaborn rarely arrived before then. With that in mind, and without giving any reason, Delaney asked Hiram Kilgore and Ward Guthrie to be present at five-thirty. Nathan and Katrina were always there early, and it would allow Delaney to prepare them for what was about to happen.

"I saw Sheriff Garrett in town a while ago," Nathan told Kate. "That means Delaney's planning a showdown tonight."

"It's going to be interesting," said Kate. "I'm wondering how they're going to force Seaborn to return all the money he's replaced with counterfeit coins."

"Maybe by lettin' him think he can get out of it by re-signing from the Silver Dollar and returning the money," Nathan said.

"You don't suppose he *can* get out of it that easily, do you?"

"No," said Nathan. "Horton Goodner, the banker, is aware of it, and I doubt he'd allow a crime of such magnitude to go unpunished."

Nathan and Kate reached the Silver Dollar at twenty minutes past five. Delaney, Kilgore, and Guthrie were already there.

"All of you gather around close," Delaney said. "I have a lot to say, and I don't want outside ears hearing it. Please don't interrupt until I'm finished."

"Seaborn's not here," said Guthrie.

"This involves Seaborn," Delaney said. "We'll have a question for him when he gets here."

Delaney began with the bank's disclosure that the Silver Dollar's deposits had resulted in massive amounts of counterfeit eagles.

"Damn it," Hiram Kilgore shouted, "why weren't we told?"

"You *have* been told," said Delaney. "Stomping around and raising hell would have resulted in allowing the culprit to take the money and run. As it is, we're going to confront him in a few minutes, with enough proof to send him to territorial prison."

"By God," Ward Guthrie shouted, "you're saying Cash Seaborn robbed us."

"Yes," said Delaney, "and I'm telling you I have the proof. Now sit down and shut up so I can fill you in on the rest of it."

Delaney spoke rapidly, and while his partner's mouthed curses, they remained silent. But the silence was temporary. When Delaney had finished, there were angry outbursts from Kilgore and Guthrie.

"Damn it," Kilgore roared, "with all this proof you got, why ain't the bastard in jail?"

"Because we don't know what he's done with our twenty thousand dollars," Delaney roared back. "We lose that and we're ruined. We're going to try and bargain with him. If he returns what he's taken and resigns, he goes free. Otherwise, we'll prosecute him to whatever extent the law allows."

"You're forgetting something," said Nathan. "There's been a crime committed and you can't promise Seaborn the law won't prosecute. Is Sheriff Garrett aware of your plan?"

"No," Delaney admitted. "All he knows is that we're going to try and negotiate for the return of our money."

Cash Seaborn paused before the Silver Dollar. From within, he could hear the angry voices of Delaney, Kilgore, and Guthrie. Across the street, leaning against an awning post, stood Sheriff Pat Garrett. Hitching up his trousers, Seaborn buttoned his coat, concealing the Remington revolver shoved under his belt.

CHAPTER 21

Southeast Texas
February 1, 1881

The sun seemed to balance on the rim of the western horizon, granting a few final moments before the coming of the night. The chill fingers of the west wind caressed Wes Tremayne, reminding him that his coat was tied behind his saddle. He hadn't eaten since supper the night before, and his belly growled with the lack of food. Without faltering, he went on, knowing that for Rebecca time was running out.

"The next good water," Doak said, "let's stop for the night."

While his companions said nothing, the thought had crossed their minds. The day had been long, and they had stopped only to rest the horses. Covertly, they eyed Rebecca, who pretended they didn't exist. The first stars were out before they found suitable water. The spring gurgled out from beneath a mass of rock at the deep end of an arroyo. There was a runoff from which the horses could drink, and enough of a rim to shield the camp from a chill wind. Rebecca eyed the rim approvingly. It might also allow Wes to get the drop on the outlaws when he caught up to them. Despite her predicament, she smiled to herself, aware of how much she had changed. Her first days with Wes had been fraught with terror, for it had seemed death was stalking him, never more than a heartbeat away. Now, having seen him shot down before her eyes, she didn't doubt that he lived or that he would be coming for her. One of the outlaws had a small fire going, and it was Doak who shouted at her.

"You! Gather some wood for the fire."

The three of them sat on the rocks near the spring, passing around a bottle. There was no way Rebecca could reach the horses without being seen, so they weren't concerned about her escaping. Beyond the spring's runoff, she gathered damp leaves and piled them on the small fire. As the flames bit into the leaves, smoke billowed up into the evening sky in great clouds. It was Sellers who finally took notice of what she was doing.

"Damn you," Sellers shouted, "stop that."

He ran to the fire and kicked the smoking mound of leaves, scattering them.

"I didn't see that much wood," said Rebecca innocently, "but there's plenty of leaves."

"Git away from the fire," said Sellers.

"What's bitin' you, Sellers?" Doak asked, taking another drink from the bottle.

"Damn you," said Sellers, "it was you told her to feed the fire. The fool woman sent up enough smoke to be seen in Dodge City."

"Maybe," Burris said, "but so what? The Comanches ain't a threat no more. Nobody else is likely to be interested."

But someone was interested. A few miles away, Wes Tremayne eyed the distant smoke and set out to reach it. The outlaws would never be so careless. The smoke meant Rebecca was still alive.

Lincoln, New Mexico
August 1, 1881

Cash Seaborn entered the Silver Dollar, pausing just inside the door. Nearest him sat Nathan and Kate, while directly ahead of him his three partners waited.

"Come on in and set down, Cash," Delaney said. "We have something to discuss with you."

"I'm comfortable where I am," said Seaborn. "Since when do you find it necessary to include the house dealers in our discussions?"

"This particular discussion involves them," Delaney said. "You're responsible for that. The bank has informed us of peculiar circumstances surrounding our account. All evidence points to you, Cash, and there's more than enough to convict you. Return the money to us, resign, and you can walk away a free man."

"I don't know what you're talking about," said Seaborn. "You've drummed this up to boot me out, to take what's mine."

Seaborn had purposely remained near the door. None of his partners, as far as he knew, was armed with anything more lethal than a derringer, and he was out of range. The only threat to him was Nathan Stone, who was seated. The arm of his chair would slow his draw. Seaborn took a step forward, as though to join his partners, but suddenly turned on Nathan and Kate, a pistol in his hand. The first slug ripped into the tabletop, while the second struck the arm of a chair. The ricochet struck Kate McDowell in the head. Nathan rolled out of his chair and came up shooting. He fired twice, and both slugs tore into Cash Seaborn, who stumbled into a table, hung there a moment, then collapsing on the floor.

"Damn it," Hiram Kilgore shouted, "you've killed him. Now we'll never get our twenty thousand."

But Nathan didn't hear. Kate had slid out of her chair and lay on the floor. Nathan knelt beside her, knowing she was dead. Sheriff Garrett burst through the door, a gun in his hand. He looked from Seaborn to Kate, holstered his gun, and removed his hat. The three saloon owners had gotten to their feet, and it was Delaney who spoke.

"We tried to reason with him, Sheriff, but he pulled a gun and started shooting. He was shooting at Stone, and hit the woman by mistake. Stone returned fire."

"Stone didn't have to kill him," Kilgore growled. "Wounded, he could have talked."

It was a shameful, foolish thing to have said, and in an instant, Nathan had seized the front of Kilgore's shirt, standing him on his toes.

"You greedy damned fool," said Nathan through clenched teeth, "all that matters to you is money. I wish to God it was you layin' there with a hole in your skull, instead of Kate."

He shoved Kilgore across a table, and amid a tangle of chairs, he thunked headfirst to the floor.

"That's enough, Stone," Sheriff Garrett said.

Drawn by the shots, other men crowded into the saloon.

One of them was Jubal Park, whose cabinet shop served as a funeral parlor when needed.

"Jubal," said Sheriff Garrett, "have these bodies taken to your place and made ready for burying."

"Only if the county's payin'," Jubal said. "I ain't gettin' stuck for no more funerals."

"Prepare the lady for burying," said Nathan, "and do it proper. I'll pay."

"We'll pay for Seaborn," Delaney said.

"Speak for yourself," said Kilgore. "Livin' or dead, he ain't gettin' another *peso* out of me."

"Everybody to the bar," Ward Guthrie shouted. "Drinks are on the house."

That got their attention, and as the bodies were being removed, Delaney hung back and spoke to Nathan.

"This has been a most regrettable incident. Will you deal tonight?"

"No," said Nathan. "Not tonight or any other night. Tomorrow, after the buying, I'll be riding on."

Nathan said no more, for Ward Guthrie and Hiram Kilgore were approaching, and as he turned away, he heard Guthrie speak to Delaney.

"Come on, Jess. Leave it with the bartenders. We're goin' up to Scaborn's quarters and rip the place apart. He's stashed that money somewhere."

Southeast Texas
February 1, 1881

Exhausted, weak from hunger, Wes looked down on the outlaw camp from the brush that grew along the rim. The outlaws were passing around a bottle. Wes was barely able to see Rebecca, for she had distanced herself from them. Somehow she must be made aware that Wes was alive. From one of the loops on his gunbelt, he took a cartridge and, carefully judging the distance, threw it. It fell in the sand just inches from Rebecca. Using her body to hide her movements from the outlaws, she drew the .38 Colt from beneath her shirt, hoping Wes could see that she was armed. While she had no idea what he might attempt, she didn't believe he could successfully defend himself against three gunmen. Even in the pale moonlight, Wes had seen the pistol and knew they hadn't disarmed her. There was no cover that would allow him to descend the arroyo's rim without being seen, and he circled around to the shallow end. He ground his teeth in frustration, for lack of a means of communicating with Rebecca. Her accuracy with a gun— or lack of it—wouldn't matter if they made their move together. She would distract the outlaws, allowing him the edge he needed. Now he had but one choice, and that was to go in shooting. But that all changed in an instant.

"Woman," Sellers shouted, "git over here."

"No," said Rebecca defiantly. "If you want me, then you'll have to come and get me."

"Then I'll come an' git you," Sellers said, "and I'll take you first."

"Come on," said Rebecca, "if you're man enough."

Wes took a deep breath. She was speaking for his benefit, drawing one of the outlaws away, reducing the odds. From his position, Wes couldn't see any of them. He waited, depending on his ears. It was Rebecca who gave him his cue, when she spoke.

"I have a gun, and I'll shoot."

Sellers laughed. "Sure you will. If you had a gun, you'd of used it before now."

The stillness of the night was shattered by the roar of a gun, and Wes was off and running. In the shocked silence following the shot, Sellers cried out.

"I . . . I'm . . . shot."

Doak and Burris were on their feet, reaching for their guns, when Wes shouted his challenge.

"Hold it. You're covered."

But the outlaws ignored the warning and began firing. Wes gunned them down, and as he turned toward Rebecca she came running to meet him.

"I saw them shoot you," she cried, "but I . . . I knew you'd be coming for me, if . . . if . . . you were still alive."

"My head hurt like nine kinds of hell," said Wes, "but I got here as soon as I could. The smoke helped."

"Help me," Sellers cried. "I'm . . . gut-shot."

"I'm sorry," said Rebecca, "but you didn't believe me when I said I had a gun."

"Mister," Wes said, "I'm doin' as well by you as you did

by me. You'll lay there and take your chances with the coyotes and buzzards."

Wes released the horses belonging to the outlaws. He then saddled his own horse and Rebecca's, and with Frank Bell's horses on lead ropes, they rode out.

Lincoln, New Mexico
August 2, 1881

Nathan rode behind the hearse taking Kate to the cemetery. Drawn by four matched blacks, the macabre vehicle made its way past the old adobe jail from which Billy the Kid had so recently shot his way to freedom for the last time. Sheriff Pat Garrett and Jess Delaney were among the few mourners. The minister was waiting, and the service was brief. Without a word, Nathan mounted his horse and rode away. Empty had refused to follow the hearse, joining Nathan on his way back through town. Following the Rio Grande south, he reined up and looked back. It was yet another town in which he had the uneasy feeling he was leaving part of himself.

"Well, Empty," he said aloud. "Where do we go from here? Molly's in El Paso?"

With Kate strong on his mind, he wasn't ready to resume his relationship with Molly Horrell, but if he returned to El Paso, would he have any choice? That reminded him of a similar situation in New Orleans, where Vivian Stafford awaited him at the McQueen place. Would he ever see Barnabas and Bess McQueen again?

"Damn it," he growled, "I'm boxing myself in."

Unwilling to ride farther without resolving the problem, he dismounted. Picketing the grulla so that it might graze, he sat down, his back to a pine, to think. He was forced to admit that he wasn't ready to settle down, and however strongly he felt about any woman, life on the trail became more difficult when she accompanied him. He had never forgotten how Eulie Prater had frowned on his fondness for saloon gambling. While Eulie's remains rested in a grave near New Orleans, it seemed to Nathan there was a little of her in every woman. Could a woman ever be satisfied with a man whose first love was a deck of cards?

"Empty," said Nathan, getting to his feet, "we won't be goin' back to El Paso any time soon, and I reckon that goes for New Orleans, too. I don't know what's goin' to cure me of this wanderlust. A slug between the eyes, maybe."

Nathan mounted the grulla and, with Empty following, rode west, toward Arizona Territory.

Beaumont, Texas
February 4, 1881

"We're still on time," Wes said as they rode into Beaumont. "If Barnabas McQueen's already here, we can turn these horses over to him and save tonight's livery bill."

"We only have to find the sheriff's office," said Rebecca. "It seems Frank Bell knows a lot of lawmen."

"Not a bad idea," Wes said, "with so many rustlers. There's the sheriff's office."

Sheriff Waddy McLean stood up behind his desk, as Wes and Rebecca entered.

"I'm Wes Tremayne," said Wes, "and this is Rebecca. We're with Frank Bell, and we have some horses for Barnabas McQueen of New Orleans. Mr. Bell said you'd know if Mr. McQueen's here, and if he is, where we can find him."

"Pleased to meet you," said the sheriff. "I'm Waddy McLean, and the way Bell uses me, I ought to be collectin' wages. McQueen's here. You'll find him at the Beaumont Hotel, I reckon. If he ain't there, put the horses up at Elkins Livery, near the track. McQueen's other horses are stabled there. If you miss McQueen, I'll tell him you're here. Where will you be stayin'?"

"We'll stay at the Beaumont Hotel," Wes said.

Leaving all the horses at the Elkins Livery, Wes and Rebecca registered at the Beaumont Hotel.

"I'm looking for Barnabas McQueen," said Wes.

"The McQueens are in room nine," the desk clerk said. "They may be in the dining room now, having breakfast."

But when Wes knocked, the door was opened immediately.

"Mr. McQueen," said Wes, "I'm Wes Tremayne, and this

is Rebecca. We're with Frank Bell and we've brought your horses. They're at Elkins Livery."

"Much obliged," McQueen said. "This is Bess. We were about to go to breakfast. Will you join us?"

"Yes, sir," said Wes. "We'd like that."

"Hold on," McQueen said, "and I'll get Vivian."

He knocked on a door across the hall, and the girl who returned with him left Wes staring and Rebecca envious.

"This is Vivian Stafford," said McQueen. "Vivian, this is Wes and Rebecca. They'll be going to breakfast with us."

Wes and Rebecca said little during the meal, listening to the McQueens talk about their horses, races they had won, and races they hoped to win. In the course of the conversation, McQueen got around to praising Vivian for all her winning rides. Wes regarded her with new interest, while Rebecca scarcely regarded her at all.

"I'm riding in races tomorrow and Sunday," Vivian said. "Are you going to stay?"

"Yes," said Wes, avoiding Rebecca's eyes. "I'd like to see you ... the horses ... run."

"We'll race Modelo tomorrow," Vivian said, "and Petalo on Sunday. This will be the first time for Modelo to run here, and there'll be good odds. Be sure to place your bets."

Following breakfast, Wes and Rebecca went to their room, and Rebecca exploded.

"You didn't ask *me* if I wanted to stay for the races."

"I wasn't aware that I had to ask your permission for *anything*," said Wes coldly.

"I'm not going," Rebecca said, just as coldly.

"Then don't," said Wes. "You can set here till moss grows on the north side of you, for all I care."

Furious, she threw herself face down on the bed. Wes got up, pulled on his boots, buckled on his gunbelt, and grabbed his hat.

"Where are you going?" she demanded.

"Out," he said. "I'm betting every dollar I have on Modelo."

"That's a damn lie," she cried. "You're betting it on Vivian Stafford."

"Have it your way," said Wes. "She's riding the horse."

Southwestern New Mexico
August 5, 1881

Nathan rode as far south as he dared, careful not to cross the border into Mexico, but seeking a less mountainous terrain. Soon he came upon the ruts of what he suspected was the old Butterfield Overland Mail Route.* But there was something more.

"Empty," said Nathan, "these are fresh tracks. There's a wagon with four outriders up ahead of us. Who can they be, and where are they going?"

It was an unlikely time and place for anyone on legitimate business, for New Mexico and Arizona were—although recognized by the Union—still territories. From El Paso to Yuma, there was hundreds of miles of Mexican border, a haven for thieves and killers who had ridden beyond the reach of the law. Nathan rode cautiously, reining up when he heard cursing. He dismounted and advanced, leading the horse.

"By God," a voice bawled, "get your backs under that pole and heave."

Four Mexicans wearing leg irons threw their combined weight under a long pole, seeking to lift a wagon whose left rear wheel had shattered. Four men stood beside their saddled horses, Winchesters at the ready, while the man shouting orders stood with his hands on his hips. Again he spoke.

"Halsell, you and Thacker get ready to pile those stones under the axle when they lift the wagon."

"Damn it, Childress," one of the men grumbled, "I didn't hire on to git down in the dirt with a bunch of Mexes."

"Do as you're told, Thacker," Childress shouted, "or by God, I'll have you shot for insubordination."

The Mexicans threw their weight behind the pole, raising the wagon, while Halsell and Thacker began laying the flat stones in place. But the stones had been hastily and poorly laid, and when the wagon was let down, the column tumbled. The hapless Mexicans looked at Childress, and he motioned for them to raise the wagon again.

*Authorized by Congress, the Butterfield Overland Mail operated from September 15, 1858 until March 1, 1861. The route was 2,795 miles, from St. Louis to San Francisco.

"Maybe you'd oughta have a couple of the Mexes stack them rocks. Colonel," one of the other guards said, "and have Halsell and Thacker help lift the wagon. That don't take no brains."

"When I want advice from you, Colcord, I'll ask for it," said Childress. "You and Beal get your backs under that pole and help raise the wagon."

Unwillingly they did as ordered, and the pile of stones supported the wagon. Nathan advanced, while Empty backed off, growling. It was enough to get the attention of Childress, and he turned, his hand on the butt of his revolver. When he spoke, it was without friendliness.

"Who are you?"

"Stone," said Nathan. "I'm Nathan Stone."

"And your business?"

"My business is my business," Nathan said. "Who are you?"

"I am Colonel Barkley Childress, United States Army, retired."

"Sorry I can't say I'm pleased to meet you," said Nathan. "Why are those four men in irons?"

"They are slaves," Childress said. "I bought them in Mexico, and they are mine to do with as I see fit. I am taking them to Tucson, where they will be sold. Are you satisfied?"

"No," said Nathan. "The days of slavery are over. You or whoever has the key to those leg irons—set those men free. You're in violation of federal law."

"Federal law be damned," Childress shouted. "New Mexico and Arizona are territories. Who is going to enforce federal law? You?"

"If need be," said Nathan.

Childress was in a poor position, for his men—Halsell, Thacker, Colcord, and Beal—had laid aside their Winchesters when Childress had ordered them to help with the repair of the wagon. While each man was armed with a revolver, Nathan Stone had twin Colts thonged down, and he wasn't in the least intimidated.

Childress laughed. "How ironic. I believe this is referred to as a Mexican standoff. We must negotiate, I suppose."

"No," said Nathan. "You don't negotiate a man's freedom or his life. I'm ordering you one more time to set those men free."

"If I refuse," Childress said, "are you going to shoot me?"

"If I must," said Nathan. "I've shot better men."

Childress had moved his right hand closer to the butt of his pistol, and believed he had an edge. That was his first mistake. He immediately made the second one, snatching the weapon from its holster. One of Nathan's Colts roared and Childress dropped his gun. While the four hired guns were armed, they froze, for each man found himself looking into the deadly bore of Nathan Stone's Colt.

"Now," said Nathan, "who's going to unlock those leg irons?"

"Damn you," Childress said through gritted teeth, "you've broken my arm."

"I could just as easily have killed you," said Nathan, "but I'm saving that. Now, if you don't turn those four men loose, I'll break your other arm. Then if you still need some convincing, I'll gut-shoot you."

Awkwardly, using his left hand, Childress loosed a leather thong from his belt. At the end of it was a single key.

"Here," he said, flinging the key at Thacker. "Unlock the leg irons."

"Not yet," said Nathan. "The four of you toss your weapons over here. *Then* you'll unlock the leg irons."

Sullenly the four removed their weapons from their holsters and pitched the guns at Nathan's feet.

"Now," Nathan said, "remove those leg irons."

One by one, the four Mexicans were freed. While they apparently didn't understand what was being said, they fully understood the Colt in Nathan's hand and the fact that the hated shackles were being removed. And once freed, it was to Nathan that they looked.

"Libre, Mejicanos," said Nathan, pointing south.

They understood. Like frightened quail, they vanished into the underbrush. When the four were well on their way toward the border, Nathan gathered the discarded weapons and, looping his bandanna through the trigger guards, hung the weapons from his saddle horn. Careful to keep the men covered, he took the Winchesters, shoving one into the saddle boot of each man's mount. He then gathered the reins of the four horses and backed away.

"I am not one to forget," Childress said. "We'll meet again."

"You'll find your horses and weapons somewhere ahead," said Nathan. "Replace the wagon wheel, and you won't be afoot. I'd suggest you leave the mules hitched to the wagon. If anybody gets ambitious, I'll be watching my backtrail, and it'll be your last mule ride."

Leading the four horses, Nathan circled wide. Empty awaited him on the trail ahead, and again Nathan rode west.

Beaumont, Texas
February 5, 1881

Saturday, the day of the first race, Rebecca still sulked, and it didn't help her disposition when Wes left her to have breakfast with the McQueens and Vivian Stafford.

"The odds were ten to one," Wes told McQueen.

McQueen laughed. "Better take them while you can get them. Modelo's about to make some changes."

Wes thought Vivian Stafford looked a bit uncertain, and he wondered if he had been wise, betting all his money on Modelo. Winning, he'd have five thousand dollars. Losing, Rebecca would never let him forget. After breakfast, he returned to the hotel, kicked off his boots, and lay down to rest. Rebecca pretended to be asleep, but curiosity got the best of her, and she spoke.

"I suppose you bet on the horse. Or was it the rider?"

"Both," Wes said. "When Modelo wins, I'll have five thousand dollars."

"Suppose he loses," said Rebecca. "Then what do you get?"

"A kiss from the rider," Wes said recklessly, "but I don't expect to lose. McQueen's horses are winners."

Despite Rebecca's dislike for Vivian Stafford, she was there for the race. In competition with fourteen other horses, Modelo beat his closest rival by two lengths. Wes, in his excitement, grabbed Vivian in a bear hug. When he went to collect his money, Rebecca followed. Despite her anger, she was impressed. Many a man labored a lifetime and never saw so much money all at one time.

"I suppose you're going to bet all that on tomorrow's race," she said.

"Yes," he said with a straight face, "and I aim to sell our horses and saddles. When I add that to all this—"

"I can hang around the saloons tonight, selling my body," she said.

He looked at her, half believing, and despite herself she laughed.

"I aim to salt most of this away against hard times," he told her. "I reckon I'll risk five hundred on tomorrow's race."

"I'll go with you," said Rebecca. "I still have money from the sale of those mules. Do you still want to work for Frank Bell, now that you have so much money?"

"Yes," he said. "I want to become friends with those Lipan Apaches and learn how they gentle horses."

CHAPTER 22

Southwestern New Mexico
August 7, 1881

Nathan rode thirty miles before picketing the four horses. He left them near water, where they could graze, but far enough ahead that their owners would be fortunate to get to them before sundown. The terrain was rough, and the wagon, once they had it repaired, would be slow going. Nathan rode on to the next water before making camp. Childress and his men couldn't possibly catch up to them, and if they did, Empty would announce their coming well in advance.

Nathan arose at first light and, after a hurried breakfast, rode west. Empty trotted well ahead. The terrain began to change, and by late afternoon Nathan began seeing literal forests of sagauro that seemed to flourish only in southern Arizona. Many stood taller than a man on horseback, marching up slopes like soldiers, their arms lifted to the heavens of brilliant blue. Nathan reined up.

"Well, Empty, we're in Arizona, but where do we go from here?"

There was Tucson, within a day's ride, or Phoenix a day or more beyond, somewhere to the northwest. He couldn't help remembering the outlaw town on the Gila River, beyond Tucson. There, he and other unfortunates had toiled in virtual slavery, until they had taken control and destroyed their captors. He wondered if the place had become a ghost town, but he had no intention of returning there.*

"Empty," he said, "I think we'll drift a little farther south and have us a look at Tombstone. I've heard a lot about it."

*The Killing Season (Book 2)

Tombstone, Arizona Territory
August 8, 1881

As Nathan rode into town, he couldn't believe his eyes. A familiar figure had stepped out of a mercantile, shouldering a sack of grain. Nathan reined up, shouting a greeting.

"Mel Holt, you old tin-star varmint, what are you doin' here?"

"I could ask you the same thing," Holt said. He dropped the sack of grain and came to meet Nathan, a grin on his rugged face.

"I last saw you in Little Rock," said Nathan. "You helped me corral some thieves and recover Barnabas McQueen's horses. We raced McQueen's Diablo and won big time. You were going back to Fort Smith to turn in your badge and buy a place in South Texas."

"Places and people change," Holt said. "Ride out to my place for supper and I'll tell you all about it."

Holt hoisted the sack of grain up, mounted his horse and led out. Nathan followed. Empty trotting alongside, as they headed north. Free of town, Nathan caught up.

"Come on," said Nathan. "Talk."

"I reckon there's some things I should tell you before we reach the house," Holt said. "Do you remember Susie Horrell?"

"Yes," said Nathan. "Sister to Molly."

"I wanted Susie and she wanted me," Holt said, "but you know the Horrells. They got no interest in anything except shootin' anybody that looks like a Higgins or speaks kindly of one. Mart told me to get the hell away and to stay away. It was quit the country or spend all my time fightin' Susie's kin, so here we are. I got a blessed plenty of shootin' and bein' shot at while I was a deputy marshal in Fort Smith."

"Congratulations, Mel," said Nathan. "You're smarter than you look."

Holt laughed. "I know. I count my blessings every day."

They reined up at Holt's barn, and when they had unsaddled and rubbed down their horses, they started for the log house. It looked well built, and there was real glass in the windows. Mel Holt was a Texan, tried and true, and Nathan was amazed at how much the man reminded him of Byron Silver. Susie met them at the door.

"Susie," Holt said, "you remember Nathan Stone, don't you?"

"Yes," said Susie, "although I've never met him. But he doesn't look anything like the Horrells described him. There are no horns, no spike tail, and no cloven hooves."

Nathan laughed. "With all due respect to your kin, Susie, I reckon they see everybody in that light, if he ain't a Horrell."

"That's the God's truth, if it was ever spoken," Holt said.

They all laughed, appreciating the humor and its proximity to the actuality.

"Wash up and go to the table," said Susie. "The coffee's ready, and I'll have supper in a few minutes."

The dining table was in the kitchen. There was a wood stove, a split-log floor, and the table and chairs had been hand crafted from pine. The plates, cups, and saucers were of bone china, while the eating tools were silver plated. On a big glass plate was two-thirds of a chocolate cake.

"Stay out of the cake," Susie warned. "I have a beef roast and potatoes coming."

"Tarnation," said Nathan. "If I'd known all this was waitin', I'd have been here a mite sooner."

"We're glad you're here," Susie said.

"Yeah," Holt agreed. "It's good to see a friendly face. I hope you'll stay awhile."

"Maybe I will," said Nathan, "but I'll have to find something to occupy my time. All I know is how to pull a gun and deal cards."

"You've come to the right place, then," Holt said. "The town's full of saloons, and the country's split into two factions."

"Yes," said Susie. "The rustlers against the rest of us."

"What about the law?" Nathan asked.

"John Behan's sheriff," said Holt, "and in June, Virgil Earp was appointed marshal."

"Then I reckon Wyatt's here, too," Nathan said.

"Hell, they're all here," said Holt. "Wyatt's deputy sheriff of Tombstone, and he owns a piece of the Oriental Saloon, the classiest place in town."

"Wyatt doesn't think too highly of me," Nathan said. "In Dodge, I had to shoot a no-account gambler, after Earp had ordered me to leave him be."

"Some of us don't think too highly of Wyatt Earp," said

Susie. "He left his wife, and he's just married another woman."

"That's the least of our worries, where Earp's concerned," Holt said. "The man has a lust for power. Since coming here, he's tried twice to be appointed Cochise County sheriff. Earp tried to influence the county commissioners through a shady deal with the Clantons and the McLaurys, and it blew up in his face."

"Who are the Clantons and McLaurys?" Nathan asked.

"Thieves," said Holt. "Cattle, horses, mules. They were caught with six army mules and had changed the U.S., brands to a D.8. That's one of their lesser crimes."

"What was Earp doing with these varmints?" Nathan asked.

"It's a pretty accepted fact that the Clantons and McLaurys are friendly to every outlaw in the territory. The Benson stage was held up and a man was killed. Earp believed if he could bring the robbers to justice, it would help his chances of becoming sheriff in the next election. He was satisfied that Jim Crane, Billy Leonard, and Harry Head had been responsible for the stage robbery and the killing. He was also aware that these men were on good terms with the Clantons and McLaurys. There was twelve hundred dollars reward on each of the three robbers. Wyatt Earp met with Ike Clanton and Frank McLaury, and offered them the reward—thirty-six hundred dollars—if they would turn in the three stage robbers. Earp wanted to personally capture them."

"My God," said Nathan. "And they agreed?"

"That's the word," Holt said, "but only if the rewards would be paid for the outlaws, dead or alive, and that Earp kept his mouth shut about the betrayal by Ike Clanton and Frank McLaury."

"I've never liked Earp," said Nathan, "but I never believed he'd stoop that low just to gain advantage."

"He didn't gain any advantage," Holt said. "Before Clanton and McLaury could lure the stage robbers within Earp's reach, the men were killed by horse thieves. After that, the Clantons and McLaury's began threatening the Earps."

"That's not hard to figure," said Nathan. "The Clantons and McLaurys had revealed their connection to outlaws, and they rightly suspected they couldn't trust Earp, knowin' his ambition to become a lawman."*

---

*Wyatt Earp's alliance with Ike Clanton and Frank McLaury was admitted by Earp in his testimony before Wells Spicer, October 30 1881.

"That's the way I see it," Holt said. "There's been threats flung from both sides, and the time's comin' when there'll be gunplay."

"Supper's getting cold," said Susie. "I fed your dog on the back porch."

"I'm obliged," Nathan said. "It's been a while since we've had decent grub. I reckon there's nothin' I've got to say that stands as tall as that beef roast."

There was no more conversation until they were into the chocolate cake and a second pot of coffee. Susie spoke.

"If you're going to be here awhile, you're welcome to stay with us. We have room."

"I'm obliged," said Nathan, "but that wouldn't be wise. I don't know that Earp would trouble you on my account, but he might. There must be a good boardinghouse in town that won't object to Empty, my dog."

"You're still welcome to stay with us," Holt said. "I can't imagine a man carrying a grudge from another time and another town. I own this place free and clear, and nobody's goin' to tell me who can or can't bunk here. Not with the Clanton and McLaury ranches bein' friendly to outlaws."

"No," said Nathan. "Stay out of it if you can. I aim to find me a saloon that needs a house dealer, and I'll be more comfortable in a boardinghouse nearby."

"In that case," Holt said, "try Inez McMartin's place on Third Street. As for saloons, the New Orleans is one of the better ones. By that, I mean there's no whorehouse on the second floor. Sorry, Susie."

"Mel Holt, stop acting like I'm one of those prissy town women," said Susie. "I knew what a bawdy house was, time I was twelve."

Nathan laughed, and Holt looked a little sheepish. Susie came to his rescue, speaking to Nathan.

"You're welcome to eat with us anytime, but if you do eat in town, the New Orleans Restaurant is right next to the saloon. I've been there. They're both on Fourth Street, next to Brown's Grocery."

"I'll ride in before dark," Nathan said. "With so much rustling going on, how are you making out?"

"Better than most," said Holt. "When we first came here, I casually mentioned that I'd been a deputy marshal. And I have a brand that nobody can alter with a running iron or cinch ring."

Nathan laughed. "I'll want to see that."

"It's the M H connected," Holt said. "The fore leg of the M is connected to the upper hindleg of the H. I haven't lost a cow."

"We don't have that many," said Susie.

"If they can't change your brand," Nathan said, "they'll wait for your natural increase and come after your unbranded calves."

"Our best crop won't be along until spring," said Holt. "If you're still here, and these rustlers are still helping themselves, I'll hire you to side me."

"If Susie will feed me regular, like she did today," Nathan said, "I'll track down that bunch of rustlers for nothing."

Beaumont, Texas
February 8, 1881

"Wes," said McQueen, "if you and Rebecca are ever in New Orleans, come visit us."

"We will," Wes replied.

"Sorry you didn't get better odds on Petalo, Sunday," said Vivian. "He's run here before."

The McQueens and Vivian rode east, toward New Orleans, while Wes and Rebecca took the trail west.

"The town was nice, for a while," Rebecca said, "but I'm ready to get back to the Bell ranch. I grew up in the city, but I'm losing my feel for it."

"You're becoming a frontier woman," said Wes.

Medina, Texas
February 13, 1881

"There was hell to pay while you were gone," Frank Bell said when Wes and Rebecca returned to the ranch. "Night riders hit the Beckham ranch. They took six horses and shot down one of Beckham's riders."

"Did anybody trail them?" Wes asked.

"Beckham and his four riders started after them," said Bell, "but two of the thieves stayed on the backtrail. They killed Beckham's *segundo* and wounded two others, one of 'em Beckham. The thieves took the horses and headed for the border."

"I reckon the nearest law is in San Antonio," Wes said.

"Yes," said Bell, "and a sheriff's posse couldn't of got on the trail until morning. The thieves could have been near the border by then. We can't count on the law. We'll have to stomp our own snakes, so I rode into San Antone and hired three more men."

"I don't like the looks of them," Martha Bell said. "I wonder if they aren't outlaws themselves."

"Aw, Martha," said Bell, "this is the frontier. It takes men with the bark on, just to stay alive. They're in the bunkhouse, if you'd like to meet them."

"I reckon I'd better," Wes said. "Have you told them about me?"

"Yes," said Bell. "You'll continue to take orders from me."

"The truth," Martha Bell said, "is that Frank doesn't trust them too far, and neither do I."

"Now, Martha," said Bell, "they're hard men, but that's what it takes when the law's spread too thin. They're all ex-bounty hunters."

"What are their names?" Wes asked.

"Font Gerdes, Wolf Strum, and Oz Withers," said Bell.

"I'll let 'em know I'm here, and say howdy," said Wes. "We need to lay some plans. That bunch of night riders may hit us next."

The bunkhouse was large enough to house thirty riders, and Wes wondered why Bell hadn't hired more men, and why he hadn't done it sooner. Heads drooping, three horses stood at the hitch rail. They should have been unsaddled and in the barn or corral. When Wes entered the bunkhouse, the men sat on their bunks, smoking and passing around a bottle. Wes stood there, his thumbs hooked in his belt, saying nothing.

"You got somethin' to say," one of the trio said, "then say it."

"It's a sorry excuse for a man that leaves his horse saddled and tied up in the middle of the day," said Wes.

"Wal," said one of the three, "you must be the younker Bell was tellin' us about. We been waitin' fer you. Unsaddle them broncs, rub 'em down, and fork 'em some hay."

The three laughed uproariously. Wes waited until they were silent, and then he spoke.

"I'm Wes Tremayne, and I don't take orders from you. See to your own horses."

"It don't pleasure me none, meetin' you," said one of the men, getting to his feet. "I'm Wolf Strum, and I don't take orders from any hombre that can't enforce 'em."

"I wouldn't expect you to," Wes said.

He drove the toe of his right boot into Strum's crotch. With a grunt, Strum's head came down and Wes slammed a hard right to his chin. Strum tumbled back into one of the bunks, striking his head against the wall. Gerdes and Withers had their weapons halfway out of their holsters when they froze. Wes had them covered. Strum sat up, rubbing his chin.

"I don't aim to give any of you orders," said Wes, "but if the time ever comes when I have to, then I want you to know I can damn well stand behind them."

"There's somethin' we're wantin' you to know," Strum said. "We'll do what we was hired to do, but if you ride with us, it's at your own risk. When lead starts to fly, there's a chance you might stop a bad one."

"I'll keep that in mind," said Wes. "Ridin' with the three of you, I can understand how that might happen."

Wes was between the trio and the door and, keeping them covered, he backed out. He then turned to the house he shared with Rebecca.

"Well?" said Rebecca.

"We talked," Wes said.

"I'm glad you won't be chasing those rustlers alone," said Rebecca.

"Yeah," Wes said. "I'll sleep better, knowin' they're on the job."

Tombstone, Arizona Territory
August 9, 1881

Nathan took a room at Inez McMartin's rooming house on Third Street. Right across the street was the roofed stalls of the O.K. Corral, where Nathan stabled his horse. Just beyond those stalls, fronting Fourth Street, were the cor-

ral's open stalls. On the far side of Fourth was the New
Orleans Saloon. It seemed one of the less gaudy establishments in town, and adjoining it on the left was the New
Orleans Restaurant. It wasn't quite eleven o'clock in the
morning, the best time to find a saloon owner on the prem-
ises, so Nathan stepped through the batwing doors and
went directly to the bar.

"It's a mite early for a drink," Nathan said. "I'm here
to talk to the owner."

"Talk," said the man, leaning his elbows on the bar. "I'm
Norris Lanham."

"I'm Nathan Stone. I'm a fair-to-middlin' dealer looking
for work."

"There are gaudier places than mine," Lanham said.
"Why did you come here?"

"It looks like the kind of place where I'd be comfortable," said Nathan. "I've dealt for the house at the fancy
places, and they seem to draw all the troublemakers."

Lanham laughed. "You know Doc Holliday's in town,
then."

"No," Nathan said, "I didn't know. But I saw him shoot
up a saloon in Dallas, Texas, and another in Las Vegas,
New Mexico, and he's hell on wheels at the poker table."

"He ain't been in here," Lanham. "Earp owns a piece
of the Oriental, and Holliday spends most of his time there.
I can use another house dealer, as long as you're comfortable with my rules. No drinking, no slick dealing, and no
gunplay without cause. Your cut is twenty percent."

"Your rules are my rules," Nathan said, "and the percentage is fair."

"Good," said Lanham. "We'll get along. The bartender
will take over in a few minutes. Then we'll go next door
for dinner. My wife, Elsie, runs the restaurant."

"I'd like to talk to her about feeding my dog," Nathan
said. "He's a hound and his name is Empty. He doesn't
like saloons."

"He's smarter than most men," said Lanham. "I'm sure
he can eat in the kitchen."

Lanham dressed like a gambling man, and Nathan liked
his looks. He appeared to be in his fifties, with silvery hair
and direct brown eyes. He sported a leather vest over a
white boiled shirt, a black string tie, and striped trousers.

"Take your dog around to the back of the restaurant,"

Lanham said when they left the saloon. "I'll bring Elsie out back to meet you and feed the dog. Then we'll eat."

"My land," said Elsie after she had met Nathan, "your poor dog looks half starved."

"It's the nature of the beast, ma'am," Nathan said. "He's a hound, and he looks like a rack of bones all the time. That's why his name is Empty."

"You may have to change his name after a while," said Elsie. "We serve three meals every day, and there's always leftovers. When you come to eat, just bring him around to the kitchen door."

Nathan laughed. "I won't have to bring him. After you've fed him the first time, he'll be here on his own."

Nathan and the saloon owner sat down to eat before the restaurant became crowded, and while Norris Lanham didn't speak quite as openly as Mel and Susie Holt, he supplied much of the background on Tombstone and the people who lived there.

"With Virgil the marshal and Wyatt a deputy sheriff, you're a mite deep in Earps," said Nathan. "Who usually shows up if you need a lawman?"

"Usually Sheriff John Behan," Lanham said. "Virgil's been here a time or two."

"I knew Wyatt when he was a lawman in Dodge," said Nathan. "I don't know any of his brothers."

"Virgil and Morgan are all right," Lanham said, "but I believe they're often influenced by Wyatt."

While the saloon owner had said nothing negative about Wyatt Earp, he had implied much, none of it lost on Nathan Stone. Dinner finished, they talked for a few minutes more over coffee.

"I'd like one free night," said Nathan. "Sunday, if possible."

"Sunday it is," Lanham said. "Most of my regulars are cowboys, sheepmen, and a few miners. Sunday's my slow night. When can you start?"

"Tonight," said Nathan. "Six o'clock early enough?"

"Six o'clock Monday through Thursday," Lanham said. "Friday and Saturday nights, come in at seven. Those nights we're open until three the next morning."

Nathan's first night at the New Orleans Saloon was uneventful. After eleven o'clock, there was no demand for a house dealer. The few patrons seemed content to hunch

over the tables, nursing their beers. A few minutes before
midnight, Nathan was leaning on the bar, talking to the
barkeep, when a stranger in a dark suit entered the saloon.

"Sheriff Behan," said the barkeep under his breath.

Behan approached the bar, nodded to the barkeep, and
eyed Nathan questioningly.

"I'm Nathan Stone," said Nathan. "House dealer."

"Sheriff John Behan," the lawman said. "I always like
to know who the dealers are."

"I don't blame you," Nathan said. "I was sheriff in
Dodge for a while and, my friend, I don't envy you your
job."

Behan laughed. "Believe it or not, there are some who'd
like to have it."

He moved on, a quiet man dressed all in black, like a
preacher or undertaker, with a black bow tie over a white
boiled shirt.

Wednesday night, Nathan's second night at the New Orleans, began quietly. At six-thirty, a distant church bell
chimed, summoning the faithful to prayer meeting. It offered a contrast in a town fraught with strife, and for a
moment it reminded Nathan of his childhood. Long ago, in
Virginia, there had been a church on the town square, and
in its tower a great brass bell . . .

"Damn," said the barkeep when four men shouldered
their way into the saloon, "it's the Clantons and the
McLaurys."

"Bottle an' four glasses," said one of the four as they
approached the bar.

He dropped his money on the bar and took the tray with
bottle and glasses. The four made their way to a table.

"That's Ike and Billy Clanton with their backs to us,"
the barkeep said, "and the two that's facin' us is Frank and
Tom McLaury."

The barkeep's voice trailed off, for Tom and Frank
McLaury were watching. Not until the four eventually left
the saloon did the barkeep speak again.

"There's been a cuss fight goin' on all summer, with the
Clantons and McLaurys on one side and the Earps on the
other. I hope there's none of 'em in here when they start
pullin' guns."

"You really think it's coming to that?" Nathan asked.

"Yeah," said the barkeep, "and I ain't by myself. Most ever'body knows it's comin'. We just ain't sure of the time and place."

"I've heard some talk," Nathan said. "What position is the town taking?"

"Most folks ain't takin' sides," said the barkeep. "Some—the church-going' bunch—is down on Wyatt Earp. He run out on his wife and married another woman."*

The following Sunday, Nathan rode out to Mel Holt's ranch for dinner. Empty had identified them as friend and took his place on the back porch.

"Well," said Holt, "I reckon you've jumped in amongst 'em. How is it?"

Nathan laughed. "No trouble yet. A pair of Clantons and the McLaurys came in and shared a bottle."

"There's rumors of more rustlers comin' to the territory," Holt said, "and they're all bein' sheltered by the Clantons and the McLaurys."

The first trouble involving Nathan Stone took place not in the saloon but in the New Orleans Restaurant next door. Nathan had gone there for supper, and to his surprise Doc Holliday took the table next to his. The waitress who brought Holliday his coffee appeared nervous, and her trembling hand lost its grip. The cup struck the table, splashing coffee all over the front of Holliday's boiled shirt, bringing him to his feet in an instant. Cursing, he seized the frightened waitress by the arm and she screamed.

"Let her go, Holliday," Nathan said.

In a single motion Holliday turned and went for his gun, only to find himself looking into the muzzle of Nathan Stone's Colt.

"I think you owe the lady an apology for your ungentlemanly conduct," said Nathan.

Furious, Holliday looked as though he might pull the gun, although Nathan already had him covered, but Elsie Lanham intervened.

"Is there a problem here," Elsie inquired.

"I don't think so," said Nathan. "Mr. Holliday was a

---

*Earp deserted Mattie, his second wife, in 1882. She went on to become a prostitute, and at the age of thirty committed suicide on July 3, 1888, in Pinal, Arizona.

mite upset when his coffee was spilled, but he's gotten over it. Haven't you, Holliday?"

"Yes," Holliday choked, almost in a whisper.

"I'll wait on you myself," said Elsie, "and if you'll bring your soiled shirt to me, I will see that it's washed and ironed."

"Never mind," Holliday said in his clipped, emotionless voice. "I am leaving."

Seizing his top hat and cane, Holliday stalked out the door without looking back.

"I'm sorry," the offending waitress sobbed. "I was afraid of him."

"Nothing to be sorry for," said Nathan. "Elsie, it was an accident. He may not come back, and if he doesn't, you won't be hurt."

"I agree," Elsie said, "but I'm not all that sure about you. He's a dangerous man."

"When the occasion calls for it," said Nathan, "so am I."

CHAPTER 23

Medina, Texas
March 1, 1881

Tameka and Wovoka, the Lipan Apaches Frank Bell employed to gentle his horses, had a hut of their own, and Wes Tremayne spent much of his free time there, listening to the aged Indians talk about horses. Having spent most of their lives near the white man, the old ones spoke English well and they seemed amused at Wes Tremayne's interest. Wes spoke to them regarding the three men Frank Bell had hired, and found them sharing his own suspicions.

"We know of them," said Wovoka. "They steal from us three summers ago."

"You should have hunted them down," Wes said. "Why didn't you?"

"We still with Lipan tribe," said Tameka. "Have treaty with white man. Chief say we not fight."

"A treaty with the white man shouldn't allow white outlaws to steal from you," Wes said. "You're not living with the tribe now. I believe these and other whites will steal from Frank Bell as they once stole from your people. Will you not fight?"

"We fight," said Wovoka. "We will."

"You have the Winchester, the long gun?"

"*Si,*" they replied in a single voice.

"Starting tonight," said Wes, "here is what I wish you to do."

Quickly, Wes laid out his plan for protecting the horses, and the old Indians nodded in satisfaction. Wes then went on to the house, where he would make Frank Bell aware of as much of the plan as he wished the rancher to know.

"Mr. Bell," Wes said, "I have a plan to protect the horses."

"Let's hear it," said Bell.

"At night, move all the horses into one of the barns.

Post Gerdes, Withers, and Strum outside with Winchesters. Order them to shoot anybody approaching the barn between dusk and dawn."

"I reckon that's about all we can do," said Bell. "Where are you plannin' to be?"

"Out there in the dark, with a Winchester," Wes said. "I'll go wherever I'm needed the most. If the rustlers strike, we'll have to hit them as hard as we can, because there'll be no tracking them until dawn."

"I'll take a Winchester and join you, then," said Bell.

"No," Wes said. "You may be needed to defend the house. Until this is settled, I'd like Rebecca to spend her nights there with you and Martha."

Bell was quick to agree, while Rebecca was reluctant.

"Why can't I bring my gun and come with you?"

"Because I don't know what to expect," said Wes. "If I end up shooting at shadows, I want to be sure you're not one of them."

Wes had suggested that Bell relay orders to Gerdes, Strum, and Withers, and Bell did so. Well before dark, Tameka and Wovoka, armed with Winchesters, took the position Wes had assigned them. After supper, Wes took his Winchester and left the Bell house, disappearing into the gathering darkness.

"I hope it all works out according to his plans," said Rebecca.

"He seems like a resourceful young man," Martha Bell said.

After five quiet nights, Frank Bell began to doubt the outlaws would strike.

"Somebody has to report to them," said Wes. "They'll want to know where the horses are being kept and what kind of defense you have planned."

"How do you suppose they'd be learning that?" Bell asked.

"I reckon we'll know more about that after the attack," said Wes.

Outwardly there was no charge in the ranch routine, except that all the horses were now being taken into one of the barns at night. The three men Frank Bell had hired were dutifully taking their positions at dusk. The Indian horse trainers retired to their hut at the end of the day. Only Wes Tremayne knew that the pair of Lipan Apaches crept out into the night with their deadly Winchesters, their eyes on the trio standing watch at the barn. The attack came late on a Sunday night. Winchesters roared in the darkness and ranch house windows exploded with a tinkling crash. Seizing his own Winchester, Frank Bell fired at muzzle flashes. He doubted the effectiveness of his fire until somewhere beyond the line of marauders another Winchester cut loose. Wes Tremayne! They had a cross fire going!

"Back off and ride," somebody shouted.

The attack on the house ended as abruptly as it had begun. Frank Bell ceased firing, and in the silence that followed, there were footsteps on the back porch.

"Hold your fire," Wes said. "I'm comin' in."

He came in, Winchester under his arm, and Rebecca ran to him.

"What about the horses?" Bell asked.

"Let's go have a look," said Wes. "There was some shooting near the barn."

One of the big barn doors stood open, and a horse nickered.

"Tameka," Wes called. "Wovoka."

Two figures separated themselves from the shadows, Winchesters at the ready.

"What's the meaning of this?" Bell asked.

"I told them of the thieves," said Wes, "and asked them to watch the barn, to guard against the rustlers."

"That's what I expected of Gerdes, Strum, and Withers," Bell said. "Where are they?"

"Them rustlers," said Wovoka. "Them steal, them die."

He vanished into the shadows, Tameka following.

"Come on, Mr. Bell," Wes said. "They have something to show you."

The clouds slipped away and a pale quarter moon added its light to that of the distant twinkling stars. They reached Withers' body first. The three horses he had taken had been tethered to a pine limb, and were nickering their fear at the smell of blood. Gates and Strum were soon found in similar positions, just as dead, near the horses they had taken.

"Well, by God," said Bell, "while the rest of the bunch was blastin' hell out of the house, these three varmints was takin' the horses."

"Yes," Wes said, "the attack on the house was a diversion. The three at the barn were part of the gang and were taking the horses."

"I played right into their hands when I hired the varmints," said Bell.

"It couldn't have worked out better if you'd planned it," Wes said. "We were able to take them on our terms."

"But how did you know? How did Tameka and Wovoka . . . ?"

"I didn't know anything for sure," said Wes. "I've had enough dealings with outlaws that I didn't trust the men you had hired, and when I spoke to Tameka and Wovoka, they recognized Gerdes, Strum, and Withers as horse thieves who had stolen from the Lipan Apaches in the past. They saw a chance to even an old score, and I had them watching the three hombres you hired."

"Well, hell, you could of told me, and—"

"It would have been the word of two old Indians against that of three white men," Wes finished. "Now you can see with your own eyes what these men were about to do. Is there any doubt in your mind?"

"None," said Bell. "I just wish we could have gunned down the others."

"You don't know that we didn't hit some of them," Wes said. "We were shooting at their muzzle flashes. Come first light, we'll take a look."

"There'll be tracks," said Bell. "Since they didn't get away with any horses, there ain't much reason for 'em ridin' for the border. Let's go after the varmints."

"I'd agree," Wes said, "but we'd be leaving the ranch and the horses unprotected."

"Yesterday, I'd have felt that way myself," said Bell, "but no more. I reckon Wovoka and Tameka are worth a dozen white men, even if I knew that many I could trust."

"Give them the run of the ranch, with the authority they need," Wes said. "These old ones take pride in the horses they have gentled, and they'll greet horse thieves with lead, just as they did tonight."

"I believe it," said Bell. "There's a hell of a lot more to them than just horse savvy. I aim to visit that Lipan village and hire some more of them, if they'll come."

Tombstone, Arizona Territory
September 15, 1881

During his off hours, Nathan made it a point to visit the elegant Oriental Saloon. On one of those occasions, he encountered both Wyatt Earp and Doc Holliday. Neither man had anything to say, but when Nathan's eyes met theirs, there was no mistaking the open hostility. Nathan had a beer and left the saloon.

"Rustling's on the upswing," Mel said when Nathan next visited the Holts. "Virgil and the rest of the Earps has been accusin' the McLaurys and the Clantons."

"I know," said Nathan. "I've been hearing the same talk. You're right. I reckon some powder will be burnt before this is over."

Norris Lanham had some advice for Nathan.

"We can't keep them out of the saloon, Nathan, but we can avoid getting sucked into the fight. Don't give any one of them an excuse to pull a gun."

"Suppose I catch one of them slick dealing?"

"You'll have to call them on that," said Norris. "Just try to avoid killing anybody. I'd not want you shot in the back as a grudge killing."

"You think they'd resort to that over a poker hand?"

"Probably not the Earps or Holliday," Norris said. "I suppose it's a matter of pride with them, but not so with the McLaurys and the Clantons. They were here long before the Earps and Holliday arrived, and there were plenty of unsolved murders, every one of them from ambush."

"Holiday and the Earps are pushing their luck, then," said Nathan. "It's one thing to have a man face you in an even break, and another to have him shoot you in the back."

"True," Lanham said, "but such an ambush could backfire. If Holliday or one of the Earps were ambushed, there wouldn't be much doubt as to the guilty parties. That would result in open season on the Clantons and McLaurys, and they would become outlaws, to be shot on sight."

"Then the Earps and Holliday are trying to push the Clantons and McLaurys into an open fight," said Nathan.

"I wouldn't want you crediting me with the possibility," Lanham replied, "but can you come up with anything else that makes sense?"

"No," said Nathan. "There's a reason for everything, and only a damn fool gets himself gunned down in another man's fight. I'm going to just stand back and watch this one from the sidelines. What's Holliday's stake in this, besides his being friendly with Wyatt Earp?"

"Holliday has more cause for a grudge than the Earps," Lanham said. "For the past several years, there's been a rash of stage holdups. Last March, the McLaurys took the stand and testified against Holliday, implicating him in a stage robbery in which two men were killed. Holliday was acquitted, but it resulted in his everlasting hatred for Frank and Tom McLaury."

"That's one part of this running feud that makes sense," said Nathan. "I saw Holliday walk into a saloon in Las Vegas, New Mexico and shoot a man tending bar. Nobody knew why. I reckoned it was a grudge shooting."

"Many a man started out carrying a grudge," Lanham said, "and by the time he has satisfied his grudge, he's become a killer with a reputation that follows him the rest of his life."

"That's the gospel truth," said Nathan. "I know at least one man who's ridden that trail. It's a hard life, and there's only one escape. I recall some words—maybe from the Bible—that says a man who lives by the sword dies by it. I reckon those words apply to a gun."

"I'm afraid they do," Lanham said, his eyes on the well-used twin Colts thonged to Nathan's hips

Tombstone, Arizona Territory
October 25, 1881

Nathan was on the street when Tom McLaury and Ike Clanton drove a wagon into town for supplies. Holliday discovered the pair was in town and began cursing them as they began loading the wagon at Brown's Grocery, next to the New Orleans Restaurant. Norris Lanham stepped out of the restaurant, joining Nathan.

"Who's the hombre siding Holliday?" Nathan asked.

"Morgan Earp," said Lanham.

Tombstone, Arizona Territory
October 26, 1881

Nathan was awakened by gunfire at first light. Empty was reared up on his hind legs, looking out the window. Nathan got up and looked out, but saw nobody.

"We're awake now, Empty," Nathan said. "We might as well have breakfast."

Empty was let into the kitchen to be fed, and Nathan entered the New Orleans Restaurant, where Norris Lanham was already seated. Nathan pulled out a chair and sat down across the table from the saloon owner.

"I heard shooting," said Nathan. "I reckoned the fight had started."

"No," Lanham said. "I don't know what that shooting was about, but there was other trouble last night. Last night, while Ike Clanton was eating supper, Holliday took to cussing him and challenged him to a fight. Holliday was backed by the Earps. But Ike wasn't armed and just walked away. Later, I hear Ike was pistol whipped by Virgil Earp. There's Tom McLaury at that table over yonder against the wall. I'm hoping he'll finish eating and leave before Holliday and the Earps show up."

McLaury did finish his meal and leave the restaurant, only to meet Wyatt Earp in the street.

"Wyatt," said McLaury, "I ain't wantin' a fight."

"Well, you're damn sure going to get one," Earp replied, drawing his revolver.

"No," said McLaury, his hands up.

Earp slapped McLaury with his left hand and then clubbed him on the head with his gun, knocking him down. For a moment, Earp glared at the fallen Tom McLaury in disgust. Finally, he holstered his weapon and walked away.

"Damn him," Nathan said, through clenched teeth.

Lanham laughed. "I take it you don't think much of the he-coon of the Earp clan."

Nathan said nothing. Empty was waiting for him at the corner of the building and the two of them started back to Inez McMartin's rooming house. There he stretched out on the bed and by dinnertime was thoroughly bored.

"Come on, Empty," said Nathan. "We might as well go back to the restaurant and eat."

Across the street from the restaurant, Nathan paused. Next to the restaurant, in front of Brown's Grocery, Wyatt Earp had a horse by the bridle, backing it off the boardwalk.

"Damn you," Frank McLaury said, emerging from the store, "take your hands off my horse."

"Then keep him off the boardwalk," Earp snapped, backing the animal into the street. "It's against the town ordinance."

Cursing Earp, McLaury mounted the horse and rode toward the O.K. Corral, where he tied the animal.

"Billy Clanton and Frank McLaury rode in a little while ago," said Norris Lanham, who had witnessed the exchange. "The Clantons and McLaurys are all here. All hell's goin' to bust loose before this day's done."

"I've seen enough damn feuds to last me a lifetime," Nathan said. "I aim to have me a good dinner, go back to the rooming house, and not do a blasted thing until seven o'clock tonight."

"Come on," said Lanham, "and I'll join you for dinner."

Nathan put the Clantons, McLaurys, and Earps out of his mind, spending an enjoyable hour in the restaurant. Afterward, thinking of his old habit of reading newspapers, he left the restaurant, bound for the office of the Tombstone *Epitaph*, which fronted Fremont Street to the north. When he left the *Epitaph* office, the sun told him it was near three o'clock in the afternoon. Near the west end of Fremont Street, near C. S. Fly's Lodging House, the Clantons and McLaurys had gathered. At that moment, turning the corner of Fourth and Fremont, came the Earps and Doc Holliday. Beside Wyatt Earp strode Holliday, with the ugly snout of a shotgun extending beneath his long coat. Beside Doc, like angels of death in their long black coats, stalked Virgil and Morgan Earp. Both Morgan and Doc had been deputized for the occasion, and the four men wore the star of lawmen. Nathan Stone paused where he was, unable to return to his rooming house without crossing Fremont. He watched in grim fascination as the Earps and Holliday drew closer to the Clantons and the McLaurys. Death was only seconds away.

Medina, Texas
July 1, 1881

"If Vivian Stafford can ride and win races, then so can I," said Rebecca Tuttle. "All I need is experience. Mr. Bell has already promised me a chance, as soon as we find a horse I like."

"While I'm chasing rustlers, you'll be out somewhere breaking your neck," Wes said.

"I've ridden every horse Tameka and Wovoka have gentled since we've been here," said Rebecca. "I've ridden them with only a saddle blanket, and I haven't been hurt once."

"Well, I don't want you riding alone," Wes said. "I've been seeing tracks, and I'd bet my saddle it's that bunch of rustlers."

"They haven't bothered us since they attacked the house, when Tameka and Wovoka killed three of them near the barn," said Rebecca.

"No," Wes replied, "but Bell told me riders from some of the other ranches have been shot at. They'll get around to us, now that Bell's hired four more Lipan Apaches to defend the place. I took for them to be especially eager to ambush those Indian riders. Bell says these Apaches can track a man across solid rock."

"All the more reason for the rustlers to leave us alone," said Rebecca. "These Apaches don't sound like the kind to be taken by surprise."

"Maybe not," Wes said, "but I'm thinking those outlaws might shoot up the house or dry-gulch one of us. That would force Bell and the Apaches to go after them. Even these Apaches can be outgunned if there's enough outlaws laying for them."

"Perhaps it won't come to that," said Rebecca. "Mr. Bell has asked for help from the Texas Rangers."

"I don't look for them to be of much help," Wes said. "There's just too much territory for so few men."

On Saturday, July 2, near suppertime, a dusty rider reined up before Frank Bell's ranch house. A thonged-down Colt rode low on his right hip. Unblinking eyes looked at them from beneath the brim of a weatherworn

Stetson. His Levi's, blue flannel shirt, and scuffed boots might have belonged to any cowboy in south Texas. He spoke.

"I'm looking for Frank Bell."

"You're looking at him," said Bell.

"I'm Ranger Bodie West," the stranger said. "I'm answering your call for help."

"Step down and come in," said Bell. "We're about to set down to supper. I'll see that your horse is rubbed down, fed, and watered. The gent here with me is Wes Tremayne, one of my riders."

"I'll see to your horse," Wes said.

"I'm obliged," said West, dismounting. His eyes rested on Wes a long moment before he followed Bell into the house.

Wes led the horse to the barn, where he unsaddled the animal and rubbed him down. He then turned the horse into the corral. It went immediately to the water trough and drank its fill. Then it rolled in the corral dust and got up and headed for the hay manger mounted on the side of the barn.

"It's nearly full of hay," said Wes. "That should be enough for you."

When Wes reached the ranch house, Bell and West were already at the table, drinking coffee.

"By the time you wash up," Martha Bell said, "supper will be on the table."

When Wes reached the table, Martha and Rebecca were bringing in the food. Bodie West stood up and bowed.

"This is Martha and Rebecca," said Bell, forgetting to mention who was who.

"I'm Frank's missus," Martha said. "Sometimes he forgets."

They all laughed at Bell's expense, and there was little conversation until the meal was finished. Ranger Bodie West was the first to speak.

"Ma'am, I haven't had a feed like this since I was last at my mama's table."

"Thank you," said Martha Bell. "We're pleased to have you with us."

"Before we get down to business," West said, "I have to satisfy my curiosity, and I'm hoping I won't be out of line. Mr. Tremayne, you remind me of someone. He's probably the best friend the Texas Rangers ever had, and he should be wearing a Ranger shield. His name is Nathan Stone. Take twenty years off him, and the two of you could be twins. Are you in any way related to such a man?"

"I know of nobody by that name," said Wes. "My family is dead. I spent most of my early years in an orphanage."

"Sorry," West said. "Forgive my prying."

"Mr. West," said Bell, changing the subject, "we're having a problem with rustlers in these parts, and aside from three of 'em my men gunned down a few weeks back, they're always off and gone across the border before we can catch them. What's to be done?"

"The Rangers are spread mighty thin," West said, "and usually by the time we can get a man on the case, the rustlers have crossed the border. I can spend a few days with you, and if they strike lead a posse after them. But if they strike at night—and generally they do—I'm as handicapped as you are. By the time it's light enough to trail them, they are already near enough to the border to outride us."

"That's honest talk," said Bell. "There's three other ranches within ridin' distance of us, and I reckon we can gather a posse of our own. But I got to tell you, if we're able to ride these varmints down, we aim to shoot to kill. I want it said plain that the law's on our side before we salt these varmints down."

"You'll get no argument from the Rangers," West said, "and if anything is ever said to the contrary, I'll stand behind you. The one thing I can't do is sanction your chasing them across the border. There's an agreement between Washington and Mexico City that says we must respect one another's borders."

"Suppose we ran this bunch across the river," said Wes, "gunned them down, and rode back into Texas without the Mexicans catching us?"

"You might get away with it," West said, "but it wouldn't be worth the risk. If you were caught by Mexican authorities, it would be blown up into an international incident. You might be tried, convicted, and executed. Being in violation of the agreement with the Mexicans, there would be little any of us could do to save you."

"You got nothing to worry about," said Bell. "I'd never ask any man that's ridin' for me to take such a risk as that."

"I'm glad to hear it," West said. "There is one thing I can and will do, though. I can send an official notice to the Mexican border patrol, complaining about this continual rustling. I'd bet a horse and saddle that Mexican stock is being rustled across the border and sold in this country. So it could be a mutual problem the Mexicans are as anxious to solve as we are."

"I hope you're right," said Bell, "and we'll appreciate whatever you can do."

"I'm going to visit some of the other ranchers in the area," said Ranger Bodie West the following morning. "Maybe all of you can get together and organize an around-the-clock posse."

"We're obliged to you for ridin' by," Frank Bell said.

"There's not enough of them to be of any help to us," said Wes when the Ranger had ridden away. "We'll have to stomp our own snakes."

Medina, Texas
July 15, 1881

Two weeks after the Ranger's visit, the rustlers began their night attacks on the area ranches, and Frank Bell acquired—among others—the very horse Rebecca Tuttle had been waiting for.

"He's built to run," said Bell. "Fifteen hands, stocky, deep muscled, and as sturdy legged as they come. He's got that deep chest, low withers, and powerful hindquarters. His neck's thick, while his head's broad and short."*

"Him fly like *aguila*," Tomeka said.

"Eagle," said Bell. "I reckon that suits him."

"I want to ride him in the races," Rebecca said. "Tameka, Wovoka, will you gentle him for me?"

After the black horse had been Indian gentled, Rebecca spent virtually all her time with him. She galloped him wildly across the plains, using only a saddle blanket, and

---

*This is the horse that became noted for its fleetness in a quarter-mile run, but not until 1941, when it became a registered breed, was it referred to as a "quarter horse."

the horse grew fond of her. Then rustlers struck the Calloway ranch in the late afternoon, and two cowboys died.

"The varmints didn't take a single horse or cow," Frank Bell said angrily. "They just wanted to make us all even more jumpy than we already are."

"No more long rides alone, Rebecca," said Wes.

"Eagle runs like the wind," Rebecca said. "They can't catch me."

"A slug from a Winchester can," said Bell.

Rebecca yielded, and picked a quarter-mile stretch along the Medina River, in sight of the Bell ranch house. On a Thursday evening in mid-September, Bell and Wes sat on the back porch and watched Rebecca astride Eagle, thundering along the river.

"She's a natural," Bell said. "I believe she can ride and win."

Suddenly, from across the river, there were distant rifle shots. Nickering in pain and fear, the black horse reared.

"Damn it," Wes shouted, "loose the reins! Loose the reins!"

Shaken, Rebecca did exactly the opposite, and as the reins tightened, Eagle reared all the more. Losing his balance, he fell on his back, all his massive weight on the slight rider beneath him. The horse rolled, came to his feet, and stood sniffing anxiously at his fallen companion. But Rebecca Tuttle lay silent, unmoving. Disregarding the possibility of more fire, Wes Tremayne ran toward her, his heart in his throat and tears in his eyes.

CHAPTER 24

Tombstone, Arizona Territory
October 26, 1881

There was little Nathan could do but watch as the feuding factions came together in a vacant lot between McDonald's Assay Office and C. S. Fly's Lodging House. Ike and Billy Clanton, Billy Claiborne, and the McLaury brothers were approached by Doc Holliday and Virgil, Morgan, and Wyatt Earp. Tom McLaury stood behind his horse; but for a Winchester in his saddle boot, he was unarmed. Doc Holliday stood opposite him, a pistol under his belt and a shotgun beneath his long coat. There was a light wind from the west and Nathan could hear their every word. Wyatt Earp spoke first.

"All you sons of bitches have been looking for a fight, and now you can have it."

"No," Ike Clanton shouted, "I'm unarmed."

"Up with your hands," Virgil shouted.

"Don't shoot me," Billy Clanton cried, throwing up his hands. "I don't want to fight."

"I ain't armed," Tom McLaury declared, opening his coat.

At point-blank range, Morgan Earp shot Billy Clanton in the chest, while Wyatt drew his pistol and pumped lead into Frank McLaury's stomach.

"Stop the shooting!" Ike Clanton shouted. Still unarmed, he seized Wyatt Earp's left arm, but Earp broke loose.

"The fighting has now commenced," Wyatt said. "Fight, damn you, or get out of the way."

Ike Clanton, with Billy Claiborne on his heels, fled to Fly's Photograph Gallery, behind the C. S. Fly Lodging House. When Tom McLaury's horse shied at the gunfire, Holliday raised his shotgun and shot Tom in the right side. He staggered a few steps and fell. Mortally wounded, Billy Clanton and Frank McLaury drew their guns and managed to wound Morgan and Virgil Earp and Doc Holliday. His right wrist broken by a bullet, Billy Clanton lay on his back, firing with his weapon braced on his knee. Then a final slug struck him in the stomach. The tragedy had taken less than thirty seconds. The McLaury brothers and Billy Clanton were dead, and of the Earp faction, only Wyatt hadn't been hit. Nathan watched as the dead were carried away. Slowly, Sheriff John Behan made his way down Fremont Street toward the bloody scene. He paused before the *Epitaph* office, and almost apologetically, he spoke.

"I tried to disarm them, but it had gone too far. It had to happen, and my God, it has."

Quickly, Nathan crossed Fremont and, passing through a vacant lot, went between Fly's Photograph Gallery and the open stalls of the O.K. Corral. He was then able to get to Inez McMartin's Rooming House without meeting anyone. Half a block away, he could see the scene of the shooting. A crowd had gathered, and more were coming. He hoped nobody had seen him before the Tombstone *Epitaph* office on Fremont. Beyond a doubt there would be an inquest, probably a trial, and the last thing he wanted was to become embroiled in any affair that involved Holliday and the Earps. Obviously, the Earps had intended to kill their adversaries and had gunned them down without mercy, even as Billy Clanton and the McLaurys had not fought back until they had been mortally wounded. Nathan had seen too many such feuds to believe the fight was over. There would be more killings, probably from ambush.*

"Empty," said Nathan, "we'll be having supper a mite late."

He stretched out on the bed, not wishing to venture back

---

*December 28, 1881, just before midnight, Virgil Earp left the Oriental Saloon. As he crossed the street there were two shotgun blasts. After removal of the buckshot and four inches of bone, he survived. He died of pneumonia in Goldfield, Nevada, in 1905.

March 18, 1881, Morgan Earp was playing a Saturday night game of billiards in the Campbell and Hatch Billiard Parlor in Tombstone. Suddenly there were two shots from the back door, and a slug shattered Morgan's spinal column. Wyatt was narrowly missed by the second shot. Morgan Earp died less than an hour later.

November 14, 1882, Billy Claiborne was gunned down in Tombstone; he had been involved in a failed ambush. In 1887, near Bonita, Arizona, Ike Clanton was shot for cattle rustling.

out on to the street until everybody's curiosity had been satisfied. As the westering sun gave way to the coming of the night, Nathan and Empty made their way around the rear of Fly's Photo Gallery and past the roofed stalls of the O.K. Corral. Reaching the New Orleans Restaurant, they parted company, the hound going to the back door where Elsie Lanham would be expecting him, and Nathan entering the restaurant. The eating establishment was crowded, and the only topic of conversation seemed to be the recent gunfight. Norris Lanham sat alone at a table, nursing a cup of coffee. He nodded, and Nathan took a seat. He said nothing until Nathan had ordered his meal and was sipping coffee.

"I hear you saw the Earps and Holliday enforcing Tombstone law."

"Unfortunately," said Nathan. "I saw them shoot some gents who had their hands up, some of them unarmed."

"There'll be an inquest," Lanham said. "Is that what you're going to tell the coroner's jury?"

"I don't aim to tell the coroner's jury anything," said Nathan. "With them facing me, I'm not afraid of Holliday or the Earps, but it's foolish to antagonize a bunch of killers when it serves no good purpose."

"An excellent point," Lanham said. "I wouldn't want this repeated, but Virgil's going to lose his star within a few weeks. His having deputized his brother Morgan and Holliday for what obviously was a grudge fight has left the town of Tombstone in an embarrassing position. You can expect the newspapers here to present this in the best possible light, with the Earps and Holliday upholding the law."

"The press can make or break a man," said Nathan. "After this, I reckon Holliday and the Earps will be nine feet tall and a yard wide."

"You can count on it," Lanham said. "In little towns like Tombstone, the editors of the newspapers serve as stringers, feeding news to larger papers in other parts of the territory. They generally get paid by the word, so they juice it up as much as they can. I don't doubt there'll be an inquest before a coroner's jury, or that Holliday and the Earps will take the rap for the killings. But it's all a formality. It'll all be smoothed over and legalized in the hope that one of these factions will leave and the other will follow. When do you aim to ride out?"

"Tomorrow," said Nathan. "I reckon it'll take a few days to get all the legal machinery in motion. If somebody wants to make plaster saints of Holliday and the Earps, they won't need or want my testimony. If I thought any of them were about to get what they all deserve, I'd stay. But even before talking to you, I had my doubts."

"Wherever you are," Lanham said, "pick up a newspaper. I believe you'll discover that Holliday and the Earps were lawmen, acting only in the best interests of the good citizens of Tombstone."

Tombstone, Arizona Territory
October 27, 1881

"We're sorry to see you go," said Elsie Lanham as she brought Nathan's breakfast. I gave Empty an extra portion. I'll miss him at the back door at meal time."

"No more than he'll miss you," Nathan said. "I'll miss you, too, and if I ever get back to Tombstone, you can bet we'll be taking our meals here."

Before Nathan left the restaurant, Norris Lanham arrived with an edition of the local paper, the Tombstone *Epitaph*. The story was front-page news. Nathan ran his eyes over the columns until he found a heading that read: "Earp Brothers Justified."

> *The feeling among the best class of our citizens is that the Marshal was entirely justified in his efforts to disarm these men, and that being fired upon, they had to defend themselves, which they did most bravely . . .*

There was more, but Nathan didn't bother reading it. Norris Lanham had been correct in his assessment of the situation, and Nathan felt better about his decision to ride on.

"You can see how the town fathers are going to handle it," said Lanham.

"Yeah," Nathan said. "It takes a brave bunch to gun down men who are unarmed or have their hands up."

Leaving the restaurant, the first person Nathan saw was Mel Holt. Reining up, he hooked a leg around the saddle horn and spoke.

"We reckoned you'd ride out on Sunday, but Susie wants you for supper tonight. This is her eighteenth birthday, so she's old enough that the Horrells can't come looking for her. She's baked another cake for the occasion."

"The truth is," said Nathan, "I'd planned on seeing you and Susie today, before I ride on. I'll get my horse and ride back with you when you're ready."

"I'm ready when you are," Holt said. "I just rode in looking for you."

Susie Holt was glad to see Nathan, but some of the joy went out of her when she learned he was about to leave.

"I hate to see you go," she said. "Mel's told me so much about you that with you here, I felt almost . . . like we had family close by."

"I'll stay tonight," said Nathan, dreading the time when he must leave these two good friends.

Breakfast became a memorable occasion, and Nathan made the most of it, unsure as to when he would sit before such a bounty again.

"I've packed some food for you to take with you," Susie said, "and something extra for Empty."

"We're obliged," said Nathan.

When the moment of parting came, and as they stepped out the door Empty bounded up on the front porch. He knew he and Nathan were about to leave these friends.

"I'm going to miss you, Empty," Susie said; kneeling, she threw her arms around him. "Don't you forget me, you big old hungry bag of bones."

"Don't forget where we live," said Holt, offering his hand.

Nathan shook Holt's hand long and hard, not knowing if he would ever see either of them again. He often had premonitions, and he had one now. Swallowing hard, he mounted the grulla and rode away, Empty following. Still vivid in his mind were the brutal killings he had witnessed the day before. From the little he had read in the *Epitaph*, he believed Norris Lanham was right, that the entire affair would be glossed over. From what he had seen with his own eyes, there had been no heroes in that dusty alley a few yards above the O.K. Corral. The men acting in the name of the law had come to settle a grudge that had been festering for months, and they had come with killing on their minds.

Medina, Texas
September 15, 1881

Wes Tremayne fell on his knees beside Rebecca, and when she tried to speak, there was bloody froth on her lips.

"It ... wasn't Eagle's ... fault ..." she whispered.

She died then, and in that moment Wes Tremayne learned a terrible truth about himself. He had believed he had come to grips with his emotions, that nothing could touch him to the heart, but the loss of Rebecca affected him as nothing else ever had. Dry eyed, he had seen both his grandparents buried. Now, not caring that Frank Bell was present, he wept long and hard until no tears remained.

"I'll get some blankets," said Bell, "and we'll take her to the house."

The night that followed was long and hard, for Wes Tremayne never slept. He sat at Frank Bell's kitchen table, drinking coffee. The Bells were up well before dawn, Martha to begin breakfast, Frank to talk to Wes.

"Unless you got other ideas," Bell said, "we can bury her yonder by the river, under that big cottonwood."

"That's as good a place as any," said Wes. "Let's do it as soon as possible, because I want to be on my way."

"You're going after them?"

"After whoever fired those shots," Wes said.

"They're likely headed for the border," said Bell.

"That doesn't matter to me," Wes said. "I'll chase them to hell and go in after them if that's the only way."

During the short time at the Bell ranch, Rebecca Tuttle had become friends with everybody there, including the Lipan Apaches. Tameka and Wovoka dug the grave, and from the family Bible, Frank Bell read the words. The service was short. After saddling his horse, Wes rode back to the house.

"I can send some of the Lipans with you, if you want," said Bell.

"I'm obliged," Wes said, "but I'd rather you didn't. You'll be needing them to protect your ranch and your stock."

"We hope you'll come back," said Martha Bell. "You'll always be welcome."

Wes rode on across the river, seeking the position from which the unseen rifleman had fired the shots. Eventually he found five shell casings near the place from which the outlaw had done the shooting. From the sign, it appeared the rifleman had fired from a left-handed position. While it wasn't much to go on, there was a good chance his pistol rode on his left hip, or possibly butt forward on his right hip, for a cross-hand draw. In either case, it was something to remember. As Wes had quickly learned, an unconventional draw might be the most memorable thing about a man. Quickly he found where the man had picketed his horse, and he had no difficulty following the tracks that led downriver. The outlaws never bothered concealing their tracks, depending on the nearness of the border to discourage any and all pursuit. That, Wes thought, was about to change, as he rode grimly on. It came as no surprise when he learned that the solitary horseman had crossed the Medina River and his trail led due south. But circumstances changed quickly. The rider dismounted and, leading the horse, turned eastward. The animal favored the left-front leg; its lameness had forced the rider to change his destination. He now seemed bound for San Antonio, and Wes kneed his horse into a slow gallop. While Wes wasn't sure how far he was from San Antonio, he believed it was farther than a man on foot could walk, even if he had walked all night. The tracks seemed fresh, and Wes had to consider the possibility of an ambush. When he was unable to see beyond a rise or through thickets and brush, he rode wide, paralleling the trail until the way was again clear. When Wes dismounted to rest his horse, he studied the tracks of the man he pursued. Spur rowels dug deep into the sand and appeared to be of the cartwheel variety, popular among Mexican riders. Wes rode on, reining up when a cow bawled somewhere ahead. There were more bovine laments, and Wes rode on until he was within sight of the cow camp. There was the smell of wood smoke from a branding fire, mingled with the stink of scorched hair and hide. Wes reined up well out of gun range, for the man he was trailing might be among these cowboys. His horse nickered and one within the camp answered, alerting them to his presence.

"Hello the camp," Wes shouted. "I'm friendly."

"Ride in," one of the men responded.

Wes rode in, reining up near the branding fire. It was time to introduce himself and explain his reason for being there.

"I'm Wes Tremayne, from the Frank Bell ranch. I'm following a man who fired on the ranch late yesterday, causing a woman to be killed. I believe this man is part of a band of rustlers who have been hounding ranchers in the area."

"I'm Jess Whittaker," said an elderly man in range clothes, "and this is Rafter W. We had our share of rustling. The gent you're chasin' was here sometime last night. If you can catch the varmint, we'd be interested in makin' his acquaintance. He took a prime cow hoss from our remuda, leavin' us a crow bait."

"When I settle with this hombre, I'll turn your horse loose," Wes said.

Backstepping his horse, Wes rode wide of the camp and began looking for the trail of the elusive rider. He rode in a circle, and when he crossed the trail, it had again turned due south.

"We got us some ridin' to do, *amigo*," said Wes to his horse. "He's still ahead of us, on a fresh mount."

Wes rode on, resting and watering his horse, painfully aware that he seemed no closer to his adversary. In his haste and fury, he had brought no supplies. In his saddlebags was only a quantity of jerked beef. The sun slid slowly down the western horizon toward the rim, where it would soon disappear in a moonless night sky, and Wes had no choice but to make camp for the night. When he reached a spring, he unsaddled the horse, picketing it on the little graze there was. Leaving his saddle beside the spring, he spread his blankets above it in a concealing thicket. He was learning the ways of the frontier, the means of staying alive.

Southern New Mexico Territory
November 2, 1881

Nathan felt a little guilty as he rode north, again avoiding El Paso.

"Empty," he said, "I'm just not ready to tie myself down to a woman. Not even one as pretty as Molly Horrell. I reckon· we'll just follow the Rio north, and from Pueblo take the train to Dodge."

Nathan reached the Rio Grande a hundred and seventy miles north of El Paso. There he made camp for the night and cooked supper for Empty and himself. He was about to douse the cookfire when he heard the rumble of a wagon somewhere to the south. Quickly he put out the fire and stood facing downriver until he could see the approaching wagon. A man in town clothes and a top hat controlled the reins of the four-mule team. Beside him sat a woman whose gown seemed totally unsuited to the frontier, but the Winchester rifle across her knees looked all business. But the six riders accompanying the wagon were all the more out of place, for they were soldiers in Union blue. The lead rider, with the silver bars of a captain riding the epaulets of his blue coat, raised his right hand. The rest of the soldiers reined up, and the wagon rumbled to a halt. The captain spoke.

"I must ask you to identify yourself, sir, and state your business."

"I'm Nathan Stone," said Nathan, "and I can't see that my business is any of yours."

Something about the man didn't ring true, and Nathan didn't like him. The nearest military outpost would have to be at El Paso, and with Indians no longer a threat, how did a civilian-driven wagon command a six-man escort? It was the woman who spoke, further deepening the mystery.

"Captain, I don't believe he's a threat to us. Darkness is only minutes away. Perhaps we can spend the night here. Have you any objection, Mr. Stone?"

"None," said Nathan, "as long as your soldiers back off. I don't like being regarded as a fugitive."

She laughed. "I am Kathleen La Mie, and this is my husband, André. The soldiers—"

"Madam," the captain snapped, "I am capable of introducing myself and my men."

"Then do so," the woman replied, and the officer fought to control himself before he finally spoke.

"I am Captain Kendall. This is Sergeant Gannon, Corporal Walton, and Privates Olson, Baird, and Ponder."

"Where is your outpost?" Nathan inquired.

"I don't regard that as any of your business," said Kendall.

"Maybe it's more of my business than you think," Nathan said, his cold eyes meeting Kendall's. "I know most of the commanding officers at the Texas outposts, and some of the other personnel, but I don't recall ever seeing you."

"I am newly assigned to the outpost at Houston," said Kendall. "Are you satisfied?"

"No," Nathan replied. "What are you doing in New Mexico?"

"We are a military escort," said Kendall, barely controlling his temper. "Indians—"

"Indians haven't been a threat since 1874," Nathan said. "Try again."

"Captain," said Kathleen La Mie, "I see no need for secrecy. Mr. Stone, we are bound for Colorado. The wagon's cargo is vintage French wine, in quart bottles, twelve of them to a case."

"For that you need a military escort?" Nathan asked.

"We believed so," she said. "It's worth a fortune."

"Then why wagon it eight hundred miles across country?" Nathan asked. "Why didn't you take it from New Orleans to St. Louis by steamboat, and from there on to Colorado by train?"

"We had our reasons," said André La Mie, speaking for the first time.

"Now," Kathleen said, "if you're satisfied, we'll make camp, and after supper, you may sample our vintage wine."

"I'm obliged," said Nathan, "but I'm not much of a wine drinker."

La Mie stepped down from the wagon box and began unharnessing the teams. Kendall and his men dismounted and unsaddled their horses. Kathleen La Mie started a fire and got supper under way. Kendall and his men settled down, waiting for the food to be prepared. It was uncharacteristic of the military, dawdling about a civilian camp, and with darkness falling, a potential enemy could see the fire from a great distance. Not liking or trusting these strangers, Empty had disappeared. Nathan sat with his back against a pine, and he was aware that the soldiers—if that's what they were—had their eyes on him. Nathan gave as good as he got. He kept his eyes on Captain Kendall, and the more he saw of the man the more suspicious he became. The sleeves of Kendall's officers coat were much too short, and instead of regulation boots he wore cowman's boots with pointed toes and high, undershot heels.

"Captain," said Nathan, "you're setting a poor example for your men. Those boots you're wearing aren't regulation."

"Mind your own damn business, Stone," Kendall replied.

One of the privates laughed, and Kendall cast him a dirty look. Kathleen La Mie paused at the supper fire, her eyes on Kendall. She spoke.

"André, break out a bottle of wine, and starting with Mr.

Stone, pour all of us some. Perhaps it will relax us for the meal."

La Mie let down the wagon's tailgate and, standing on it, began fumbling around inside the wagon. He emerged with a fancy quart bottle of green glass with a green and gold label. He continued pawing around until he produced a box, from which he removed a dozen glass goblets. These he placed on the wagon's tailgate, carefully filling each glass with wine.

"You may go first, Mr. Stone," said Kit. "You are our guest."

Nathan went to the wagon, downed a glass of wine, and returned to his former position. The wine was no better or worse than what could be had in almost any saloon on the frontier, and his suspicion grew all the more. While he had no idea what these people were transporting, he was now virtually certain the wine was only a cover. The La Mies had been all too anxious for him to sample the wine. Eventually, this bunch had to sleep, and if they posted a guard, Nathan intended to discover the secret within that wagon. He did his best to conceal his suspicion and to appear amiable. While the others partook of the wine, Kathleen La Mie had her eyes on Nathan. Finally she spoke.

"Well, Mr. Stone, what is your opinion of our vintage wine?"

"I'm impressed," Nathan lied, "but I can't believe you're taking it all the way to Colorado just to sell it to the saloons."

She laughed. "Hardly, Mr. Stone. Because of the mines, Colorado has wealthy men to whom price is no object. We will sell to the highest bidder, by the bottle or by the case."

"It's out of my reach, then," said Nathan, "and I'm obliged for the sample. I reckon I'll turn in, so I can get an early start in the morning."

Taking his saddle, Nathan led his horse upriver a hundred yards. There he settled down for the night. Later there would be a moon, offering enough light for him to learn the secret of the wagon—or to be shot should he be discovered. Empty crept out of the brush and lay down beside Nathan, and there they waited until an hour past moonrise. The camp downriver became quiet, the silence unbroken but for the horses and mules cropping grass. Slowly Nathan made his way along the river bank, keeping within the shadows until he could see the sleeping camp. Moonlight bled through the trees, isolating those who slept in pools of shadow. But only seven of them slept, and that meant one man was on watch. Nathan waited patiently, his eyes on the wagon, until the sentry took a draw from his quirly. Nathan grinned in the darkness. The man was within the shadow of the wagon, his back to a rear wheel, but each time he took a draw from his smoke, the small glow gave away his position. Nathan continued along the river bank until he was well beyond the camp. He then had to cross a clearing and make his way to the wagon, bringing him in behind the man on watch. Once he was able to buffalo the sentry, he would have only until the man regained his senses. In that short interval, he must investigate the contents of the wagon, return to his horse, and make his escape. While the six in uniform were just poor excuses for soldiers, they looked like the kind who could and would shoot to kill. Nathan reached the side of the wagon opposite the sentry, and on hands and knees, began making his way under the old Studebaker.*

"Damn," the sentry muttered, getting to his feet. The fire had fallen from his smoke, and he brushed it from his clothing. Again he sat down, his back to the wheel; using his hat to shield the flame, he relighted his quirly.

It wasn't easy, slugging a man through the spokes of a wagon wheel, but Nathan did it. But his victim was only stunned, and Nathan was forced to hit him again. Some of the sleeping men, should they awaken, would easily be able to see Nathan at the tailgate of the wagon, but it was a chance he'd have to take. All of them were between him and his grazing horse, leaving him in a perilous position should he be discovered. The wagon's canvas pucker was drawn, affording him little room to do more than investigate with his hands. He quickly discovered there were wooden cases stacked high as the wagon bows allowed, and the only choice he had was to remove a bottle from the case André La Mie had already opened. Carefully he lifted out a bottle and froze, for the cold muzzle of a gun was just behind his left ear.

"Don't you even breathe, Stone," said Kendall. "There's nothin' I'd like better than to just blow your brains out right now, but you got some talkin' to do first."

---

*A freight wagon common to the plains, first built by the Studebaker brothers in 1852.

CHAPTER 25

Wes never seemed to gain on the lone horseman, and a few miles west of Uvalde the tracks merged with those of five other horses. The six riders continued on together, and it was obvious they were bound for the border. Even more curious were the tracks of yet another horse that had galloped in from the east. This rider seemed in pursuit of the first six, yet Wes doubted he was part of the gang. Who was he and what was the purpose of his pursuit? Wes had ridden only another mile or two when he saw a rider approaching from the south. He reined up, waiting, and soon recognized Texas Ranger Bodie West.

"Lost them at the border," said West in disgust, slapping his dusty hat against his thigh. "They hit Bell's place, I reckon?"

"One of them did," Wes said. "I didn't know about the others until all of them came together back yonder a ways."

"They didn't rustle any stock," said West. "Word I got was, they had shot up half a dozen ranches. Nothing but harassment."

"A hell of a lot more than that at the Bell ranch," Wes said.

"Somebody hurt?"

"Somebody dead," said Wes. "Rebecca."

"My God," West said, removing his hat. "The little lady. Tell me about it."

He listened, swearing under his breath as Wes told him the tragic story. When Wes had finished, the young Ranger spoke. His voice was brittle and savage, and his eyes like live coals.

"Remember, I told you not to chase them across the border?"

"Yes," Wes said, "I remember."

"That was Bodie West, Texas ranger, talking. Now you're about to hear from Bodie West, the man, the Texan. Ride the bastards down, if you have to run them all the way to Mexico City. Make them pay in blood."

"I aim to," said Wes. "I've just learned that a man can ride headlong into a thing that stands taller than the United States Congress and the president, all stacked up in a pile."

"Amen," West said. "Good luck."

He rode forth, not looking back. Wes kicked his horse into a lope and continued on toward the border. When he reached the Rio Grande, it was no more than a trickle. He rode across and found a profusion of tracks where the men he pursued had reined up. He could almost see them as they looked back across the river, smirking. He rested his horse, allowed the animal to drink, and rode on into the wilds of Mexico. He doubted they would attempt to ambush him, for they wouldn't be expecting pursuit. Eventually they had to hole up. Wes had no idea which of the men had fired the shots that had resulted in Rebecca's death, but it didn't matter. He would gun them all down.

Half a dozen miles south of the border, in a secluded cabin, six men sat around a table, sharing a bottle. A fire blazed on the hearth, and a Mexican woman patiently turned a spit on which a beef haunch sizzled.

"Them ranchers won't be expectin' us again so soon," one of the men said. "I say we run off some more hosses tomorrow night."

"You ain't bossin' this outfit, Snake," one of his companions said. "Bell ain't got more than two hosses on his place, and some of the others got none."

"I know I ain't the boss," Snake said, "but by God, I oughta be. Ellerbee's a damn fool, havin' us hide out with Winchesters, pourin' lead at them ranchers. All we're doin' is lettin' 'em know we're still around. Why should they buy more stock, knowin' we're just waitin' to rustle it?"

"Stompin' around and squallin' at us won't change anything, Snake," said a companion. "Why don't you jump on Ellerbee and lay your advice on him?"

They all laughed uproariously.

"Maybe I will," Snake growled.

"Humo," the Mexican woman shouted. *"Humo."*

The room was filling with smoke as it wafted down in great clouds.

"Damn it," somebody shouted, "this place is afire."

"Ah, hell," said Snake, "the chimney ain't drawin' right. Open the shutters, some of you, while I git on the roof an' run a pole down the chimney."

Having covered the chimney with his coat, Wes Tremayne was awaiting just such a move by the outlaws. When Snake left the cabin, Wes got a stranglehold on him with a brawny left arm. Once, twice, three times the knife in his right hand was driven into the struggling outlaw's chest. Quickly, Wes dragged the body around to the side of the cabin. The others wouldn't discover it until they were outside, and then it would be too late.

"Damn it, Snake," one of the outlaws shouted, "what are you doin' up there? Smoke's gittin' worse."

Wes had concealed himself within rifle range, prepared for the inevitable finale. What he hadn't counted on was the presence of the woman, and she was first out the door. Wes held his fire. With his first shot, the element of surprise would be gone. Fortunately, the woman backed away from the cabin, attempting to see what was obstructing the chimney. Coughing and wheezing, the outlaws came out, rubbing their eyes. Wes fired as rapidly as he could jack shells into the firing chamber of the Winchester. The five outlaws died on their feet, without getting off a single shot. The Mexican woman ran screeching into the brush, and Wes lit out on the run toward his waiting horse. For sure, if there were more of the outlaws, the terrified woman would get word to them. Worse, the cabin wasn't that far from the border, and the shots might have been heard by the Mexican border patrol. From the rise where he had first spotted the cabin, Wes reined up and looked back. There were the bodies of the dead outlaws and no sign of the woman. He felt no remorse, for his mind was full of Rebecca when she had lay dying. His words were for her, as he spoke aloud, and his voice broke.

"Vaya con Dios, Querido. I can do no more."

Once more he looked back toward the distant cabin as three horsemen entered the clearing. From their sombreros, he judged they were Mexican. He kept his horse at a slow gallop until he crossed the Rio Grande and was again in Texas.

New Mexico Territory
November 3, 1881

Nathan had no choice. He returned the wine bottle to the case from which he'd taken it and backed away from the wagon. By then the rest of the camp was fully awake, and it was the woman—Kit La Mie—who took charge.

"It is regrettable, Mr. Stone, that you obviously do not believe what you were told."

"I had trouble sleeping," Nathan said. "I just wanted another shot of that wine."

"I might have accepted that if you had asked, but your actions suggest something entirely different. Who sent you after us?"

Nathan laughed. "And *your* actions suggest a guilty conscience, Mrs. La Mie."

"He ain't the kind to talk," said Kendall. "Let me pistol whip the bastard."

"That's a mite heavyhanded for military discipline, Captain Kendall," Nathan said.

"Hell," said one of the privates, "Captain Kendall ain't had time to learn. He ain't been in that uniform but two weeks."

"Damn you, Baird," Kendall said, "shut your mouth."

"All of you hold your tongues," Kit La Mie snapped, "or I'll dismiss the lot of you."

"Mrs. La Mie," said Nathan, "you can drop the playacting for my benefit. I've forgotten more soldiering than these saloon rats will ever know."

"I daresay you have," Kit La Mie said, "and that's created a problem for you, Stone. I had hoped we wouldn't have to kill you."

"You murdered the soldiers who once wore those uniforms," said Nathan. "What's one more dead man?"

"Damn it, Kit," André shouted, "he knows about the nitro."

"He does now, you fool," said Kit.

Nathan now knew enough to buy time, to bargain for his life, and he laughed in their faces before he spoke.

"You didn't stand a chance of getting away with it. Only the government's allowed to have nitroglycerin. You'll never be able to dispose of it."

"It won't make any difference to you, federal man," said André. "You'll be dead."

"Wrong," Nathan said. "If I don't telegraph Washington from Pueblo, it's all of you who'll be dead."

"Hell," said Kendall, "he's bluffing."

Nathan laughed. "Can you afford to risk it, Captain?"

His words dripped with sarcasm, and Kendall would have shot Nathan point blank if André La Mie hadn't seized his arm. The slug blasted into the ground at Nathan's feet.

"Damn you, Kendall," said La Mie, "he's right. We can't afford to risk it. He was able to trail us this far, and he knows about the soldiers. We'll have to take him with us. He may be useful as a hostage, if the federals are waiting for us in Pueblo."

"How in hell are the federals goin' to know we're bound for Pueblo?" Gannon wanted to know.

"They know you and your bunch bushwhacked those soldiers," said André, "and they were able to get Stone here well ahead of us. Why shouldn't they know the rest?"

"He's right," Kit said. "Kendall, you keep Stone covered. André, get behind him and take his weapons. He goes with us."

But none of them were aware of Empty, and using the shadows for cover, the dog had crept under the wagon. He waited until André was between Nathan and the wagon and then darted out, sinking his teeth into La Mie's leg. La Mie howled in pain, and Nathan used the distraction to good advantage. He turned, his left arm seizing La Mie, while a cocked Colt appeared like magic in his right hand. When he spoke, his voice was cold, deadly.

"Now, Mrs. La Mie, you tell your play soldiers to lift their weapons and throw them over yonder in the brush. One bad move and André's backbone—assuming he has one—won't be his any longer."

"You heard him," said Kit La Mie. "Dispose of your weapons."

"No, by God," Kendall shouted.

He pulled the trigger, and again his slug tore into the ground, for Nathan had shot him in the right shoulder. His pistol thudded to the ground.

"Anybody else?" Nathan asked.

The others carefully drew their weapons and tossed them away.

"André is going to walk me to my horse," said Nathan. "Whether or not he's able to walk back will depend on the rest of you varmints. Let's go, André."

Using La Mie as a shield, Nathan backed away from them until he was lost in shadows beneath sheltering trees. Reaching his horse, he hit La Mie upside the head with the muzzle of his Colt and eased the unconscious man to the ground. Quickly he saddled his horse and rode north, Empty a fleeting shadow ahead of him.

"He's gone," La Mie shouted, regaining his senses. "Get him."

"Get him yourself," Kendall bawled. "I'm shot."

Nathan reined up, listening to them curse one another.

"We can't be more than a hundred and fifty miles south of Santa Fe, Empty. There'll be soldiers and the telegraph. That much nitroglycerin calls for a telegram to Byron Silver in Washington."

Confusion reined at the wagon, as André La Mie staggered back into the clearing. Not one of the pseudo soldiers had made a move to go after Nathan, and Kit La Mie was in a fury. She turned on the still-shaken André.

"Since he's escaped," she said, "we'll have to abandon the wagon, take a pair of the mules, and ride."

"Like hell," said the phony Sergeant Gannon. "You promised us a cut when this wagonload of stuff was sold, and we bushwhacked that soldier escort to git it. Now we just ain't about to give it up. You, missy, git over yonder and patch up Kendall's wound. Come mornin', we're takin' this wagon north, like we planned, and we ain't gonna be takin' it slow."

"You damn fools," André said, "all that wagon needs is one good jolt, and there'll be bits of you scattered all over the territory."

"Maybe," said Gannon, "but you promised us money. Big money. And we ain't of a mind to be done out of it by you not havin' the sand to see it through."

Even the wounded Kendall joined the others in a chorus of angry approval.

"We're not risking federal prison for the likes of you," Kit La Mie said, "and we're not risking being scattered all over New Mexico by the careless handling of that wagonload of nitroglycerin. Now you find Stone and silence him and we'll go on from there."

"Hell," said Private Ponder, "we can't trail him in the dark."

"You'd better give it a shot," André La Mie said. "A man on a good horse can be in Santa Fe by late tomorrow."

"He's right," said Kit. "Allow Stone to reach a town where there's a lawman, and the lot of you will be backed up against a wall, facing real soldiers with loaded rifles."

Half a dozen miles north, Nathan reined up, listening. The La Mies and their cut throat bunch had two choices. They could follow him with the intention of silencing him, or they could abandon the wagonload of deadly explosive and escape.

"They'll be followin' us, Empty," said Nathan. "That woman's a regular wampus kitty with three-inch claws, and I expect that bunch of make-believe soldiers has been promised part of the spoils. I reckon we could stay ahead of the varmints, but it purely rubs me the wrong way to tuck my tail and run. We're a good seven hours from first light. We'll just settle down and wait for them."

San Antonio, Texas
September 20, 1881

Wes had no trouble finding the Texas Ranger outpost, and Bodie West didn't seem in the least surprised to see him.

"I'd like to leave a message for Frank Bell," Wes said.

"Write it out," said Bodie. "I'll see that he gets it."

Taking the pencil and paper that Bodie offered, Wes wrote:

Mr. Bell, Rebecca has been avenged. There are six less skunks to bother you. Wes.

"It's not private," Wes said, passing the message to the Ranger. "Read it."

West read it quickly and extended his hand. Wes took it.

"You won't be riding back to Bell's, I reckon," said West.

"No," Wes said. "I left Rebecca there, and it'll be hard enough, forgetting, without it all bein' so . . . close to me."

"I understand," said West. "I'll get your message to Bell, and I promise nobody else will ever see it."

"I'm obliged," Wes said. "I'll see you again before I ride out."

"Do that," said West. "Meet me here in the morning, and I'll buy your breakfast."

While Wes didn't hold much with saloons, they occasionally served as a means of occupying one's mind, crowding out unpleasant or painful memories. Wes had developed a liking for poker and always won more than he lost, so he made the rounds of the better saloons. He was invited upstairs at the Cattleman's Emporium, but the near-naked girls on the floor distracted him and he soon left. He sat in on a poker game at the Star and took three pots in a row. One of the other men got up and leaned across the table, his hard eyes on Wes. Finally he spoke.

"Pilgrim, I been settin' here for two hours. I ain't won a pot, and I'm within a *peso* of bein' broke."

"You couldn't have had much to start with," said Wes, "if I've cleaned you out with three hands. How much did you lose? I'll give it back."

That struck the onlookers as hilariously funny, and they laughed and shouted.

"Hell, Shorty," said one of the men, "I didn't know you was needful of charity. I'll put some *pesos* in the hat fer you."

That started a whole new round of bully-ragging, and Wes regretted ever having said anything. He slid back his chair and stood up.

"Where the hell you think you're goin?" Shorty demanded. "You owe me a chance to recoup my losses."

"I owe you nothing," said Wes. "If you're broke, it's time you folded."

"Don't git throwed and stomped, Shorty," somebody shouted. "I'll stake you."

"So will I," said a second voice.

"And I," a third voice cut in.

Double eagles rang against the tabletop until Shorty had a hundred dollars.

"Deal me in," said Shorty triumphantly.

While Wes didn't win, Shorty quickly lost half his stake to three other men. When Wes won a fourth and fifth pot, Shorty got to his feet, his eyes shooting sparks of rage.

"Damn you," he snarled, "there ain't no honest way a man can win like you're doin'."

He went for his gun but was painfully slow. Wes already had him covered with his Colt, cocked and steady.

"I could have killed you," said Wes, "but I've no reason to. Get out of here."

"Shorty," somebody said, "go on home. This ain't your day."

There was nervous laughter that quickly died away. Without a word, Shorty left the saloon, and Wes spoke to the men who remained.

"Those of you who want to recoup your losses, sit down," said Wes.

"That's white of you," said one of the men. "Shorty's had a mite too much to drink. It don't do nothin' for a man's judgment when he's handlin' the cards."

Wes played five more hands, losing four of them.

"My luck's run out," Wes said. "I'm folding."

His winnings had been modest and his conduct acceptable, and he vowed to avoid saloon poker tables. At least for a while. It was late enough in the day to have supper, and he left the saloon with that in mind. Suddenly there was a shot, and slug ripped along his left side, just above the belt. A second slug slammed into the door frame as Wes dropped to his knees, his Colt spitting flame. The shots had come from between two store buildings across the street. Evening shadows had crept in, and while Wes couldn't see the person who was firing at him, the muzzle flashes were plain enough. There were no more shots, and men boiled out of the saloon. While the lead had only burned a painful furrow along his left side, Wes was bleeding like a stuck hog. Nobody had to ask what had happened, for his white shirt was drenched with blood.

"He's been hit," a voice shouted needlessly. "Somebody git the doc."

"Some of you have a look across the street, between those buildings," said Wes. "I might have hit him."

Half a dozen men hastened to obey. Excited shouts announced their discovery and when they returned, two of them bore the body of Shorty.

"The damn muleheaded little varmint," somebody said. "He purely didn't know how to lose."

The doctor arrived first and led Wes back into the saloon.

There he removed his bloody shirt, and had his wound tended. Outside, the sheriff questioned the men who had witnessed the incident in the saloon and satisfied himself that the shooting of Shorty had been justified. Ranger Bodie West was there, and while he said little, he observed much. While Wes Tremayne had been firing at muzzle flashes, he had hit his adversary twice, and the two wounds could have been covered with a man's hand. He waited until the sheriff had talked to Wes, and when Wes finally left the saloon, West was waiting for him on the boardwalk.

"I haven't had supper," said West. "Have you?"

"No," Wes said. "That's where I was going when he cut down on me. Now I'm not sure I can eat."

"Come on," said West, "and give it a try. I can say tonight what I'd intended saying in the morning at breakfast."

"I reckon I need to talk," Wes said. "I just killed a man I didn't know, for a reason that didn't amount to a hill of beans."

"When a man's shooting at you with killing on his mind," said West, "you don't have time to study his reasoning. You do exactly what you did awhile ago. You kill him before he kills you. It doesn't get any simpler than that."

When their steaks had been ordered and they were sipping coffee, Bodie West spoke his mind.

"Sheriff Lyle Tidwell was in town yesterday," West said, "and I learned what you did for him in Lampasas."

"He needed help," said Wes, "and I had nothing better to do. Anyway, Rebecca and me had just ... come to an understanding and needed to settle down for a while. The town was mighty nice to us, and I won't forget them."

Muzzle first, he extended the Colt the town had presented him, and West studied the weapon with appreciation. He returned it to Wes, and then he spoke.

"Wes, I'd like to see you become a Texas Ranger."

"I'm flattered," said Wes "but I don't feel like I'm worthy."

"We've lost too many good men who felt that way," West said. "I'm thinking of one in particular. He's godawful sudden with a pistol, the fastest I ever saw. In defense of his life, he's been forced to kill. Men are constantly calling him out to test his fast draw. He refuses to stand on the side of the law because he feels he'd be hiding his killings behind a badge."

"I kind of understand that," said Wes. "How would it

look, a Ranger killing men for no reason other than defending his fast draw?"

"No worse than you doing the same thing as a civilian," West replied. "Damn it, you can't become the protector of every idiot looking for a reputation as a fast draw. When you become a Ranger, you'll become known for your activities on the side of the law."

"But that won't stop the fast-draws wanting to call me out, to gain a reputation at my expense," said Wes.

"No," West agreed, "but it could discourage some of them. As a civilian, without a lawman's badge, you're fair game. There's no law against killing you, as long as it's a fair fight. On the other hand, nothing short of a damn fool guns down a Ranger. Even if he beats you, he becomes a fugitive, and sooner or later we'll get him. Not many men want a reputation that puts them on the wrong side of the law. There'll always be a few, such as John Wesley Hardin, who'll buck the odds. But they can't win. Hardin's in Huntsville territorial prison, and he has a lot of years ahead of him."

"You make a pretty convincing case," said Wes, "but there are plenty of hombres with a fast gun. Why me?"

"It takes more than a fast gun," West replied. "It takes nerve, a man who thinks on his feet, one who isn't afraid to stand alone. As a Ranger, you'll belong to an elite force of men who often ride alone. Not by choice, but of necessity, because there are never enough of us."

"And you believe I'm man enough to wear a hat that big?"

"I do," said West. "I saw you ride after a bunch of killers alone, and you came back alive. Sheriff Tidwell told me how you stood up to Ike Blocker and his outlaws, forcing Blocker to call you out and then gunning him down. You're already performing the duties of a Ranger; all you need is the oath and the badge."

"I gambled and won," Wes said. "Blocker might have come after me with his entire gang and they'd have shot me full of holes."

"You used good judgement," said West. "You correctly judged Blocker, and when you stood up to him the rest of the gang left the territory. That's why I'm interested in you."

"I like your style, Bodie West," said Wes. "I reckon I could do worse than become a Texas Ranger."

"*Bueno,*" West said.

The Ranger offered his hand and Wes took it, thankful he was being judged on his deeds without regard for his youth. John Wesley Tremayne was still two months shy of his fifteenth birthday.

New Mexico Territory
November 3, 1881

Despite the darkness, Kendall and his pseudo soldiers rode out in pursuit of Nathan Stone. Kendall was in a foul mood, favoring his wounded shoulder, and there was virtually no conversation. André and Kit La Mie watched them disappear into the shadows.

"They'll never catch up to Stone," and André.

"It won't matter to us one way or the other," Kit replied. "I suspect Stone can take of the lot of them with one hand behind his back."

"For the short time he was here," said André bitterly, "you developed a damned high opinion of him."

"I know a man when I see one," Kit said. "If I had *him* siding me . . ."

Nathan lay with his head on his saddle, his hat tipped over his eyes. The only sound was the occasional chirp of a sleepy bird and the unbroken rhythm of the grulla cropping grass. Empty got up, growling softly.

"Thanks, pard," Nathan said to the dog. "They made better time than I expected."

He listened until he could hear the sound of their coming. Removing his Winchester from the saddle boot, he bellied down behind a boulder facing downriver. Moonset was an hour away, and the river bank, but for stirrup-high undergrowth, was clear for at least three hundred yards. The men who hunted him must cross that clearing unless they were smart enough to ride clear of it. Nathan counted on their impatience to prevail over their better judgment, and he wasn't disappointed. They rode two abreast, and he waited until they were well within range. He then shot one of the lead riders out of the saddle. It was all the warning they were going to get.

CHAPTER 26

*San Antonio, Texas,
September 22, 1881*

For several days, Bodie West talked and Wes Tremayne listened.

"You'll be going to El Paso," West said, "and there's plenty you need to know about the situation there. It's a border town and, as you'd expect, it's as much Mexican as it is Anglo. Ranger Jim Gillett is there now, working under cover, but he'll be leaving us sometime in December. You'll be replacing him, and you will also be working under cover."

"Are you saying El Paso has no law except for the Rangers?" Wes asked.

"Oh, they have a city marshal, but he's part of the problem," said West. "On April tenth, Dallas Stoudenmire became city marshal. Four days later there was an ugly affair in the streets—Anglos and Mexicans shouted at one another over the recent murder of a pair of Mexicans. Stoudenmire owns the Globe Restaurant there, and while he was eating there was a shooting. A couple of Mexican-hating drunks—George Campbell and John Hale—started cussing Gus Krempkau, a man they considered friendly to the Mexicans. After hard words, Hale shot Krempkau. Stoudenmire, carrying two revolvers, charged into the street and began firing at Hale. But his shots went wild and one of them struck a Mexican in the back. Stoudenmire's aim improved some and he shot John Hale through the head. George Campbell had threatened Stoudenmire on more than one occasion, but when he saw Hale die, Campbell tried to escape. But the mortally wounded Krempkau had drawn his revolver and emptied it at Campbell. One of Krempkau's slugs broke Campbell's wrist, while another ripped into his foot. Stoudenmire then shot Campbell in the stomach. Both he and the Mexican died the next day."

"So Stoudenmire is on the bad side of the Mexicans," said Wes.

"Worse than that," West replied. "He's managed to get on the bad side of everybody. Three days after killing the Mexican, Stoudenmire shot and killed Bill Johnson. Enemies of Stoudenmire had managed to get Johnson drunk and had put him up to ambushing Dallas."

"Stoudenmire was blamed for defending himself in an ambush?"

"To some extent," said West. "Johnson was a former marshal, with many friends, and he was seen by many as a victim, a pawn used by Stoudenmire's enemies."

"So Ranger Jim Gillette went to El Paso at Stoudenmire's request?"

"My God, no," West replied. "Dallas Stoudenmire has too much pride. He'd rather be dead and in hell than ask for help, especially from us. He was once a member of Company B of the Texas Rangers."

"So who asked for Ranger help?"

"I'm not at liberty to say," said West. "All I can tell you is that Gillett's not there to protect Stoudenmire—the man has too many enemies. If that wasn't enough, he has a real problem with the bottle. He carries two revolvers and a snub-nosed hideout gun, and when he's roaring drunk he has a habit of firing his guns in the street, often in the middle of the night. We figure it's just a matter of time until Stoudenmire's enemies get the best of him. When that happens, Gillett's there to keep the peace. You'll join him—and eventually replace him—for the same purpose."

"Nobody is to know I'm a Ranger, then," said Wes.

"Only Jim Gillett," West said. "Take a room at Granny Boudleaux's boardinghouse, and you'll find Gillett there."

"How far am I to go toward saving Stoudenmire's hide?" Wes asked.

"Ask Gillett's advice on that," said West. "Far as I'm concerned, don't take any slugs aimed at him. He'll get it eventually, and every Ranger in Texas can't save him."

So Wes Tremayne took the oath, received his badge and Bible, and prepared to ride west to El Paso.

New Mexico Territory
November 3, 1881

Nathan emptied two saddles. The remaining four riders wheeled their horses and rode frantically back the way they had come.

"I think they got the message, Empty," Nathan said, returning his Winchester to the saddle boot. "We'll ride on to Santa Fe and report that wagonload of nitroglycerin."

Santa Fe, New Mexico
November 4, 1881

Nathan rode into Santa Fe two hours before sundown and went immediately to the telegraph office. He wrote a message, addressing it to twenty-one, Office of the Attorney General, Washington. It was brief.

Urgent you contact me at Santa Fe.

He signed his name, paid for the telegram, and took a chair by the door.

"You ain't likely to git an answer before tomorrow," the telegrapher said.

"Maybe not," said Nathan, "but I'll wait awhile."

He had waited less than fifteen minutes when the instrument began to chatter. When the telegrapher had taken the message, he stood up, a puzzled expression on his face.

"Well?" Nathan said.

"Wasn't to you," the telegrapher said. "It's to me. Washington's orderin' me to turn the key over to you. Do you know the code?"

"Yes," said Nathan.

"Take over, then," the telegrapher said.

Nathan sat down at the desk and brought the instrument to life. He identified himself and asked permission to send; it was promptly granted. Quickly he telegraphed the details as he knew them. The response, when it came, was startling. It was addressed to Deputy United States James Blanchard, Santa Fe, New Mexico, and said:

Nathan Stone is an emissary of the government of the United States stop. You are to act upon information supplied by Stone in recovery of government property stop. Person or persons involved in theft wanted for murder stop. This is your authorization to arrest on federal John Doe warrants all parties involved stop. Confirm receipt and understanding stop.

It was signed Byron Silver, Office of the Attorney General, Washington. But there was more. The second message was intended for Nathan; it said:

Assist United States in recovery and arrests stop. When mission accomplished wire me and I will meet you in Dodge.

Nathan telegraphed his acceptance and the instrument became silent. He then wrote out Silver's message to the U.S. marshal in a more legible manner and turned to the curious telegrapher.

"I'm obliged for the use of your key, pardner. Sorry I can't tell you what this is all about, but I reckon you'll be hearing after it's over."

When Nathan reached the U.S. Marshal's office, he introduced himself and passed the telegraphed message to Jim Blanchard.

"I've never encountered anything like this," said the lawman after reading the strange telegram.

"Let me tell you the story as I told it to Silver," Nathan said. "Then you're welcome to telegraph Washington to confirm it all. Silver and I have been friends for a long time."

"You talk," said Blanchard, "and I'll listen."

Nathan told the story from start to finish, including the killing of two of the men who had pursued him.

"So there's still six of them," Blanchard said.

"Yes," said Nathan, "but they know I've reached Santa Fe and I expect them to run for it, abandoning the wagon."

"But we can't count on that," Blanchard said. "If they murdered the military escort—six men—they have a big stake in this wagonload of explosive. While they can't outrun us with the wagon, they can always hole up and ambush us. That would buy them some time to try and get the wagon out of the territory."

"If they've abandoned the wagon," said Nathan, "we'll need mules."

"I'll get a couple of teams and the necessary harness at the livery," Blanchard said. "I see no point in riding after them today. It'll be dark in another hour, and if they're waiting to bushwhack us, we'd be asking for it."

"You're right," said Nathan. "If they're trying to get away, taking the wagon with them, they won't get far. It'll be slow going because nitroglycerin is volatile stuff. Jolt that wagon too hard and there'll be an explosion that'll rattle the windows in California."

"I'll telegraph Washington and confirm what we're going to do," Blanchard said, "and make arrangements with the livery for mules and harness. Meet me here at the office in the morning at first light and I'll have some men deputized to ride with us."

El Paso, Texas
October 2, 1881

The ride from San Antonio had been almost six hundred miles, and Wes had taken his time, sparing his horse. He arrived on Sunday afternoon, and following a bountiful meal at a cafe, went looking for Granny Boudleaux's boarding house. Removing his hat, he stepped through the front door and encountered a very pretty girl:

"I reckon," he said, eyeing her with appreciation, "you ain't Granny."

Her eyes twinkled and she laughed. "No, I ain't. I'm Molly Horrell, Granny's partner. Do you want her, or will I do?"

"Much as I want to meet Granny," said Wes, "I can wait. I'm Wes Tremayne, and I want a room."

"Day, week, or month?"

"A month," Wes said. "I like the surroundings."

"Meals—breakfast and supper—are fifty cents a day extra," she said.

"I'll take the meals too," said Wes.

"Breakfast's at seven and supper's at five," she said. "There's fried chicken tonight."

"I'll be there at four-thirty," said Wes.

"I'll show you to your room," Molly said, "unless you must tend your horse."

"My horse is at the livery," said Wes. "I always see to him first. Do I look that much like a shorthorn?"

"I'm sorry," she said. "I didn't realize how that sounded. Come on and I'll show you to your room."

In the hall, they met Granny Boudleaux, and Molly performed the introductions. For a long moment, Granny looked critically at Wes.

"I see you somewhere before," she said.

"I've never been in El Paso in my life, until now," said Wes.

Molly led Wes to his room, unlocked the door, and presented him with his key. When he had closed the door, he sat down on the bed and kicked off his boots. Stretching out, he thought of what Granny Boudleaux had said about having seen him before. Strangely, it reminded him of a similar conversation with Ranger Bodie West. Who was this stranger who so strongly resembled Wes Tremayne?

Supper at Granny Boudleaux's was an interesting affair. Including Wes, Granny had a total of fifteen boarders, all of them men. Several were drummers, but most of the others appeared to be clerks from the shops in town. Wes had wondered how he'd recognize Jim Gillett, but Molly Horrell took care of that. When everybody was seated at the long table, she introduced them to Wes, and Wes to them. Jim Gillett only nodded, and there wasn't a thing to draw undue attention to him. He had a thonged-down Colt on his right hip, but for the time and place, that wasn't unusual. Gillett seemed in no hurry, nor did Wes, but they finished within seconds of one another. When Gillett started down the hall, Wes followed. Concealed in his hand, Wes had the star-in-a-circle shield of the Texas Rangers, and when he caught up to Gillett he flashed the badge.

"I'm in room nine," said Gillett. "Give me a few minutes. Knock twice, pause, and then knock again."

Wes went on to his room, number 11, and waited for what he judged was a quarter of an hour. He then stepped out into the hall, and being sure he was unseen, knocked twice, paused, and then knocked again. Gillett opened the door, closing it quickly when Wes was inside. The two had already been introduced, but when Gillett offered his hand, Wes took it. Gillett stood an inch or two over six feet, with gray eyes and hair black as a crow's wing. He looked to be maybe twenty-five. He sat down on the bed while Wes took the only chair.*

"I reckon you was told about the situation here, before you left San Antone," Gillett said.

"Some," said Wes. "Why don't you tell me how you see it?"

"Was I you," Gillett said, "I wouldn't walk too close to Stoudenmire. The varmint just naturally attracts enemies like a tall oak draws lightnin' bolts."

"I was told there's trouble between Anglos and Mexicans," said Wes. "Does Stoudenmire figure into that?"

"To some extent," Gillett said. "He sure don't like 'em, and right after he became city marshal he shot one in the back."

"Accidentally, I heard," said Wes.

"I don't doubt that," Gillett said. "He carries three guns, includin' a hideout, and he ain't the world's best shot, even when he's sober. He's got a running feud going with the Manning brothers and he's always where anybody can get at him. He operates the Globe Restaurant, a place his brother-in-law willed him. It'd be damned easy to bushwhack him, just any day or night you could choose."

"We're not here to save Stoudenmire from being dry gulched, and there's nothing we can do to keep Anglos and Mexicans from hating one another," said Wes. "Exactly why *are* we here?"

"We're here to prevent a total breakdown of law and order," Gillett said. "Rangers in town have a calming effect, but we don't make our presence known until the need arises. During the next few days, spend some time in the Globe Restaurant and get acquainted with Dallas Stoudenmire. Then you'll have some better idea as to why people in this town are gettin' spooked."

---

*James Gillett was born November 4, 1856 in Austin. He was a Ranger for six and a half years.

Santa Fe, New Mexico
November 5, 1881

With Empty trotting beside him, Nathan reached the U.S. marshal's office just as Blanchard and four deputies arrived.

"Stone," said the lawmen, "these are deputies Pryor, Sowell, Wells, and Lytle. We'll ride by the livery for the mules and harness. How are you fixed for grub?"

"Enough in my saddlebag for three days," Nathan said. "When we've recovered the wagon, I'll have to ride back to Santa Fe ahead of you. I must ride to Pueblo and take the train to Dodge City for a meeting there."

"Let's ride, then," said Blanchard. "How far to the wagon?"

"Unless they've moved it," Nathan said, "maybe a hundred and fifty miles. We won't reach it until sometime tomorrow."

Just before noon of their second day on the trail, with Nathan in the lead, the posse reined up.

"We're not more than an hour away from where I left the wagon," Nathan said. "Let's rest the horses here and let my dog range on ahead. He'll warn us if there's an ambush."

"From what you've told me," said Blanchard, "that's what I expect. If this bunch went to the trouble of killing a military escort in south Texas, they're not likely to back off at this point. Their only way out is to kill all of us."

"They're not going to do that," Nathan said. "An ambush is effective only when it's a total surprise."

"You got an almighty lot of confidence in that dog of yours," said Pryor.

"I should," Nathan replied. "He's saved my life often enough."

When Empty returned, Nathan rode to meet him, and the dog growled. Nathan rode back to meet the posse.

"Well?" Blanchard asked.

"They're waiting for us," said Nathan. "All of you wait here. I'll follow Empty and see where they're holed up. Then we'll go after them."

They didn't question him, and Nathan rode away, following Empty.

"This is the strangest damn situation I ever seen," Wells said. "Who *is* this hombre that just shows up out of nowhere, with us follerin' him, and him follerin' his old hound?"

"Strange as it all seems," said Deputy U.S. Marshal Jim Blanchard, "it's real enough to have the attorney general's office in Washington on top of it. This Nathan Stone makes some big tracks. I wired the office in Washington, and the government's sidin' him all the way. That's good enough for me."

Nathan rode on, reining up when Empty came back to meet him. He dismounted and, following the dog, continued on foot. When he eventually saw the wagon, it had definitely been moved, for it sat in a clearing. There was no sign of the mules. Beyond the clearing, to the south, was a rise. At various points along the slope and near the foot of it were upthrusts of stone, every one large enough to conceal a man with a gun. Nathan watched from the brush, not having revealed himself. It would be simple enough to send three men to the east and three to the west, bringing them in behind those who lay in wait, setting up a murderous cross fire. Nathan made his way back to his horse, mounted, and then rode back to meet the posse.

"We can divide our forces, swing wide to east and west, and flank them," Nathan told them. "They're bellied down behind some rocks beyond the wagon. You're representing the law, Marshal. When we have them covered, call on them to surrender."

"They ain't likely to," said Blanchard. "What then?"

"We shoot," Nathan said. "These are thieves and killers, and you have federal John Doe warrants for their arrest. I can get them changed to execution warrants if need be. I don't like John Doe execution warrants, if there's any doubts, but I have none."

"Those people told you their names," said Pryor. "Why the John Doe warrants?"

"The names they gave me may or may not be their names," Nathan said, "but they're guilty of a crime, and it's real enough. Marshal, you take two men and ride to the east. I'll take two, and ride to the west. Give us half an hour to get into position, and then call out your challenge. Just be sure you're in range, and if they don't surrender, shoot."

"Pryor, you and Sowell come with me," said Blanchard.
They rode out, and Nathan nodded to Wells and Lytle.
They followed him as he rode to the west, swinging wide
to avoid the ambush ahead. Nathan thought the lot of them
were a little squeamish, a little uncertain, as they neared a
showdown. This had been Byron Silver's idea, bringing in
the law, and Nathan only hoped the posse held up under
fire. He seriously doubted there would be any surrender
when one of the charges against them would be murder.
They came out on the southern slope of the ridge, and
there they left their horses. There was plenty of cover, and
Nathan led them far enough that they could see several of
the men who lay in wait. Nathan couldn't see Blanchard
and his men, but it stood to reason they should be in position. Just when it seemed Blanchard would never shout a
challenge, the marshal did.

"This is Deputy U.S. Marshal Jim Blanchard. You people
are under arrest. Drop your weapons and come out with
your hands up."

The response was immediate, as rifles roared and slugs
sang above their heads like angry bees. Nathan was the
first to return fire, and someone cried out in pain. There
was a crash of gunfire from Blanchard's position as he and
his men bought it. There were more cries of pain and grad-
ually the firing from below ceased.

"This is André La Mie," a voice shouted. "My wife and
I are unarmed. We're done."

"Come on," Blanchard said, "but keep your hands up."

Slowly they came up the slope, their hands shoulder high.

"We're glad to see you, Marshal," said Kit La Mie.
"Those men have been holding us against our will."

"Tell it to the judge," Blanchard replied. "I know what's
in that wagon over yonder. It was taken from an army
escort and six solders were killed. The army's wiring me
more information, and I reckon they'll be wanting to question you folks. Pryor, you and Sowell find the horses that
belonged to this bunch. We'll need two of them."

"We'd better see if any of those other four varmints are
still alive," said Nathan. "If it's all the same to the rest of
you, Empty and me will take a look."

"By all means," Blanchard said.

If some of the outlaws were playing possum, it could
prove a deadly task, and Nathan thought they all looked

relieved. It would be safe enough, with Empty going ahead of him, and he went on down the slope. Three of the men were dead and the fourth had been gut-shot. Nathan went on to the wagon, opened the canvas pucker, and looked inside. Nothing had been bothered, as best he could tell. He walked back up the slope. Pryor and Sowell had found the horses belonging to the outlaws, and had brought two of them for André and Kit La Mie.

"Three of the men are dead," said Nathan, "and the fourth won't be around for long."

"Wells, you and Lytle get those mules harnessed to that wagon," Blanchard ordered.

"You don't have anything on us," André La Mie said. "We were traveling with those men against our will."

"That's not what you told me," said Nathan. "You and the wampus kitty were bossing those fake soldiers around like you owned them, and I had to kill two of them just to get away from you. I reckon you don't know anything about that wagonload of explosives, either."

"We've never seen you before in our lives," Kit La Mie said haughtily, "and we have absolutely no idea what's in that wagon. It'll be your word against ours."

"We'll be getting a telegraphed report and descriptions from federal authorities," said Nathan. "Maybe we can refresh your memory."

"Pryor," Blanchard said, "you'll take first turn with the wagon. One of the others will spell you after a couple of hours. You got to take it slow, avoiding rocks and drop offs."

Lytle waved his hat, indicating the mules were hitched and the wagon was ready to go. Blanchard nodded to Pryor and Sowell and they rode out, André and Kit La Mie ahead of them. Blanchard had held back to speak to Nathan.

"Stone, I don't doubt that pair's everything you say they are, but you heard what they said. They're slick as calf slobber, and if it's goin' to be your word against theirs, I want you around until I got this nailed down. There's slick-tongued lawyers that could get them off scot-free and leave me lookin' like a prime fool."

"I understand your position," Nathan said, "and I won't leave Santa Fe until you have the evidence you need. Since I telegraphed Washington and got all this started, I'll have to see it through. I'm sure the government wants that nitroglycerin, but if a soldier escort was murdered, somebody will have to account for that."

"I'll feel a lot better when we get some official word as to what happened," Blanchard said. "Have you considered how all of this is goin' to look if that wagon is loaded with nothing but French wine?"

"I've thought of the possibility," said Nathan, "but nothing that's happened makes any sense if there's anything less than nitroglycerin in that wagon. I can't imagine them trying to kill me over a wagonload of wine, and you were right in the midst of a fight to the death today. I think we're going to find some dead men on their backtrail."

"Well," Blanchard said, "let's get on back to Santa Fe and see if anything's come in on the telegraph."

Santa Fe, New Mexico
November 20, 1881

The return to Santa Fe was slow and laborious because of the heavily loaded wagon and the need to avoid rough terrain. Nathan and Blanchard went immediately to the telegraph office.

"I never seen so much telegraph business," the telegrapher said.

He brought out a sheaf of yellow paper on which he had scribbled messages. Every one had been dated, and he handed them to Blanchard.

"You have them dated and in order," said Blanchard. "Good."

"Spread 'em out on that table over yonder," the telegrapher said. "If you got trouble readin' my writin', maybe I can figger it out."

"This is what I'm wantin' to see," said Blanchard. "It covers the killin' of the soldier escort near Galveston Bay, and backs up what you said about this bunch stealin' a load of nitroglycerin."

"What about descriptions?" Nathan asked.

"We're comin' to that, I think," said Blanchard. "Here, read some of this."

"Tarnation," Nathan said, after reading some of the material, "this bunch has been in trouble with the law before.

André and Kit La Mie have used a whole passel of names. All the hombres they had posin' as soldiers were killers. They're all wanted in Texas."

"This is lookin' more solid all the time," said Blanchard. "We got to supply our sworn testimony that these six men actually died. You got to account for the two you shot, and we can all testify to the killin' of the other four that tried to ambush us. The military will be sendin' for any that was took alive."

"I think we ought to telegraph Washington that six of the bunch are dead, and that the La Mies—or whoever they are have been locked up. I expect there'll be soldiers from Fort Elliott, Texas, or from Fort Dodge, Kansas, comin' to take this La Mie pair off your hands. I reckon you'll get some recognition from this."

"I don't figure I'm due any," said Blanchard. "It was you that started all this."

"I don't want any credit," Nathan replied. "I was able to get Washington involved only because these people had committed crimes against the United States, and because I have a friend in the attorney general's office. It's no more than he would expect of me, and when you get the final word as to how this will be resolved, I'll be riding on."

When Blanchard telegraphed Washington that the nitroglycerin had been recovered and that André and Kit La Mie were in custody, the response was rapid and brief:

Suspects in custody being extradited to Texas stop. Military escort coming from Fort Elliott to claim recovered federal property and suspects.

The telegram was signed with Byron Silver's name.

"Well," said Nathan, "it's time I was riding on. You have my sworn testimony."

"Go ahead," Blanchard said. "I'm satisfied we've handled this properly."

Nathan had one more telegram to send. Addressing it to twenty-one, Office of the Attorney General, Washington, he wrote:

Will meet you in Dodge December first.

He paid for the telegram, and with Empty following, rode north toward Pueblo.

CHAPTER 27

Wes Tremayne didn't talk to Jim Gillett for almost a week. The second conversation came about after a raid by the Sandlin gang, when a Mexican wrangler was killed. Gillett nodded to Wes in the hall after supper, and they went on to Gillett's room.

"I reckon you've heard about the outlaw raid on the Collier ranch yesterday," Gillett said.

"Yeah," said Wes, "I heard. I reckon the killing of another Mexican won't help the situation around here."

"It won't change anything, one way or the other," Gillett said. "I figured this would be as good a time as any to tell you about the Sandlin gang. Cord Sandlin built himself an empire across the border, just beyond Ciudad Juarez, and El Paso's come to expect a certain amount of hell raising from him. I understand he's bought off the Mexican authorities and has an outlaw band of more than thirty men."

"There's law on this side of the border," said Wes. "Why hasn't nobody stood up to Sandlin and his bunch?"

"Somebody has," Gillett said. "Five years ago—before I came here—they murdered Sheriff McCormick."

"I reckon nobody's challenged them since then," said Wes.

"No," Gillett said, "and with good reason. Not a man in this town is willing to join a sheriff's posse to ride after the Sandlin gang. Sandlin got the word out that any man going after the gang would be marked for death, including the county sheriff or city marshal."

"Maybe he's bluffing," said Wes.

"Sheriff McCormick gambled on that," Gillett said, "and all it got him was a six-foot hole in the bone orchard."

"Sandlin has his way," said Wes, "because everybody's afraid of him, including the Rangers."

"Hell, kid," Gillett said, "that Ranger star don't make a man bulletproof. In case you ain't been told, you're not allowed to cross the border after outlaws. Some kind of border deal between the United States and Mexico. If that ain't reason enough to stay the hell out of the land of chili peppers, Sandlin's come up with a stronger one. He's put a bounty of a hundred dollars on any lawman crossing the river. My God, many a Mex would backshoot his own brother for that kind of money."

"You're not very inspiring, Gillett."

"I don't aim to be," said Gillett. "Don't ever let noble thoughts get the best of your common sense. Get yourself gunned down in a fight you can't win, and within six months, nobody on either side of the border will remember or care who you were."

"I'll keep that in mind," Wes said. "Anything else?"

"Only what I suggested last time," said Gillett. "Spend some time in the Globe and get to know Dallas Stoudenmire."

"So I inherit him when you leave," Wes said.

"Not just him," said Gillett. "The whole damn town. My resignation is effective the day after Christmas."

But trouble didn't wait for Gillett's departure.

El Paso, Texas
December 16, 1881

In the small hours of the morning, Wes was awakened by the distant crash of gunfire. In his sock feet, he crossed the hall and tapped on Gillett's door. Quickly Gillett opened the door and Wes slipped inside. Except for his boots, Gillett was dressed.

"I reckon you heard the shooting," Wes said.

"I heard it," said Gillett, "but you'll have to get used to that. It's the city marshal's job. Rangers don't enforce town law unless we're called in for that purpose, and that's not our reason for being here. There are exceptions, of course. If somebody's shot and killed Stoudenmire, then we'll have to restore and maintain the peace until a new town marshal is appointed. It's after three o'clock, and our presence in town would only reveal us without serving any good purpose. We'll skip Granny's breakfast and eat at the Globe. Whatever took place this morning will be the topic of conversation."

When Wes and Gillett reached the Globe, the place was

crowded, and they soon discovered the reason. Seated at a table with a dozen other men, Stoudenmire was recounting what had happened during the night.

"It happened outside my boardin' house, about three o'clock this morning," Stoudenmire was saying. "Some varmint tried to ambush me. I'd of got him, but he was so close his muzzle flashes blinded me. I cut down on him, but he got away in the dark."*

"Hell," somebody said quietly, "Stoudenmire was likely owl-eyed drunk, an' done all the shootin' himself, throwin' lead at a man that wasn't there."

"That's pretty much how it is," said Gillett when he and Wes had left the restaurant. "Nobody's quite sure whether Stoudenmire fought his way out of an attempted ambush, or whether he was just drunk and shootin' at shadows."

Pueblo, Colorado
November 23, 1881

Nathan went to the railroad depot and arranged for a boxcar for his horse as far as Dodge on the next westbound, which would depart at six o'clock the next morning.

"Make yourself at home in the bunkhouse," said the dispatcher, who well remembered Nathan from his days with the railroad.

"I will," Nathan said, "and I'm obliged."

Reaching the bunkhouse, the first man Nathan encountered was Harley Stafford.

"Well, by God," said Nathan, "I thought you was through ridin' anything that didn't have four legs and a tail."

"I thought so, too," Harley replied, "but I'm as fiddle-footed as you are. I missed the locomotive whistles, riding the rails, shooting and being shot at."

"Vivian didn't raise hell when you left?"

"No," said Harley. "She said all men are no damned good, that you and me are birds of a feather."

"Tarnation," Nathan said, "I don't know whether to be flattered or insulted."

---

*Joe King attempted to ambush Stoudenmire, whose return shots missed. King escaped.

"She never understood why you rode away," said Harley, "but I did. A woman wants ties, but to a man they become chains. When I left New Orleans, I felt like I'd just broke jail."

"I've never heard it said any better than that," Nathan replied. "I'll be taking the eastbound with you as far as Dodge."

"If you're after your old job," said Harley, "you'll have to fight me for it."

"Relax," Nathan said. "I'm meeting a friend there."

"I won't tell Vivian," said Harley, closing his left eye in a slow wink.

"Send her a telegram," Nathan said. "I don't care, and I'm sure she won't."

"Aw, hell," said Harley. "I was hopin' to see her a little jealous. Now we'll never find out if she cares a damn for anything or anybody but them fast horses."

"You'll have to conduct your experiments without me," Nathan said. "The last thing I want is a jealous female tied to my shirttail."

"I'll drink to that," said Harley. "We got the rest of today and tonight. Let's have us a big supper and then visit all the saloons."

"My dog don't like saloons," Nathan said.

"Leave him at the depot with the dispatcher," said Harley.

"He don't like trains," Nathan said, "and I doubt he's all that fond of the dispatcher."

Harley laughed. "How's he goin' to get to Dodge? Lope alongside the train?"

"Except for saloons," said Nathan, "he'll go where I go. We'll get supper and then go from there."

They had supper at a cafe where Nathan had eaten before, where the cook fed Empty in the kitchen.

"After supper," said Nathan, "let's find a billiard parlor. I'm a mite tired of saloons. I always end up shootin' my way out."

"Suits me," Harley said, "but most billiard parlors are saloons with a billiard table or two in the back."

Being a Wednesday night, the town was at low ebb. Nathan and Harley, after a few games of billiards, gave it up and returned to the railroad bunkhouse. The crew for the morning's eastbound was there, none of them men Nathan

knew. Nathan and Harley chose adjoining bunks and
Empty curled up on the floor between them.

"Empty's already spooked," Nathan said. "He knows,
when we go to a depot, we'll be boardin' a train, and he
hates that."

Harley laughed. "You don't need a woman to cater to,
'cause you got that hound."

"He's never got me in near as much trouble as women
have," said Nathan.

Nathan and Harley arose at four o'clock the following
morning, had breakfast, and were ready when the eastbound left at six. The train rattled across the plains, bound
for Dodge City, five hours away.

"How are things with the railroad?" Nathan asked.

"Better than usual," said Harley. "We haven't had a
train robbery since I came back."

"Is Foster Hagerman still in the saddle at Dodge?"

"So far as the railroad's concerned," Harley said, "but
he quit the town council. That affair with Wyatt Earp as
policeman did it."

"Earp, two of his brothers, and Doc Holliday started a
shootout at Tombstone, Arizona, back in October," said
Nathan. "They killed three men."

"I read about that," Harley said. "It made the papers in
Kansas City. Sounds like the Earps and Holliday finally
done somethin' right."

"Not unless you favor gunning down unarmed men," said
Nathan. "I was there and I saw it happen."

"The Earps and Holliday must be leadin' charmed lives,"
Harley said. "Four days after the shooting, there was a
coroner's inquest and nobody was charged."

"I'm not surprised," said Nathan. "I left town before
they could rope me into going to court and testifying."

Dodge City, Kansas
November 24, 1881

The first person they saw after stepping off the train was
Foster Hagerman.

"It's good to see you again," he said, taking Nathan's

hand. "I have a message for you from Byron Silver. He wants you to telegraph him in care of the dispatcher in Kansas City."

"I've come all the way here to meet him," Nathan said. "I hope that hasn't changed."

"Let's telegraph him and find out," said Hagerman.

Hagerman sat down at the instrument, requested and received permission, and sent a short message:

Stone in Dodge awaiting your reply.

"Why don't you go on to the Dodge House," Hagerman said. "I'll meet you tonight at six, and we'll eat at Delmonico's. They'll likely have to track Silver down, and you may not get an answer today."

"Come on," said Harley, "and hang around Dodge for a while. I'm off for the rest of the week, and I don't aim to sleep through it all."

Nathan checked into the Dodge House, and a few minutes before six, he and Harley left for Delmonico's. Empty bounded on ahead, for the cooks remembered him from the days Nathan had worked for the railroad.

"Well," said Hagerman, when he arrived, "for the first time in my life I was wrong. You got an answer to your telegram. Silver's in Kansas City and you're to meet him there as soon as you can. He'll leave word with the dispatcher as to where you can find him."

"If my memory serves me right," Nathan said, "there won't be another eastbound until eleven o'clock tomorrow."

"Right," said Hagerman, "so let's settle down, have us a steak, with plenty of onions, potatoes, coffee, and apple pie."

When they were down to final cups of coffee, Nathan spoke.

"There'll come a time when I may have to ask one of you to do a favor for me, and I'd like your promise that, should it become necessary, you'll do it."

"You've got my promise," said Hagerman.

"And mine," Harley added.

"My friends are scattered all over," said Nathan, "and when I've ridden that last trail, I want them to know I've cashed in, gone west."

"Hell," Hagerman said, "you're still a young man."

"A slug has no respect for youth," said Nathan. "I only want you to send telegrams, and there's just two words you'll have to remember. Omega Three."

"Omega's the last word in the Greek alphabet," said Hagerman, "but why the three?"

"That's a location," Nathan said. "If it happens around here, I'll want you to send the message to Silver in Washington, to Barnabas McQueen in New Orleans, and to a girl—Molly Horrell—in El Paso. Before the need arises, all of them will be given the same message I'm giving you. Then if I take the fall far away from here, you'll have someone who can tell you what became of me. If you receive a message that reads *Omega One,* you'll know to contact McQueen in New Orleans. If it reads *Omega Two,* you'll know to contact Molly Horrell in El Paso. Either of you will be *Omega Three,* while Silver is *Omega Four.*"

"My God, Nathan," said Harley, "it sounds like you know something we don't."

"No," Nathan replied, "I'm just accepting something you don't want to accept. I aim to hold Silver to this same promise because I never know when I'll cash in, running some errand for him. I don't want my bones bleaching on some lonesome trail, without my few friends knowing where I am and what became of me."

"He has another of those errands waiting for you," said Hagerman. "That's why you'll be meeting him in Kansas City. You're the only man I know who works for nothing, for the government."

"I'm not working for the government," Nathan said. "I'm doing a favor for a friend."

The evening ended on a somber note, and Nathan and Harley returned to their rooms at the Dodge House.

"I'll join you for breakfast," said Harley.

"Do that," Nathan replied. "I'm counting on it."

"One thing more," said Harley. "How do you aim to get your message to McQueen? I was just bully-raggin' you about Vivian forgetting you. She hasn't, and if you tell her and the McQueens what you just told Hagerman and me, Vivian will come looking for you."

"I've considered that," Nathan replied. "I aim to send Barnabas a letter, swearing him to silence where Vivian is concerned. She has no business with me, and if I live to be a hundred, I'll still feel better about her being with the McQueens."

"You're a thoughtful, generous man, Nathan," said Harley, "and it's a damn shame that you're passing through this world with so few men knowing you. I'm glad our trails crossed, if only for a little while. Goodnight."

Nathan's eyes clouded and a lump rose in his throat. Empty following, he went on down the hall to his room.

When Nathan and Harley reached Delmonico's for breakfast, Foster Hagerman was already there, drinking coffee.

"It's not often I get to eat in such good company," said Hagerman, "so I'm taking full advantage of it."

"Nathan," Harley said when they were seated, "in your travels, have you come across a young hombre name of Wesley Tremayne? The kid can't be a day over sixteen, if he's that, and he's chain lightning with a Colt."

"I haven't seen him," said Nathan. "It's an unusual name that I've heard only once, and that was long ago. What does he mean to you?"

"He was kind of special to us both," Hagerman said. "He rode a freight in here, green as grass, with nothing but the clothes on his back. Vic Irwin hired him as swamper at the Alhambra Saloon. Harley met him there and talked me into hiring him as a baggage clerk. Harley also taught him Morse code and how to use a gun, and I promoted him to railroad security. He killed some hombres that needed killing, including a pair that held up a train, and people started hounding him, testing his fast gun. Newspaper men started meeting the trains, hoping to see him shoot somebody. The kid had a horse and had learned to ride, and one night he just rode away, and we haven't seen him since."

"I kind of know how he felt," said Nathan. "I've had to shoot men I've never laid eyes on before, just to keep them from shooting me. There are men all over the frontier who'd give five years of their lives for a shot at me. In the back, if necessary."

"I hope you'll meet him one day," Harley said. "I saw him kill a man—his first—on the street, here in Dodge, and he reminded me of you. He wasn't the last bit afraid, and his eyes, my God! They looked for the world like blue ice."

"If we ever meet," said Nathan uneasily, "I hope it's on

friendly terms. I have more than enough hombres gunning for me."

Nathan and Empty were at the depot when the eleven o'clock eastbound rolled in, and Nathan watched as the locomotive backed onto the side track, coupling on the box-car with Nathan's horse.

"Come on, Empty," Nathan said. "I know this is against your religion, but if you're goin' with me, there's no other way."

Nathan climbed the steps into the passenger car, and with a look of resignation in his eyes Empty followed.

Kansas City, Missouri
November 25, 1881

Nathan called on the dispatcher and the message he was given was brief. It said:

Kansas City Hotel nine.

Nathan led his horse out of the boxcar and, with Empty following, rode to the hotel. Having no idea how long he would be with Silver, he stabled the horse at a livery across the street.

"Stay with the horse, Empty," he commanded.

Reaching the door to Room 9, he knocked twice, waited a moment, then knocked a third time.

"Identify yourself," said a voice from within.

"Nathan Stone, you old *paisano*."

The door was opened and Nathan stepped inside. Silver closed and bolted the door.

"You must have something almighty important cooking," Nathan said. "I told you I'd be in Dodge December first."

Silver laughed. "I know, but I counted on you being curious enough to get there a week early, which you did. I decided there was no point in me going to Dodge when you could just as easily come here. Anyway, I'd like you to do some investigating, and it will take you into Missouri. I suppose you're familiar with Jesse James?"

"I should be," said Nathan. "Jesse threatened to shoot me if we ever met again."*

"You never told me about that," Silver said.

"I didn't want you lying awake nights, worrying about me," said Nathan. "I kind of got in the way, back in Nevada, Missouri, during a bank robbery. Frank and Jesse ended up without a dollar and with a posse on their trail."

Silver laughed. "I can see how that might have upset them. With Jesse threatening to shoot you, what I am about to say may sound a bit strange. I'd like you to help us track him down and, if possible, take him alive."

"Tarnation," said Nathan, "why can't you ever come up with somethin' easy, such as turning lead into gold ingots? How can you expect to take Jesse James alive when there's a ten-thousand-dollar bounty on him, dead or alive?"

"The reward is being offered by Governor Thomas Crittenden, and that is a problem. While the State of Missouri only wants him out of circulation by any means, the Treasury of the United States would like him taken alive. Much of the money he's taken from train robberies was intended for government outposts, military payrolls, and such. The Treasury believes Jesse has most of this money squirreled away somewhere, and that if he is taken alive, they might plea bargain for its return."

"And just how the hell am I supposed to take Jesse James alive?"

"You're not expected to do that," Silver said. "We know he's holed up somewhere in Missouri, and all we want you to do is tell us where. Governor Crittenden is cooperating with us, but not to the extent he's willing to back off on the reward. There'll be a hundred men ready to ride when we hear from you."

"How much time do I have?"

"We don't know," said Silver. "Almost daily, there are telegrams seeking to claim the reward, from people who are willing to produce a dead body. Ten thousand dollars could tempt a man's own family. Judas sold out for thirty pieces of silver."

"I trailed the James gang once," Nathan said, "but that was after they'd robbed a bank and I had a trail to follow. When was their most recent robbery?"

*The Dawn of Fury (Book 1)

"Four months ago," said Silver. "On July 15, they boarded a Chicago, Rock Island & Pacific train at a stop just out of Kansas City. They killed two men, including a conductor, forced their way into the express car, and pistol-whipped the messenger. They took his key, emptied the safe, and disappeared into the darkness."

"No more recent robberies?"

"None that we know of," Silver said. "In fact, this is the only robbery attributed to Frank and Jesse since the shoot-out at Northfield, where they got nothing and three of the Youngers were captured."

"So they could be anywhere," said Nathan. "Not just in Missouri."

"Yes," Silver agreed, "but they have friends in Missouri. There are literally thousands of God-fearing people who would hide Frank and Jesse and would consider it an honor. I realize what I'm asking will be difficult, if not impossible. I'm only asking that you try."

"I'm willing to do that," said Nathan, "but before I do, I want to ask a favor of you. Not for now, but later."

"If it's within my power," Silver said, "you know I'll do it."

"It's within your power," said Nathan. "All it will involve is three telegrams. Just remember that you're *Omega Four,* and you'll be contacting *Omega One, Two,* and *Three.*"

He then told Silver what he had told Harley Stafford and Foster Hagerman.

"*Omega One, Two,* and *Three* is McQueen in New Orleans, Molly Horrell in El Paso, and Harley Stafford or Foster Hagerman in Dodge."

"Right," said Nathan, "and each of them will be told to telegraph you. The *Omega* code will tell you where I am. Or was."

"You're serious, aren't you?"

"Never more serious in my life," Nathan said. "Every man is born with the seeds of death within him. All that's lacking is the time and place."

"When this Jesse James thing is behind us," said Silver, "why don't we travel down to the McQueens' place in New Orleans and spend some time there?"

"I have a good reason for not going there," Nathan said. "Her name's Vivian Stafford. She's Harley's sister and she traveled with me for a while. I don't want to kick any sleeping dogs, if you know what I mean."

"I know what you mean," said Silver, "but I think they deserve to hear it from you on this *Omega* code. Wouldn't you like to see them again?"

"I reckon I would," Nathan said, "but I had such a hell of a time escaping from Vivian last time, I don't like the thought of goin' through it again."

Silver laughed. "You've been on the frontier a dozen years, shootin' and being shot at, and you expect me to believe you're scared of one helpless female?"

"Helpless, hell," said Nathan. "Give her a little encouragement and she'll follow you back to Washington."

"Maybe I will," Silver said. "Are we going or not?"

"I reckon we'll go," said Nathan. "I need to talk to Barnabas instead of writing him a letter."

"Telegraph me from St. Louis when you're ready," Silver said. "I'll meet you there."

El Paso, Texas
December 17, 1881

Almost immediately following the ambush, Dallas Stoudenmire began looking with suspicion on men who seemed to have no means of support. Eventually, while Wes was having coffee in the Globe Restaurant, Stoudenmire stopped at his table.

"I've been seein' you around for a while, pilgrim. You lookin' for work or just passing through?"

"Neither," Wes said. "While I really don't consider it any of your business, I gamble for a living. Any objection to that?"

"No," said Stoudenmire, "as long as you keep it honest. Frankly, I ain't seen many that could make a livin' without slick dealing. Maybe you're the exception."

"Maybe I am," Wes said. "Until you get some complaints, why don't you just accept that?"

Stoudenmire's face reddened and he walked away without another word, but wherever he found Wes, Stoudenmire continued to eye him with suspicion. So Wes began playing an occasional hand of poker, winning more than he lost. It was in the Rio Grande Saloon that he first saw Frank Wooten and his daughter, Renita. Wooten had lost steadily, and Wes took the pot that cleaned him out.

"Deal me in," said Wooten desperately. "I can cover it."

It was then that Wes became aware of the girl. She sat in a chair against the wall, and when Wooten spoke to her, it was loud enough for everyone to hear.

"Gimme the ring, girl."

"No," the girl cried, "it's my mama's."

"Damn it," Wooten shouted, "gimme the ring."

Wooten hit her then, so hard the chair tipped over sideways. Before Frank Wooten could make another move, half a dozen men were on him. Bruised and bloody, he was thrown through the batwing doors and out into the dusty street. Weeping, the girl got to her feet. She was starvation thin, with auburn hair and big brown eyes. She fixed them on Wes; her nose dripping blood, she approached the table.

"Please," she said, "will you help me?"

CHAPTER 28

Liberty, Missouri
December 1, 1881

Nathan spent three days with Silver and, when his friend departed, he rode to Liberty, the seat of Clay County, where Jesse James had been born. He expected hostility and ran headlong into it immediately and from a most unexpected source. He opened the door to the sheriff's office, and the tall, thin man who greeted him there wore a deputy's badge.

"The sheriff's laid up sick. I'm Deputy Tobe Willis. What can I do for you?"

"I'm Nathan Stone, and I'm thinking of writing a book on Frank and Jesse James."

"You don't look like no book writer to me," said Willis. "You look like one of them damn bounty hunters. Git out."

"I'm no bounty hunter," Nathan said, as calmly as he could.

"They all say that," said Willis, "an' I'm tellin' you what I told the others. Git out."

Nathan left, and word spread quickly. When Nathan and Empty stopped at a cafe, the cook was openly hostile.

"The dog's welcome," he said, "but you ain't."

They were turned away at every hotel and boardinghouse in the county; with only few supplies on hand, Nathan rode back to Kansas City.

"Damn it," he said aloud, "Silver's fixed us good this time."

He rode to Eppie Bolivar's boardinghouse, where he had often stayed before, and was welcomed. Empty remembered Eppie and went immediately to the back porch, positioning himself just outside the door.

"I've never seen another dog like him," said Eppie, greeting Nathan, "so it had to be you."

"I'm glad to see a friendly face," Nathan said. "I've been

to Liberty, trying to gather some information on Jesse James, but nobody will talk. We were unwelcome at every cafe, hotel, and boardinghouse."

"My God," said Eppie, "you're more fortunate than most. Two bounty hunters have been shot and killed. Shot in the back."

"I'm not bounty hunting," Nathan said.

"No matter," said Eppie. "Anybody asking about Frank and Jesse gets the same treatment. Two newspaper fellows were here from Chicago and were beaten within an inch of their lives. Pistol-whipped, they spent a week in the hospital before they could leave."

"For a pair of outlaws and killers, the James boys stand mighty tall," Nathan said.

"I agree," said Eppie, "but I have to keep my mouth shut. I'm too old and frail for a pistol-whipping."

"I haven't read the Kansas City papers for a while," Nathan said. "What position are they taking toward the James gang?"

"They haven't taken a position," said Eppie. "They mostly just report what happens, like the reporters from Chicago being beaten. Old wounds go deep, Nathan, and there are too many who remember that Frank and Jesse fought for the Confederacy."

"So did I," Nathan said, "and I can understand why such feeling still runs high here in Missouri. But even if stealing and killing can be justified during the war, there's no logical and sensible way it can continue, when the war's over."

"That's how I see it," said Eppie, "but I dare not say it too loud, and neither should you. Why must you pursue Frank and Jesse? There's already an enormous reward, and if that's not enough, what can *you* do?"

"I don't know," Nathan said. "I promised a friend for reasons that I can't tell you. I don't know that I can do anything, but I must try."

El Paso, Texas
December 17, 1881

The girl took Wes by surprise. While she was older than he, she seemed to have placed her confidence in him, perhaps because he was nearer her own age. He took her hand and, without a word, led her out the back door of the saloon. Nobody came after them, and in the alley, Wes spoke to her.

"Tell me where you live, and I'll take you there."

"No," she said. "He'll beat me."

"He's your father?"

"My stepfather," she told him. "My mama's dead. His name is Frank Wooten."

"What's your name?"

"Renita."

"What am I going to do with you?" Wes asked.

"Take me with you," said Renita. "I can cook, clean, and wash."

"I don't doubt you can," Wes said, "but if you have a father—even a stepfather—I may find myself in big trouble. How old are you?"

"Seventeen."

"Not old enough," said Wes. "He'll have the law after us."

"I'm not going back to him. If you don't want me, I'll ... I'll run away."

"I'll take you to my boardinghouse and get you a room," Wes said. "I don't see anything wrong with that. Wait here until I get my horse."

"Can't I go with you?"

"No," said Wes. "My horse is tied in front of the saloon. I'll get him, and we'll ride down this alley a ways."

Wes went back through the saloon, where the poker game had resumed without any sign of the girl's stepfather. Nobody gave Wes a second look, and he left the saloon, and stepped out on the boardwalk. Wooten still sat in the street, rubbing his head. Dallas Stoudenmire came down the boardwalk, pausing to look at Wooten.

"Why are you settin' there in the street?" Stoudenmire asked.

"Because they throwed me out of the damn saloon," said Wooten. "Do you reckon I'm settin' here because I like the view?"

"Don't you smart-mouth me," Stoudenmire said. "I'll haul your carcass to jail if you don't get up from there and be on your way."

"Them slick-dealin' bastards in there cleaned me out," said Wooten. "I ain't even got the price of a room for the night."

"Then I'll fix you up with one," Stoudenmire said. "Get up."

Wooten struggled to his feet and stood there weaving back and forth. He staggered toward Stoudenmire and would have fallen if the town marshal hadn't caught him.

"Hell," said Stoudenmire, "you're drunk as a coot. You can sleep it off in jail."

"Ain't goin' nowhere," Wooten said, his speech slurred. "Not without my girl."

"I don't see anybody but you," said Stoudenmire, "and you're drunk. Let's go."

He hustled Wooten off in the direction of the jail. Wes untied his horse and led him around the building to the alley. Renita was hunched up as close to the building as she was able to get.

"Did you see him?" she asked fearfully.

"Yes," said Wes, "and he's being taken to jail. He told the town marshal he had no place to stay tonight, and he's drunk."

"He's always drunk," Renita said. "We slept in an old store building last night, and it had big rats."

"I'll see that you do better than that," said Wes. "Here, I'll boost you up on my horse."

Wes lifted her up, amazed at how little she weighed. Mounting behind her, he trotted his horse down the alley to the next cross street. From there, he took back streets until he reached Granny Boudleaux's boardinghouse. It was near suppertime, and Granny was in the kitchen. Molly Horrell met them in the front parlor.

"Molly," said Wes, "this is Renita, and she needs a room for a while. I'll pay for it."

"She can have the room next to yours," Molly said. "That should be convenient for the both of you."

For a moment she studied Renita, and the girl blushed, for she understood the implication of what Molly had said. Wes glared at Molly, took the key she offered, and, without a word, led Renita down the hall.

"Here's your key," said Wes. "Go in, lie down, and rest. I'll knock on your door at suppertime, and we'll go to the dining room together."

"No," Renita said. "I ... I'm not fit. This is the only dress I have, and there's nothing under it except me."

"Your breakfast and supper is included in the price of

the room," said Wes, "and you have to eat. You don't look
like you've had a decent meal in a week."

"Longer than that," Renita said. "Frank drinks and gam-
bles his money away, when he has any. He sold two horses,
and now he's broke again."

"Where would the likes of him get horses to sell?"
Wes asked.

"He stole them at a ranch north of here," said Renita.

"Go on in there and lock your door," Wes said. "Don't
open it until I come for you. My name is Wes."

Her eyes met his, and she swallowed hard, unable to speak.
Wes waited until she had locked the door before going to his
room. Wes sat down on the bed, wondering what he was
going to do with her, but he had already decided he wasn't
going to allow the drunken Frank Wooten to reclaim her. He
waited an hour before knocking on her door, and found she
had used the wash basin and pitcher of water to good advantage. Her hair somehow looked better, and she had washed
her face and hands. They reached the dining room a bit early
and encountered Granny Boudleaux.

"Granny," said Wes, "this is Renita. I found her in town,
and she had no place to go, so I paid Molly a month's
room and board."

"You good boy, Wes," Granny said, and she then placed
her arm around the thin shoulders of Renita. "Welcome,
pequeno muchacha. You starved. You eat."

Wes could have kissed the old Cajun woman, for the
warm welcome brought a smile to Renita's face as she took
her place beside Wes at the table. The girl was indeed
starved, and after she had been introduced to the other
boarders, she ate like she hadn't seen food in weeks.
Granny beamed, urging her to eat. Molly Horrell continually brought food to the table, but the cold eyes of Wes
Tremayne met hers, and she said nothing. Wes took his
time, wanting Renita to eat her fill. When he was sure she
had, he excused himself, and so did Renita. She followed
him down the hall and paused before her door.

"Except for Granny," he said, "you know what they're
all thinking, don't you?"

"Yes," she said, "and I don't care. I was starving, and
I've had to fight Frank off me since before mama died.
You helped me when there was nobody else."

He said nothing. Unlocking the door for her, he handed

her the key. Suddenly, like a striking bird, she leaned forward and kissed him. Then she was gone, closing the door behind her. Wes stood there a moment. He would be a while, forgetting Rebecca Tuttle, if he ever did. But when he reached his room, he sat down on the bed, thinking. In this lonely girl he had befriended, there was a spark that was something more than gratitude, a spark that might become a flame.

Sedalia, Missouri
January 2, 1882

Having spent a month in Missouri, Nathan had accomplished only one thing. He had been fired upon twice from ambush and had narrowly missed being hit both times. When he grew weary of sleeping on the ground and eating his own hurriedly cooked meals, he retreated to Eppie Bolivar's boardinghouse in Kansas City. There he rested, reading the Kansas City newspaper, seeking some clue that might help him solve a mystery that began to seem more and more impossible.

"Nathan," said Eppie, "you're not even sure that Jesse James is in Missouri. There is evidence aplenty that Frank and Jesse left the state for more than four years. What proof do you have that they're even here?"

"I've had my doubts," Nathan said, "but if they're not here somewhere, why is everybody so damn hostile? I can't find them if they're not here, but I've already just missed being the guest of honor at two ambushes."

"How long are you going to pursue this before giving it up as a lost cause?" Eppie asked. "What is it going to accomplish for your friend if you're shot dead?"

"I'll give it a few more weeks," said Nathan. "I hate to give up."

But all Nathan's enemies weren't friends of the James boys. Leaving Sedalia, he rode south to Springfield. He was just emerging from the newspaper office when he ran headlong into Amy Limbaugh. She looked older and harder, and her eyes were brimming with hate.

"You!" she hissed.

"Me," said Nathan mildly. "I was hoping while you were doing time, you had bitten yourself and died of the poison."

"You murdering bastard," she shouted.

"I never shot anybody that wasn't shootin' at me," said Nathan, "and you know it."

"I don't care what your reason was," she gritted. "You killed my brother and I won't be satisfied until you're dead."

"Then don't expect any slack from me because you're a woman," said Nathan. "Come gunning for me, and I'll kill you as readily as I would if you were a man. Just remember, ma'am, I don't make threats. When I tell you something, take it as a promise."

Nathan left her standing there, hating him, and entered the mercantile for grain for his horse. When he stepped out of the mercantile, a slug ripped into the sack of grain he carried under his arm. She was across the street, under a saloon awning, holding a Colt with both hands. The weapon roared again, and the slug burned a furrow across Nathan's left hip. He drew his Colt and fired once, and she stumbled back against the saloon wall. Her Colt sagged, clattering to the boardwalk, and the cursing Amy Limbaugh stood there with blood soaking the left side of her shirt. Men came on the run, some of them with their hands on their weapons, all of them looking murderously at Nathan Stone. The sheriff was among the first to arrive, and all he seemed to see was Amy Limbaugh's bloody shirt. He drew his Colt, advancing toward Nathan.

"Sheriff," Nathan said, holstering his Colt, "I only defended myself. See the hole in this sack of grain, and the bloody welt across my thigh? She fired at me twice, before I pulled my gun, and I can prove she served time for trying to ambush me in Jefferson City."

"I wasn't sheriff then," the lawman said, "but I seem to recall the incident. Damn it, Amy, ain't you learnt nothing?"

"Yes," she cried. "I've learned if I want him dead, I'll have to kill him myself."

"Mister," said the sheriff, "I'll take her to jail and have her patched up. I'll hold her until you've had a chance to leave town. Or you can press charges if you want. With her record, she'll go back to prison."

"I'm not interested in sending her back to prison," Nathan said. "When it comes to her learning anything, there's no hope for her. Save prison for those smart enough to learn from their mistakes. Lock her up for a while, and if you have any influence with her family, tell them I won't spare her again."

Nathan slung the sack of grain across the rump of his horse and stepped into the saddle. Some of the men who had gathered were shouting at him, their hands on the butts of their revolvers. Before riding away, Nathan spoke.

"She planned to kill me, and I only defended myself. I urge all of you to keep that in mind. Pursue me and I'll kill you. Sheriff, you remember that too."

"I aim to," said the sheriff. "The rest of you, go on about your business. You ride after this hombre, prepare yourself for whatever he dishes out. I won't get involved."

Nathan rode out, heading north, uncertain as to what would be his next move.

El Paso, Texas
December 18, 1881

Cautioning Renita to remain in her room, Wes rode to town the next morning after breakfast. He wanted to know if Frank Wooten had been released from jail, and learned that he had been. By listening to talk, he also learned that Dallas Stoudenmire had ordered Wooten out of town. But nobody seemed to know where Frank Wooten was. Wes returned to Granny Boudleaux's boardinghouse to find Renita watching for him, a question in her eyes.

"He's been let out of jail and ordered out of town," said Wes, "and nobody seems to know where he is. We'll sit tight, and I'll have another look tomorrow."

The following day, Wes waited until near noon before riding into town. When he rode past the carpenter's shop, two men were putting the finishing touches on a coffin. Reining up, Wes spoke.

"Who's it for?"

"Gent name of Wooten," said one of the men. "Somebody found him strung up just north of here."

"Where is he now?" Wes asked. "I used to know a man named Wooten."

"He's at the undertaker's," one of the carpenters said. "They don't aim to plant him if the county won't pay."

Wes reined up before the undertaker's, dismounted, and went in.

"You have an hombre here name of Wooten," Wes said. "Mind if I look at him?"

"Go ahead," said the undertaker hopefully. "Are you family or friend?"

"Neither," Wes said. "I once knew a gent name of Wooten and I wonder if this could be him. He owed me money."

"If he is," said the undertaker, "you're still out of luck. He didn't have a dime on him and the county is balking at burying him."

Frank Wooten was stretched out on a wooden pallet. Pinned to his coat was a ragged piece of paper, and scrawled on it in pencil there were two words: *Horse thief.*

Wes left before the eager undertaker could get to him again. He remembered what Renita had said about Wooten stealing horses somewhere north of town. It seemed Wooten had gone back for more horses and had encountered a vindictive rancher. Wes rode back to the boardinghouse and broke the news to Renita.

"It's a terrible way to feel," the girl said, "but I'm glad he's gone. When I think of him, all I can recall is him hurting me."

"I can't fault you for feeling that way," said Wes. "My mother died when I was born and I never knew my father. When my grandparents—my mother's mother and father—were gone, I was sent to an orphanage. I ran away from there and I've made my own way ever since."

"Now that Frank Wooten's gone, and can't come looking for me, can I . . . may I . . . stay with you?"

"I reckon," Wes said, "but I'd feel better if you were of age. How long until you'll be eighteen?"

"The fourth of next April," said Renita. "Not quite three and a half months. Can't I just say that I'm eighteen until I actually am?"

"That's not a bad idea," Wes said. "It might stop all these foolish looks we're gettin' in the dining room."

"If I'm going to be eighteen, why can't we share the same room? They think we are already."

"Do you think you're ready for that?" Wes asked. "Do you know what it means?"

"Yes, I know what it means, and I'm ready for it. Since

I was ten, I've had to fight men who wanted me when I didn't want them. You're not like any of them,. You were kind to me without asking anything in return."

"I just don't want you believing you have feelings for me when it's only gratitude," said Wes. "I helped you because I saw your need, not to take advantage of you. You don't owe me anything. I'm a gambler. I'm not sure I'm that much better than Frank Wooten was. Please keep that in mind."

"I will not," she said. "Frank had a weakness for whiskey, and the more he drank, the worse his skill with the cards became. You don't drink whiskey, and you have money for food and a nice place to live. Frank never had that, and he killed my mama by being always on the move. He just wore her out, and he was wearing me out. Until I met you, I didn't care if I lived or died. You're young, but you're a man. Frank was much older, and he was never a man. I want to stay with you if you'll have me."

"I'll answer that by taking you to town and buying you some new clothes. Horse and saddle too, if you can ride," said Wes.

"I can ride, but I hate for you to spend so much on me. I'm not used to it. I never had new clothes. Just mama's hand-me-downs, and after she took up with Frank, not even that."

Nobody seemed to recall that Renita had been with Frank Wooten, and the trip to town was uneventful. Wes bought a bay horse and saddle for Renita, and they stabled the horse alongside his. When they returned to the boardinghouse, Wes made it a point to seek out Granny Boudleaux.

"Granny, starting tonight, Renita's moving in with me, so we won't need the room she has. She has no family, and neither do I."

"Is good," Granny said. "Is what we all expect."

They bypassed Renita's room, and Wes unlocked the door to his. He piled all their purchases on the bed and turned to the girl.

"Do you want me to leave while you try them on?" he asked.

"No," she said. "You bought them, and you have the right to be the first to see me wear them. Besides, the bed's not that wide. We'll be—"

"A mite crowded," Wes finished.

The dress she wore was faded white in places, and she wore nothing else. She tried on the different dresses, trying to see herself in the small oval mirror over the dresser.

"How do I look?" she asked anxiously.

"Grand," said Wes.

"I feel like a queen," she said. "Which one should I wear for supper?"

"Your choice," said Wes. "You look wonderful in them all. I'm looking forward to us going to supper."

"So am I," she said, "but not nearly as much as I'm looking forward to tonight. How long since I've been able to lie down unafraid?"

The day after Christmas, Jim Gillett resigned from the Texas Rangers. Wes spent a few minutes with Gillett after breakfast.

"I'll be around El Paso for a while," said Gillett. "I'm thinking of ranching."

Wes laughed. "Are you sure you want to raise stock this near the border?"

"Maybe not," Gillett said. "The truth is, I have my eye on a woman, and she comes from a good family here in El Paso."

"Good luck," said Wes.

Kansas City, Missouri
March 31, 1882

The first genuine lead Nathan eventually found was in a short paragraph he read in a Kansas City newspaper. A former member of the James gang had been captured, and in a bid for a lighter sentence had revealed that Jesse James was indeed living in Missouri as Thomas Howard. The outlaw had been captured near Marysville, Kansas. Nathan rode to a number of small towns in eastern Kansas, especially those that were county seats. There he pored over records of registered voters, spoke to newspaper editors, and sought courthouse records that might reveal men named Howard. Few being aware of the alias, there was no way of knowing the Thomas Howard Nathan sought was Jesse James, and so there was no hostility. Unfortunately, there was no Jesse James either. Not one of the

Howards proved to be the man Nathan was seeking. Most were older men who had lived in the same house all their lives, while it was a known fact that Jesse James had left Missouri for at least four years. Since Nathan had taken Eppie Bolivar into his confidence, he often talked to her about his frustrations.

"You don't *know* that Jesse's using an alias," said Eppie. "this outlaw they captured may have just told the law what they wanted to hear."

Nathan sighed. "I know. He may not be in Missouri, either. I had hoped that if this varmint was telling the truth, that Jesse might be hiding somewhere near where this outlaw was captured. But if I keep moving in that direction, I'll have to go into Abilene, Wichita, and beyond. My God, it'd take me forever."

"Then why not take some of the towns on the Missouri side," Eppie suggested. "Most of the robberies took place in Missouri. And have you noticed that almost without fail, the James gang never went too far from the scenes of their crimes?"

"Maybe you have something there, Eppie," said Nathan. "I've been beatin' the bushes in Kansas, when Jesse James is holed up in Missouri. There's only been one robbery by the James gang since the shoot-out at Northfield, in September 1876. On July 15, 1881, a Chicago, Rock Island & Pacific train was boarded by the James gang at Cameron and Winston. Both these towns are north of Kansas City, and both are in Missouri. Damn it, I should have started with them."

"Not necessarily," Eppie said. "Both those towns are small towns. A man living under an alias should be in a town large enough that he doesn't attract attention to himself. Why don't you try St. Joseph?"

"Eppie," said Nathan, "you're a caution. I've been too close to this thing. I'm going to St. Joseph, and if I draw a blank there, I'm going to give it up for a lost cause."

St. Joseph, Missouri
April 2, 1882

It was Sunday, so the courthouse, the post office, and the newspaper office all were closed.

"We've waited this long, Empty," said Nathan, "so I reckon we can wait another day. Maybe tomorrow something will happen."

CHAPTER 29

El Paso, Texas
March 1, 1882

In the weeks following Jim Gillett's departure from the Rangers, Wes Tremayne spent most of his days in the various saloons, sharpening his skills as a gambler. It began to have its inevitable effect on Renita.

"Why must you spend so much time in the saloons?" she complained. "I hate them."

"Because I must have something to do," said Wes. "El Paso is home to rustlers and outlaws from both sides of the border, and unless I obviously have some other way of making a living, I'll be suspected of being one of them."

"Then let's go somewhere else," she suggested.

There it was. Wes sighed and told her the truth—that as a Ranger, he had been sent to this tumultuous border town.

"There's some kind of change in the wind," said Wes. "I aim to ride it out."

But Wes had begun making enemies, most of them among the men who lived on both sides of the border. In Mexico, they abided by no rules, and wanted none. Armijo Barboncio's hand was quick with cards or gun, and his quick temper made for an unholy trilogy. Few Saturdays passed that didn't find him in El Paso's Acme Saloon, involved in a poker game. Wes had observed Barboncio's adeptness with the cards before, and was virtually certain the man was cheating, but he wanted to take part in a game to be sure. The Saturday afternoon he sat in Dallas Stoudenmire was there, and appeared to be the big loser. After yet another losing hand, Stoudenmire turned hard eyes on Barboncio and said exactly the wrong thing.

"Mex—if that's what you are—them cards is dancin' to your tune a mite too often."

"You are implying that I cheat, *señor*?"

"Implying, hell," said Stoudenmire brashly. "I'm accusin' you."

Stoudenmire had slid back his chair far enough to get to his gun, but never completed his draw. He found himself staring into the deadly muzzle of Barboncio's cocked Colt.

"You will apologize—take water—or I kill you," Barboncio said grimly.

"I ... I reckon I was wrong," Stoudenmire stammered. "My apologies."

Barboncio laughed, holstered his revolver, and tipped back his sombrero. Stoudenmire slid back his chair, got up, and quickly left the saloon. Observers backed away, all of them feeling less like men in the face of Stoudenmire's cowardice. It was Barboncio's turn to deal, and with a smirk he did so. When it came time to show their hands, Barboncio had a straight diamond flush.

"By God," said one of the losers, "it's the first time I ever seen a man draw two damn straight flushes in one day."

"It's not difficult," Wes said quietly, "when you're bottom dealing."

What followed happened in less than a heartbeat. Armijo Barboncio was swift as a striking rattler, but died with his gun in his hand. Wes Tremayne had fired only once, and Barboncio had drawn first.

"My God," somebody cried, "what happened?"

"Somebody get the marshal," a bartender shouted.

But nobody bothered with Stoudenmire. Two bartenders removed Barboncio's body to a storage room near the back door. The game was over and Wes was about to leave the saloon when he saw Jim Gillett near the back door. Gillett nodded and Wes followed him out the back door.

"You've put your foot in it, kid," said Gillett. "The little sidewinder you shot was part of the Sandlin gang. You won't be safe anywhere in this town. They'll get you."

"Maybe," Wes said. "but it had to be done. Stoudenmire made me sick to my gut."

"Stoudenmire's finished as a lawman," said Gillett.

"Who do you reckon will replace him?"

"Me, maybe," Gillett said. "My name's in the pot."

Wes laughed. "You've been telling me how hell's goin' to bust loose here at any time, and now you're wantin' to take Stoudenmire's job. Why?"

"Call it vanity, I reckon," said Gillett. "Bein' a Ranger, my hands were tied. I've had to play second fiddle to

Stoudenmire. I'll side you when I can, but watch your back."

To nobody's surprise, a little more than a year after becoming city marshal, Stoudenmire resigned. Taking his place was former Texas Ranger Jim Gillett.

St. Joseph, Missouri
April 3, 1882

On a quiet street in St. Joseph, Jesse James lived under the alias Thomas Howard. A robbery was being planned, and the Fords—Bob and Charlie—were staying at the James residence. Charlie, having ridden with the James gang before, had no trouble getting Bob into the gang. For some time, Robert Ford had considered murdering Jesse James, and had once met with the governor of Missouri to discuss it. Governor Crittendon had promised a large reward and a full pardon. It was right after breakfast on a Monday morning.

"Jesse," said Bob, "Charlie and me are goin' to the barn to tend the horses."

"Go on," Jesse replied, "but come on back as soon as you can. We have planning to be done for that bank job tomorrow."

The Ford brothers went on to the barn, returning to the house at half-past eight.

"That picture's hanging crooked," said Jesse.

He removed his coat, unbuckled his gunbelt, and climbed onto a chair to straighten the picture. Charlie Ford nodded at Bob and they drew and cocked their pistols. The ominous sound warned Jesse, and he started to turn. But Bob Ford shot him in the back of the head, and Jesse James was dead when he hit the floor. Jesse's wife ran screaming into the room. That and the sound of the shot alerted the neighbors. Charlie and Bob Ford ran from the house, bound for the telegraph office. Nathan Stone was on his way to the local newspaper when the commotion drew his attention.

"I shot Jesse James!" Robert Ford shouted, standing before the telegraph office. "He's dead! Jesse James is dead, and I killed him!"

Robert Ford went on into the telegraph office, where he sent a telegram to Governor Crittendon, claiming the reward. He then went outside where his brother Charlie waited, and they led the curious back to the house where Jesse James lay dead. Nathan followed, not believing what he was hearing. The sheriff soon arrived, and in deference to Jesse's grief-stricken wife, forced the curious to leave.

"Sheriff," Nathan said, "I don't want to intrude at such a time, but I do need to know whether or not this dead man is Jesse James. Where will the body be taken?"

"To the undertaker's," said the lawman, "over yonder next to the jail. Stick around, and when he's laid out, I'll get you in to see him."

Nathan waited more than two hours for the body to be laid out at the undertaker's. The curious were allowed to file past the wooden coffin, and when Nathan reached it, he saw a young man with a black, bushy beard. He had seen Jesse James only once, more than ten years ago, and he just wasn't sure this man was the notorious outlaw. Leaving the undertaker's, Nathan found a crowd had gathered. Charlie and Robert Ford had their backs against the wall of the jail and were bombarded with angry shouts and curses.*

"Break it up," the sheriff shouted. "You two," he said, turning to the Fords, "get out of town."

"I'm waiting for a telegram from the governor," Bob Ford protested.

"Damn you and the governor," said the sheriff angrily. "Get out of here before I jail the both of you."

St. Joseph, Missouri
April 4, 1882

Jesse's grieving wife soon convinced everybody, including Nathan Stone, that Jesse James had been shot and killed.

---

* For a while, Robert Ford returned to the home of his parents in Richmond, Missouri, but was met with widespread contempt and scorn. Charlie had the same problem, and just two years later, in 1884, he committed suicide. Robert Ford was ridiculed wherever he went, and after two years in P. T. Barnum's freak show, began to drink and gamble excessively. On June 8, 1892, in Creede, Colorado, Ed O. Kelly killed Bob Ford with a shotgun.

Nathan went to the telegraph office and sent a message to Byron Silver in Washington.

Jesse James shot and killed in Saint Joseph on April third.

Nathan signed his name, paid for the telegram, and awaited an answer. He received it an hour later.

Meet me in Saint Louis at Pioneer.

There was no signature, but Nathan needed none. He and Silver had stayed at the old Pioneer Hotel before. Nathan rode back through Kansas City and said goodbye to Eppie. He and Empty then headed east, toward St. Louis.

El Paso, Texas
July 29, 1882

There was more trouble involving Dallas Stoudenmire in the Acme Saloon. Will Page, who had at one time been Stoudenmire's deputy, got into a fight with Billy Bell. Stoudenmire broke up the fight and persuaded Page to go with him to Doyle's Concert Hall. There the two spent the evening drinking, returning to the Acme Saloon near midnight. Almost immediately they started arguing, and Stoudenmire drew a gun. Page struck the weapon just as it went off, and it blasted lead in the ceiling. Stoudenmire then drew a second revolver, but before he could fire he was confronted by city marshal Jim Gillett, who had a shotgun. Gillett then marched the troublesome pair to jail, where he locked them up for the night.

"I wish I'd seen that," Wes Tremayne said later.

"Better that you didn't" Jim Gillett replied. "After gunning down one of the Sandlin gang, you have no business in town after dark."

"That's been awhile," said Wes. "I think I've lived that down."

"I don't think so," Gillett said. "They're waiting for the right time and place."

Renita had grown weary of spending all her time at

Granny's boardinghouse, so Wes had agreed to take her into town on Saturday afternoons. The first two trips behind them, Wes began to relax, but not for long. They were riding past a livery barn, when suddenly there was the roar of a Winchester from the loft. The first slug struck Wes in the left shoulder, driving him from the saddle. The second shot narrowly missed Renita, but only because she all but fell out of the saddle trying to reach Wes.

"Get away from me!" he shouted.

A third slug kicked dirt in his face, and although he had no specific target, his Colt spat fire. Then the firing ceased, and Renita came running to him.

"You're hurt," she cried.

"But I'm alive," said Wes. "Damn it, you could have been killed getting to me."

Jim Gillett came galloping toward them, his Winchester at the ready.

"Where was he holed up?" Gillett asked.

"In the livery loft," said Wes. "The varmint wasn't just after me. He was shooting at Renita, too."

"You'd better ride on in and let the doc patch you up. I'll nose around and see if I can find any tracks."

Renita mounted her horse and, with some difficulty, Wes mounted his. They rode on into town, reining up at the doctor's office. Doctor Winslow asked no questions, for it was a time and place where a day seldom passed without at least one gunshot wound. When his wound had been bandaged, Wes paid the doctor two dollars. Just as he and Renita stepped out the door, Jim Gillett rode up.

"The sidewinder was afoot," Gillett said. "Plenty of tracks around the barn, but no way of knowing which were his."

"About what I expected," said Wes. "Next time, I'll just have to be ready and go get him before he can escape."

"Next time," Gillett said, "he may get you dead center with the first shot."

"Oh, I wish we didn't have to stay here," said Renita when Gillett had gone.

"We don't have to," Wes said. "I'm just not the kind to back off from a fight."

"Even when they're firing from cover and you don't know when they'll strike next?"

"Even then," said Wes.

"I know you have your pride, but pride's no good to a dead man, and a dead man's of no use to me."

"I've been dry-gulched before," Wes said, "by hombres who did a hell of a lot better job of it, and I'm still alive. I'm more afraid of them shooting you than hitting me."

"I'm afraid for you," she said, "and you're afraid for me. I'm glad you're afraid for me. Since mama died, you're the only one who's cared."

Having finished their shopping, Wes took a different way back to Granny Boudleaux's.

"Next time," said Renita, "let's ride as far from all the buildings as we can."

"We will, going and coming," Wes said, "but we'll be afoot and in plain sight on the boardwalks."

"Then after this, I won't go to town as often," said Renita. "I'll be more satisfied at Granny's."

But there was no safety, even at Granny Boudleaux's, for that very night riders came in close, shattering windows with gunfire.

"This is going to be difficult," Jim Gillett said, when he came to investigate. "We'll be hard pressed for defense because we'll never know when they're coming."

"It's me they're after," said Wes, "and I'll take care of the defense. Every night after dark I'll be outside with a shotgun. Let them try that again, and I'll empty some saddles."

"All my windows gone," Granny lamented.

"I'll pay to have them replaced," said Wes.

"That's no more than you should do," Molly Horrell said. "Perhaps you should consider moving somewhere else."

"Maybe I should," said Wes, meeting her eyes, "and I will, if my defense fails."

"No," Granny said firmly. "We no let *bastardo* outlaws drive our people away."

St. Louis, Missouri
April 10, 1882

When Nathan and Empty reached St. Louis, Silver was already there. As so often was the case, he was in Room

21 at the Pioneer Hotel. Nathan knocked twice, paused, and knocked a third time.

"Who is it?" a voice inquired.

"You damn well know who it is," said Nathan. "Let me in."

The door opened just enough for Nathan and Empty to enter. When they had, it was quickly closed.

Silver laughed. "Where have you been? I got here yesterday."

"I stayed an extra day in St. Joseph," said Nathan. "I was only ambushed twice, and I reckoned there might be a few more wantin' a shot at me."

"Now, now," Silver said, "let's not be bitter. You did the best you could. Even the government doesn't expect more than that."

"Well, God forbid that I should disappoint them," said Nathan. "Are you sure you've got no more phantom outlaws for me to track down?"

"Not at the moment," Silver said cheerfully. "Maybe when I return to Washington. It's a shame you didn't get to Jesse in time, but Frank's surrendered. If there's any money left from the robberies, he may be willing to give it up for a more lenient sentence."

"It's even more of a shame you didn't think of that before I wasted four months of my life looking for Jesse," said Nathan.

"It is," Silver agreed. "I'm good, but I'm not perfect."

Conversation lagged. Nathan sat down on the bed and drew off his boots. Empty sat on the oval rug, regarding Silver in a quizzical manner.

Silver laughed. "Look at him. He's getting more like you every day, sittin' there just looking right through you, and you don't know what the hell he's thinking."

"I know what he's thinking," Nathan said. "He's thinking it's time he was fed. We've been on short rations since Christmas, because those damn people in Missouri wouldn't sell us grub."

"Oh, is that all?" said Silver. "If I feed you, will your sweet disposition return?"

"Maybe," Nathan said. "Why don't you try?"

"Come on," said Silver. "Both of you. After we eat, we can buy passage on the boat to St. Louis."

"I'm taking my horse," Nathan said, "because I don't

know how long I'll stay at the McQueens'. When I'm ready to go, I aim to go."

New Orleans
April 16, 1882

Silver rented a horse and saddle, and with Nathan astride his grulla, they set out for the McQueen place. Recognizing familiar territory, Empty ran on ahead. Spring had come early to New Orleans, and the mighty oaks wore mantles of green, while wildflowers had sprung up in the fields and along the road. They rode past the horse barn, and under the spreading oak where Eulie Prater had been buried was the unmistakable mound of a second grave. Nathan's heart was in his throat, for he didn't want to know who slept there beside Eulie. McQueen had acquired some more dogs, and they came loping around the house—four of them—baying their heads off.

"You dogs," McQueen bawled, "here!"

Reluctantly they reversed themselves and started back to the house. Nathan and Silver rode around to the back porch, as they always had. Empty was already at the back door, expecting Bess McQueen to greet him. But it was Vivian who greeted him, and when they stepped down to take the big hand of Barnabas McQueen, there was something different about him. To Nathan, it seemed almost as though Barnabas wished they hadn't come, and for some reason, Vivian's eyes refused to meet his. Something was wrong. Bad wrong.

"Barnabas," Nathan said, "what's wrong? Where's Bess?"

"Over yonder . . . by the horse barn," said Barnabas, choking on the words.

"When . . . how . . . ?"

"She died . . . two weeks . . . after Harley left," McQueen said. "Sudden. She took sick and three days . . . later . . . she was gone."

"God," said Nathan. "I'm sorry to hear that."

"So am I," Silver said. "She was a great lady."

"You might as well come on in," said Barnabas. "The

place won't be as neat as it used to be. Vivian and me . . .
we've been away . . ."

All of them sat down at the kitchen table, but Empty
walked on through the house in search of Bess. Returning
to the kitchen, he regarded them all with sad eyes. He then
sat down at the kitchen door and howled mournfully.

"Oh, God, Empty," said Nathan, "stop it."

"Nathan," Barnabas said, "there's . . . there's been some
changes. We should have gotten word to you . . ."

"You didn't know where I was," said Nathan. "Tell me."

"I . . . me . . . Vivian and me . . . are husband and wife,"
Barnabas said, his eyes on his folded hands. "We were so
. . . lost without Bess, and we . . ."

Nathan said nothing as memories came flooding back.
Memories of Vivian from the day he had first seen her in
Dodge, half-starved, seeking her brother.

"Congratulations," said Nathan, having trouble with the
word.

"Amen to that," Silver added.

There was a painful silence. Nathan's eyes were on Vivian, and the harder she tried not look at him, the more
surely it seemed that she must. Finally she got to her feet,
leaned across the table toward him, and the dam broke.

"Damn it, Nathan, why did you have to come back, just
. . . just when I thought I . . . I was free of you . . ."

"You are free of me," Nathan said. "I . . . I have a
woman in El Paso. I . . . I thought you ought to know . . .
I'm . . . on my way there . . ."

They were the hardest words he had ever spoken, but
they were for her, for Barnabas. He got to his feet, put
on his hat, and took Barnabas McQueen's hand for the
last time.

"So long, Barnabas."

Vivian stood there in silence, tears streaming down her
pale cheeks. Nathan stepped out the back door, with Silver
and Empty behind him. Nathan and Silver mounted and
rode away without looking back. Empty paused, looking
back toward the McQueen house, and then back toward
the distant riders. Reluctantly he turned away, trotting to
catch up to the horses.

"My God," said Silver, when they were well away from
the house, "who would ever have thought . . ."

"I'd give anything if we'd never come here," Nathan

said. "I may have spoiled whatever slim chance they might have had."

"You did the right thing," said Silver. "You left Barnabas believing you hadn't come to take Vivian away, and you left Vivian believing you'd thrown her over for another girl. Give them time, and that'll draw them together. I know what that cost you, *amigo*. You're one *bueno hombre*. The question is, where do we go from here?"

"I'm going to El Paso," Nathan said. "You're welcome to ride along."

"I'm obliged for the offer," said Silver, "but I can't see it accomplishing anything. It's a good thousand miles from here, and I'd use up the rest of my leave just getting there. I reckon I'll leave this horse and saddle at the livery and take the next boat north. I hope when our trails cross again, it'll be under better circumstances."

Nathan and Empty waited at the landing until Silver had boarded the steamboat. Without a backward look, Nathan Stone rode out of New Orleans for the last time. Riding west into the setting sun, he felt suddenly free. While he regretted losing Vivian, he now knew she had become a burden without his realizing it. He felt some obligation to her, but now she belonged to Barnabas McQueen.

"Empty," said Nathan, "we're goin' near Houston, so I reckon we'll stop long enough to see Captain Dillard of the Texas Rangers."

Houston, Texas
April 23, 1882

"It's near suppertime, Captain, and I'm buying," Nathan said.

"I'll take you up on that," said Captain Dillard.

The two old friends spent an hour in a cafe, and when they parted company, they had planned to meet for breakfast the following morning before Nathan again rode west.

"Is Bodie West still in south Texas?" Nathan asked, as they sat down to breakfast.

"Yes," said Captain Dillard. "He's in Austin or San Antonio. Most likely San Antone."

"Good," Nathan said. "I'd like to see him again. He was a friend to Captain Jennings."

"If there's any one thing I dislike about the Rangers," said Captain Dillard, "it's all the old friends who have died in the line of duty. Among them, Sage Jennings."

"He won't be forgotten," Nathan agreed.

San Antonio, Texas
April 26, 1882

"Nathan," said Ranger Bodie West, "it's good to see you again."

"Good to see you," Nathan replied, taking West's hand. "What's happened since I was last here?"

West laughed. "You won't believe it. In 1879, Ben Thompson ran for city marshal of Austin and was defeated. He ran again in 1881 and was elected."

"Tarnation," said Nathan. "I reckon I'll have to stay awhile and watch Ben work. I'd say if he can use his gun as well for the law as he has against it, he'll be one hell of a lawman."

"He has potential," West said, "if only he can control his temper. A gun is a lot like money. It can serve you well if it's properly used, or it can get you into all kinds of trouble if you don't know how to handle it."

To Nathan's surprise, Ben Thompson appeared to be an excellent lawman. Rarely did he have to resort to his gun, for his reputation was enough. One Saturday evening in San Antonio, Nathan and Ben were having supper when King Fisher came in.

"Thunderation," said Fisher, wringing Nathan's hand. "I been wonderin' what became of you. Remember when we cleaned up on that horse race? My God, my luck's never been that good again. Are you aimin' to be here July fourth?"

Nathan laughed. "I haven't planned that far ahead. Another horse race?"

"Damn right," Fisher said. "When you get enough of Ben, ride down to the ranch for a while. I got me a horse to enter in that July fourth race. Just wait till you see him."

"I'll stay a while," said Nathan. "Where'd you get the horse?"

"He's a rustler," Thompson said. "You didn't know that?"

"Shut up, Thompson," said Fisher.

Fisher's horse was a black, reminding Nathan of Barnabas McQueen's Diablo. Fisher had hired an Indian rider, and the black won the race with good odds. But on July 11, Thompson and Jack Harris renewed an old feud. King Fisher explained it to Nathan.

"It started over a gambling incident in 1880," Fisher said. "Harris, along with Joe Foster and Billy Simms, own and operate the Vaudeville Theatre and Gambling Saloon, the wildest and most popular place in San Antone. Let's get over there before Thompson does something foolish."

When they reached the saloon, Thompson stood outside on the boardwalk in conversation with another man.

"That's Billy Simms," Fisher said, "a longtime friend of Ben's."

Simms went back into the saloon, and Thompson turned his attention to Nathan and King Fisher.

"Ben," said Fisher, "you're city marshal of Austin. Don't forget that."

"City marshal be damned," Thompson said. "I'm here to settle with Harris, but I can't find him."

But Jack Harris had entered the saloon by the back door, and was told by one of the saloon's employees that Thompson was outside and had been looking for him. Harris got a shotgun from behind the bar and positioned himself behind the door nearest Thompson. Several saloon patrons, not wishing to be caught up in a shoot out, rushed outside.

"Jack has a gun," one of them shouted to Thompson.

"Come on," Harris taunted from inside. "I'm ready for you."

But Thompson drew and fired through the blinds. The slug ricocheted and ripped into Harris's right lung. A second shot by Thompson missed, but Harris was finished.

"Damn it, Ben," King Fisher said, "why did you do that?"

"I owed him," said Thompson, "and I pay my debts."

"What do you aim to do now?" Nathan asked.

"The only thing I can do," said Thompson. "I'm turning myself in. Then I'll resign as marshal of Austin."

Jack Harris, mortally wounded, died that night.

CHAPTER 30

El Paso, Texas
August 15, 1882

Two weeks passed before the night riders struck again. Patiently, from dusk to dawn, Wes had kept watch, armed with a shotgun. When the marauders began firing from the predawn darkness, Wes answered their muzzle flashes with a bellow from the shotgun. His responses drew their fire, but he was bellied down and a poor target. He fired twice, reloaded and fired twice more. There was no more return fire. Quietly, Wes made his way into the house, confident the outlaws had pulled out.

"You alive," Granny said from the darkness. "Good."

"More alive than some of them, I think," said Wes. "Come daylight, I'll have a look."

But within minutes, there was a clatter of hooves, followed by a knock on the door.

"Who are you?" Wes inquired.

"Jim Gillett. Sounded like a war in progress out here."

Wes opened the door and Gillett stepped inside.

"Granny's in the kitchen making coffee," said Wes. "Time we have some, it should be light enough to see. I had only muzzle flashes to shoot at, but I may have got one of them. They didn't stay long."

Renita was already at the kitchen table, and when she spoke it was more to Gillett than to Wes.

"How long will this terrible thing go on?"

"Don't look for it to end any time soon," Gillett said. "With Wes fighting back, it may get a lot worse."

"I've only started to fight," said Wes. "I'll be out there with the shotgun the next time, the time after that, and the time after that, until they get enough."

"Or until they kill you," Renita said.

"Or until they kill me," Wes echoed. "The very first thing I learned when I came west is that if you won't fight you're branded a coward."

"I suppose that's worse than being shot dead," said Renita.

"On the frontier it is," Gillett said.

Nothing more was said, and when the first gray fingers of dawn touched the eastern horizon, Gillett and Wes left the house to search the grounds. They didn't have to search too long or hard. The first man lay belly down.

"God Almighty," said Gillett, when he rolled the dead man over. His face was gone.

"Here's another," Wes shouted.

The second man hadn't fared any better, for he had taken a load of buckshot in the chest. A search of the grounds produced no more bodies.

"You've got to be the luckiest hombre alive," said Gillett.

"I prefer to think of myself as careful," Wes replied.

"Go on being careful," said Gillett, "but don't rule out luck. You've accounted for no less than three of the Sandlin gang, and they'll be wanting you almighty bad."

"Do you want me to plant these two varmints?"

"No," Gillett said. "We'll let the country bury them."

Gillett rode back to town and Wes returned to the house.

"How many you get?" Granny wanted to know.

"Two," said Wes.

"My God," Molly Horrell said, recalling Nathan Stone's experience, "you'll have to run for your life."

"I'm not the running kind," said Wes. "I hear there's thirty men in the Sandlin gang. That means I only have to shoot twenty-seven more."

They could only look at him in amazement, for he was deadly serious.

San Antonio, Texas
August 15, 1882

"My God," Nathan said, "why don't you suggest something simple, like me running for governor of the state of Texas?"

Bodie West laughed. "I don't have that much influence, but I can get you appointed city marshal of Austin, to replace Ben Thompson. It pays pretty well, and you'll be right here with friends. Come on, damn it. They need a good man, and there's nobody around here as qualified as you. It'll only be for the rest of Thompson's term, and there'll be an election a year from this November. You'll be out of it the following January."

"A little more than fifteen months," said Nathan. "I reckon I can stand it that along."

El Paso, Texas
September 18, 1882

Monday was usually a slow day in town, and Wes had spent the afternoon engaged in draw poker in the Manning Brothers Saloon. Actually, it was a partnership, involving J. W. Jones, Frank, Doc, and Jim Manning. There had been a long-standing feud between Dallas Stoudenmire and the Mannings, and during the day there had been hard words between Doc Manning and Dallas Stoudenmire. Just before six o'clock in the evening, the poker game stalled as Stoudenmire came in and began cursing the Mannings. J. W. Jones, trying to make peace, approached Jim Manning.

"Jim, go find Frank, and all of you settle this thing."

Jim Manning nodded and went out to look for his brother Frank, but he situation worsened. Dallas Stoudenmire and Doc Mannings stood toe to toe, with Stoudenmire doing most of the cursing.

"Ease up, gents," said J. W. Jones, stepping between the two men.

But when Jones pushed them apart, both men drew guns. Manning fired first, shooting over Jones's shoulder. The slug ripped through Stoudenmire's arm and chest and, dropping his gun, Stoudenmire stumbled backward into the door. Manning pressed his advantage, firing a second time, but the slug didn't penetrate Stoudenmire's body. Instead, it struck some folded papers in Stoudenmire's shirt pocket, and only knocked the wind out of him. The fight continued outside on the boardwalk as the men struggled, each seeking an advantage. Stoudenmire finally got his hands on his belly gun and shot Doc Manning in the arm. Manning dropped his gun, but wrestled Stoudenmire, preventing him from firing another shot. As they cursed and fought, Jim Manning returned with a Colt in his hand. He began firing at Stoudenmire, and while his first shot missed, the second one didn't. It struck Stoudenmire behind his left ear, and he died on his feet. Doc Manning seized one of the fallen weapons, straddled the body, and began pistol-whipping the dead man.

"Stop it, Doc!" Jim Gillett shouted. With considerable effort, he separated Manning from the dead Stoudenmire. Gillett then appealed to the bystanders. "Jake, get somebody to help, and tote Stoudenmire over to the undertaker's."

Ignoring the Mannings, Gillett went into the saloon and began questioning the patrons about the fight.

"It looked about equal," said Wes, when Gillett got to him.

"You charging me, Marshal?" Doc Manning asked, as Gillett left the saloon.

"No," said Gillett shortly. Mounting his horse, he rode away.

Austin, Texas
August 16, 1882

When Nathan answered the knock on the door of his hotel room, he was surprised to find Ranger Bodie West standing there.

"I'll be in town tonight," West said. "What about supper?"

"I never miss it," said Nathan. "Does the invite include Empty?"

"It does," West said, "if I have to pay for him to have a place at the table."

They had supper at a cafe where Nathan had eaten before, and Empty was fed in the kitchen. When the meal was finished, Nathan spoke.

"I haven't heard from King Fisher in a while. Is he keeping his hands clean?"

West laughed. "He has no choice. He's acting deputy sheriff of Uvalde County."

"The hell he is," said Nathan. "When did this happen?"

"In the fall of 1881," West said.

"I've seen him since then," said Nathan, "and he said nothing about it."

"When you saw him last, he was with Ben Thompson," West said, "about the time Ben was forced to resign as Austin's city marshal. That's a sore spot with Ben, and I'd say that's why Fisher didn't tell you about his own appointment. He's taking it seriously, I'm told, and is talking about running for sheriff of Uvalde County two years from now."

"I'll have to get down there for a visit," said Nathan. "Maybe around Christmas, or the first of the year."

"I'll help you get a few days off after the first of the year," West said. "Christmas is generally a time when all kinds of hell break loose and lawmen are needed most."

Uvalde, Texas
January 10, 1883

"Bein' a lawman don't take as much time as I allowed it would," Fisher said.

"I'm glad to see you get such an appointment," said Nathan. "I let Bodie West talk me into finishing Ben's term in Austin, and it hasn't been half bad. I think it's discouraged a few ambitious hombres who wanted to become fast guns at my expense. For a while it seemed everywhere I went, somebody was forcing me into a gunfight, and I was killing men I didn't even know. It was that or risk having them kill me."

"I know how it is," Fisher said. "It's shoot or be shot."

Three days after Nathan's arrival, Fisher was called on to investigate a stage holdup. Nathan rode with him to the scene and accompanied him as he began trailing the pair of suspects.

"It looks like they're headed for the Leona River," said Fisher. "The only nearby town is Leakey, and there's only two or three ranches strung out along the river."

"I'll back your play," Nathan said, "if you need me."

They reined up where the tracks crossed the river.

"Looks like the Hannehan ranch," said Fisher. "Just Jim and Tom Hannehan and their mother. I reckon we might as well ride over there and be done with it."

Fisher rode on across the river, Nathan following. When

they approached the ranch, two men stepped out on the porch.

"You Hannehans are under arrest," Fisher shouted.

One of the men went for his gun, but Fisher drew and shot him. An elderly woman stepped out the door and knelt beside the dead man.

"Damn you," she cried, her voice breaking, "you've killed Tom."

"Sorry, ma'am," said Fisher, "he shouldn't have gone for his gun. I've trailed the two of them from the scene of a stage holdup. I'll be taking Jim with me. Where's the loot you took from the stage, Jim?"

"In the barn," Jim said sullenly. "I'll get it."

"I'll go with you," said Fisher.

Nathan remained with the distraught Mrs. Hannehan until King Fisher and Jim Hannehan returned with the stolen money.

"I'll be taking Jim with me, ma'am," Fisher said. "Do you want us to help bury Tom before we go?"

"No," said Mrs. Hannehan, looking Fisher in the eye. "I reckon you've done enough for me."*

There was no conversation as Fisher and Nathan, accompanied by the handcuffed Jim Hannehan, rode back to Uvalde.

"There are parts of bein' a lawman I purely don't like," King Fisher said when the unfortunate Hannehan had been locked in a cell.

El Paso, Texas
December 2, 1882

When the Sandlin gang struck again, it was in a devastating manner that nobody was expecting. Twelve-year-old Jody Connors rode in at dawn, his frantic cries alerting the town.

"What is it, boy?" Jim Gillett inquired.

"They took my pa and my brothers, Jeff and Jory," the boy panted.

*It was said, following King Fisher's death, that Mrs. Hannehan came to the cemetery on each anniversary of Tom's death, piled brush on Fisher's grave, and lit a brush fire.

"Who took them?" Gillett asked.

"I don't know. They wore masks. Ma says hurry."

"I'll gather some men," said Gillett.

Wes rode in, having come to have breakfast with Gillett.

"Trouble at the Connor ranch," Gillett shouted, to the men attracted by Jody Connors's arrival. "Who'll ride with me?"

"I will," said Wes.

Quickly, a dozen men gathered, and they followed Jody Connors north. Reaching the ranch, they found Mrs. Connors on the porch with a shotgun.

"They rode west, sheriff," she shouted.

"They're headed for the border," said Wes, galloping his horse alongside Gillett's.

Slowly but surely, the trail veered southwest, and then due west. But as they neared the Rio Grande, their quest abruptly ended. Revolving grotesquely in the breeze, three men hung from a branch of a cottonwood. Standing on his saddle, Gillett cut the ropes and the three bodies were lowered to the ground. Pinned to one of the dead men's shirt was a scrap of paper. Scrawled on it in pencil was a message:

Three of yours for three of ours.

Jim Gillett looked at Wes. It was clear enough. The Sandlin gang had extracted payment in kind for the three outlaws Wes had killed, and the significance of it wasn't lost on the rest of the men who had accompanied Gillett. Some of them were already looking at Wes with disapproving eyes.

"Some of you stay here with these men," Gillett said. "Mrs. Connors will have to be told about this, and I'll see if they have a wagon we can use. If they don't, then I'll send one from town."

"No use in all of us settin' out here with three dead men," somebody growled.

"Then two of you stay until I can get a wagon out here for the bodies," said Gillett. "Harris, how about you and Phillips?"

The two men nodded and the others mounted and rode hurriedly away, for obviously they were uncomfortable in the presence of death. Wes remained, and when Gillett started for the Connors ranch, Wes rode with him.

"I reckon you know what this is building up to," Gillett said.

"Yes," said Wes. "Every time we kill one of the Sandlin bunch, they'll ride across the river and kill somebody on our side, and they won't be particular."

"You're goin' to become unpopular in a hurry," Gillett said, "because you've managed to gun down three of the Sandlin gang. Since they can't get their hands on you, it appears they'll kill any and everybody."

"Then maybe I'd better give them a stronger reason for coming after me," said Wes. "Maybe I'd better begin wearin' this Ranger shield instead of keeping it in my pocket."

"That won't accomplish anything," Gillett replied. "The Sandlin gang knows Rangers aren't allowed to follow them south of the border."

"Then I'm going to do what I should have done before now," said Wes. "I'm resigning from the Rangers. Then I can follow these outlaws anywhere I please, without the Rangers or the State of Texas being at fault."

"That's just partially true," Gillett said. "As a civilian, you're still not permitted to go into Mexico without official permission."

"Then I reckon it'll be between me and the federals in Washington," said Wes. "I just can't believe the State of Texas will object to me getting these damn outlaws any way that I can."

"Neither can I," Gillett said, "unless you're captured in Mexico and Washington gets involved. Mexico could officially give them hell, and they'd pass it along to Austin."

"How can I return this Ranger shield and get word of my resignation to Bodie West?" Wes asked.

"Get your parcel ready and give it to the stage driver, along with ten dollars," said Gillett. "It won't hurt if you tell West in your letter what you're up against here in El Paso. In fact, if you're serious about resigning, what's the point in staying here? Sandlin and his bunch won't follow you."

"The first and most difficult thing I had to learn," Wes said, "is that a man—if he's to go on considering himself a man—can't run from a fight. I've been beaten bloody, had the hell stomped out of me, but I've never run and I won't now."

"Well, now," said Gillett, "that's an admirable thing as long as you can live with it, but being shot dead by a gang of outlaws is a mite more permanent than havin' your tail feathers ripped out, hand to hand."

They were nearing the Connors ranch and the conversation came to an end. Standing on the front porch, Mrs. Connors appeared not to have moved, for she still cradled the shotgun in her right arm. Wes and Gillett reined up and, dismounting, Gillett spoke.

"Ma'am, there's no good way to tell you this. They're all dead. Do you have a wagon we can use to bring them in?"

"Yes," she said, in an emotionless voice. "Mules are in the barn, and the wagon's in a shed behind it."

Wes and Gillett hitched the mules to the wagon and set out on their macabre mission. Gillett drove the wagon, his horse on a lead rope behind it.

"That woman's got a hard way to go," said Wes. "What will she do, with a ranch, and her menfolk dead?"

"Sell out, if she can find a buyer," Gillett said, "but that ain't likely. Some of these places are just ten-cow outfits, in debt to the bank."

After loading the three dead men in the wagon, Gillett and Wes set out for the ranch house. When Gillett reined up, Mrs. Connors was waiting. She fixed her eyes on the dead, and when she spoke, her bitter words sent chills up Wes Tremayne's spine.

"They worked from daylight to dark, never hurt nobody, and look what they got for it."

"Ma'am," said Gillett, "we'll be glad to dig the graves if you'll show us where you'll be wanting them. I can drive to town for some coffins."

"Dig the graves over yonder beyond the barn, under the big oak," she said. "I'll get some blankets for them. They didn't have no luxuries when they was alive, and I reckon they wouldn't want none now that they're dead."

Gillett drove on to the barn. In a tackroom they found picks and shovels.

"I'd have paid for the coffins," said Wes.

"I'm glad you didn't make the offer," Gillett said. "All she has left is the rags of her pride, and I'd not want to take that from her."

There were rocks in the soil, and digging the graves took them three hours.

"I'll go to the house and see if she wants to be present for the burying," said Gillett.

Mrs. Connors answered Gillett's knock and stood there waiting, saying nothing.

"The graves are ready, ma'am," Gillett said. "Do you want to be present?"

"I reckon not," said Mrs. Connors. "Me and young Jody is sorrowful enough. After the burying, I'll go read the Word over them."

When the three men had been buried, Gillett drove the wagon back to the barn and unharnessed the mules. He and Wes then rode on to the house.

"We're done, ma'am," Gillett said. "Is there anything else we can do?"

"No," she said. "We're obliged to you for seeing to their needs."

"Call on me," said Gillett, "if there's anything more I can do."

"There's plenty I can do, and I aim to do it," Wes said, as they rode back to town.

Austin, Texas
March 9, 1883

"I'm here to testify in court tomorrow," said King Fisher. "I reckon we have time to win a bundle at the poker tables tonight."

Nathan laughed. "I don't always win. First time you're with me on a bad day, you'll be cured. Let's have supper first, while we still have money."

"After that," Fisher said, "let's go to the Cattleman's Emporium. I want to visit the upstairs, where the naked women are."

"They're there to distract you," said Nathan, "to take your mind off the game."

"I reckon they got the right idea," Fisher replied. "When a naked woman can't capture a man's attention, the varmint might as well lay down and let somebody shovel dirt in his face."

Nathan and Fisher reached the Cattleman's Emporium just after ten o'clock, and to their surprise, when they climbed the stairs to the upper level, there sat Ben Thompson. His top hat was tilted back on his head and on the table before him was a bottle, a glass, and a substantial pile of poker chips.

"Thompson," said Nathan, "I didn't know you were in town."

"I purposely avoided you," Thompson replied. "Every time I come to this town I get in trouble with the law, and you're wearin' the badge. You've done me some favors, and I'm trying to avoid shooting you."

"Thanks," said Nathan. "We're here because Fisher wants to see the naked women."

"I never mix business with pleasure," Thompson said, "and gambling is business."

"Well, I aim to play a few hands of poker," said Nathan. "I've seen all these women before."

The trio spent the rest of the day in the Cattleman's Emporium, and near suppertime, when they departed, Thompson was the big winner.

"I'm on a roll," Thompson said. "After supper, I'm going back up there."

"I didn't do bad myself," said Fisher, "considerin' I was mixing business with a considerable amount of pleasure. But I reckon I'll call it a day. I got to be in court early tomorrow."

Thompson laughed. "I ought to get up and go with you, King. It'll be the first time you've ever been in court when you wasn't on trial for shootin' somebody."

"You should talk, Thompson," King Fisher said. "Why I remember—"

"Oh hell," said Nathan, "if there was any justice, both of you would be doing life in Huntsville prison."

Following King Fisher's day in court, he again accompanied Nathan and Ben Thompson to the Cattlemen's Emporium.

"I can't understand why they keep allowing you in here, Ben," said Fisher. "You don't come to look at the women, and when you leave, you always have a sackful of Emporium money."

"I bought a membership in the place," Thompson said.

"Cost me a thousand dollars. I come here as often as I can, to win back some of my money."

The following morning, before King Fisher was to return to Uvalde, the three friends had breakfast.

"Thompson," said King Fisher, "why don't you ride back with me? We can spend one night in San Antone, and go to the Vaudeville Variety Theatre."

"My God, King," Nathan said, "Ben's got no business in there. Have you forgotten he killed Jack Harris, one of the owners, two years ago?"

"No," said Fisher, "I haven't forgotten, but Ben was acquitted. Hell, Jack was after him with a shotgun."

"Yeah," Thompson agreed, "I ain't often shot anybody that wasn't trying to shoot me. If I avoided every place I've had to shoot some varmint, I'd have to go back east and look for work selling dry goods. It's been a while since I've been to San Antone. I reckon I'll go along with King."

After breakfast, Nathan watched them ride out, unaware that he was seeing the two of them alive for the last time.

El Paso, Texas
January 15, 1883

"You'll have to wait for a letter from Bodie West, accepting your resignation from the Rangers," said Jim Gillett. "If I may ask, when you're officially free, what do you aim to do?"

"I aim to see that the Sandlin gang learns I no longer live at Granny Boudleaux's," Wes replied. "I'll take my meals there, and Renita will be there, but I'll spend my nights along the border and riding to some of the surrounding ranches. I aim to see that nobody else is murdered by the Sandlin gang while they're trying to get to me."

"By God," said Gillett, "I've never seen one hombre so damned determined to get himself killed. There's hundreds of miles of border, and while you're settin' at one place, those outlaws will cross somewhere else."

"Maybe," Wes said, "but they won't be able to back me into a corner, killing someone else trying to get to me."

"You're overlooking something, Wes," said Gillett.

"Sooner or later, with you riding at night, you're going to have another fight with the Sandlin gang. I'd bet the little that I have, and all I hope to have, that Sandlin will murder some more innocent people, like he did the Connors men. While the Sandlin bunch may not be able to find you, you won't be able to find them, either. Are you prepared to take the responsibility for their murders, as a means of retribution for members of the gang that you've killed?"

"I realize they can pile all that on me," Wes said, "but if somebody doesn't go after the Sandlin gang, are they going to be allowed to have their way forever? I think, if you'll recall, this bunch of varmints was stealing and killing before I ever killed any of them. If I back off and leave them alone, you're just as good as telling them they have a license to steal and kill as often as they like. There's a price on everything, Jim, and sooner or later the people of southwest Texas will have to pay. Running from a fight only puts it off until another time. Don't you see that?"

CHAPTER 31

San Antonio, Texas
March 11, 1884.

When they reached San Antonio, Ben Thompson and King Fisher visited a saloon and saw a play that had just opened at the Turner Hall Opera House. Finally, a few minutes past ten o'clock that night, they went to the Vaudeville Variety Theater. There, two years ago, Thompson had killed Jack Harris, one of the owners.

"Let's have a drink at the bar," Thompson suggested, "before we go upstairs to watch the show."

They then climbed the stairs to their box seats to watch the show. No sooner had they reached their seats when they were joined by Jacob Coy, Joe Foster, and Billy Simms, the former partners of Jack Harris.

"Ben," said King Fisher, "let's go. We can see the show some other time."

"Damn the show," Thompson said. "This bunch has come after a dose of the medicine I spooned out to old Jack two years ago."

"You had no call to shoot Jack," said Joe Foster. "It ain't over."

"You got that right," Thompson replied. "I'll send you to hell with old Jack."

"Thompson," said Jacob Coy, the bouncer, "stop causing trouble or I'll boot you out of here."

"Not till I'm done with old Joe," Thompson replied.

Thompson slapped Foster and, drawing his revolver, cocked it and shoved the muzzle into Foster's mouth. Jacob Coy seized the cylinder of the revolver, and Foster fought with Ben.

"Ben," said Fisher, "let's get out of here while we can."

But it was too late. While scuffling with Foster, Ben managed to get off just one shot, which struck Foster in the leg. Seconds later, gunfire, from shotguns and rifles, erupted from an adjoining box. Ben Thompson and King Fisher died in a hail of lead. King Fisher had never drawn his revolver, but had been hit thirteen times in the head, chest, and leg. Ben Thompson had fired only once, but had been hit nine times. When the city marshal arrived, the dead bodies of Ben Thompson and King Fisher lay sprawled in the box from which they had come to see a variety show. On their faces were numerous powder burns. There were no weapons in evidence.

"Marshal," said Jacob Coy, "Thompson started a fight with Joe, and before I was able to break it up the shootin' started from that box over yonder."

"And I suppose you have no idea who did the shooting," the lawman said.

"No," said Coy. "Whoever it was, they shot Joe. We got to get him to the doc."

Word of the shooting in San Antonio was quickly telegraphed, and it was Bodie West who told Nathan Stone.

"I reckon there was nothing said about who did the killings," Nathan said.

"No," said West. "An ambush is a cowardly act, the last resort of men who don't have the guts for a stand-up fight. Jacob Coy, Joe Foster, and Billy Simms were with Thompson and King Fisher in a box on the balcony of the Vaudeville Variety Theater. Joe Foster was wounded and his leg is to be amputated. Coy and Simms have left town."

Nathan removed the city marshal's badge from his shirt and passed it to West.

"Nathan," said West, "you're an excellent lawman. Stay here."

"King Fisher was a good lawman," Nathan said grimly, "and you see what it did for him. Him and Thompson had their faults, but by God they didn't deserve to die like that, with nobody to avenge them."

"So you're about to take on another vendetta," said West. "Let me remind you there is no conclusive evidence as to who did the killings. You're the last man I'd ever want to see on the wrong side of the law."

Nathan said nothing. He checked out of his hotel and went to the livery for his horse, but before he could leave Austin, the Austin *Statesman* had a special edition on the streets, covering the killings. There were no facts beyond the little Bodie West had learned by telegraph. Most of the four-page newspaper consisted of excerpts from the lives of Thompson and Fisher, while an editorial on page one condemned the city of San Antonio for allowing the ambush of two prominent Texans in a single day.

San Antonio, Texas
March 12, 1884

Nathan went first to the Vaudeville Variety Theatre, inquiring about Joe Foster, Billy Simms, and Jacob Coy.

"Mr. Simms and Mr. Coy are out of town," he was told by a bartender. "Mr. Fisher is in the hospital."

"What can you tell me about the shooting here yesterday?" Nathan asked.

"Nothing," said the bartender. "I wasn't here."

Nathan went next to the city marshal's office, where he spoke with the deputy on duty, Ira Dement.

"We have no suspects," Dement said. "All we know is that both men were shot at very close range, from a box next to and slightly above theirs."

"Then the three men in the box with Thompson and Fisher should have seen whoever did the shooting," said Nathan.

"Not necessarily," Dement replied. "The show hadn't started and the theater was still dark. None of the three with Thompson and Fisher saw anyone, so they testified. All we got from them was that suddenly there was a roar of gunfire. All they claim to have seen was muzzle flashes."*

"I was told Foster's in the hospital," said Nathan. "Am I allowed to talk to him?"

"No," Dement said. "The bone in Foster's leg was shattered and the doctor had to amputate it. The shock was too great, and Foster died early this morning."

Nathan considered going to the Ranger outpost, but after considering what Bodie West had told him, he changed his mind. Leaving his horse at a nearby livery, he rented a room for himself and Empty. He then spent the rest of the day and most of the night visiting various saloons and listening to talk. But he learned nothing of any value.

*There's no record that the killers of Ben Thompson and King Fisher were ever found.

                *   *   *

    While Nathan was in no mood for breakfast, he ate anyway, lingering over coffee. He thought back to the time, now almost eight years ago, when Wild Bill Hickok had died in Deadwood, Dakota Territory. His death had been as senseless as those of Ben Thompson and King Fisher. Jesse James, while admittedly an outlaw and killer, had died with a slug in the back of his head. King Fisher had been just thirty years old, Ben Thompson forty-two, and Hickok thirty-nine.

    "My God," said Nathan aloud, "I'm thirty-seven years old. I've been a wanderer for eighteen years. How much longer do I have?"

    Suddenly he felt old, alone, forsaken. Suppose he hung up his guns, called it quits, tried to settle down? He thought of El Paso, of Granny Boudleaux's boardinghouse, of Molly Horrell. She was still a young woman, beautiful by anybody's standards, and he suddenly wanted to see her, if she still waited. He left the cafe and mounted his horse. He was more aware than ever of his own mortality, and with an eerie sense that his time was short, he rode west, toward El Paso.

El Paso, Texas
March 24, 1884

    Since the hanging of the three Connors men, there had been a continued feeling of unease. Wes Tremayne made it a point not to be seen entering or leaving Granny's boardinghouse, and despite his haunting the border at night, he hadn't encountered the Sandlin gang. Renita became more distant, and even when Wes was there, they seldom spoke. To spare Wes the possible danger of riding in during daylight, Granny had begun feeding him breakfast before first light and supper well after dark. He had grown lean and hard, his eyes squinted from lack of sleep, and he carried his Winchester wherever he went, even to the table.

    "Rub him down and feed him a double ration of grain," Nathan said, turning his tired horse over to the hostler at the livery. "It's been a long trail. Store my saddle in your tackroom. I may not be riding for a while."

Having been gone for so long, Nathan was a bit reluctant to just walk into Granny Boudleaux's place unannounced, but he needn't have worried. When he arrived, the old Cajun woman was sweeping the front steps.

"Nathan Stone," she cried. "You come back!"

"Yes," said Nathan, "I'm back. Maybe I can stay awhile this time."

"You sneak in quiet," Granny said. "Molly in kitchen."

Molly was in the kitchen, but Renita Wooten was with her. The younger girl's face went white when she saw Nathan. Seeing her fear, Molly turned.

"Nathan!" Molly cried. "Nathan!"

Nathan hadn't been sure how she would receive him, and her response exceeded his wildest expectations. She threw her arms around him, laughing and weeping. Renita, who had no idea who he was, had retreated into the dining room. Granny came in, shoving Renita back into the kitchen.

"Nathan," said Granny, "this Renita. She Wes Tremayne's woman."

Nathan grinned at Renita, who was blushing furiously and glaring at Granny.

"A pleasure to meet you, Renita," Nathan said. "I've been hearing about Wes. I'd like to meet him."

"He don't come in daytime," said Granny helpfully. "Sandlin outlaws watch for him, and in the dark he hunt for them."

"What?" Nathan exclaimed. "He's after the Sandlin gang! Why?"

"Because he killed three of them," said Renita, speaking for the first time. "He won't leave here. They're hunting him and he's hunting them."

Nathan laughed. "He makes me feel like a coward. He must be some kind of man."

"He not a man," Granny said. "He just a boy."

"He's as much a man as anybody in Texas, or anywhere else," said Renita hotly.

"I won't argue with that," Nathan said. "I left here a while ago, after killing one of the Sandlin gang. It was that or start an ongoing feud with them."

"Wes is a strong man," said Renita, "but he's not as smart as you. He has this feud going and he won't run out on it. They're going to kill him."

"He sounds like he'll take a lot of killing," Nathan said.

"You see him tonight," said Granny.

"I'm looking forward to it," Nathan replied.

Wes Tremayne rode along the river, resting at intervals, his eyes constantly on the trees and undergrowth that lined the south bank. For months he had seen nobody, and it seemed as though his vigil had become a fruitless one. Despite himself, there were times when he dozed, for he allowed himself only the hours between dusk and midnight for sleeping. He eyed the sun occasionally, as the golden disc slipped toward the western horizon. When he judged it was dark enough, he took a roundabout way to Granny's boardinghouse, riding behind it.

"You come in," Granny said, from the darkness of the porch. "Someone wait to see you."

Wes came in with the Winchester under his arm. In but a few weeks, he would be eighteen years old, but he looked older. When Nathan Stone stood up to greet him, he was as tall as Nathan. His eyes met Nathan's for only a moment, before dropping to the *buscadera* rig with its two matched Colts. When his eyes again met Nathan's, there was unmistakable respect in them.

"I'm Nathan Stone," said Nathan, offering his hand.

"Wes Tremayne," Wes replied, taking his hand. "I've heard of you."

"And I've heard of you," said Nathan. "You have friends in Dodge. Foster Hagerman and Harley Stafford spoke well of you.

"I'm obliged to them," Wes said. "Bodie West, a friend of mine, told me a little about you."

"Wes," said Granny, "we already have supper. You eat."

Wes was hungry and he wolfed his food, eager to continue the conversation with this newly discovered gunfighter. Nathan said nothing, waiting, and didn't speak again until Wes had finished eating.

"Now," Nathan said, "I'd be interested in hearing about this running fight with the Sandlin gang."

Wes played down his own role, eliminating most of the details, and it took prompting from Molly and Renita before Nathan began to get the entire story. He listened in amazement, for this young hellion had walked headlong into a situation Nathan Stone had avoided by just riding away. He half-hoped his ignominous retreat wouldn't be brought up, but it was.

"Wes," said Granny, "you just go away like Nathan did, and the outlaws forget you."

"I may wish I had done just that before it's over, Granny," Wes said, "but it's time I was getting back outside."

Nodding to Nathan, he took his Winchester and left.

Conversation lagged after that. It was Molly who made the first move. She got up, nodded to Nathan, and made her way down the hall. He soon followed, found the door to the room unlocked, and went inside. She was waiting for him, and for an hour not a word was spoken. When she finally did speak, it was the very last thing he expected.

"Nathan, the boy is the spitting image of you, and I get the feeling he's the same kind of hard-headed idealist you were twenty years ago."

"Damn it," Nathan said, kicking the covers off and sitting up, "what are you trying to say?"

"Ever since Wes Tremayne came here," said Molly, "he's reminded me of someone I felt I ought to know. Granny's spoken of it too, so it's not just a fancy of my own. What can you do to fill in the missing years? Doesn't the name mean anything to you?"

Nathan sat on the edge of the bed, his head in his hands, thinking. When he finally spoke, his voice was so soft she barely heard him.

"St. Louis, February of 1866. Molly Tremayne . . ."

"You're Wes Tremayne's father, aren't you?"

"My God," said Nathan. "My God, it must be, but . . . how was I to know . . . ?"

"But he doesn't know about you," Molly said. "Why doesn't he?"

"Because she didn't want him to know," said Nathan. "She must have hated me . . ."

"Tell me, Nathan," Molly said. "You've been running from her all these years and now she's going to haunt you . . . through him. You must talk."

Nathan began to talk, slowly at first, but the words tumbled out, as his emotions took control. He talked for an hour, until at last he was silent, drained.

"Don't you think he should be told?" Molly asked.

"My God, no!" said Nathan. "She didn't want him knowing or she would have told him about me. I'll respect her wishes."

"Is it that," Molly asked softly, "or is it that you're afraid he'll hate you, if and when he knows who you are?"

"No," said Nathan, "it would be his right to hate me, because he doesn't know all the story. I was as ignorant as a nineteen-year-old can be when I met Molly Tremayne. I'd joined the Confederacy when I was just fifteen, and I'd never been with a woman in all my life. Molly was older than me and she just took my breath away. I'd spent two nights with her before I got around to telling her why I couldn't stay . . . what I had to do."

"So she told you to go to hell, to get out and stay gone."

"She told me that and more," said Nathan. "But it was what she wanted, against the oath I'd taken on my father's grave."

"So that's where Wes Tremayne gets his stubbornness," Molly said. "That's why he's so determined to stop the Sandlin gang. He feels responsible for the three men the Sandlin gang hanged, and now he's living up to some oath he's taken unto himself."

"I reckon he is," said Nathan, "and now that he knows I ran away from the fight he's facing, he'll be all the more determined."

"Maybe not if you tell him who you are," Molly said.

"Damn it, no," said Nathan. "If Molly Tremayne hated me that much, I reckon she's entitled to take her revenge any way she can. I don't know how you'll manage it, but you have spent more time with Granny than I have. Before she figures out who Wes is, shut her mouth, will you?"

"I'll try," Molly said, "but it won't be easy."

"Have you heard about King Fisher?" Nathan asked. "He's dead."

"Far as I'm concerned," she replied, "he was dead the day I walked out on him."

Struck by the coldness in her voice, Nathan said no more, and it was Molly who broke the prolonged silence.

"Nathan?"

"What is it?"

"Molly Tremayne," she said. "Was the first Molly anything . . . like me?"

"Not really," said Nathan. "She was beautiful, just as you're beautiful. At the risk of soundin' like a damn fool,

I'd have to say the first Molly took advantage and had her way with me."

Molly laughed. "That does sound strange, coming from you. The woman's supposed to say that."

"Oh, hell," said Nathan, "that didn't come out like I meant for it to. Have you ever wanted something so much, had your mind made up as to how it would be, that you hated the person who didn't live up to your dream?"

"Of course I have," she said. "That's how I felt about you when you rode away to avoid the Sandlin gang. But it wasn't just the Sandlin gang, was it? You were a rolling stone, and you weren't quite ready for a clinging vine."

"Damn it," said Nathan, genuinely irritated, "you could find work in a medicine show, reading minds."

She laughed. "But I'm not like the first Molly. I believed you'd come back, and now you have. Will you ride away again?"

"No," he said. "I've been killing men and having men try to kill me for eighteen long years. I'm tired. Tired of having men—even kids—that I don't know, trying to kill me, just to prove they're faster with a gun. That's what bothers me about young Wes. Before I associated the name, before I knew who he was, all I heard was how quick he is with a gun. Maybe that's what bothered Molly Tremayne, why she never told him about me. She didn't want him riding vengeance trails, a gun in his hand and a lonely grave ahead of him."

"You feel that's what you've been doing?"

"I reckon," he replied. "What do I have to show for those eighteen years, except the men that I've left dead? All my friends have lived by the gun, and most of them are dead by it."

"So you're going to settle here, across the river from the Sandlin gang?"

"Why not? I can't name a town on the frontier where I can be sure I won't meet an hombre wantin' to kill me to prove he has a faster gun."

"What will you do in El Paso?"

"I don't know," said Nathan. "I have enough money so that I don't have to do anything, unless I want to. I aim to stay out of the saloons, and if I play poker, I'll stay with low-stakes games."

"I like the sound of that," Molly said. "Since I'm partners with Granny, why don't we just stay here for a while?"

"That might be wise," said Nathan. "Wes doesn't know who I am, but I'd like to stay close enough to side him if he needs me."

"He's so much like you," Molly said. "Don't be surprised if he refuses any help."

In the days that followed, Nathan continued spending as much time with Wes as he could, without the boy becoming suspicious. But Wes Tremayne never wavered in his determination to destroy the Sandlin gang. One night after supper he raised the lid on his watch to check the time.

"That's an interesting old watch," Nathan said. "May I have a look at it?"

"It was left to me by my grandfather on my mother's side," said Wes, handing the old time piece to Nathan.

Nathan had caught just a glimpse of the photograph in the lid of the watch, and as he looked at it more closely, there was no mistaking the well-remembered face of the young Molly Tremayne. Nathan swallowed hard before he spoke.

"A beautiful lady, Wes. Is this your mother?"

"Yes," Wes replied. "It's all I have left of her. She died when I was born."

Nathan returned the watch to the young man who was his son. No longer was there any doubt, and among the others in the room, Molly Horrell and Granny Boudleaux had seen and understood.

A month after Nathan's arrival, the Sandlin gang struck again. They rode across the river half a dozen miles east of El Paso, murdered a rancher and his wife, and then set fire to the house. They rode away with a dozen horses, escaping across the border. Following breakfast at Granny's, Wes Tremayne broke his long-standing rule and rode into town and went right to the town marshal's office, to talk to Jim Gillett.

"All hell has busted loose," Gillett said. "The city fathers have telegraphed Austin for help from the Rangers."

"A lot of good that'll do," said Wes. "They've already had two Rangers here—you and me—and our authority ended at the border. A Ranger can't be everywhere at once. I was riding the river west of town, and the Sandlin

bunch crossed the border a dozen miles to the east. I
learned of it when I saw the glow from the burning house,
and long before I could get there, the varmints had taken
the horses and were back across the river."

"There's just one way to get at the Sandlin gang," Gillett
replied, "and that's to lure them across the river for some
definite purpose, but that can blow up in your face."

"Yeah," said Wes. "Like when they hung the Connors
men."

"Exactly," Gillett said. "Then you'll have the whole
county giving you hell because you were responsible for
enticing the outlaws across the river. When I took the marshal's badge, I thought I could make a difference here. But
I'm not allowed to do what has to be done, and I'm giving
it up."

"When are you leaving?"

"Just as soon as I can be replaced," said Gillett. "The
town council was after me this morning before breakfast.
They wanted to know where the hell I was when Eli Dan-
vers and his wife were murdered and their ranch house set
afire. I had no way of knowing the Sandlin gang was coming, and even if I had known, they could have crossed the
border anywhere along a fifty-mile stretch. Damn it, I'm
one man with one gun. Let them send for the Rangers."

"I'll take the badge for a while," Wes said, "if you can
arrange it."

"I can arrange it, but are you sure that's what you want?
I'd feel like I'm signing your death warrant."

"I believe I can lure that bunch of owl hoots across the
river," said Wes. "They want me, and I've kept out of their
reach, waiting for them to make a move. Well, they made
it, and I was too far away to make any difference. They
have to think they can get their hands on me."

"So you aim to set a trap with yourself as bait," Gillett
said. "There's just one of you, same as there's just one of
me. They can always spring the trap, take the bait, and just
ride back across the river."

"They can try," said Wes. "Get me the badge and let
me try."

Gillett had no trouble getting Wes appointed as town
marshal, but nobody at Granny Boudleaux's favored it.
Only Nathan Stone kept his silence.

"They'll kill you," Renita predicted. "The only reason they haven't already is that they couldn't find you."

"She right," said Granny. "You young, have pretty woman. Why you want to die?"

"Wes," Molly said, "you and Renita could make a new start somewhere else, far from the border. You don't owe this town anything."

"I don't run from a fight," said Wes, "however unfair or uncertain it may be."

Wes Tremayne refused to change his mind, and Molly tried to get Nathan to intervene.

"I didn't see you trying to talk sense to him," she said.

"No," said Nathan, "and you won't. He's enough like me that it wouldn't make a bit of difference. He knows I ran out on a fight once, and the Sandlin gang has been a threat ever since."

"Then if he won't take Renita and leave here," Molly said, "why don't we get away from here?"

"No," said Nathan. "The kid's right. I ran away once. I won't do it again."

"You're going to get yourself killed alongside him," Molly said.

"I aim to be here if he has need of me," said Nathan.

"I have need of you alive," Molly said. "Doesn't that mean anything to you?"

"Sure it does," said Nathan, "but I have to make up those wasted years. Is that so hard to understand?"

"I understand perfectly," Molly said. "He's going to get himself shot dead, and you'll be right there beside him. Well, if I'm going to have to live without you, we'll start now. I'm moving to another room. You can sleep by yourself."

She slammed the door with a finality that shook Nathan but did nothing to weaken his resolve. He sighed, tugged off his boots, and stretched out on the bed.

CHAPTER 32

Wes Tremayne found himself in an increasingly precarious position with Renita. After her outburst following his appointment as town marshal, she said little to him unless she was forced to. To make matters worse, outlaws—presumably the Sandlin gang—raided yet another ranch, and while nobody was killed, all the stock was rustled. A week later, the town's request for Ranger assistance was answered when ranger Tom Webb arrived. He was a young man, not more than twenty-five, and Wes liked him immediately.

"A company of rangers couldn't solve this town's problems," Wes told him.

Webb laughed. "Be a little more specific."

Wes told him of having shot three of the Sandlin gang, only to have them cross the river and murder three innocent people.

"I've ridden this border as thoroughly as one man can do it," said Wes, "and it makes no difference where I am. The outlaws are always somewhere else, and when they strike they're back across the border before I can get to them. I reckon you're aware that you're not allowed to cross the river?"

"Yes," Webb said. "That's the first thing I was told."

"Two elements must come together," said Wes. "First, they must be lured across the river, and then we must have some idea as to where they are. They're over here plenty often, but I've never been able to get to them. I never know where they'll cross."

"Maybe we can set a trap with enough bait to bring them to a specific location," Webb said. "Are they partial to cattle or horses?"

"Horses," said Wes.

"Suppose we had a holding pen, and in it fifty or more horses. Wouldn't that draw them across the river?"

"I reckon it would," Wes said. "It might be the only way to draw them to a specific place. Even then we'd have to stake it out day and night."

"Exactly," said Webb, "but wouldn't that be better than constantly riding the border, never knowing when or where they're going to strike?"

"It would," Wes replied. "It's the best proposal I've heard."

"We'll begin by riding to the different ranches," said Webb, "and asking for horses. We'll ask each rancher to contribute what he can, along with necessary hay and grain. The horses will be kept only as long as it takes to lure the outlaws across the river."

"While we're asking for horses to bait the trap," Wes said, "I believe we should ask for men to ride after the outlaws. I've heard there may be thirty or more outlaws in the Sandlin gang. That's heavy odds, even for a Ranger."

"Heavy odds for anybody," said Webb. "We'll definitely need help."

"I think then you'll find out just how much folks around here want to be rid of the Sandlin gang," Wes said. "I've heard that Sandlin has a standing reward of a hundred pesos for any man taking up arms against the Sandlin gang. Nobody's likely to forget how three men were hanged and they hadn't done anything."

"I can see the deck is pretty well stacked against us," said Webb, "but if nobody's willing to join us in the fight, we'll have to risk it alone. The trouble is, we'll be risking a holding pen full of borrowed horses. If something goes wrong, and they're lost, there'll be hell to pay. Not just here, but in Austin."

"If there's just you and me against the entire Sandlin gang," Wes said, "the very last thing we'll have to worry about is the horses. We'll both be shot dead."

"Tomorrow," said Webb, "we'll start calling on ranches."

When Wes returned to Granny Boudleaux's at the end of the day, he said nothing to anyone about the newly arrived Ranger, and nothing about the plan to lure the Sandlin gang within reach. Renita was still out of sorts with him, and while he wasn't aware of the reason, he was aware that there was a problem between Nathan and Molly Horrell. Where did it all end, when a man began conducting himself according to the wants of a woman?

Tom Webb and Wes visited three ranches without gathering a single horse.

"I need the hosses I got," said one rancher after another. "I can't afford to send 'em to a holdin' pen, to do nothin' but eat their heads off."

"You need the horses you have," Wes said, "but if the Sandlin gang rode across the river and took them, what would you do?"

Nobody had an answer to such a question, but they countered it with one of their own.

"Suppose we let you pen up our stock, and the outlaws gunned you down and took 'em anyway?"

The second half of the day was as unproductive as the first, and the sun was less than an hour high when Wes and Webb returned to town.

"I still think your plan's a good one," Wes said, "but none of these people are willing to risk even one horse. Where do we go from here?"

"Tomorrow," said Webb, "we'll call on the mayor and the town council. Hell, even a Ranger can't perform miracles. If the ranchers won't cooperate, then the town will have to supply the necessary horses."

"That I'll have to see," Wes said. "They're quick to give you hell when the outlaws steal and kill, but nobody's willing to lift a hand to help."

After supper, when it was too dark to be seen, Wes went out on the front porch and sat down on the steps. Nathan got up and followed, leaving Molly Horrell glaring at him. He said nothing, taking a seat at the other end of the steps. If there was a conversation, Wes would have to begin it. Eventually he did.

"How well do you know Harley Stafford?"

"Pretty well," Nathan said. "We were in the war together. After that, I lost track of him until I found him again in Deadwood, Dakota Territory."

"That's where Hickok was killed."

"Yes," said Nathan, "I was there. Wild Bill was a friend of mine."

"I've read about him," Wes said. "I wondered if any of it was true."

"Probably not," said Nathan. "He liked to laugh, to drink, and to gamble. In Denver, after a saloon fight, I spent the night in jail with him."

"Is it true that Jesse James was shot from behind by a member of his own gang?"

"It's true," Nathan said. "Robert Ford did it for the reward."

"Whatever Jesse James was," said Wes, "Robert Ford is still a coward. What became of him?"

"He's looked on with contempt everywhere he goes," Nathan said. "I hear he's on tour with a stage company, telling how he shot Jesse James, but it's not working out. He's been run off the stage just about everywhere."

"I read the newspaper stories about Ben Thompson and King Fisher being ambushed," said Wes. "Did you know either of them?"

"I knew them both," Nathan said. "I spent the day with them in Austin, the day before they were killed."

"Nobody went after their killers?"

"I was there the next day," said Nathan, "but there was no evidence."

"But you did try."

"Yes," Nathan said, "I tried."

"A man never has enough friends," said Wes.

"I agree," Nathan replied. "Most of mine are dead."

"But you have a dog. I've seen Granny feeding him."

"That's Empty," said Nathan. "His Daddy was Cotton Blossom, a blue tick hound from Virginia."

As though on cue, Empty trotted up the steps and sat down between them. Suddenly the dog growled deep in his throat. Nathan lunged at Wes and the two of them went off the steps together as lead chunked into the wooden steps where they had been sitting. Despite his poor position, Nathan came up with his Colt spitting lead, firing at the muzzle flashes. Beside him, like an echo, Wes was returning fire. As quickly as it began, it was all over, and the silence seemed all the more intense. Empty had taken refuge in the shadows of the porch, and he trotted down the steps.

"They're gone or they're dead," said Nathan. "Otherwise, Empty would warn us."

"He saved us," Wes said, "but how did you know?"

"That was his somebody's-out-there-with-a-gun growl. He's saved me more times than I can remember. Come daylight, we'll go out there and look around."

The front door opened and most of the boarders came

out, for the hour was early. It was Granny who asked the obvious question.

"Wes? Nathan? You not be hurt?"

"We're all right, Granny," Nathan said.

Renita came to Wes and stood beside him, trembling, but Nathan didn't see Molly. It was a fair conclusion, he decided, that she didn't care if he was alive or dead, but that did not matter. If he hadn't been there on the steps with Wes, Empty wouldn't have been on hand with his warning, and Wes Tremayne would be dead.

The next morning, after breakfast, Nathan and Wes went outside to search the area from which the gunfire had come.

"They crept up on foot," Nathan said, "depending on the darkness."

"If they were part of the Sandlin gang," said Wes, "they had to leave their horses somewhere."

"Likely in the livery," Nathan said. "They probably hoofed it back to town and spent the night at one of the hotels."

"I hadn't thought of that," said Wes. "Since I don't know who's a member of the gang, they can ride in and out of town as they please."

"That further allows them to spy on you, knowing your every move before you make it," Nathan said.

"I heard the shooting last night," said Ranger Tom Webb, "but I had no idea you were the target."

"I was," Wes replied. "Nathan Stone and me were on the porch at the boardinghouse and we both returned fire, but we didn't get any of them."

"Is that the Nathan Stone I've heard so much about?"

"I reckon," said Wes. "I don't know of any other."

"He's highly respected among Texas Rangers," Webb said. "He tracked down and shot the varmint who ambushed Ranger Sage Jennings. I've heard he was the third oldest man in the Rangers and that before he died, he gave Stone his shield with a three inscribed on the back. Not many men can claim such an honor."

Wes digested this new information in silence. At first, he hadn't thought too highly of Stone for having run away from the Sandlin gang, but after the attack the night before, and having seen Stone under fire, his opinion rapidly changed. Stone had told him only a little about himself—mostly about friends who were dead—and then only when Wes had pressed him. The man was no braggart, and his movements of the night before were testimony to his ability with a revolver. The dog had warned them only split seconds before the shooting had started, yet Stone had been able to save himself and Wes. Seconds before Wes had gotten off a shot, despite Stone's disadvantage, he had come up shooting. There was all the evidence Wes Tremayne needed to believe that Nathan Stone had walked with the likes of Wild Bill Hickok, Ben Thompson, and King Fisher.

"I reckon we'll know this morning if our plan using horses for outlaw bait is going to be accepted," said Webb.

"I hope the town will go along with it," Wes replied, coming back to their problem at hand. "It's our only hope, short of riding the border again."

Wes and Webb began by calling on the mayor, Daniel Hutchins, who handled their request in the manner of all politicians.

"You'll have to take your request before the town council," said Hutchins. "The next meeting is May 20."

El Paso, Texas
May 20, 1884

There were twelve men on the town council, eleven of whom were present. Tom Webb took just five minutes explaining their proposal, and it required just five minutes more for the council to kill the idea.

"We simply don't have the money," said Mayor Hutchins.

"I reckon you didn't know that when we talked to you a month ago," Wes said.

"We are following procedure," said Hutchins stiffly.

"Maybe you don't understand what we're proposing," Tom Webb said. "All we want is maybe fifty horses we can keep in a holding pen to attract these outlaws. Nobody's asking you to buy these horses. They can be borrowed or rented stock, to be returned when the need for them is done."

"You do not understand the magnitude of what you are proposing," said Hutchins. "If we have no money to actually buy these animals, neither do we have the money to replace them should they be lost."

"You're considering the possibility that, despite our efforts, the outlaws may actually take the horses," Webb said.

"Of course we are," said Hutchins. "By your own admission, you have been unable to deputize men who will assist you. We hear that the Sandlin gang may consist of thirty or more men. Who are the two of you to stand against such a number?"

"The fact that the two of us are willing to take a stand should count for something," Wes said.

"Oh, it does," said Hutchins, "and don't think us ungrateful. But we are practical men, and there is the obvious risk that both of you will die, leaving us with the awesome responsibility of paying for the stolen horses."

"We understand," Wes said, "The possibility of us being shot dead is of considerable less importance than how you hombres would pay for the stolen horses."

"Your sarcasm is unwarranted, Mr. Tremayne," said Hutchins. "Your request will be considered again on November 20, when the budget for the next fiscal year is proposed."

"That's six months away," Tom Webb said. "That's time enough for a lot of stock to be stolen, and men to die."

"The subject is closed until November 20," said Hutchins.

"I'm not surprised," Wes said, when they were again on the street. "Those varmints all come up for reelection November 13."

"They're gambling there'll be no more rustling and killing between now and then," said Webb. "That could unseat the lot of them."

"That's a comforting thought," Wes said, "but it's of no help to us now."

"Too bad," said Webb. "I don't know how else to get those outlaws across the border so that we can get our hands on them."

"I do," Wes said. "I'll ride over there and shoot a couple of them. The rest will follow me anywhere."

"I can only remind you of what you once reminded me," said Webb. "Legally, we're not allowed across the border."

"So I'll cross illegally," Wes said. "Will the Sandlin gang call on the Rangers and have me arrested?"

"No," said Webb, "they'll do exactly what you expect. They'll go after you with fire in their eyes and guns in their hands. But how do you plan to find them? An entire army can hide in the wilds of Mexico and never be rooted out."

"I'll let them know I'm coming, and let them find me," Wes said. "Nathan Stone gave me an idea. He said Sandlin's bunch probably has spies right here in town. I'll spread the word that I'm going after them, so they'll be looking for me."

"My God," said Webb, "with that kind of sand, you should be a Texas Ranger."

"I was," Wes said, "but I gave it up. Now I can do what I must."

"You'll scare hell out of Hutchins and the town council. They'll be expecting trouble from Washington if you're caught or killed."

"It's up to me to see that I'm not caught or killed," Wes said. "What I aim to do will be done long before the next meeting of the town council."

Nobody had to warn Wes Tremayne of the hazards of what he proposed. While planting word of his intentions in various saloons for benefit of the outlaws, he carefully avoided speaking of his plans at Granny Boudleaux's. Better that none of them knew what he proposed to do until it was done. He allowed the outlaws a week to learn of his coming, and when he rode out at dawn, only Tom Webb was aware of his dangerous mission.

Old Mexico
June 2, 1884

Crossing the Rio Grande, Wes rode eastward for what he believed was ten miles. He dared not get too far into this wild country, lest he be trapped, for the outlaws knew the land, while he did not. He rode carefully, watching his backtrail and the terrain ahead, but saw nobody. Finally he wheeled his horse and rode back the way he had come, and reaching the point where he had crossed the river, he followed it westward a dozen miles. Still he saw no riders, no evidence that the outlaws had taken the bait. Frustrated, he rode on across the river, and on the Texas side found Tom Webb waiting.

"I can't understand it," Wes said. "I gave them a week to get the word."

"They got it," said Webb, "but must have suspected a trap. We'll have to be a lot more convincing than that."

But others had gotten the word as well. Renita and Wes had a falling-out all over again, while Molly Horrell regarded Nathan as though she suspected he'd had a hand in it. Finally, Wes was called before the town council, where he was censured for violation of federal law.

"You could well have caused an international incident," said Mayor Hutchins, "leaving the town of El Paso liable for penalties from Washington. How dare you represent us in such a manner?"

"This is your lucky day," Wes said, getting to his feet. "As of now, I'm through representing this town in any manner."

Removing his badge, he dropped it into a pitcher of water on the mayor's desk. Then he walked out. Tom Webb, who hadn't attended the meeting, was waiting for him.

"You have the look of an hombre that's just told somebody to go to hell," said Webb.

"Thirteen of them," Wes replied. "The mayor and his coyote council."

"You have the right idea," said Webb. "They ask for help, but they do nothing, and then tie our hands so we can do nothing. I'm riding back to Austin and telling them what's going on here. The Rangers can take me off this assignment or take my badge."

"I'm finished," Wes said. "The Sandlin gang can have El Paso for breakfast as far as I'm concerned."

There was excitement at Granny Boudleaux's when Wes broke the news.

"Now that you can't be accused of running from the Sandlin gang," Renita said, "there is no reason why we can't go somewhere else."

"No," said Wes, "I reckon they've given up on me."

After supper, for the first time in weeks, Molly Horrell sought out Nathan, and she had a question for him.

"Now that the danger from the Sandlin gang is past, can't we leave here?"

"I suppose we can," Nathan said.

But the running feud with the Sandlin gang wasn't over. A week after Wes had quit and a new town marshal—Buchanan Reynolds—had been appointed by the mayor and town council, the outlaws struck again. They rode through town shooting out windows, and before they left, they took every horse from the horse barn near the wagon yard. The new town marshal hadn't fired a shot. Short tempers returned to Granny Boudleaux's as Renita and Molly became more intense in their efforts to persuade Wes and Nathan to leave El Paso.

"No," Wes said. "I aim to stay awhile. Through Christmas, anyway."

The town remained quiet, and two days before Christmas, Wes and Renita were riding to the general store. Granny Boudleaux and Molly Horrell followed in a buckboard, needing to replenish supplies for the holiday. There were several vacant store buildings on the edge of town, and from the flat roof of one, a rifle cut loose. The first slug caught Wes in the upper left arm, while the second stung his cheek. In an instant, he was off his horse and running toward the store building. Two more slugs kicked up dirt ahead of Wes before panic seized the bushwhacker and he tried to escape. But he had waited too long. The roof sloped toward the back of the building, and just as the killer dropped to the ground, Wes shot him. He tried to raise the Winchester but could not. He stumbled back and fell, the weapon still clutched in his dead hands. Wes returned to his horse, blood dripping from his left elbow.

"You're hurt!" Renita cried.

"Nothing serious," said Wes. "I'll have the doc patch me up."

Granny had reined up the team. She and Molly said nothing, and Wes spoke to them.

"There was only one, and I got him. Go ahead into town. I'll report to the new town marshal."

Wes mounted his horse and rode on, Renita beside him.

"Oh, God," Molly groaned, "the Sandlin thing is about to start all over again."

"But they shoot Wes," said Granny, "and he shoot them. What else he do?"

Wes reported the shooting to Reynolds, the new town marshal, and then stopped at the doctor's office. By the time he was finished there, and ready to join Renita at the store, the dead bushwhacker had been brought to the marshal's office in a wagon.

"Hell," a bystander said, "this hombre's been hangin' around the Acme Saloon for as long as I can remember."

"Yeah," said another, "he was always here, and he always had money."

It vindicated Nathan Stone's suspicions, Wes decided. The Sandlin gang did have men in town, and that meant Sandlin would soon know that Wes Tremayne had killed a fourth member of the gang. He prepared himself for trouble, and it wasn't long in coming. The next morning, an hour before dawn, there was a single shot. Lead slammed into the front door at Granny Boudleaux's. Somewhere outside, Empty barked.

"It's safe to go out," said Nathan. "That was a warning, for some reason."

Wes opened the door and looked out, but there was nobody in sight. Then he saw the dagger driven into the door. It secured a piece of paper upon which a grim message had been scrawled. It said:

We are coming for you.

There was no hiding the warning, for others had seen Wes remove it. Closing the door, he went back inside, dropping the warning on the dining table. Let them all read it and give him hell. He no longer cared.

"Wes," Renita cried, "it's not too late. Can't we just ride away?"

"No," said Wes shortly. "They've called me out, and I'm going."

Taking a second Colt, he shoved it under his belt, and with his Winchester under his still-bandaged arm, he went to saddle his horse.

"Please," Renita cried, "isn't there something we can do to stop it?"

"Only he can stop it," said Nathan, "and he'll die before he'll run."

Nathan started down the hall to a room he no longer shared with Molly, but this time she followed him. His Winchester leaned in a corner, and he made sure it was fully loaded. He then buckled on the *buscadera* rig with its two deadly Colts. From his saddle bag he took shells and began filling his pockets.

"It had to be him or me, didn't it?"

Molly Horrell stood in the doorway, tears streaking her cheeks.

"I never said that," Nathan replied.

"You didn't have to," said Molly. "You've stayed here because of him, knowing that it would come to this. What I wanted didn't matter."

"It mattered," Nathan said, "but I owed him eighteen years, and I don't have nearly enough time to make it up."

Without another word, she stepped aside. Nathan went down the hall, his Winchester in his left hand. Molly followed, standing with Granny and Renita on the front porch as Nathan walked to the stable. He saddled the grulla, mounted, and rode toward town. Well before he got there, the shooting started. The main street appeared deserted, but at the western end of it stood Wes Tremayne. The bushwhackers were hidden at intervals along the street, and while their victim wasn't yet within range, they were firing, kicking up dirt a dozen feet ahead of him. If he chose to advance, he would be caught in a deadly cross fire, a gauntlet of lead. Empty had followed Nathan, and from the corner of his eye he could see the dog as he kept close to the buildings along the street. The eyes of the outlaws were on Wes Tremayne, and as they prepared to fire they moved to better positions. Well within range, Nathan opened fire with the Winchester. He cut down three of the outlaws before the others turned on him. A slug broke his left arm, and he dropped the Winchester. Drawing his right-hand Colt, he continued firing.

At the other end of the street, Wes Tremayne was cocking the Winchester, firing as he ran. He saw Nathan fall to his knees, saw dust puff from his shirt, as the slugs tore into him. Nathan dropped the empty Colt, and managing to reach the weapon on his left hip with his good right hand, he dropped another of the outlaws. He fired once more, the slug kicking up dust a few yards ahead of him. Finally the Colt sagged in his weary hand and dropped to the dusty street. Bleeding from a dozen wounds, dying, Nathan Stone fell across the weapons that had served him so well. There was a clatter of hooves as what remained of the Sandlin gang rode away.

Wes Tremayne walked slowly toward Nathan, but he paused, for Empty was already there. His teeth bared, he stood ready to defend this man with whom he had traveled the long trails, a master who could no longer defend himself. That was the scene that greeted Molly Horrell, Renita, and Granny when they arrived in a buckboard. Molly stepped down to the dusty street and ran to Nathan, weeping. With a strange moan, Empty backed off, allowing her to kneel beside Nathan. When there were no more tears, she looked up and her eyes met those of Wes Tremayne, those ice blue eyes that were Nathan Stone's.

"Why?" Wes asked. "Why did he do it? This wasn't his fight."

"Oh, but it was," said Molly, her voice trembling. "He tried to make up for eighteen years today. Your mother never wanted you to know, and he respected her wishes, but you deserve to know. Nathan Stone was your father."

Wes still held the Winchester, and he dropped it in the dust at his feet. He dropped to his knees as tears rolled down his dusty cheeks. When he finally got to his feet, he stood, looking up toward the rising sun. When he spoke, his voice was cold.

"They're going to die," he said. "I swear before God, they'll die. I'll hunt them down to the last man."

Nathan's body was taken to Granny Boudleaux's, where he spent his last night in her parlor.

"We bury him behind the house," said Granny. "He one of us, and he sleep forever there."

Nobody slept that night, as Nathan lay dead in the parlor. Molly told Wes all she knew about Nathan Stone.

"He has friends he wanted telegraphed," Molly said. "One is Barnabas McQueen in New Orleans. Another is Byron Silver, at the attorney general's office in Washington. And in Dodge City, there's Foster Hagerman and Harley Stafford."

"You can contact the others," said Wes, "but let me telegraph Foster Hagerman and Harley Stafford. They're my friends, and I especially want them to know who I really am."

"Then address the telegram to Omega Three," Molly

said. "It's what Nathan wanted. I know he'd want you to have his Winchester and the Colts, because they were given to him by Captain Sage Jennings of the Texas Rangers. There's a Ranger shield that belonged to the captain, and a watch given him by Byron Silver. He has a considerable amount of money in the bank, and that's yours, too."

"No," said Wes. "I want the other things, but I want you to have the money."

Empty had howled most of the night, and had to be shut up in the house until Nathan had been buried. Wes already had his horse saddled and waiting. In the boot was Nathan's Winchester, and Wes had the *buscadera* rig, with its twin Colts, belted around his lean middle.

"Turn Empty loose, Granny," Wes said. "I'd like to see him again before I go."

Empty came out and sat down at the head of Nathan's grave, and he didn't object when Wes ruffled his ears. He then turned to face Renita, who wept silent tears.

"I'll be back," he said, "if you'll wait. I'm taking my father's weapons and his name, and I must pay a debt for him."

"I'll wait," the girl cried.

Wes mounted his horse and rode away, and that's when Empty began howling. While Wes wasn't aware of it, the mournful howls of the hound drifted back over the years to that long ago time in Virginia, when Cotton Blossom, Empty's sire, had howled over the remains of Malachi, an old black man who had long served Nathan Stone's family.

"He lost," said Granny Boudleaux, her eyes on the grieving dog.

But Empty had a choice to make, and as Cotton Blossom had done, so long ago, he made it. He ceased howling and trotted a few steps along the way that Wes had ridden. He paused, looking back, and then turned away. He barked once, and in the distance Wes reined up, waiting for him.

"Wes," said Molly aloud, "you're truly the son of Nathan Stone. You could never have been anything else. God help you as you cross that river into Cord Sandlin's border empire."

Appendix

Gunfights—1880

Billy the Kid	January 10	Fort Sumner, NM
John Webb	March 2	Las Vegas, NM
Dave Rudabaugh	April 30	Las Vegas, NM
George Flatt	June 19	Caldwell, KS
Frank Hunt	June 19	Caldwell, KS
Frank Leslie	June 22	Tombstone, AZ
Billy Thompson	June 26	Ogallala, Neb
Jesse Evans	July 3	Presidio, TX
Curly Bill Brocius	October 28	Tombstone, AZ
D. L. Anderson	November 29–31	White Oaks, NM
Billy The Kid	November 29–31	White Oaks, NM
Dave Rudabaugh	November 30–31	White Oaks, NM
D. L. Anderson	December 19	Fort Sumner, NM
Lon Chambers	December 19	Fort Sumner, NM
Pat Garrett	December 19	Fort Sumner, NM
Billy The Kid	December 19	Fort Sumner, NM
Tom O'Folliard	December 19	Fort Sumner, NM
Dave Rudabaugh	December 19	Fort Sumner, NM
Charlie Bowdre	December 23	Stinking Springs, NM
Pat Garrett	December 23	Stinking Springs, NM
Billy the Kid	December 23	Stinking Springs, NM
Dave Rudabaugh	December 23	Stinking Springs, NM
Tom Pickett	December 23	Stinking Springs, NM

Gunfights—1881

Port Stockton	January 10	Farmington, NM
John O'Rourke	January 14	Charlestone, AZ
Luke Short	January 25	Tombstone, AZ
Jim Crane	March 15	Contention, AZ
Harry Head	March 15	Contention, AZ

Bill Leonard	March 15	Contention, AZ
Jesse James	April 3	St. Joseph, MO
James Masterson	April 9	Dodge City,
Dallas Stoudenmire	April 14	El Paso, TX
James Masterson	April 16	Dodge City, KS
James Masterson	April 17	Dodge City, KS
Sam Cummins	April 17	El Paso, TX
Billy The Kid	April 28	Fort Sumner, NM
Robert Olinger	April 28	Fort Sumner, NM
Jeff Davis Milton	May 16	Dodge City, KS
William Breakenridge	May 25	Galeyville, AZ
Curly Bill Brocius	May 25	Galeyville, AZ
Pat Garrett	July 14	Fort Sumner, NM
Billy The Kid	July 14	Fort Sumner, NM
Dave Rudabaugh	September 19	Las Vegas, NM
John Joshua Webb	September 19	Las Vegas, NM
William Claiborne	October 26	Tombstone, AZ
Ike Clanton	October 26	Tombstone, AZ
Morgan Earp	October 26	Tombstone, AZ
Virgil Earp	October 26	Tombstone, AZ
Wyatt Earp	October 26	Tombstone, AZ
Doc Holliday	October 26	Tombstone, AZ
Billy Clanton	October 26	Tombstone, AZ
Frank McLaury	October 26	Tombstone, AZ
Thomas McLaury	October 26	Tombstone, AZ
Michael Meagher	December 17	Caldwell, KS
James Sherman	December 17	Caldwell, KS
Frank Stillwell	December 28	Tombstone, AZ

Gunfights—1882

Robert Ford	January 3	Bay County, MO
Samuel Cummings	February 14	El Paso, TX
James Manning	February 14	El Paso, TX
Florentino Cruz	March 18	Tombstone, AZ
Frank Stillwell	March 18	Tombstone, AZ
Wyatt Earp	March 20	Tucson, AZ
Warren Earp	March 20	Tucson, AZ
Doc Holliday	March 20	Tombstone, AZ
Jack Johnson	March 20	Tucson, AZ
Sherman McMasters	March 20	Tucson, AZ
Frank Stillwell	March 20	Tucson, AZ

Florentino Cruz	March 22	Tombstone, AZ
Wyatt Earp	March 22	Tombstone, AZ
Warren Earp	March 22	Tombstone, AZ
Doc Holliday	March 22	Tombstone, AZ
Jack Johnson	March 22	Tombstone, AZ
Sherman McMasters	March 22	Tombstone, AZ
Frank Stillwell	March 22	Tucson, AZ
Jesse James	April 3	St. Joseph, MO
Robert Ford	April 3	St. Joseph, MO
Ben Thompson	July 11	San Antonio, TX
Dallas Stoudenmire	July 29	El Paso, TX
Dallas Stoudenmire	September 18	El Paso, TX
James Manning	September 18	El Paso, TX
William Claiborne	November 14	Tombstone, AZ
Frank Leslie	November 14	Tombstone, AZ

Gunfights—1883

Henry Newton Brown	April 11	Hunnewell, KS
Cassius Hollister	April 11	Hunnewell, KS
Ben Robertson	April 11	Hunnewell, KS
Luke Short	April 30	Dodge City, KS
Henry Newton Brown	May 14	Caldwell, KS
Lon Chambers	September 29	Coolidge, KS
Cassius Hollister	November 21	Caldwell, KS
Henry Newton Brown	December 15	Caldwell, KS

Gunfights—1884

Jack Watson	February 7	Montrose, CO
King Fisher	March 11	San Antonio, TX
Ben Thompson	March 11	San Antonio, TX
Henry Newton Brown	April 30	Medicine Lodge, KS
Ben Robertson	April 30	Medicine Lodge, KS
Mysterious Dave Mather	July 18	Dodge City, KS
Mysterious Dave Mather	July 21	Dodge City, KS
James Miller	July 30	Plum Creek, TX

Doc Holliday	August 19	Leadville, CO
Bill Tilghman	October 16	Dodge City, KS
Cassius Hollister	October 18	Hunnewell, KS
Elfego Baca	November 30– December 2	Frisco, NM

Gunfights—1885

Jesse Lee Hall	February 9	Las Islas crossing of the Rio Grande
Mysterious Dave Mather	May 10	Ashland, KS
Heck Thomas	September 6	Dexter, TX

Gunfights—1886

| Dave Rudabaugh | February 18 | Parral, Mexico |
| Joe Stinson | June 24 | Santa Fe, NM |

Also available in hardcover from
the *USA Today* bestselling series

Tucker's Reckoning:
A Ralph Compton Novel

by Matthew P. Mayo

In the two years since his wife and daughter died,
Samuel Tucker has wandered, drunk and increasingly
bereft of a reason to go on—until he sees two men
gun down a third and finds himself implicated in the
murder of the man he saw killed.

But Emma Farraday, the victim's niece, believes in his
innocence—and the two must reveal the machinations
of some wealthy and powerful men to prove it. If they
don't, Emma could lose the family ranch and Tucker
could lose his life—just when he's found a new
reason to live...

**Available wherever books are sold or at
penguin.com**